MW00700776

CRUDE INTENT

AN ALEX SHERIDAN THRILLER

ELIZABETH JEFFETT

DEFIANCE PRESS
& PUBLISHING

Crude Intent: An Alex Sheridan Thriller

(Defiance Press & Publishing, LLC)

Printed in the United States of America

10 9 8 7 6 5 4 3 2 1

ISBN-13: 978-1-948035-65-1 (Hardcover)
ISBN-13: 978-1-948035-66-8 (eBook)

Edited by Janet Musick
Cover designed by Spomenka Bojanic
Interior designed by Debbi Stocco

Published by Defiance Press and Publishing, LLC

Bulk orders of this book may be obtained by contacting Defiance Press and Publishing, LLC at: www.defiancepress.com.

Public Relations Dept. – Defiance Press & Publishing, LLC
281-581-9300
pr@defiancepress.com

Defiance Press & Publishing, LLC
281-581-9300
info@defiancepress.com

DEDICATION

Live your dreams…
With love to
Austin and Katie Smith
William Jeffett and Margaret Metras

ACKNOWLEDGMENTS

Many friends and acquaintances shared with me their expertise that positively contributed to this novel, *Crude Intent*. It is impossible to name them all, but thank you for your time and assistance. Sincere appreciation to the following: My dear book club friends, who read the novel and made thoughtful suggestions, including Beth, Deezy, Ginny, Dabney, Cara and Julie. Martha and Reed Williams, my business partners, who had the oil and gas lease in the Thompson Divide, in Colorado. Deputy Michael Buglione, with the Pitkin County Sheriff's Department, who shared his time and expertise. Members of the Garfield County Attorney General's Office in Glenwood Springs, Colorado; volunteers at Colorado Mountain Rescue; Wild Well Control, Inc., the fire-fighting company from Houston and their engineers. Expert legal opinions were provided by Attorney Edwin V. "Bubba" King and Attorney Tom Rafter. Drs. Tom Sudela and Rick Weiner shared their highly respected medical opinions. Sally Giddons Stephenson for her first round of editing and Jan Keeling and Bonnie Smith for their contributions. Heather Siler, David Thomas Roberts, and his team at Defiance Press have done an amazing job, along with my talented editor Janet Musick.

I would like to recognize my mother, Nancy P. Jeffett, who passed away before this could be released. She was a huge inspiration and a tremendous mother, as well as a world class business woman who demonstrated how to be a great entrepreneur and a lovely person. I also want to thank my amazing father, Frank A. Jeffett, who was an author, poet and renaissance man; Dr. William F. Jeffett, my brother, who is a brilliant writer, art historian, and curator, and a huge personal supporter; and my children, Austin Jeffett Smith and Katherine M. Smith, who I love beyond measure; and their father, Charles F. Smith, Jr.

IF...

If you can keep your head when all about you
Are losing theirs and blaming it on you;
If you can trust yourself when all men doubt you,
But make allowance for their doubting too;
If you can wait and not be tired by waiting,
Or being lied about, don't deal in lies,
Or being hated, don't give way to hating,
And yet don't look too good, nor talk too wise;

If you can dream—and not make dreams your master;
If you can think—and not make thoughts your aim;
If you can meet with Triumph and Disaster
And treat those two impostors just the same;
If you can bear to hear the truth you've spoken
Twisted by knaves to make a trap for fools,
Or watch the things you gave your life to, broken,
And stoop and build 'em up with worn-out tools;

If you can make one heap of all your winnings
And risk it on one turn of pitch-and-toss,
And lose, and start again at your beginnings
And never breathe a word about your loss;
If you can force your heart and nerve and sinew
To serve your turn long after they are gone,
And so hold on when there is nothing in you
Except the Will which says to them: "Hold on!"

If you can talk with crowds and keep your virtue,
Or walk with Kings—nor lose the common touch,
If neither foes nor loving friends can hurt you,
If all men count with you, but none too much;
If you can fill the unforgiving minute
With sixty seconds' worth of distance run,
Yours is the Earth and everything that's in it,
And—which is more—you'll be a Man, my son!

—RUDYARD KIPLING

PROLOGUE

A clean-cut young man wearing a long black coat and woolen gray scarf, looking more like a law clerk than the courier he is, scales the formidable steps of the Denver Courthouse. Snowflakes swirl like moths through the pastel sky as thunder growls in the distance. The massive courthouse doors open into a vast hall where armed guards monitor guests passing through a security scanner. The young courier removes his coat and scarf and places them with his cell phone and briefcase in plastic containers. A burly guard casually inspects the briefcase and waves the courier through the security scanner.

The young man pulls his coat and scarf back on and crams the cell phone in his pocket. He surveys the hall, eyes searching, then heads for the nearest red exit sign, leather briefcase in hand.

The door opens on a dingy staircase to the second floor, where portraits of state Supreme Court justices loom. He hurries through the silent gallery as if to avoid their penetrating eyes. He pauses when he comes to a door with a brass plaque engraved with the name "Judge J.R. Thompson." He fishes through the briefcase to retrieve a fat manila envelope, then pushes through the mahogany door and enters an office where a striking young woman sits at a large maple wood reception desk.

The desktop is void of clutter, with only an iPad resting on it. A wingback chair sits in a corner of the room next to a glass coffee table. The table surface holds several neatly placed legal journals and business magazines. Fresh lilies are arranged in a vase at the table's center, and

7

classical music plays softly in the background.

"This is for Judge Thompson," says the courier, handing the receptionist the envelope.

She smiles at him. "Are you a law student?" she inquires casually.

"Yes, at Boulder. You?" he asks.

"Me, too. I'm clerking for the summer."

The young man notices that she has deliciously smooth olive skin and striking amber eyes. He hesitates, chews the corner of his lip, and hands her a delivery receipt to sign.

"Maybe I'll see you around the library," he says, hesitating for just a moment before disappearing into the hallway.

"See you in the library." The young woman calls after him, then gets up from the desk and knocks softly on the judge's interior office door.

"Come in."

The judge's deep voice is reminiscent of Margaret Thatcher's. The clerk delivers the envelope to the judge as carefully as she would pass food to a jailed inmate.

"Can I get you fresh coffee?" the clerk asks.

The judge's gaze remains fixed on the papers on her desk. "No, thank you."

The clerk backs out cautiously.

Alone in her private office, Judge Thompson looks at the envelope. A few files lie next to the papers on her desk, but otherwise the room is impeccably neat. She opens a desk drawer, locates a wood box, and removes a large, elegant letter opener with semi-precious stones adorning the handle. With the miniature dagger, she carefully slices the envelope to reveal a wad of cash wrapped in blank white paper. The shredder hums as she quickly feeds the envelope into its teeth. Deliberately, she returns the letter opener to its case and puts the cash inside a large white envelope.

The tall, distinguished-looking judge walks over to an oil painting of the English countryside and moves it aside to reveal a wall safe. Right, left, right—in seconds, the safe unlocks. The judge's elegant hands tremble slightly as she opens the vault and stuffs the envelope inside. She closes the safe and returns to her desk.

Nearby, the courtroom is empty except for a few defendants, a court reporter, a stout security officer, and a lawyer fidgeting with files. They are all waiting for the judge, whose vacant chair dominates the courtroom.

Behind the bench and through a door are the judge's chambers, where Judge Thompson remains at her desk. A knock on the door interrupts her concentration, and she frowns.

"Come in."

A short, dark man with wire-rimmed glasses and a balding head walks in and places a file on her desk. His suit is smart.

"Your client has barely served the minimum time," observes the judge, striving to keep her voice level. They both know the history of the case.

"His record is commendable," the lawyer replies softly.

"Premeditated murder is not commendable," she says, without veiling her sarcasm. Tension thickens between them.

"I assure you, Judge, he is contrite and not a danger to anyone."

The judge notices the man's nervous twitch and incessant blinking. "He is a murderer," she says. Looking down, she reluctantly opens the file, picks up a pen, and signs a paper in it.

"Who has shown exemplary rehabilitation," the lawyer counters.

The package that arrived earlier is neither acknowledged nor discussed, but its presence is felt by both.

"Your letter to the parole board is critical," he adds calmly. Inside his immaculate suit, sweat soaks his shirt. "The governor will take care of the rest."

"If he is back in my court again, it will be for life."

"I understand. Thank you."

No eye contact or trite pleasantries are exchanged. The judge closes the file and hands it, with the signed paper inside, to the lawyer. He quickly takes it and exits.

Judge Thompson pulls a small bottle of prescription pills out of her desk drawer, swallows two, then washes down a third with tepid coffee. After letting out a heavy sigh, she puts her hands on the desk for support and stands carefully. The anxiety is worse. She adjusts her robe and heads into her courtroom.

CHAPTER 1

Alex Sheridan opened the door to the downtown Denver office building, waved warmly at the security guard, and strode confidently across the marble lobby to the elevator labeled for floors twelve to twenty-four. The glass-and-granite tower was one of the most prestigious buildings in the city.

Inside the elevator, a television flashed cable news highlights from around the world. The stock market lunged up and down like a bungee cord, and oil was priced at more than one hundred dollars a barrel. Give it time, Alex thought; it would soon reverse course and come crashing down.

She watched the screen and, just before the doors closed, a well-dressed young man stepped into the elevator and pushed the button for the twenty-third floor, one floor below Alex's office. Their eyes locked.

"Are you Ms. Sheridan?" he asked, excitement in his voice.

"Yes." She reached out and shook his proffered hand.

"I really liked the article in oil and gas magazine," he volunteered.

"Don't believe the media." She smiled, then glanced at her vibrating cell phone as an unknown number flashed on the screen. Pressing a button, she ignored the call.

A leader and maverick in the oil and gas business, Alex had recently been described by a journalist as a tycoon. One of her friendly adversaries in the oil and gas business was quoted in a profile story saying, "Her peers respect her—she is shrewd and smart, tough and honest as any man in this business." Alex Sheridan knew more about putting an oil deal together than most. In the industry, her word was gold, a rare and admirable quality.

She noted the young man having a difficult time keeping his eyes off her as he took in her long dark hair, lean muscular body, and head-turning features that camouflaged one of the best business minds in the industry.

He blushed as he realized she had caught him staring. "How is your project coming along on the Western Slope?"

She smiled, impressed that he was following her company.

"Challenging, thank you," she replied, "What part of the business are you in?"

"We're a new startup on the twenty-third floor," he told her. "We buy minerals and rework old wells."

With the advent of horizontal drilling and fracking, underground formations that had previously been inaccessible now produced record quantities of oil and natural gas. The drilling cracked open deep-level formations, allowing the oil trapped inside to flow to the surface. Fracking, a controversial technique, forced a mixture of fluids, sand, and water under extreme pressure into a shale formation, making it possible to extract oil and gas from the shale in massive amounts.

The technologies had unlocked vast reserves, creating an energy boom and, overnight, the United States had more oil and natural gas reserves than any country in the world.

"Good luck, and let me know if we can do anything to help," she said earnestly.

He nodded his thanks, then the door opened and he was gone, only the scent of his aftershave lingering.

A few moments later, Alex exited the elevator that opened directly into her world, an expansive office occupying the entire twenty-fourth floor. Dramatic black-and-white photographs, a visual history of her professional life, adorned the walls. A photo taken at a large field in the Permian Basin in West Texas showed her sitting on the back of a pickup with several weathered men in cowboy hats. She wore a frayed baseball cap and a muscle T-shirt, revealing a sculpted body that looked as if it belonged to a ballet dancer. Another photo showed her on an offshore rig in the Gulf of Mexico, with huge waves crashing against the platform as the team held on tight. In yet another, she and a striking blonde woman, with shovels in hand and broad smiles, were breaking ground for a building in downtown Denver.

A breathtaking view poured in from the floor-to-ceiling windows, and exquisite purple and pink clouds hovered on the spiny mountain peaks like floating cotton candy. In the conference room, maps lay unfurled on a gigantic boardroom-style table. Maps and seismic charts pinned to the walls showed the expanse of Sheridan Enterprises. In addition to the Colorado ventures, operations included wells in the Barnett Shale, production in numerous counties in Texas, and leases in Wyoming and the Dakotas.

A door slammed in the front office, startling Alex. The door to her office flew open as Colt Forester burst in like a hurricane. He was working-man handsome, smudged with grease and dirt, and wore a Texas-sized smile.

"You scared me," Alex said, smiling.

Closing and locking the door to her office, Colt pulled off his worn tee shirt and work gloves, and tossed his sunglasses on a table. Tousled hair and a two-day-old beard made him irresistible. He strode across the room toward her while unbuckling his belt. His hard-muscled arms enveloped her as he kissed her fiercely.

"I missed you," he said in a husky voice.

"Where have you been?" Alex pulled her mouth loose from the kiss, looking perplexed. He had been on the road for more than a week without a word.

"Drillin', baby. Fightin' with that well in the Permian Basin." He placed his stainless-steel watch on the end table by the sofa, then kissed her again, groping like a hungry bear.

"We've got major problems over at the Thompson Divide," Alex protested, as he pulled her to him and slid his hands down the back of her pants.

Located just outside the Aspen Valley, the Thompson Divide on the Western Slope of Colorado was erupting with controversy.

"Protesters are trying to shut us down," she told him. "I think it's far more serious than prior well projects."

Protesters were active and vocal in their determination to stop the drilling. A big red circle on the map indicated the importance of the multi-million-dollar project. Emotional fury around fracking and drilling had gained momentum and potentially threatened the business.

"That," he whispered, his lips and hands all over her, "can wait."

Ignoring her objections, he pressed hard against her, grabbing her perfect bottom. She could feel his full erection as he expertly slid her tee shirt over her head. She mumbled something futile, but his roguishness was too seductive. He took her hand and led her to the large sofa, where he feverishly kissed and nuzzled her breasts.

"Seriously, Colt," she protested, but her struggling was half-hearted. "They are trying to shut everything down. It's urgent!"

"I am so going to make your day," Colt promised, as he knelt in front of her.

"Fran will be here soon," she warned, referring to her reliable assistant, but her resistance was weak.

"I locked the door," he told her. He pulled at her jeans, then kissed her stomach until she quit fighting. She ran her hands through his unruly hair, conceding the conquest as she felt the need for him rising like a tsunami. The familiar terrain was intoxicating. Alex's heart ignited as Colt pulled her close to him on the sofa. They held the kiss as Colt discarded his jeans. Alex, breathless, stroked him into an erotic frenzy. Colt broke into a sweat, smothering her with his mouth.

He was all over her, gentle and forceful at the same time, burying himself in her, touching her with velvet hands, saturating her with his wildness. She moaned with ecstasy, reveling in the passion. For some time, he lay pressed to her, stroking her hair. Theirs had been a precious, yet bumpy love affair for many years.

Finally, Colt rolled off her, smiling with satisfaction. They giggled playfully.

"You think you can just barge in here and take what you want?" Alex cried in a mock display of indignation.

"I do," Colt said, patting her cheek. "Do I detect a complaint?"

Dropping to her knees, Alex searched under the sofa for her thong.

"Voila!" Colt mischievously dangled the thong, holding it high in the air.

"Give that to me," she demanded, snatching at it.

"Say please," he said, giving her another love pat.

"Stop it!" She swatted at his hand as she tried to smooth her tee shirt. "I could charge you with breaking and entering."

"Not if you climax," he laughed. "That *was* a climax when you squealed, wasn't it?"

Alex leaned over and kissed him softly. These were magical moments. She adored this carefree man-boy who danced through life on the tail of the wind. From the moment they met years before, an electric attraction and powerful love force infected their lives.

"I'm going to try to make myself presentable." She disappeared into an elaborate dressing room that housed every conceivable necessity, from makeup to athletic gear to guns.

"We have to stop meeting like this," she called out happily, brushing her hair and wiping away smudges of mascara. She vividly recalled their first meeting over a complex oil deal. It led to a love affair and business partnership neither had expected.

"Can't," he said, "you love it too much."

He was right, she thought. Theirs was a love that had survived great adversity.

"Thank goodness you're back," she said, walking over to the large mahogany desk that dominated the end of the room opposite the sofa. "There is so much to do on the wells."

Colt's phone rang a country tune as she reentered the room. He stood against the great western landscape outside the office's enormous windows, looking as solid and monumental as a Michelangelo sculpture. The sight of Colt's sculpted body, forged from handling pipe and steel, intoxicated her.

"Yeah, I'll be down there in the morning. You're first in line. The rig's on the way." He hung up.

"What did you just promise?" Alex demanded, hands on her hips and jaw set hard. Standing behind the desk with her temperature rising, she could hardly believe what she'd just heard.

"I had to squeeze in another project, but it won't take too long," he replied casually.

Alex exploded like a scud missile. "You're committed to go to the

Thompson Divide, to our project."

He shrugged. "It'll keep."

"You know it's urgent!" Alex fumed at the feeble excuse for a broken promise. She picked up some papers and waved them at him. "They are going for an injunction."

He didn't look at her. "I would have lost this other deal if I hadn't…"

"So you screw me and our project."

Colt grinned, his eyes on her. "You weren't complaining a few seconds ago."

"You're risking my project and shoehorning someone else in," she continued stubbornly.

It was his predictable pattern to slip information in after the fact, and it was not the first time he had welched on a commitment.

"Now it's all *your* project?" Colt shot back. He cinched his belt buckle hard but diverted his eyes.

Alex tightened her lips, frowning at him. "It will be if you don't hold up your end of the deal."

"Have at it. There's probably another operator you can screw!"

The cruel words hit Alex like a pipe bomb to the heart. A part of her soul crumpled as she watched Colt snatch up his things with the fury of an angry bull.

"You gave your word, Colt." She tried to soften her accusation, but his word was losing its meaning.

"Relax, Alex, you're overreacting." His tone was condescending.

"Your word means nothing anymore." The poison arrow shot out and hit its mark.

"And you're a control freak!" he shouted.

"Get out. *Now!*" Alex ordered. "Just get out!"

Colt stormed out and slammed the door, leaving a jet stream of rage in his wake.

Alex had seen an ugly pattern of excessive drinking, feeble excuses, and broken commitments accelerate over the past year. Unreliability oozed through their life like sludge through a pipe. She was sure Colt was underestimating the seriousness of the situation at the Thompson Divide. She had to change course and diffuse the volatile situation herself, but she vowed silently to remember this moment and not count on Colt Forrester again.

Now it was up to her to figure out what she could do to head off the trouble on her own.

CHAPTER 2

Alex's call to Colt's cell phone rolled straight to voicemail again. It had been more than a week since they had made ravenous love and then fought like tomcats. She was still enraged that he had deserted their project for another company's fees. As the drilling operator, he was desperately needed at their well site at the Thompson Divide. The multi-well project cost millions of dollars, and the company could not afford to wait around for Colt.

A text popped onto her screen:

Mobs of protesters today.

Alex hurled the phone across the office with vehement force.

Protesters and politicians were fighting to get a temporary restraining order to halt all drilling, and the efforts had slowed down development in the area. Alex's eyes were almost crossed from reviewing the financials related to the deal. More than ten million dollars had been spent building roads, pouring pads, and drilling test wells, all within the federal government guidelines. But working within the guidelines didn't seem to matter anymore.

The frenzy churned up by local protesters had garnered the sympathy of many within the forestry service as well as in the local community. They were determined to stop the fracking technology that had changed the world. For some, it was just automatic hatred of the entire energy industry. She knew they would not believe the truth, that she loved the forests and mountains that were her habitat, and it was paramount to her to find safe ways of operating in the environment.

The phone rang, interrupting Alex's thoughts. Hurrying over to retrieve the phone from where she had flung it, she glanced at Caller ID before accepting the call. "How are things in Big D?" she asked her closest friend, Schaeffer London.

"Denton, Texas just voted to ban fracking," replied Schaeffer, a top industry expert and long-time business partner and consultant to Alex. She made it her business to be informed about all aspects of the oil and gas industry, especially the mounting challenges it currently faced.

Alex sighed. "That's not good."

"More earthquakes were recorded in Arlington." Arlington, Texas was a suburb in the heart of the Dallas-Fort Worth metroplex. Schaeffer sounded worried, never a good sign.

"That's a big problem."

"Any word from Colt?" Schaeffer asked.

"Not yet." Alex couldn't keep the disdain out of her voice. "He's nowhere to be found. I'm so pissed at him."

"Anything I can do?"

Alex tightened her grip on her phone. "No, but his behavior is totally inexcusable, not to mention downright cruel."

"He has been so erratic this last year," Schaeffer said. "I'm sorry."

"I have to focus on our business. I can't let him destroy our Thompson Divide project. Several days ago, protesters blocked the road to the rig."

Her friend sounded sympathetic. "I'm here if you need anything."

"I'll let you know as soon as I can," Alex said, "if I don't kill him first." She ended the call.

Alex looked at the screensaver on her computer. Colt stood with his arm around her in Monument Valley near the Four Corners, the intersection of Colorado, Utah, Arizona, and New Mexico, one of the most barren and dramatic sites she had ever experienced.

She and Colt had been together for years, first as friends, then as lovers. After Alex extracted herself from an emotionally abusive marriage, she and Colt reunited as lovers and then business partners. It had been a convoluted journey, but their soul connection had been present from the time of their first encounter many years before.

The view from Alex's twenty-fourth floor office was an expansive vista of the Rocky Mountain Front Range covered in the last remnants of winter's snow. The office tower was only a block from the old headquarters where she had built her first company with her former partner, Christine Welbourne. A photo of Alex, Christine, and a tall, handsome cowboy standing by an airplane was prominently displayed on her partner's desk. The cowboy, Jake Winston, had been their friend and had helped Alex during the murder investigation.

Christine's brutal murder and the harrowing investigation that followed had almost destroyed Alex but, after facing her fears and the loss, she emerged stronger than ever. Eventually, she and Colt began their twisted journey together with a big joint venture, followed by an even more spectacular well in the Texas Panhandle. They drilled into one major formation after another, building Sheridan Enterprises into one of the most successful independent oil and gas companies in the U.S.

Alex glanced at the map on the wall. Its many red dots indicated producing wells, a large number of which had been drilled with Colt. She smiled and thought about how proud and excited Christine would have been.

Alex picked up the phone and started to call one more time, then stopped as anger mixed with fear. Colt's refusal to answer calls was childish and disturbing and, in her gut, she knew his absence was intentional. His many disappearances had become a pattern that tore at her heart. Their last parting was more painful and fractured than ever.

The phone rang, interrupting her thoughts. Alex finally answered. "Hi, Wayne."

Wayne Decker, one of her top engineers and senior manager at the Thompson Divide, muttered something. A deafening roar in the background muffled his words, but Alex thought she heard something about fur.

"I can't hear you!" she exclaimed.

"*Fire!* The well is on *fire!*" Wayne screamed over the roar.

Alex processed the information instantly and, cool as an ice cube, asked, "What happened?"

"Not sure yet!"

She found herself raising her voice to match his. "How bad is it?"

Wayne was an expert who had handled almost every kind of well disaster imaginable. "Serious!"

"Have you seen Colt?" Alex shouted as a knot of fear lodged in her gut.

"No, his truck is here but his phone rolls to voicemail."

"I can't get an answer either." The knot in her stomach tightened. "Did the blowout preventers fail?" Alex paced in front of the windows as storm clouds gathered to the north.

Wayne answered, "Not from what I can see."

Alex's brain ricocheted from one idea to the next. What happened? How did the fire start? Who was on duty? How long would it take to put out? The first order of business was putting it out. How it happened was a secondary matter. They had to protect the surrounding forest. Fire was their worst nightmare.

"Can we handle the fire?" Alex forced herself to calmness as she waited for his response.

"It's too big; the local emergency crews have been notified!"

She made a decision. "I'm coming over."

"Protestors are swarming the place. It's a zoo. Gotta go."

Alex stared silently out her windows. Could the protesters have been angry enough to destroy the well?

She moved deliberately into her closet and selected a small backpack while her mind raced. She wondered if her old friend Jake Winston, a respected business leader, would have some sage advice. His experience and friendship were invaluable, but she didn't want to send the wrong signal. His romantic interests in her were always close to the surface. She would wait until after inspecting the fire firsthand.

When necessary, Alex could live out of her office; often, it was her preference. The huge dressing area and closet were immaculately organized with every item imaginable. One section contained formal business wear. Another space housed boots, hats, and jeans. In the back, ski equipment was stored in cubbies. A huge marble steam shower was just steps from a Murphy bed in an adjacent alcove.

She opened a fake wall in the closet. Inside a secret drawer lay a piece of her history, a Colt .45 pistol that was a gift from her father. He had worn the pistol on their first hunting trip in Colorado and on

20

hundreds of other occasions. She hadn't thought to carry it in a long time, but this situation gave her pause. Those who protested at wells were often emotional, but they had never turned violent. She stuffed the weapon in her backpack and texted her pilot.

> Trey, we need to go over to Thompson Divide.
> How soon can you be here?

Trey Hunter's text came back in seconds:

> I'm on the way.

The routine responsibilities of flying for Sheridan Enterprises meant he was on call day and night. Their numerous projects required moving people around the clock.

❧

Alex pulled on weathered cowboy boots and a scuffed Barbour jacket, then texted Fran about her movements. She ended the text with:

> Not sure when I'll be back.

She knew Fran would handle the office while she was away.

Last, she texted Schaeffer with the disheartening news.

She loped up the stairs to the top of the building where the chopper waited. The Bell 407GX five-seat helicopter was a sleek black model with powerful lift and more than enough heft to get through turbulent air over the Rocky Mountains. She slid into the left seat next to Trey, gave him a warm nudge on the shoulder, then put on the headset and took the yoke. The fancy glass cockpit had a state-of-the-art Garmin instrument navigation system. In the back of the chopper lounged Trey's English bulldog, Brutus.

Trey was a mature man with a graying ponytail who had flown transport and combat missions at the tail end of the second Gulf War. He managed to survive two tours of duty and return with his body intact. His burly arms were hard from lifting weights, and a tattoo of a Coptic Orthodox cross was inked on his left bicep. The emotional trauma from his war years had been difficult, but Trey recovered and made a bumpy, yet eventually successful, transition into the civilian world. Alex trusted his experience and judgment.

"You ready?" he asked.

Alex nodded, giving a thumbs-up, and she lifted the chopper into the sky above downtown Denver. In minutes, they were near the foothills and the Front Range. Turbulent air yanked and jerked the helicopter as it made its bumpy way over snow-capped peaks. It was a short distance as the crow flies, not far from the sleepy town of Carbondale, about thirty-five miles from Aspen. In the distance, a black plume tarnished the sky.

"Oh, my God, it's our well," Alex murmured as she studied the oily smoke billowing into the atmosphere. "This is a nightmare."

Signs were abundantly displayed throughout Garfield County: "Save the Thompson Divide."

"They don't like drilling." Trey had a way of boiling issues down to a few words.

"Cars don't run on wind."

He nodded. "That's another subject."

Alex skillfully fluttered the chopper to the landing pad. It was her favorite investment, a luxury purchased for the company after a huge home-run well.

"Nice landing." In addition to being a seasoned pilot, Trey was a top-notch flight instructor.

Alex smiled at the compliment. "Thanks for the ride."

She patted Brutus before stepping down and into a waiting pickup truck. Wayne Decker greeted Alex with a big hug. Wayne had worked in the oilfields for her dad and later signed on with Alex's company when she returned to Denver. He managed a delicate balance working for Sheridan Enterprises as well as for Colt Forester. The sweat-stained cowboy hat protecting his balding head was branded with the state of Texas, and smudged fingerprints soiled the rim. The last half of his index finger was missing on his right hand, the consequence of a rig accident many years before. Wayne's weathered skin looked craggier than usual.

"What's the status?" Alex asked as they headed off the main road toward the backcountry.

"Something exploded at the wellhead. It was powerful enough to destroy the pipe and set everything on fire." Wayne's eyes were Paul Newman-blue slits that twinkled when things were good and went dark and stormy when he was worried, as he was now.

"This was intentional?"

Wayne shrugged. "Well, it definitely doesn't look like an accident to me."

Alex glared as she asked, "How do we handle it?" She had never faced a threat of this magnitude. Mechanical failures were commonplace in the industry, but deliberate destruction of property was foreign to Alex.

"Everyone's working to get it under control," he told her. "I spoke on the phone with the sheriff who's handling the investigation."

"What do they know about gas wells?"

"Not much, from what I can tell." Wayne rolled his eyes.

A worried frown appeared on Alex's forehead. "Someone could have been killed."

"Whoever is responsible wanted it destroyed." Wayne chewed on a straw as he pondered the situation. "It appears they knew enough to blow it up at a stage when it would do the most damage."

"We need the fire out before the whole forest goes up in flames. Do whatever it takes."

"Wild Well is the only company that can handle this." Wild Well Operations, a Houston-based company, specialized in extinguishing well fires around the globe.

Alex glanced over at him. "When can they get here?"

"Not soon enough. They've already been called."

"And the other wells?" she asked. Two other completed and producing wells had been drilled from the same pad and were precariously nearby.

"They haven't ignited yet."

Smoke filled the sky as if from an angry locomotive. Alex swallowed hard and let out an audible sigh. Her entire career had been focused on safe drilling practices and extreme safety measures. This fire had to be contained.

"Wild Well Operations is the best since Red Adair," Wayne said, referring to the famous man who had put out oil well fires all over the world. Wayne's reassurance didn't relieve her tension.

She fidgeted for a minute, then forced herself to stillness. "This is going to cost a fortune."

"The sheriff told us not to touch anything." Wayne chuckled. "Kind of stupid, since the fire's burning so hot it's melted almost everything."

The rutted forest road led them in the direction of the black smoke that surged above the fire. As they pulled up to the site, sign-waving crowds surrounded the area. Gazing past the protesters, Alex saw flames shooting sideways from the mangled pipe.

The wellhead and pipe had melted from the extreme heat, and local fire fighters from various Colorado agencies worked furiously to keep the surrounding forest from turning into an inferno. The air was hot and toxic. The well team managed to keep the crowds and spectators back while spraying water on the raging well. For the moment, all energy was focused on containing the flames.

A call came in on the radio. "Hold on for Alex Sheridan." Wayne passed the device like a baton.

"This is Alex Sheridan." She spoke loudly over the roar of the fire.

"Bull Hawthorn, at Wild Well Operations. How are you?"

For a moment, she was astonished. She had not expected the owner of Wild Well Operations, one of the most famous oilmen in the business, to call.

"I've been better," she said. "We have a big fire here."

"An assessor is on the way up there to determine what equipment we need to bring in," he told her in a calm tone.

"When will that be?" she asked anxiously.

"Sometime tomorrow, we hope." Hawthorn's voice didn't change at all.

"This is urgent!" Alex cried. Behind her, the well spewed fire like an erupting volcano.

"Always is. We'll take care of it." He sounded as if he were talking about a flat tire.

"Before the whole forest burns, please," she blurted, and immediately wished she hadn't sounded so sarcastic.

"After the charter flight is scheduled, we'll let you know all the details, including who'll be managing the well." His tone remained detached and polite.

"What about the equipment? Where's it coming from?"

"Some can be sourced locally. The rest will come from Houston." Hawthorn sounded like he was accustomed to urgent demands from his customers.

Ever the decisive, action-oriented woman, Alex was annoyed by the nonchalant response. "This is costing a fortune," she said, stating the obvious.

A burning well cost thousands of dollars a day. Even more disturbing was the risk to the workers who tried to put out the fire.

"Ms. Sheridan, we know what we're doing," Hawthorn said. "You're going to have to trust me."

"I'm trying, but you should see the flames and the fire. We're short on water now."

"We'll take care of it," he said again, his tone a bit more reassuring, and ended the call.

Alex turned to Wayne. "How well do you know Bull Hawthorn?" she asked doubtfully.

"He's known worldwide, best in the business. Good man all 'round."

Wayne drove through the gaggle of protesters and parked the truck a safe distance from the burning well. Not too far away stood an abandoned pickup truck. Alex's heart sank—it was Colt's. A wave of rage over his actions rippled through her, coupled with a thick fog of sadness.

They got out of the pickup, and a scruffy young man approached them. "The Thompson Divide belongs to the people, not the oil companies!" he yelled with malice.

Wanting to avoid a confrontation, Alex and Wayne walked toward Colt's pickup.

The young man, who must have seen the Sheridan Oil and Gas sign on the truck door, bird-dogged Wayne. "Get out of the national forest!" he shouted.

Wayne took two steps toward the man, spat tobacco juice in the dirt, and looked the young protester square in the face. "Son, we're going to put out the fire and protect the forest. Don't get in my way again."

The young man shrank back at Wayne's forceful but polite response.

Extinguishing well fires was a perilous business. The fires had to be extinguished at the wellhead, just above ground. The job required tons of water, which was another logistical challenge and, frequently, highly volatile explosives were used. An explosion had to be large enough to rob the fire of oxygen and, once the fire was extinguished, the well had to be capped to stop the flow of oil and gas.

Alex circled the abandoned vehicle, peering inside where Colt's hat and glasses lay on the seat. For the first time, she felt a pang of concern. Old coffee cups and a couple of empty chewing tobacco cans littered the cab floorboard, and a cigar lay in the console.

"Still no sign of Colt?" she asked.

"Nothin'." Wayne picked up an empty can and spit brown chewing tobacco into it.

"Why would he have left his truck?" Alex wondered aloud.

Wayne looked puzzled at the question. "He's a loose cannon." Colt's recent erratic behavior had not earned favor with Wayne Decker, who was doing his best to cover for Colt and convince the site team that things were under control.

"If he's goofing off somewhere, I'll shoot him," Alex said, irritably. Using a handkerchief, she looked underneath the seat and in the glove compartment.

"Sheriff said not to touch anything," Wayne reminded her.

"Just looking."

"I hope Colt didn't run into whoever did this," Wayne said, a concerned tone in his voice.

Alex closed the glove compartment, then examined the back seat and the inside of the toolbox. Nothing in or around the truck appeared out of the ordinary.

"Me, too. Have you seen Colt's pistol?"

"No sign of it." Wayne watched as she finished searching the truck.

An official Garfield County SUV screeched up to the site, kicking up dirt in a dramatic entrance. A large man in a forest-green uniform with a 9mm Glock pistol strapped to his side stepped out of the cab. His Smokey Bear-style hat cast a shadow across his face. With two large strides, the officer reached Alex and Wayne. "Sheriff Dan Salido." The officer stuck out a paw-like hand.

"Alex Sheridan." Her hand was dwarfed in his palm. "We, Sheridan Enterprises, own the well. Colt Forester is the operator," she said, trying to explain the complex business relationship. "Companies often hire separate drilling operators and we have numerous consultants and subcontractors as part of our operation."

"Wayne Decker." Wayne extended his gnarly hand with the missing fingertip. His skin looked as if it had been in formaldehyde for years.

The two men studied each other silently, as if preparing for a duel. Then Sheriff Salido turned his attention to the murky smoke billowing into the clean mountain air. His hedge-row brows furrowed.

"This is one of the reasons we don't want drilling around here." The word "we" stood out like a hot branding iron, revealing his allegiance to his local constituents. The sheriff's tall, lean form belonged in the forest, and a halo of quiet confidence surrounded him. His crisp uniform and short-cropped hair gave him a rigid, military-style appearance. Alex found him almost handsome, but she thought something hard and lonely was masked by his bravado.

"This land was leased fair and square from the federal government," Alex said, reminding him about their legitimate presence.

"That doesn't make it right," he retorted. "Before becoming sheriff, I worked as a fire jumper, and I'm acutely aware of the actions needed to fight a well fire."

Alex crossed her arms and stood her ground. "The drilling permits are on file."

"And this is my jurisdiction and my investigation." His jaw tightened.

"Then investigate who started the fire. This is arson," Alex shot back harshly.

"But *you're* responsible." The sheriff gazed down at her defiantly.

Behind Salido, Alex saw several more official county vehicles, and uniformed men swarmed the premises.

It was obvious that the volunteers, workers, and observers respected Dan Salido. Alex noticed a lot of the onlookers were definitely against fracking, basing her conclusion on the signs they carried, although she would have bet they knew little about the technology.

She also understood the sheriff's concern. It was the end of drought season and, even under the best of circumstances, the area was on high fire alert. Signs dotted the highways, warning campers of the risks. One smoldering cigarette or one lightning bolt could cause acres of forest to erupt in flames.

"This was sabotage," Alex stated as she glared at Salido. "And we'll prove it."

He sighed. "I hope you're wrong."

CHAPTER 3

The first news truck arrived at the well site while Alex was sparring with the sheriff. A reporter with carefully styled hair and a fresh spray tan positioned himself in front of the burning well with its spewing flames. As the cameras rolled, the reporter gestured toward the forest: "We are here at the disputed area in the Thompson Divide." He directed the cameraman to zoom in and focus on the voluminous smoke. "The well has been burning for hours with no end in sight in this favorite recreation area for local hikers and nature lovers," he spoke into a microphone before moving deliberately toward Alex, who was clearly the person in charge

"I'm Bruce Babcock of KMTN," he told her. "I understand you own this well?"

"Yes, it's owned by my company, Sheridan Enterprises," she answered.

"I'd like to ask you a few questions." The anchorman, whose face had been a staple on the evening news for decades, shook Alex's hand. He held the microphone toward her as the filming continued.

"We are now speaking with Alex Sheridan, the owner of the well. Ms. Sheridan, what happened here?" Babcock asked in a dramatic tone.

"That's what we'd like to know," she replied.

"This is a colossal disaster," he said. "What's your plan?"

"First, we have to contain the fire. Hundreds of emergency workers, including firefighters, county personnel, and sheriff deputies are here to assist."

He nodded. "How often do wells burn out of control like this?"

"Almost never—" Alex said before the reporter cut her off mid-sentence.

"Is this a justifiable reason to stop drilling in this area?"

Alex paused and took a deep breath. In half a second, she could drown the news anchor in facts and statistics that would make him look uninformed and unprepared. Part of her wanted to rip apart the reporter's slanted agenda and tell him what she thought about his ignorant, sensationalized journalism, but her measured side knew it was best to remain calm and collected. This was one of the moments that tested the best in Alex. Still, it took all she had to restrain her temper.

"It is best not to speculate. Our job is to put out the fire." Inside, she smoldered.

"Some say that drilling in this pristine forest can't ever be safe. Look at this fire!" His free hand waved in the direction of the burning well. An army of men from different agencies worked feverishly to contain the flames. Their hoses sprayed rivers of water on the surrounding trees as noxious fumes billowed into the once-clean air.

"The investigators will determine exactly what happened," said Alex calmly. "Drilling is safe as long as the wells aren't tampered with, Mr. Babcock."

"Tampered with?" The reporter looked appalled. "Are you suggesting this was intentional?" His voice rose with each word.

"The investigation will find the truth." The words "tampered with" had slipped out, and she couldn't take them back.

"That is a rash allegation, don't you think?" Babcock turned to the camera. "We are at the burning well site operated by Sheridan Oil and Gas. The Thompson Divide is one of the unspoiled areas of Colorado— *was* one of the unspoiled areas. KMTN is covering the incident at the contested site just outside Carbondale." The camera crew cut to the protestors, who waved signs and shouted, *No Drilling!* Cell phones held high in the air streamed the disaster to the world.

"We will get to the truth of what really happened," Alex repeated..

"How will you contain the fire before it spreads to the forest?" the news anchor demanded, turning back to her.

"Wayne!" Alex called, "can you come answer some technical questions?"

Wayne walked in their direction, weathered and brown, looking as if he had just stepped off an old western movie set.

The anchor introduced himself and shook Wayne's outstretched hand. "So, what would cause a well to burn out of control?"

Wayne looked at Alex, who nodded, encouraging him to speak freely.

"This was no accident," he said. "The only way it could burn like this is if someone set the fire."

The blunt words evoked a shocked look from the newsman. He directed the camera to focus on a group of protestors who were waving signs and chanting: "No more drilling! No more fracking! Save the Divide! Save our water!"

The crowd swarmed like angry bees. More news trucks arrived from different media outlets, discharging a wave of reporters and camera operators. They descended on Alex's group, shouting questions.

Alex's chest tightened, and her head throbbed from the fumes and the unrelenting noise as she tried to field a barrage of questions that flew at her from multiple people.

"No, this will not damage the water table. It is not anywhere near the water table," Alex said to one reporter. In her opinion, the oil and gas industry had done a poor job of educating the public about the drilling business, its risks, and its safeguards. Misinformation about fracking and many other aspects of the industry created a formidable hurdle.

Babcock corralled the sheriff. "How will you investigate the fire?" he demanded.

"Nothing can be done until we stop the burn."

Babcock looked disheartened, and Alex could tell he wanted controversy. "Will Sheridan Oil and Gas be held accountable for the damage?"

"That depends on what caused the explosion. We *will* find out what happened." The sheriff excused himself and went back to managing the fire-fighting operation.

Darkness descended on the mountains, leaving a slight glow in the western sky. The burning well could be seen for miles. Wayne Decker and Alex sat on the tailgate of his dented pickup as several of the field workers gathered around. Wayne had a silver Coors can in one hand and a piece of jerky hanging out of his mouth as he contemplated their predicament.

"Did you ever meet Red Adair?" Wayne asked Alex.

"Just once, on a drill site."

"He sure knew how to handle a fire," Wayne said, swigging his beer. "He put out a fire on a gas well in Somalia that threatened an entire field."

The field workers sat on coolers to drink their beers and listen to Alex and Wayne. Covered in grime and exhausted from the long day, they were finally taking a break.

"Where's Colt?" one young man inquired.

Alex frowned. "We're tracking him down."

Wayne reminisced as they sat in the glow of the fire. "Do you remember the Devil's Cigarette Lighter?" he asked, referring to one of the most famous well fires to ever burn—a 1961 natural gas fire in the Sahara Desert in Algeria.

"I know the legend," one of the young men answered. He pulled up a picture of the burning well on his iPhone.

"That was before you were born. The fire burned for six months," Wayne explained. "Fire from the gas well shot about one hundred forty meters into the air."

The young men listened intently. Their dreams were big and their fears almost nonexistent. They hadn't lived long enough to know to be afraid.

"It was so big that John Glenn, you know, the astronaut, could see it from space as he orbited," Wayne snorted. "Hell, it was so hot that the sand around the fire melted into glass."

Another young worker spoke up. "How did they put it out?"

"Nitroglycerin. They exploded hundreds of tons to pull the oxygen out of the air. It's not done that way anymore, but it was something to see."

Wayne's life had spanned the greatest eras in the business, from the early swashbuckling wildcatter years all the way to the present, where technology had become king. He seemed sure the Thompson Divide fire could be put out, but he could not know if the project and the company

31

would survive. Odds were that the well would be lost, as would the millions invested in seismic tests, geological studies, and infrastructure. Even more troubling was the looming environmental damage. Protecting the forest ecosystem was a vital priority.

Damn it, Alex thought angrily. Where the hell is Colt?

CHAPTER 4

In the moonless night, Wayne and Alex drove toward Carbondale, where Alex and her team regularly stayed when working at the drilling site. The small Comfort Inn just off Highway 133 had become a regular temporary home for the team. Nestled at the base of the soul-stirring, twin-summit Mount Sopris, Carbondale was a mixture of small bars and restaurants, consignment stores, and pot shops.

In one shop, a green neon window sign blinked, advertising weed for sale. Colorado's hottest industry was the legal marijuana business, and it was like the Wild West again, with untested rules and vague regulations. People hoping to cash in on the boom raced to apply for grow permits and licenses for greenhouses and pot shops. No one quite knew the best way to regulate the legalized commodity.

"What do you think about legal pot?" Alex asked Wayne to kill time on their way to Carbondale.

He exhaled. "I'll stick to chewing tobacco."

"That's not a good choice either." Alex yawned as fatigue set in after the excruciating day.

Wayne loved his chewing tobacco and wasn't the least bit concerned with the health risks. "I called ahead and got rooms," he said, changing the subject.

"Thanks." Alex's eyelids were heavy as Wayne pulled the pickup into the familiar parking lot. The warmly lit reception area of the motel was a welcome sight.

The manager, a large welcoming woman, had been there for years. "Your usual rooms," she said, handing over key cards. "Let me know if you need anything."

"Just quiet," Wayne responded in a tired voice. He escorted Alex the short distance down the dimly lit hallway to her room. "I'll be right down the hall if you need anything."

She nodded. "Thanks, Wayne. Night."

Alex's eyes felt as dry as burnt toast and her head pounded fiercely. She tossed her small backpack onto a chair, took out the Colt .45 revolver, and opened the cylinder for extra safety. She placed the pistol on the far pillow of the queen-sized bed.

A wave of gratitude for the sparse motel room away from hostile protestors and the burning well washed through Alex, followed by a troubling fear about Colt. After taking three Advils, she stripped and stepped into a hot shower. The steamy water rinsed away as much of the day as could be erased. The mud and fumes disappeared, but her anxiety over the lost well increased. What would her financial backers and investors do?

She wrapped her hair in a towel and turned on the news to discover the governor giving an interview on Channel 9. "Oh, shit," she whispered.

The governor, a distinguished graying man in his early sixties, stood before a podium on the steps of the state capitol building in Denver. Local activist groups could be seen marching on the grounds of the building, waving signs in the same places where the Occupy Wall Street protestors had squatted for months demanding justice. Drilling in Colorado was a combustible issue, and now Sheridan Oil and Gas was in the public eye.

The camera cut to the burning well, then to Alex's earlier interview at the Thompson Divide. Then came an interview with the Democratic U.S. senator from Colorado, a handsome, suited man with thinning hair and a wide smile.

"We can't overreact to one isolated incident," the senator explained reasonably. "The oil and gas industry employs thousands of people in our state. Vast numbers of people on the Western Slope, in towns like Mesa and Rifle, depend on the drilling industry. Oilfield suppliers and support businesses employ numerous men and women."

Several "boos" were audible in the background.

"Finally!" Alex exclaimed aloud. It was the first positive statement she had heard all day. There were hundreds of links in the chain between drilling rig operators and the gas pump. Skilled workers laid pipe and worked as engineers, while others drove huge disposal trucks that transported the wastewater. Lives and livelihoods depended on the successful continuation of oil and gas production in the state, and the fracking technology that had fueled the boom.

The crowd behind the senator continued its "No more fracking!" chant.

On social media, the story had gone viral. A video of the burning well was on YouTube and Twitter.

Alex was startled by the ring of the landline phone in the room.

"You all right?" Wayne asked.

She sighed. "Dead tired."

"You seen the news?"

"Yes, watching it now." She muted the volume.

"We'll get through it," he said reassuringly. "I've seen a lot worse than this."

"I'm not too good at waiting." She resisted the urge to snap at him.

Silence settled between them. Alex knew Wayne's ways, so she patiently waited for his next question.

"No word from Colt?"

"Not yet." Alex clutched at and guarded her deepest fears. Colt had been sober for some time, but there had been a few slips along the way. Half of her was afraid he was on a binge, and the other half didn't want to contemplate anything else. She finally asked the question she had been afraid to utter. "You don't think he could have gotten drunk and done something stupid at the well, like accidentally set it on fire?"

Wayne cleared his throat. "He was furious that the drilling permits were delayed again by the protestors."

"Yes, he was angry, in a way I've never seen." Alex was thinking of their last fight when Colt had stormed out in a fury.

"Better get some rest." Wayne hung up.

Alex turned off the news and crawled clean and naked between the sheets. She lay sleepless in the dark with the wall air conditioner humming a familiar lullaby. Its soothing sound brought back memories of the well sites she had visited with her father in West Texas, with fireflies dancing at sunset. This was one of the moments when her heart longed to be curled up tight in a warm blanket next to a loved one. She had chosen a wilder path, a life journey of adventure filled with awe and risk and aloneness.

It was nearly 2:00 a.m. when she finally fell into a restless sleep. She tossed and turned for a while, then a dark familiar dream returned. In the misty dream state, old memories were exhumed, and she was transported to a haunting scene that refused to stay buried.

She saw herself walking into her old Denver high-rise office. She was euphoric about new projects, and she couldn't wait to see Christine, her partner, best friend, and mentor. Their magical synergy had produced unparalleled success in oil and gas and real estate development. Alex was brimming with anticipation and ecstatic with news.

"Chris?" she called out. She rounded the corner, moving from the hallway into the office that overlooked the rugged Rocky Mountains.

The scene was always the same. A deathly silence filled the room. Chris, a brilliant woman of poise and elegance, sat statuesque in her chair in front of floor-to-ceiling windows. Everything was calm and in its place, except for the blood. Blood covered the floor like red syrup.

Alex looked directly at her partner. Her head was partially blown away by a high-caliber bullet. Blood splattered the windows and turned the room crimson.

Alex heard her own scream and jerked upright. Sweat covered her body and soaked the bed sheets. Agony lingered in the room like the odor of a rotting carcass. Her eyes searched for the familiar: dirty clothes lay on the chair and the pistol rested untouched on the pillow.

As her breathing evened, Alex shook her head, seeking coherence. The clicking and humming of the air conditioner brought her back to reality in the Comfort Inn in Carbondale.

Every time the dream resurfaced, it was as vivid as the day she had found Chris murdered in their office. The shock and horror persisted.

A long, tortuous investigation following the murder had only added to the traumatic loss. Each day the case remained unsolved, another thread in the tapestry of Alex's life unraveled. Her business was all but destroyed, leaving her financial affairs in shambles. Then the hapless police set their sights on Alex and named her as a suspect. This stab in the dark was excruciating and, even when she was cleared, the investigation dragged on. Eventually, the murder case went dormant.

Years later, a moment of divine intervention provided a vital new lead, and a determined detective, Mike Carter, would not let it go. Though they got off to a rocky start, Detective Carter's ferocious determination won Alex over, and she grew to care for him like a brother. It was his call to Alex, years after the murder, that caused her to return to Denver to help find the truth. Together they solved the mystery and arrested and prosecuted the person who had murdered Christine.

Exhaustion tortured Alex, but sleep was elusive. Somehow, the well fire had to be contained, with or without Colt.

A Jeep traveled on Highway 133 along the ancient snaky twists of the Crystal River, headed toward the picturesque towns of Redstone and Marble. The landscape was rural outside of Carbondale, and an abundance of red dirt ground, pastures dotted with lazy cows, and listing gray farmhouses bordered the river. The driver pulled the late-model vehicle into the drive by a log cabin in a secluded camping area and RV park just outside of Redstone.

Aaron Jeffries, the driver, got out of the vehicle and waited. He had the shadow scraps of being handsome, but his dark face was worn hard beyond its years. A deep crooked scar wound from his left ear down to his collarbone.

A short stocky man with red hair approached and shook Aaron's hand familiarly.

"Hi, Beaver, glad you made it," Aaron said, welcoming the redheaded man. "Where's Jason?"

"My brother's busy!" the stocky, red-haired man said in a harsh tone.

Protesters were assembling in their vehicles. A bumper sticker on the rear of one of the vans read: *No Fracking. Save Colorado.*

An enthusiastic young man with a smartphone approached Aaron and the others, proudly offering to show them a video. "The fire is all over YouTube!"

"The feds have no business in our land!" the short redheaded man proclaimed.

Most agreed with him that the federal government and their partners, the oil companies, had no right to make decisions that impacted their state, and they were determined to take any action necessary to stop the drilling.

"The forest belongs to the people, not the government," another activist chimed in.

The burning well and the sign-waving crowds made dramatic footage. "This is epic," a young woman exulted.

Jeffries, originally from Denver, was new to the area, but he was experienced in the oil and gas industry and got interested in the cause. He was living a peaceful life up in Marble, one of the more remote mountain towns in Garfield County, famous only for providing the clean white marble used for the Lincoln Memorial.

Few people knew Aaron, but he was a welcome behind-the-scenes voice against development. Like so many who moved to towns in Colorado, he had fallen in love with the area and quickly became a local.

The smiling, boisterous gatherers entered the cabin. They were a diverse set of county locals united by their common purpose. Some were in need of a cause and others liked railing against the big companies.

Aaron welcomed the group with coffee and juice as they all chatted aimlessly. Finally, he clanged a mug with a spoon and called the little meeting to order. "Thanks to all of you for your hard work. We are making progress and will prevail."

Cheers burst forth in the small cabin.

"Did you see the media coverage?" a short, weathered man in work clothes asked.

"The fire could be the key to the end of drilling in the Thompson Divide!" another said animatedly. The group grew as more people supporting the cause entered the small space.

"Do you think the fire will be enough to force the government to revoke all drilling permits in the area?" a woman asked. She was a young mom. Aaron recognized her as a teacher in a local elementary school.

"If we keep enough pressure on the government," Aaron said. "Can you rally more folks to come up to the site? We have to stop the government from issuing any more permits and we need lots of people to make our point."

The man who'd met Aaron when he arrived spoke up. "More people are coming in the morning."

"And make sure someone is tweeting everything." Aaron preferred to work behind the scenes, giving others the spotlight. He was just grateful to have this project to give him purpose.

"It will be all over social media tonight and tomorrow," a young man with a partial buzz cut stated.

The group continued to cheer and clap.

"The fire proves that drilling is dangerous!"

"Tell them to go drill in the Rhone Plateau," someone yelled.

Not far away in Rifle, Colorado, and the Rhone Plateau, hundreds of rigs dotted the mountainside. At night, hazard lights illuminated the rigs like a forest of Christmas trees. It was exactly what the group wanted to prevent in the Thompson Divide. They would not allow the government and oil companies to destroy the beautiful forest.

The men and women cheered, shook hands, and slapped backs. Volunteers agreed to various assignments. Several of the young people took responsibility for the social media campaign, and Aaron felt proud that he was able to help save the national forest. Before the supporters and protesters went away, enthusiastic and committed to the cause, he made sure the others would be strategically located when the press arrived.

Aaron had spent much time thinking about how to stop the federal government from leasing lands to the oil and gas companies. The Thompson Divide was a place covered with gnarly skinned conifers and hiking trails. It was the last place the federal government should be handing out leases. Now retired from a business career in the city, he valued dearly the opportunity to live in the wilderness, and he wasn't about to let Big Oil, a hated industry, destroy his adopted way of life. The raging fire could be used to effect changes beyond his wildest dreams.

CHAPTER 5

At 5:30 a.m., Alex left the Carbondale Comfort Inn, bought two large coffees at the gas station and, with Wayne riding shotgun, she drove along the bumpy mountain road until she reached the drilling site.

Colt's pickup remained parked in the same spot near the well. There was no way he would have just abandoned his truck, Alex thought. A little voice of fear and doubt countered: *Unless he had so much to drink that he walked away.*

Alex thought about filing a missing person's report, the next logical step, but that had its own set of complications. Colt's drinking history would probably come up, making it difficult to prove he was actually missing.

When Colt drank, he morphed into a completely different person from the one she had fallen in love with and, sometimes, he disappeared for days. There were times he ended up at another drilling operation. As an engineer, he consulted on numerous well projects that could be located anywhere from Beaumont to Midland. It was impossible to know whether he was holed up in a border town bar or just working another job.

Alex decided to take a walk around the area before the mobs of protesters arrived. The fire still burned, and firefighters worked on the outer edges of the blaze to contain it. A wooded path led into the surrounding forest. She walked in widening circles, staring at the ground in hopes of finding clues. Everyone, including the sheriff, had been so consumed by containing the fire that there was no time to look into what had actually caused the explosion.

A giant section of yellow tape encircled the perimeter of the drill site to protect the scene. The sheriff had called for backup from collaborating agencies. This well was in the county, but it was on national forest property, so the feds could get involved if there was a crime. For now, it was all in the hands of Sheriff Salido, a man who made Alex very nervous.

She searched the area, hoping to discover some detail that would help her make sense of the situation. A young buck with fuzzy antlers looked at her through the trees. She stood motionless as his huge, dark eyes studied her. Then he bolted into the remains of the morning fog.

Alex looked downward to her far left. She noticed the needle-covered floor of the forest had been disturbed, as if someone had been rolling around on the ground. A small compass lay nearby, half-buried in leaves and debris. She instantly recognized it as Colt's. He always wore the brass compass attached to his belt loop and keys. Several loose keys were scattered in the dirt. Maybe he had fought with the arsonists and was lying hurt somewhere?

Alex bent to pick up the items, then stopped herself. The compass and keys would be vital evidence, and she didn't want to taint a crime scene.

With her cell phone camera, Alex snapped multiple photos, noticing that she had no signal in this part of the drilling site. She continued to search the ground as she walked farther into the woods. Methodically, she scanned the area for evidence, but found nothing more.

As she cut through the trees, moving toward the truck, a flash of orange caught her eye. She tiptoed deftly into the area, trying not to disturb anything. A Denver Broncos logo bandana, covered in what appeared to be dried blood, lay in a ditch next to the path.

This bandana had been in Colt's back pocket since their first meeting. Alex took several more photos. The hot air was thick with smoke, and the suffocating fire made it painful to breathe.

Alex felt a stab of guilt. Something violent had happened, and she had wasted time thinking only about Colt's addiction. She had jumped to a conclusion, sure he had fallen off the wagon, and now she realized his life could be at risk. What could have happened to him, and where and how would they search for him? Did Colt accidentally stumble on someone who was sabotaging the equipment?

She made a note of the location of the orange bandana, then called the sheriff's number. Even if he seemed hostile to her cause, he needed to know about the evidence she'd found. She kept trying to reach his number as she walked in the direction of a company truck, hoping for cell service. Through an opening in the trees, she saw Wayne drinking coffee and talking to one of the team members.

She ran over to Wayne, interrupting his conversation. "Look at this." She held up the cell phone.

"What ya got?" Wayne asked, looking at the photos as she flipped through them.

"His keys with his compass and his Broncos handkerchief."

She was breathless. The air was already thin in the high altitude, and the fire had robbed it of more oxygen. "The bandana is covered with blood!" She choked out the words.

Wayne rubbed his forehead and readjusted his hat as he waited for more details.

But Alex turned away and started toward her truck. "Radio if you need anything," she said over her shoulder.

"Where are you going?" he yelled after her.

"To get more help."

Sheriff Salido pulled into the driveway of his small ranch house in a modest development on the outskirts of Carbondale. A pony grazed in the yard next to a swing set, and the garage door was half-open. Silence greeted the sheriff as he walked through the front door, and the emptiness of the house hit him like a cold wind. Just like the time before, a neighbor had called to warn him.

The drawers gaped open in the bedroom, hanging half-in and half-out. A scribbled note lay on the dresser. "*I just need more time.*"

His wife, Susie, had run away again, unable to handle the responsibilities of being a mother to their ten-year-old daughter. Salido had begun to believe that there was not enough time in this life for his wife to heal from the abuse she suffered at the hands of her father. Salido had not anticipated the intensity of the trauma that would come back to life after the birth of their beautiful little girl. Cathy's arrival in the world opened a great wound. Every painful childhood memory and fear was reborn as his wife slowly fragmented.

He took a deep breath and made a call to his assistant, Beverly.

"Will you be able to help with Cathy after school starting tomorrow? I'm not sure for how long."

"Of course. I'll call her coach to see if she can stay in the aftercare program until I get there." Beverly Doyle was the office manager and mother hen in the sheriff's office. Sadly, she was all too familiar with the sheriff's problems with his traumatized wife.

Sheriff Salido walked into the yard of the house next door and climbed the front steps. The screen door opened and a beautiful ten-year-old girl with a ponytail and braces burst onto the porch and into his arms. She had the body of a fawn and the heart of a lioness.

The neighbor woman smiled at him from under disheveled brown hair. On her hip, a plump baby with a double chin and full pink cheeks cooed irresistibly.

"Thanks for helping," Salido said gratefully.

"Any time. We had fun," the mother said, looking fondly at Cathy, who stood close by.

"Try the cookies," Cathy said joyfully, holding a cookie up to her father, crumbs around her mouth.

"She say anything?" Salido asked the neighbor, hoping for a clue to his wife's behavior.

The woman shook her head. "Nothing. I'm sorry."

Salido was half-ashamed of the thought that entered his mind: *What was so hard about taking care of a beautiful little girl and making cookies?* He would do anything in the world to help his wife feel safe, but he had tried a hundred different strategies, and nothing had helped. It was ultimately up to Susie to see if she could get to the other side of her trauma. One doctor said the healing might never happen.

Cathy handed him a cookie, a gesture that helped him ignore the incessant vibrations of his cell phone.

ᔆ

Chaos reigned at the drilling site, where a blazing column from the spewing well shot hundreds of feet into the sky. The adjacent well caught fire, adding to the disastrous situation. Hard-hatted men worked feverishly, some spraying constant streams of water from gigantic hoses to hold back the sea of flames.

Alex climbed into a company truck and sped away, kicking dirt into the air. As the truck bumped along the rutted, rocky path, protestors in vans appeared. One of the vans pulled sideways across the road in front of the truck. Alex slammed the brake to the floor. Several nearby agitators on foot began to rock the vehicle as they shouted taunts.

Alex gripped the steering wheel and blared the car horn, startling the crowd. She shifted the four-wheel drive into low gear and maneuvered around the blockade, driving over a high mound to escape the crowd, whose frustrated members continued to yell, "No more drilling!"

Alex repeatedly tried to reach the sheriff, but his number rolled to voicemail again. "Why doesn't he answer?" she asked aloud in the empty truck. She texted Trey to tell him she was on her way.

After a long, bumpy ride that seemed to go on forever, she pulled up beside the helicopter pad where Trey waited. Again, she took her seat to his left, but this time he would be flying pilot. Before taking off, she dialed an old friend.

Trey maneuvered the chopper around several thunderheads and over Independence Pass. Turbulent air jerked the chopper around, causing it to lurch erratically as Trey maneuvered effortlessly through the storms and over the mountains. They made the turbulent helicopter ride to Denver in about an hour, and he set the copter down atop the downtown office building.

"Thanks," Alex said, stepping out onto the roof, "we'll go back over to the well later today."

She waved all clear, jogged to the elevator, and descended to the garage level, where she opened the door to an espresso-colored Cayenne Porsche. The mid-size SUV barreled out into an alley and, within minutes, the GPS map showed the car winding through the streets of downtown Denver.

Alex needed someone on her side in this investigation, a trusted advocate to find out what happened to the well and to Colt. If anyone could help, it was Mike Carter, the former homicide investigator who led the investigation into her partner's murder and eventually became Alex's trusted friend.

After Christine's murder was solved, Carter left the Denver Police Department to go out on his own as a private investigator and consultant. He helped clients with missing person cases, assisted the local department with special cases, and supposedly enjoyed a less stressful life. Alex wondered if he had ever found someone to share his life with besides Tom, his gray tabby cat. Carter was a loner.

She made another attempt to reach Detective Carter. The call rolled to voicemail. "Get off the phone!" she yelled, slamming the steering wheel with the palms of her hands. Carter was probably on two lines at once; she doubted his habits had changed.

Frustrated, she followed the GPS map into a shadier part of Denver. The route led her over railroad tracks, into the northeast section, where she entered a transitional neighborhood that had once been an industrial warehouse district. At a dirty intersection under a trestle, a man wearing multiple layers of clothing pushed a rusty grocery cart filled with debris and blankets. He held up a cardboard sign that said, *Hungry.*

Alex felt a wave of sadness wash over her as she opened her window. "You know about the church mission?" she asked.

"Yes, ma'am." He was worn thin like an old blanket. Alex gave him some cash, knowing there would never be enough.

"They can help," she suggested gently. He pushed on his way, muttering to the wind as she continued to her destination.

The old industrial area had not seen prosperity in years, and there were no street numbers or signage. She came to a driveway that led to a large parking lot fenced with razor wire. Carter's old Ford Bronco was parked by an unmarked entryway. She reached through her car window and pressed a button. After a few seconds, a voice like dripping oil came through the intercom: "Security Services."

"Lafayette!" Alex cried. She could barely contain her excitement. She'd recognize that deep voice anywhere. "Is that you?" she asked with genuine delight.

The deep bass voice chuckled. She could almost feel his smile through the intercom.

"It is," he drawled.

Her heart pounded with joy, just hearing her old friend speak. The security gate rattled open as if by magic.

"Come on in this house!" Lafayette's southern accent was so warm she could almost smell cornbread on the stove. As she pulled the Cayenne into a parking space, the rolling electronic fence closed behind the car like a prison door.

The large figure of Lafayette emerged from a doorway and onto the asphalt. Lafayette was a bit bigger than a large defensive linebacker and sported a shaved head and a goatee. Despite his imposing figure, she knew the kindness in his bones and the gentleness of his heart.

Lafayette's huge grin shone like the sun. Alex jumped out of the car excitedly and buried her body against his massive form. He was the safest place she had ever been and, in turn, she had been the catalyst for changing his life. She reached up to stroke his goatee.

"Where'd this come from?"

His grin widened. "You like it?"

She nodded. "I bet the ladies love it!"

She lowered her hand from his face, realizing they had formed an unbreakable bond, like Marines who have survived a firestorm. Alex and Lafayette had survived Chris's murder, and he helped save her life as they closed in on the killer. She, in turn, helped him wade through the aftermath of the shooting death of his only son.

She stepped back to get a good view of her dear friend. "What are you doing here?" she asked, confused.

"After Carter left the homicide department, he asked me to help with surveillance and some security." Lafayette smiled and lifted a pant leg, revealing a pistol strapped right above his ankle. "I even got a permit to carry," he boomed, opening the door. He motioned for Alex to step inside.

"Look what the cat dragged in," Lafayette yelled into the cavernous warehouse. There was a light in a small office in the far back corner of the dark expanse.

Alex followed Lafayette through the emptiness. It felt like walking through a graveyard at night where shadows came to life.

"We have a visitor," Lafayette called out in the direction of the office. His voice reverberated in the hollow spaces. "He's on the phone," he explained in the rich, Delta drawl that persisted despite years in the Mile-High City.

Quietly, they slipped into the office where Carter listened to a client's complaints. Some people age like bronze, and Carter had a fine patina. As Alex remembered, his desk was littered with papers and files. A day-old cup of coffee rested on an end table, and several dated newspapers and a box of stale powdered donuts had set up shop on the coffee table. No photos, no family mementos, nothing personal.

Being with Lafayette and Carter was like coming home to a favorite old armchair, something familiar, formidable, and lumpy in the nicest way. Since her father's death and the loss of Chris, Alex considered these two men her family and guardians.

They had remained close over the years. Alex helped Lafayette receive a pardon for an accidental murder he committed when he was barely a man, a good deed that forever changed his life. He was a finely minted human being who paid dearly for a terrible mistake, serving time in Tucker Prison, a silent, violent place in a forgotten part of rural Arkansas. The pardon had given him a well-deserved second chance. Theirs was the kind of friendship that didn't require regular maintenance.

Alex shook Carter's hand while he finished up the phone conversation. "Yeah, gotta go. Got people here. Yeah, I'll call later." Carter gestured with his fingers and thumb, flapping them together to show them the caller would not stop talking. Finally, the call ended, and Carter moved deliberately from behind the desk and, without a word, gave Alex a huge hug.

"You look good for a woman with fire up her ass." They all laughed. Carter had his own way with words.

"It's not funny!" she retorted.

"I saw the protesters on the late news last night." He chuckled.

"They're certainly not the friendly sort!"

"You looked good all covered in dirt." Humor was Carter's way of managing adversity, Alex thought. "You were due for a hiccup."

"This is more than a hiccup." A frown shadowed her face.

47

"Last I read, you guys hit about a dozen wells with no setbacks. What do you expect?" Carter retorted. As they chatted, he picked up the old coffee cup, dropped it in the overflowing garbage can, then passed the box of stale donuts in Alex's direction.

She shook her head. "No, thanks."

"Forgot, you don't do sugar, right?"

"Or moldy and stale." Laughter echoed in the mostly empty warehouse.

Carter watched a familiar expression pass across Alex's face. Over the years and through Chris's murder investigation, both he and Lafayette had gotten to know Alex like their own DNA. To them, it seemed that her calm, public poker face was only a veneer.

"Wayne thinks someone blew up the well," Alex said softly.

Carter raised his eyebrows and looked at Lafayette. "Why?" It was a simple question, but one he had asked Alex so many times that—at one point in the past—she thought about punching him in the teeth. But the question always led to answers.

Carter removed his jacket, revealing a holstered gun. He moved to the corner of his desk to focus on Alex and listen intently to the story.

"Wayne thinks it was tampered with. Maybe someone put explosives at the wellhead."

He asked again, "Why?"

"Maybe because the protesters or someone behind them want to stop the drilling. The well wasn't pumping, and they don't blow up on their own. It just exploded. The rig melted, and now it's burning." Alex ticked the list off on the fingers of her left hand.

Carter took out his gun and wiped it with a cloth as he listened. "Motive?"

She shook her head. "If we have a big mess, it validates the concerns of the anti-fracking-stop-all-drilling lobby. There are hundreds of people up there who want this project to fail."

Carter followed her argument. "Anything else?"

"No. Well, yes, possibly." Her hesitation was revealing. "Colt is missing, and I think he may be in trouble."

"Why?" he asked again.

Oh, my God, here he goes again, she thought.

She flipped to the photos on her cell and handed the phone to him. "I found his keys and bandana early this morning."

"At the well?"

"Yes," she said, swiping through to the last photo, "and the bandana was bloody."

Carter wrinkled his forehead and looked at her with a concerned expression.

"It looked like there was a struggle," she added.

"Is anyone looking for him?" Carter, his face scrunched up as he processed the information, continued cleaning the pistol with an oily rag.

"Not yet. I called the sheriff but have not heard back."

"Where else could Colt be?" Carter persisted.

Alex shrugged. "Another well project...or just out of communication, the way he sometimes gets."

"You mean drinking?" Carter filled in truth between the lines of innuendo.

"Maybe, but he could be working. He mentioned some problem in the Beaumont area." She shrugged again. "But I know he was up at our well recently. One of his trucks is still at the well site."

"You want me to try to see what we can find out before the whole investigation gets botched by the local guys? They don't have a lot of experience with crime scenes."

Alex considered the offer. "That's why I'm here. We need you and I don't trust the sheriff."

"Colt could have been drunk. Maybe he went up there and accidentally set the well on fire. Maybe he was smoking," Carter mused. "Or maybe he stumbled across the people who were tampering with the well and tried to stop them."

She offered another possibility. "Or he wasn't there at all."

"What would you do if someone caught you in the act of blowing up a well?"

Alex swallowed hard. Carter saw her dark eyes become opaque. "And we had a huge fight just a few days before."

He raised an eyebrow. "Over?"

"Another job."

"That complicates everything," Lafayette chimed in.

A loud chorus of Aretha's song "Respect" coming from Alex's cell phone interrupted their conversation.

"This might be the sheriff." Alex put the phone on speaker. "Alex Sheridan," she answered.

"This is Susan Armstrong with Boyle Insurance. Ms. Sheridan?" The woman's voice was crisp, business-like.

"Yes?" Alex looked at Carter, indicating her intention to hurry the call.

"We are trying to locate Mr. Colt Forester," the other woman said.

"He's not here," Alex responded curtly.

There was a short pause, then the woman said, "My boss says that one of your wells has been reported as burning, and we have the insurance policy."

"How can I help?" Alex asked.

"We need to inspect the damage to the site and speak with Mr. Forester."

"Have you tried his cell?" Alex asked, trying to hide her frustration.

The woman's tone took on an edge of annoyance. "No answer. He took out this blow-out policy more than a month ago."

"I am not sure where he is at the moment. Just out of curiosity, remind me how much the policy is for?" Alex inquired, hoping to get some details. She knew nothing about this particular insurance policy on the well project. Of course, Colt's company had to carry insurance for liability as the well operator, and it would also cover Alex's company, Sheridan Oil and Gas, as a named insured.

"The umbrella policy is for twenty-five million, and the underlying insurance is ten million."

Carter and Lafayette looked concerned.

For one second Alex felt a flicker of doubt. Her oil and gas company had been incredibly successful over the past years, but Colt's engineering business had suffered setbacks. A few costly mistakes coupled with horrific spending habits had landed him in a cash-flow crunch. The Thompson Divide project was an opportunity to get his company out of the red and would allow him to build back his business. He was good when he was focused, but drinking had cost him on multiple fronts. Could Colt have disappeared to another project after setting the well on fire with a plan to reappear and collect the insurance money? Alex hated that the thought crossed her mind and she fought to contain her fear.

"We will send some of our people out to inspect the well." It was a statement, not a question.

Alex sighed. "No one is allowed near the well while it's burning, but send your people to the site and ask for Wayne."

Alex's mind churned as she disconnected from the call. Her silence was telling.

"That muddies the water," Carter remarked.

"Arson is not in Colt's makeup," she asserted, but could she be sure of that?

Carter raised his eyebrows doubtfully. "Tell it to the people who invested with Bernie Madoff! No one saw that coming."

"Colt's getting things under control," Alex rationalized.

Carter had seen almost every scenario in his long career. Greed and financial fear had fueled Ponzi schemes, fraud, embezzlement, and murder. He shook his head. "You know as well as anyone what people will do when they are desperate and afraid." Carter didn't believe Colt Forester was the criminal type, but it was always a possibility. "Alex, remember that Jeff Ashton murdered Christine over money, gambling debts, and fear."

"How can you even suggest that Colt is anything like Jeff Ashton?" she blurted out defensively. Her voice rose in indignation.

"I'm not saying that," he said, letting his calmness soothe things down. "But Ashton is a good example of how far desperate people will go." Jeff Ashton had been a loyal employee of Alex's partner Christine Welbourne and, after many years of investigation, Carter proved he was Christine's murderer.

Alex looked hopefully at her two friends. "Will you help me figure out what happened at the well?"

"I'm in," Lafayette said enthusiastically.

Carter looked at Lafayette. "I'm stuck here for a few days. Please go with Alex. Find someone who was with Colt and talk to his guys. Then go poke around Carbondale."

"Of course." Lafayette smiled.

"I'll be there to help as soon as possible," Carter promised.

"Thank you." Relief threaded through Alex's voice. "I knew you'd help." She eyed her surroundings. "What's going on here anyway? This place looks abandoned."

"It's a rat trap." Carter flashed a devilish smile, clearly pleased with the setup.

She chuckled. "Funny. I thought it was a warehouse."

"Trying to catch some drug dealers. Now that marijuana is legal, the entire drug game has changed."

"How so?"

Carter shrugged. "Everyone is growing pot, so the dealers have moved into heroin."

"Smack is back on the streets big time," Lafayette chimed in. "They're selling it cheap and trying to get everyone hooked."

"This is our pretend office. We're trying to catch the rats." Carter grinned.

Alex knew catching bad guys was a rush for Carter. He liked the game of cat and mouse, especially when he was the cat.

CHAPTER 6

Jake Winston, one of the leading players in land conservation in Colorado, strode into his Boulder office. Outside large glass windows, massive rock formations jutted sideways from the earth. The town of Boulder, on the edge of Denver and the Front Range, was filled with ultra-liberals and far-right conservatives, all stewing together in a boiling cauldron. Jake walked a tightrope between the factions as he spent his days trying to preserve the remaining open spaces around the state.

With Marlboro Man cowboy looks and miles of dirt under his boots, Jake made a rough but attractive vision. He flopped into a leather chair and watched the news again, smiling as Alex Sheridan gave an interview, the well blazing in the background. It looked as if his old friend and illusive love was in over her head.

A reporter described the fire in the Thompson Divide as he interviewed Alex, who was oil-smudged and tousled from the wind and fire. Her long, black hair tumbled from beneath a hard hat. He loved how she looked—dirty, beautiful, and seductive all at the same time.

Jake reflected upon Alex's monumental accomplishments. Despite the past loss of her business and the murder of her partner and their mutual friend, Chris Welbourne, she thrived. She overcame incredible odds and rebuilt her life and her company. The meanness of her manipulative, controlling husband had come close to taking her down. The police investigation and the evisceration of her business almost destroyed her, but she came back with a vengeance, becoming one of the only female owners of a major independent oil and gas company. He beamed with pride.

She leased land in the major shale formations and successfully developed wells in the brutally competitive industry. She went up against the likes of Harold Hamm from Oklahoma, a self-made billionaire, and giants like Devon Energy and EOG Resources. Money was raised with confidence, well after well was drilled, and she became one of the biggest players in the renaissance of the business. Big companies like Duke and Apache tried to buy her out, but Alex was determined to stay an independent player. Jake was proud of her and, in his own way, he would always love her.

Alex and Lafayette left Carter to his rat trap and headed for her offices to field inquiries and set up a plan to deal with the crisis.

When they arrived at Sheridan Enterprises, it was to a deluge of calls from frightened investors. The news was sensational, designed to incite fear. Alex knew that, for every concerned friend, there was a gloating competitor.

"What time are we flying over?" Lafayette asked.

"As soon as I catch up on these calls." Fran had given Alex a stack of messages, including one from the insurance company. The cutthroat oil and gas business was full of scavengers waiting to pick up the choice tidbits of a failed business or to pounce on a vulnerable company for pennies on the dollar. When small companies were short on cash, they were vulnerable. The fire in the Thompson Divide was a potentially lethal blow to Sheridan Enterprises.

"Love this view." Lafayette took in the 360-degree view of the world from downtown Denver.

"Make yourself comfortable in the guest office," Alex invited, indicating an empty office down the hall.

"I'll start putting out bait to try to find Colt," he told her, moving to the office she indicated.

Alex planned to take the chopper later in the day to check out the well and look for clues in Carbondale. She smiled. Lafayette was going to be a welcome addition to her group.

Meanwhile, the team handled concerned callers like traders in a bond pit. All the members of the Sheridan Oil and Gas team worked frantically to manage the crisis. Schaeffer London, who managed public relations for the firm, was at her desk with an iPhone, an iPad, a computer, and a landline all running in harmony. She looked intensely focused as she directed the crisis management team. Alex waved at her friend; Schaeffer was also one of the best crisis managers in the business.

"Thanks for coming so fast," Alex said with genuine relief.

The friends exchanged a warm hug. Lafayette bent down to give Schaeffer a kiss on the cheek.

"Glad to be here, but sorry about the fire." Schaeffer had been a partner in Alex's previous company, and now worked as an independent consultant for a few key members in the industry. Sheridan Enterprises was her most important client, and Alex was her dearest friend. The news of the burning well had prompted Schaeffer to take the first morning flight out of Dallas.

"You're a pleasant surprise," Schaeffer said warmly to Lafayette. "Let me take this call from CNN. We can chat later." Schaeffer was like a five-star general. She made sure the media knew things were under control. She had already created an investor campaign to reassure everyone about the stability of the company. She could handle almost anything thrown her way, and Alex trusted her with her life.

Alex motioned to Schaeffer. "When you get a break, let's talk in my office."

A pile of maps was stacked on Alex's large walnut desk, and a vase of freshly cut flowers stood on the empty side. It was the partners' desk she had shared with Christine Welbourne.

On the desk was a note from Fran. John Malone, president of Rocky Mountain Bank, which financed Sheridan Enterprises, had called several times.

Fran popped her head in. "John sounded anxious. Did you see the message?"

Alex had not heard from Malone for a while. "Yes, he probably wants to make sure everything is under control and, more important, to know if I will take the box for the Broncos game. I can call later."

She and the banker talked infrequently. Her interest payments were always on time, and John valued her business. Sheridan Oil and Gas, a subsidiary of Sheridan Enterprises, was a huge client, a feather in John's cap. There were plenty of other banks in pursuit of Alex's business—in particular, Great Western Bank, a Boulder operation that was a big oil and gas lender led by an aggressive salesman, Tebo Stephens. Other banks in the Denver and Dallas areas also courted her, but she was loyal to Rocky Mountain Bank. It had been part of a bank consolidation during the financial crisis but, if the trail was followed back far enough, it was the financial institution Christine had favored. Alex knew it was sentimental to hang on to some of the threads of her connection to Chris, but Rocky Mountain had always served them well.

Schaeffer entered and closed the door of Alex's office.

"How do you get up in the middle of the night, fly here, and look like a movie star?" Alex complimented her friend, one of those drop-dead gorgeous women who had to work extra hard to be taken seriously. Schaeffer was poured into a tight skirt and a fitted knit sweater that showed off her full breasts. For some time now, she had given up trying to dress like the men.

Alex remembered the phase when Schaeffer wore suits and horn-rimmed glasses, with her blonde hair pulled back in a tight ponytail. The studious look had done absolutely nothing to hide her sexual allure. She was a man magnet.

She ignored the compliment from Alex. "We're going to post on YouTube, Facebook, and all the other social media from the well, and show them fighting the fire. Kind of our own broadcast to offset the news bozos. What do you think?"

"I like it. Get someone to interview you—you're our secret weapon."

Schaeffer nodded. "I'm on it. Trey is taking me over. Let's catch up later."

"Thanks for being here."

Schaeffer's presence was a godsend. Their friendship was bedrock solid, something they both knew could overcome any obstacles.

"Of course." Schaeffer smiled and went to make more strategic calls as Alex called the sheriff again.

"This is Dan," Salido answered.

"Hi, Sheriff, it's Alex Sheridan."

"Finally! We need to go over a few things," he said sternly.

"Yes, I've been trying to reach you for hours, but we have another problem," Alex said, not hiding her frustration.

"Besides an out-of-control fire destroying the forest?" Sarcasm dripped off each word, revealing his displeasure.

"One of our top people, Colt Forester, our engineer, is missing," Alex explained.

"I would be missing, too, if this was my charge. Have you seen what is going on up there?" Salido snapped. "The second well is burning now."

"We're working on a plan to put the fire out." She tried to keep the resentment out of her voice.

"You better hurry." His voice darkened with every sentence.

Alex closed her eyes, praying silently for patience. "Everything possible is being done. More water trucks are on the way."

"I have called in back-up help from all of our firefighters…this is going to cost you."

"We did not cause this fire!" she exclaimed.

"But it is your well."

"And you have an obligation to conduct a fair and impartial investigation," Alex reminded him, trying not to raise her voice. She didn't want to get completely sideways with this man, but he seemed determined to blame her for the catastrophe.

"There's something else important," she added. "I found Colt's keys, compass, and a bloody handkerchief!"

"There's an arrest warrant out for Mr. Forester," he said flatly.

"For what?" she shouted. Inside, she was scared and torn. She had no idea where Colt was or what had happened to him. He had been in a full-on rage when he stormed out of her office.

"For negligence, and maybe more," the sheriff told her. "He is the operator, and this is costing millions in damage."

"Someone else did this!" she insisted.

"Nevertheless, his disappearance is highly suspicious."

Alex controlled her anger and modulated her tone to a more reasonable level. "I'm sending you the photos of the evidence I found and will meet you there in a couple of hours."

"We'll get the fire under control and then see." He added, conciliation in his voice, "I've got a lot going on."

"Me, too," she said in like tone. "We want to help."

Alex hung up and immediately called Wayne Decker. "Any news?"

Wayne sounded exhausted. "Planes with retardant and more people are on the way, but there isn't much we can do if the winds don't cooperate."

Alex turned on the news. Multiple screens installed in her office allowed her to monitor cameras from different well sites, as well as news from around the world. She looked at the camera focused on the Thompson Divide project. The screen was blank.

"What's wrong with our video feed?" she asked Wayne.

"It melted, Alex. Everything within a hundred yards of this thing is destroyed."

Alex thought for a moment, then asked, "Can you stream from your iPhone?"

"Right away."

Alex yelled to the outer office. "Can someone establish some real-time coverage of what is going on up there?"

In minutes, an aide came into her office and tuned into coverage of the catastrophe. On the screen, a woman in blue jeans and a yellow raincoat reported at a safe distance from the fire. A plane dumping water and retardant circled the burn site.

"The oil company's well is responsible for this disaster that could destroy tens of thousands of acres," the reporter expounded. She turned to a nearby group of protesters and shoved the microphone into the crowd. "This is Beaver Scott, one of the local residents." A big man with red hair stepped forward. "You are against the oil companies drilling in this area?" the reporter prodded.

"The oil companies have no business drilling in any of our national forests," Beaver spat as he yelled, "It damages the land and contaminates the water. Now, as you can see, the forest is being destroyed. It will take generations to regenerate."

The supporters behind the stubby man shouted, "Stop the drilling."

Alex listened carefully. The protesters were vehement and angry. The man being interviewed looked familiar, Alex thought, but she had seen so much repeat coverage.

Several uniformed forestry service employees worked to keep the crowd at a safe distance from the fire. "We need you to leave now," one of them said in an urgent voice. "The area is being evacuated."

"We have a right to be here," someone yelled. The rest of the protesters cheered in unison.

"The winds are shifting against us. You have to evacuate now before we all get swallowed up in the flames." Uniformed officials from the sheriff's office and members of the forestry service joined the effort to push the crowd back.

Forest fires had a way of circling around and surrounding their victims. One large wildfire in Colorado had killed an entire group of firefighters trapped by surrounding flames.

Alex watched in horror as the situation took on ghastly proportions. There was no way the helicopter would be able to land anywhere near the fire. Trey would have to put the chopper down near Glenwood, then she and Lafayette would have to drive up to the site.

"There's nothing more we can do now except pray for the wind to stop!" shouted someone behind the reporter. "We need more water!"

Alex knew he was right, but something had to be done to get the heat off of Colt and prove foul play.

CHAPTER 7

District Attorney Robert Portland inhabited a modest government office in Glenwood Springs, just ten miles from Carbondale. Garfield County was mostly rural, and Bob was a big fish in a small pond. A large yard sign with his name on it rested in a corner, and a pile of bumper stickers was stacked on his desk along with a multitude of current case files. His recent election had been closely contested.

"Another one of the protesters wants to talk to you," said his personal assistant, exasperated from the relentless calls pouring in from constituents. The callers were on every side of the fracking issue, as well as the oil and gas industry many of them depended on for their livelihood.

"Take a message," Portland barked.

"She's called three times and sounds upset." Whatever their point of view, the constituents were emotional and mostly angry.

"Make an excuse," he said in an edgy tone. A deluge of complaints had swamped the office. The locals were adamant about the importance of drilling in the area, as their jobs depended on it. Others were vehemently opposed to all things related to the oil and gas business.

Regardless of a donor's point of view, his votes had depended on campaign contributions. A big contributor had stopped by to remind him of just that. Several checks from supporters lay on his desk.

"That man from the Sloanes' office called again."

Portland swallowed hard. The biggest money had come from companies and industries owned by a single source, the Sloane family.

They owned land and minerals and operations all over the West. "Thanks…make an excuse."

The Sloane family, rumored to be the largest resource owner in the United States, controlled massive coal mines in the East and natural gas reserves in immeasurable quantities in the West. The brother-sister team owned more shale oil formations than any other entity in the country, and were estimated to be worth billions more than any other private enterprise. They had invested heavily in Bob Portland.

"Thought you might be interested in this article." The PA passed Portland a copy of an article out of *Oil and Gas Report* magazine featuring Mackenzie "Mack" Sloane, considered one of the hardest women in the business. A less-than-flattering photo showed her husky form standing on a drilling platform.

"Wouldn't want to be left alone in the dark with her," Portland said caustically. The article was an in-depth story about Mack Sloane.

Shunned by her mother, Mack had been raised by the Sloane patriarch and treated like a first son since the day she was born. She was home-schooled with her brothers and taught every aspect of the business by her infamous father. When they were young, one of the brothers mysteriously died in a fall down an old mining shaft, and the rumor circulated that ten-year-old Mack had pushed him. No investigation took place.

Sweat broke out on Portland's palms as he read the article.

After attending the Colorado School of Mines, where she received a master's degree in engineering, she was sent to the North Sea for a "hands-on" graduate degree in deep sea drilling. Mack, now in her sixties—who still had similarities to a Mack truck—was the decision-maker for the powerful Sloane family. She had never married and was inseparable from her little brother, who hovered in the shadows. It was also common knowledge that she had the demeanor of a rattlesnake with plenty of stories to support the allegation.

Bob Portland tried to stay neutral, but it was impossible. Campaign contributions poured in from a hundred different sources, all of which could be traced back to the Sloanes. Behind the scenes, armies of lawyers and accountants did the work while energy experts fronted and managed their affairs. The Sloane money moved around the globe from one industry to another in so many different currencies to layer upon layer of shell corporations that even the IRS couldn't follow it. From the local city council and county commissioners to the president, unmarked Sloane money held the power.

"Mr. Brandt is on the line," the receptionist called.

At one time, Bob Portland naively thought he could run successfully on merit, but his first campaign proved otherwise. The next time around, he received a polite invitation to meet with the Sloanes' representative, Ferrell Brandt, a menacing, rodent-like lawyer. The message was clear—the votes he needed could be delivered and, in return, his help would be expected when issues vital to their companies and investments were at stake.

A trickle of sweat ran down Portland's spine to the small of his back. His heart pounded as his pulse raced. Slowly, he took three deep breaths. "Good afternoon," he answered cautiously. "What can I do for you, Mr. Brandt?"

"I trust you have seen the fire up on the Thompson Divide?" Ferrell Brandt asked. He had not lost his distinctive Queens accent.

Bob Portland knew this wasn't small talk. He could clearly envision the lawyer's eyes blinking out of control and his nose sniffing like a rat as he sat behind his desk working the strings. "Yes, I hope they get it under control." He wiped his forehead with a handkerchief.

"What can be done to stop Sheridan Oil and Gas?" Before Portland could respond, Brandt continued, "Issue some kind of restraining order to suspend drilling in that area."

"Alex Sheridan is well respected and the lease is on federal land, Mr. Brandt," Portland said.

"We are aware of its location, Bob." Brandt spit the "B" out like a bitter taste. There was an edge of condescension in his voice, as if Bob Portland was not quite sharp enough to understand the situation.

Portland pretended to ignore the insults.

"It's YOUR jurisdiction." Brandt's voice was firm. The two men understood and loathed each other. If Portland ever wanted to see someone skewered, it would be Ferrell Brandt but, for the moment, his scrotum was in the small man's vise-like fingers.

"There is an arrest warrant out for the operator, Colt Forester," Portland said, throwing Brandt a bone.

"That's not enough."

"I will see what can be done," Bob acquiesced.

"They have to have broken some law. The forest is on fire. Clearly, they were reckless," Brandt continued, spinning his story.

Bob pressed the fingers of his right hand to his forehead. "I'll let you know what we find."

"Of course you will. We'll take care of the feds." Brandt ended the call abruptly.

Brandt already had a call in to his friends who handled mineral leases on federal lands. The government staffers, with a little financial motivation, could tie up a project forever, demanding more paperwork than any small company could handle. If the company managed to comply by building more roads or working around an endangered species, they just moved the goal posts. Years could pass as the drilling companies jumped through hoops while the clock ticked down on their lease options.

Brandt knew more than anyone about how the system worked. Hell, he had designed most of the policies. At one time, he was a feared lawyer for the federal government. After he was assigned to perform a forensic audit of the Sloane family's intricate dealings, he was quickly hired away by the wealthy outfit. The audit never gained traction.

For years, Brandt had been secretly investigating every aspect of Sheridan Enterprises, detailing as many holdings as he could uncover. Alex Sheridan's leases and assets were enviable. If the Sloane machine could put financial pressure from different directions on the company and hit it while it was in a weakened position from the fire, there would be a chance of scavenging some of the most valuable shale holdings.

Brandt picked up another file on Rocky Mountain Bank and made his next move. The chairman of the board, Rutgers Johnson—who controlled most of Alex Sheridan's loans—would do his bidding.

"Mr. Johnson, please," he told the assistant. Brandt thumped his fingers on the file and his eyes blinked like windshield wipers.

"May I tell him who's calling?"

"Ferrell Brandt."

There was barely a pause before a woman answered. "Good afternoon, Mr. Brandt. He'll only be a moment."

Brandt didn't have to wait long before a jovial voice said, "Ferrell, how are you?" Johnson was gun-oil smooth. His personal fortune exploded as he invested alongside the Sloane family, with Brandt facilitating the deals.

"I guess you've seen the news about the Thompson Divide fire."

Johnson responded with a sigh of fake sympathy. "Yes, tragic situation."

"Those loans should be reviewed," Brandt said, steel in his voice.

"Sheridan has an impeccable balance sheet." Johnson held Alex Sheridan in high regard. She had come as close as anyone to losing everything, but had clawed her way back from a pile of debt and built a top-notch company.

"Call the loan," Brandt ordered.

"I will talk to Fred Malone."

"Call the goddamn loan," Brandt insisted.

"I understand." Johnson was putty in the hands of the moneyed, and the president, Fred Malone, was his hatchet man.

Brandt pondered his next move. He knew the county commissioner was in everyone's back pocket. Of course, one never knew if he could be trusted. He had taken promise money from so many people on opposite sides of issues that it was hard to know what he could deliver.

Brandt, with the help of other front people like influential power broker Nancy Parker, was systematically amassing land holdings all around the oil-rich regions. Eventually, he would not only have valuable mineral rights underground, but also surface rights worth millions. This much land, all surreptitiously owned by corporations controlled by the Sloane family, could be turned into billions. They had employed a similar methodology to take control of vast tracts in the Bakken in North Dakota and the Barnett Shale in Texas. It was his job to complete the acquisitions before others figured out who was dealing behind the scenes.

Brandt called Nancy Parker. The squeeze play began.

"Make sure no water well permits are given to Sheridan Oil."

"I'll take care of it." Nancy, brilliant and corrupt, replied from the back of the expensive sedan that was her mobile office.

"How much is the consulting fee?" Brandt asked.

"Two hundred thousand—" Nancy began.

The number didn't faze him. "And no permits anywhere in this district."

"—and a kicker for me on the backend!" she added.

Nancy knew how to manage the county commissioner, of this Brandt was certain.

The county commissioner held total control in his district in an unincorporated area outside Denver. Shale oil formations had recently been verified and, even more important, there was water. Without water, there was no fracking and, without fracking, the shale oil was trapped and inaccessible. Without fracking, the boom would bust.

Brandt inhaled a deep, confident breath. Nancy would take care of everything; she never let him down. One call to the governor's office, and the dominoes would tumble.

After Trey dropped her at Glenwood, Alex drove to the well site, where multitudes, including the sheriff, were gathered. Wayne was talking with the advance team engineer from the Wild Well Operations crew. The man was dressed in a bright orange suit and wore a hard hat in the same color, evidently the uniform of the team. Alex knew everyone was exhausted and on high alert. The relentless wind had them stymied. For the time being, thousands of gallons of water were being sprayed on the site with the hope of keeping the area from being totally consumed by the forest fire.

Alex grabbed an asbestos suit. She carried another in her arms as she interrupted the sheriff.

"Here! Come with me," she ordered.

"You can't go in there," Salido said, incredulous.

"You have to see the evidence before it's lost." Alex trudged toward the burning well, ignoring the yellow crime scene tape.

A man in an orange suit approached. "You can't go any further, ma'am." But Alex brushed by him as if she had not heard a word. "You can't go in there," the man repeated more forcefully.

"I own this well."

The sheriff protested, but her courage challenged the best of his ego. She was pretty sure he was not about to let a woman walk into the inferno ahead of him. She also knew he could not afford to have anyone hurt on his watch.

"Follow me." Fearlessly, she forged ahead, Salido trailing her.

In their asbestos suits, they disappeared into the forest of flames. Several men in hard hats tried to stop them, but Alex rebuffed them. They dashed through a ring of fire and were momentarily beyond the flames. They had only a few minutes before the winds might change and devour them. The sheriff panted as he tried to keep up with Alex and breathe through the smoke.

Alex tried to remember the path, retracing the steps she had taken earlier. They circled and backtracked frantically in the thick, toxic haze. Alex searched anxiously for something familiar. Could she be lost?

The blaze closed in around them and Sheriff Salido tugged at her arm, motioning her to leave before the fire swallowed them. Just then, Alex signaled the sheriff, pointing to the Broncos logo on the cloth covered in blood. She couldn't see the compass, but the sheriff put the bandana into an evidence bag, along with the scattered keys.

They nimbly escaped from the forest, past the well, and out to the trucks. They removed their protective headgear, but the smoke was overpowering. A paramedic ran over with oxygen.

"That wasn't your brightest move." Wayne glared at Alex.

The sheriff held up the bag with the handkerchief.

"That's Colt's, for sure," Wayne confirmed, pointing his nubby finger at the handkerchief.

Alex gasped for air as her head began to spin. "We have to find Colt," she said, pointing at the evidence bag. Then her eyes rolled back in her head.

Alex came to, wide-eyed and disoriented. She was in an ambulance. "What am I doing here?" She ripped an oxygen mask from her face.

"You'll be just fine." The angelic voice came from a young paramedic who was monitoring her oxygen level.

Alex rolled off the gurney, still feeling faint and lightheaded.

The paramedic put a hand on her arm. "You need more oxygen."

"Thanks, I'm okay." Ignoring the advice, Alex opened the door and jumped out.

Outside the ambulance, trucks and service vehicles were parked at odd angles. The emergency vehicles had all retreated a safe distance from the epicenter of the well blaze and the shifting winds. Tons of water sprayed the flames, but it was like trying to hold back the sea. Shades of an evening sky purpled the horizon. Another day, and they were further away from subduing the fire and finding out the truth about Colt.

As Wayne approached, looking as rough as worn sandpaper, Alex noticed Schaeffer recording footage for YouTube.

"Trey is on his way up with Lafayette," Wayne said. "He'll have the chopper waiting for you."

Alex glared at him. "I can't leave."

"I'm on top of this," he told her.

Alex trusted him with her life. "Thanks, Wayne; I have other fires I need to put out back in Denver."

Sleepless nights and the heat from the fire had snuffed her energy. Her limbs were heavy as anvils, and the intense heat and lack of oxygen left her head throbbing.

Lafayette arrived on the scene. Heads turned and people stared at the big man wearing a bowler hat and dark sunglasses. "Wow, this is some fire."

Wayne and Lafayette shook hands.

Lafayette offered Alex a hand. "You ready?" he asked as he opened the passenger door to the truck and helped her into the seat.

"Thank you for coming," Alex said, relieved that Lafayette had arrived.

"Of course." They rumbled off in the direction of Trey and the waiting chopper. As he drove, Lafayette studied the surroundings, taking note of the protesters.

"We need to scour Main Street and hit all the bars in Carbondale. I'm texting you a picture of Colt right now. See if any of the bartenders have seen him." Alex hunched her shoulders. "And, if he's not in the area, we have to find out where he's gone."

Lafayette nodded. "We'll make sure he's not at another project.

Carter's working on that."

"Good. We can't start a manhunt if he's been drinking somewhere."

"I know what to do." Lafayette gave her a reassuring look. "We *will* find him."

"Thank you."

Downtown Denver lit up the night as the chopper hovered down to rest on top of Alex's office building.

"Do you need a ride home?" Trey asked, still speaking into his headset.

"No, I'm staying here." The office was her safe house. Alex spent less and less time at her midrise penthouse in the upscale residential neighborhood of Cherry Creek. Everything she needed or could ever want was in the office, her command central and the heartbeat of her world.

"Are you sure? I can drive you."

"I'll be fine." She reached across and gave him a fist-bump. It took superhuman energy just to gather up her backpack and lift her boots, which felt as if they were filled with cement.

"Hope you can rest. I'm on call until you tell me different." Trey was intensely private and deeply compassionate. When he wasn't flying for Sheridan Oil, he volunteered as a pilot for emergency burn cases. One of his closest buddies in the Gulf War had been incinerated in a downed chopper. Trey had tried to pull him from the burning wreckage, but the heat had been too intense.

One of his special rescues was Brutus, his seventy-five-pound slug of an English bulldog who flew everywhere with him. Lying on a cushion in the back of the chopper, Brutus, the gentle giant, looked up sleepily at Alex. He rarely made noise and could easily be overlooked, except for an occasional grunt or growl while dreaming. He snorted when he was happy and spent most of his canine career bringing joy to those around him.

Brutus lifted his huge, gentle paw, offering to shake goodbye to Alex, who scratched him under his neck. Brutus wore an official service animal vest and had earned his rightful status when a nurse rescued him from a burning warehouse near a hospital. The nurse bandaged Brutus's pads, badly burned from the scorching floor, and called Trey. No one was sure who had rescued whom, but man and dog both thrived in the safety of unconditional love.

Alex waved to the pair, then walked to a metal door and entered a dark stairwell, making her way down to the fire-door entry for the twenty-fourth floor. She inserted a security card that allowed access into a hallway that snaked around until it came to the safety of the Sheridan Enterprises office. She sighed with pleasure as the large door opened silently, and a wave of relief came over her; finally, she was home. All was dark except for a light beam that streamed from her personal office out onto the hallway carpet, casting an eerie yellow glow on the wall.

A shadow moved, and a rustling sound sent her to her knees. She froze in her tracks, listening. The cold, hard nozzle of her pistol was easy to find in her backpack. She clamped her hands around the grip and took the ready position, back to the wall. For seconds, her heart seemed to stop. She cocked the hammer, hearing the reassuring click. Unconsciously, she held her breath. Her heart thudded as if the air had been sucked out of the room.

"Who's there?" she demanded.

"Don't shoot!" a familiar voice called out. "It's me!"

"Oh, shit!" She instantly lowered the barrel and released the hammer, aiming at the floor. "What are you doing here?" she asked harshly.

Alex trembled with anger. She wanted to get up but felt frozen in place. Tears welled up on the edges of her eyelids, and a large fat drop ran down her cheek.

"Damn it, Jake! I could have killed you," she said angrily.

Jake Winston stepped out of the shadows and walked over to put his hands on her shoulders. "I'm sorry I scared you," he said, pulling her up to him and holding her. His enormous basketball player physique loomed over her. Just being close brought back warm memories.

"How did you get in?" Her tone was a little less edgy.

"Fran, let me in. She said I could wait for you."

"I appreciate the advance warning," she said sarcastically.

Fran, a mother hen to Alex, had a special corner in her heart for Jake.

"I sent a text," Jake said.

Alex shrugged and turned toward her office. "No cell service most of the day."

"Rough day up there? It's all over media." Jake kept his arm around her shoulders as they entered her office. The feel of his skin brought back memories from a time when they were more than friends.

She unloaded the pistol, quickly wiped it clean, and put it in its drawer. The adrenaline rush left her shaky. "I can't believe you're here."

Jake grinned at her. "Thought you might need some moral support."

"Something to drink? There's some soda and juice in the fridge." Alex located a bottle of scotch and poured a double into a stemless wine glass. She rummaged around the refrigerator, found a dried-up half lemon, and added ice from the freezer. She let the cooling whisky work its magic.

"No, thanks." He picked up the remote and turned on the television. "Where's Colt?" he asked.

Alex and Jake danced on a tight wire between romance and friendship. Ever present, the ashes of love fluttered between them. But, after Chris's murder and Alex's return to Denver, she had followed her heart and ended up in a passionate love affair with Colt Forester instead.

"I don't know." Her tone was a bit exasperated. "He would not be happy to see you here."

The stormy triangle persisted. Colt's jealousy and Jake's lingering devotion made for a toxic cocktail. Based on Colt's complaints to Alex, she knew he felt certain that Jake was waiting in the wings. He was right.

Jake embraced her affectionately. "Should I leave?" he asked coyly.

"I'm grateful you're here." His arms felt warm and safe. Jake had been a part of both Chris's and Alex's lives, and he would always hold a place in her heart. He was a man she loved, but timing had never been an ally.

"Couldn't miss the fire." He turned up the volume on the news to hear the latest report.

Alex walked over to the windows. Her discarded cowboy boots landed with a thud. "I've seen all I can stand for one day."

"You seem pretty worried." Jake watched Alex thoughtfully. "Maybe more than just the fire?"

"Yes," she said, sighing. "I'm concerned about the finances. Some of the investors called today. The well is all but lost, and the bank isn't going to want to loan millions more without this one producing. Wild Well Operations might be able to salvage it, but it's a long shot that is costing us—we're bleeding money."

"And?" He knew there was more.

Alex forced the words out. "Colt is AWOL."

"Booze again?" His tone was neutral, but a shadow fell across his weathered face as he lowered himself to the couch.

"Who knows?" Her heart ached from the reality of Colt's deception and lies and secret darkness. Her loyalty was a double-edged sword. She knew it would be best for her to leave him and let him go through his journey alone.

"Do you need help?"

Alex crossed the room to him, grateful for his offer. "Carter and Lafayette are looking for Colt."

"How long are you going to torture yourself?" Jake had listened to and consoled Alex on numerous occasions following one of Colt's episodes. It had become a classic tale like *Jane Eyre*, but she knew he always hoped for a different ending.

"I think he could be in trouble, but it's impossible to be sure." Alex settled on the couch next to Jake. "One minute I'm crying and the next, I'm in a rage. It's like the little boy who cried wolf." She paused, trying to hold back her emotions. "I found his keys, compass, and a bloody bandana at the well site, but who's to know? I'm trying to let the sheriff do his job and not let my mind go crazy."

He gazed at her steadily. "How can I help?"

"You're here." Alex loved him for that. He was here now just as he had been her strength in the wake of Chris's murder.

"I can stay for a while." Jake took off his hat and boots, lifted his legs onto the cushions, and beckoned for her to lie down next to him on the sofa. She slid in beside him—perfect fit. He switched off the light and held her close.

"Thanks for being here for me," she whispered, finally able to relax.

It seemed like a miracle that they had been placed in each other's lives. His friendship with Chris had led them to this moment. Gratitude radiated through her.

"Always," he murmured, his voice muffled against her hair.

CHAPTER 8

The sound of someone moving pulled Alex back to consciousness. Her office clock read 12:30 a.m.

In the night shadows, Jake stood, boots on, car keys in hand.

Alex unconsciously smoothed her hair, then asked, "What are you doing?"

"Trying not to wake you," he said, smiling down at her. "I have to go home."

"You can stay," she told him, a little half-heartedly.

"I know you mean it, for now anyway, but Colt will call or come back, and then you'll evaporate." He leaned down and kissed her on the cheek. "Why don't you call when you've figured things out?"

They'd had this conversation before. "You mean everything to me," she persisted.

"Just...not quite enough." He picked up his hat.

Alex sighed and tried to stifle a rising tide of exasperation. There was no way she could have this conversation again. Not with a well blazing out of control, and not in the middle of the night. She got up to walk Jake to the door.

"You know where to find me." His feelings were clear. "I want you to share my life, and you want Colt."

"I'm too exhausted to talk right now." How could he possibly think that badgering her at this hour about their love life was a successful strategy?

"No time is good, but fair enough." Jake hugged her gently.

She sighed "Can we talk after this disaster is behind me?"

"I hope the Wild Well people can save your project." He stepped away from her and reached for the door handle.

"Thanks for coming."

He didn't respond, just stepped into the dark hall.

After Jake vanished into the night, Alex made herself a cup of hot tea, but it did nothing to create calm. She was tired and sleepless at the same time, and a friendship with Jake was beginning to look like a fantasy. She felt deeply connected to him, but the power of Colt's emotions was all she could manage at one time.

"Where the hell is he?" she said aloud to no one. Everything about Colt was intense. His personality was massive, his business dramatic, and his lovemaking an impossible blend of fireworks and soft music. Even now, a part of her ached for his touch. But his intense package was wrapped in chaos; every juncture was a mine field and, from one moment to the next, there was always a new crisis.

Alex searched her computer for the operating agreement she had with Colt's drilling company. She printed a copy to review. Colt's business was forever on the verge of blowing into the stratosphere or imploding. Fueled by the drinking, he was in constant upheaval in both his personal and business life. Bills piled up, important matters were left undone, and meetings were missed. Next came the excuses and the blackouts. The pattern was exhausting. The roller-coaster highs were irresistible, though—like riding his motorcycle in snowstorms and impetuous trips to new places. Then it crashed to a halt.

In the darkness of her office, with Jake's presence still lingering, Alex sat on the couch, perplexed and a little frightened. Unavoidable responsibilities lay before her. Lives and livelihoods were at stake, and she could not afford to be sucked into the vortex of Colt's chaos. She would absolutely not let another man derail her life.

The business contract lay before her and, as she read it, she knew her relationship with Colt would have to end.

She scribbled to-do notes on a pad: Call Carter first thing tomorrow and delegate the search for Colt to him; call Wayne and ask him to handle the Wild Well Operations fire team so she could focus on saving the well and her business; email and ask her lawyer to review the operating agreement and insurance coverage with Colt; draft a termination agreement; and ask Fran for phone numbers of all investors to contact. With a plan and a list in place, her mind slowed and her eyelids grew heavy. Finally, she napped fitfully.

The sun peeked its nose over the mountains and revealed dusty fuchsia clouds hanging low in the eastern sky. Alex texted Wayne Decker for an update. The burning well had to be left in his trusted hands as she faced the responsibilities that lay ahead. In another message, she asked Carter and Lafayette to take over the investigation into the sabotage and the search for Colt.

An alarm on her phone sounded, reminding her to check in for her flight to Dallas. She reviewed the file and looked at the beautiful embossed invitation. Months before, she had accepted the prestigious invitation from the Energy Business Council of Dallas/Fort Worth to be on a panel at one of the most important oil and gas industry events in North America.

While she put on a robe, the printer spit out notes for her speech. She was honored to be a part of the hydraulic fracking debate that was extremely controversial. The distinguished panel from the oil and gas industry included the CEO of ExxonMobil, which was headquartered in the greater Dallas area.

Alex padded barefoot to the main entrance of her office. A small bronze sculpture of Athena, the goddess of wisdom, stood on the corner of the reception table. Alex unlocked the front door and picked up the *Financial Times*, which reported that the Russians were invading Ukraine. They had annexed…no, *stolen* Crimea, she thought.

The BBC gave the morning report as Alex shrugged off her robe and walked into the shower to prepare for an exciting day. Hot water poured over her face as steam filled the dressing area adjacent to her large office. In the shower, she hummed a tune as, in the office, orange light from a brilliant sunrise streamed in through the filtered glass.

Out of earshot, her cell phone rang unanswered.

Alex stepped out of the shower, dried her hair with a towel, and slipped back into the thin white cotton robe.

She did not hear the man's voice call out from the reception area.

"Ms. Sheridan? Hello?"

Unaware of the intruder, she walked over to the partners' desk to look over the data from the well fire.

"Hello, is there anyone here?" The deep, warm voice startled Alex as a man strolled through the open door into her office. The clock read 7:05 a.m.

Alex jumped to her feet, the towel falling off her hair, her hand clasping the lapels of the gaping robe.

"No one answered when I knocked." He smiled a devilish smile and studied her robe and towel attire.

"Can I help you?" she asked.

"Angus Hawthorn, Wild Well Operations. My guys call me Bull."

Oh, my God, she thought. Her mind raced. What was he doing here? She was barely dressed and standing in front of a legendary oil man who had worked with the famous Red Adair. Adair had developed the techniques of putting out treacherous and massive well fires, and was possibly the most famous man in the industry's history.

Her mouth opened and no words came out for what seemed like minutes. Then, like molasses, the words seeped out. "I wasn't expecting anyone."

"That I can see. Want to help you with that fire," he said casually, his eyes twinkling as he cracked a grin. As he unbuttoned his jacket, he said, "I left a message that I would be coming by early."

"Sorry, my messages went AWOL yesterday."

"Am I interrupting?" He removed an Indiana Jones-style hat and took a sip from a Starbucks cup he had brought with him.

"No," Alex stammered. "Alex Sheridan. Thank you for coming." She gathered the robe around her with one hand as she offered her other to shake his outstretched hand.

She had received no messages from late the previous evening, and half her emails had not come through while she was out of cell range. It was a moot point now. Angus "Bull" Hawthorn stood in her office, gazing innocently at her.

In an instant, she took in the data. He stood well over six feet and was all muscle, like a rodeo bull. Piercing indigo eyes contrasted against pink-tan skin, and a full head of damp, silver-grey hair was combed

75

straight back behind his ears. He was impeccably groomed in starched jeans, a pinpoint oxford shirt, and scuffed black cowboy boots. A cross between roughneck, field hand, and East Coast preppy, he looked as if he had studied oil well fires at Harvard.

She backed away and looked at her desk as she strategized about how to excuse herself.

"I can come back later," he offered.

She cast a sideways glance at his face, but she quickly looked away, blushing.

She shook her head. "No, just give me a moment. Would you like coffee?" It was the best she could do.

"Sure." He leered at her playfully and dropped his empty cup in the trash. "I'll make some while you get dressed," he suggested. "So I don't get distracted," he added.

"The Keurig is over there." Alex pointed in the direction of the kitchen and coffee maker. "I'll just be a minute."

She dashed into the dressing room. As the door closed behind her, she leaned against the wall for support. Breathe, she thought.

Alex's heart pounded like a sledgehammer. It was almost comical that Bull Hawthorn was making her coffee. She slithered into tight pencil jeans and pulled on knee-high western riding boots and a fitted white top. She cinched the low-rider jeans with a black belt that sported a large silver LONE STAR belt buckle. Quickly, she applied makeup.

"You take cream?" Bull called from her office.

"Black, thanks." Chanel No. 22 and light pink lip color completed her transformation. Her still-wet hair hung past her shoulders as she strode back into the room.

Bull Hawthorn raised an eyebrow as she reappeared. "Wow! Houdini would be impressed." Steam from the hot coffee snaked into the air as he handed her a cup, and they sat down at a table by the window overlooking Denver.

"You have quite a little fire going on up there, Ms. Sheridan."

Alex noticed Bull surveying her body. He was professional, but he was all man, and he was taking in every detail of the landscape.

"Alex, please," she told him. "But you can handle it?"

Bull nodded. "Yeah, if you accept our agreement."

76

"Of course."

He took a sip of coffee before saying, "Safety is our priority—we don't cut corners."

Alex gave him a level stare. "I understand."

"So you need to know on the front end that you have to turn the well over to us."

"Sure," she said. "But we have final say?"

"No." Bull shook his head. "Once we sign this agreement, we take over full responsibility. We run the show."

Alex looked a bit skeptical. "I see."

He set his cup on the table and looked at her sternly. "That means no running around the site, okay? I heard what you did yesterday."

"We have a missing man."

"I can't have you or anyone else jeopardizing our effort; don't want anyone hurt on my watch." His dark eyes locked hers into an unblinking stare.

"I had to show the sheriff some evidence before it was lost in the fire." Alex hated the defensive tone of her voice.

"No exceptions," he declared. "We take complete control, then do what we deem necessary to manage the well. After the fire is out, we give it back to you."

She shrugged. "Is the well salvageable?"

"It's too soon to tell, but that is the goal, always."

"We can't lose this project." She didn't want to think about what would happen if they did.

"We're on it. The special equipment and team is on the way to the Thompson Divide right now." He ran a hand through his silver hair. "We'll know more tomorrow." His calm demeanor and confidence was like a shot of morphine.

"Thank you for coming by. Sorry I was so upset when we first spoke on the phone."

"Fires are scary business."

"They are," she agreed. "I've heard a lot about you."

"Some good, I hope." he said, a devilish twinkle in his eyes.

"All good."

He cracked a wide smile. "Can't believe everything you hear;

nothing's all good." He looked away with a hint of shyness. "We do whatever it takes."

Alex tried not to sound anxious. "Will you be going to our well?"

"Oh, no, you don't want me in the way of those guys," he said with a captivating smile. "I just collect the money." There was a simple humility about his presence. "This is going to be an expensive operation. I like customers to know what we are up against and what it will cost."

"I appreciate that."

After rummaging around in his briefcase, Bull retrieved a file filled with papers that he laid out in duplicate on the coffee table. The documents detailed his company's responsibilities and showed an initial fee of $350,000.

While Alex read the documents, Bull moved over to the large floor-to-ceiling windows and contemplated the mountainous view that Alex enjoyed daily.

Alex signed the necessary papers, authorizing him to proceed.

"I'll be in touch with our people, who are coordinating with Wayne Decker," he said.

She shook his hand. "The money will be wired right away."

"No hurry. I know you're good for it." She knew he'd probably already run a background check to make sure.

A wave of relief rippled through Alex. Having Bull officially on board and in charge of managing the disaster was the first critical step. Now she only had to make new financial arrangements to handle the cash requirements. A large team of men and equipment would be descending on the well site, and she was footing the bill. As the operator, Colt's company should have been responsible for many of the expenses, but he was out of the picture and the fire couldn't wait. Her simmering fury over his untimely disappearance was hard to suppress. Colt had deserted an appalling disaster and might even be responsible for it.

Bull spoke. "I've known Wayne Decker a long time. He is my kind of man, knows how to run a well site."

"He thinks it could have been sabotaged."

"We'll know a lot more once the fire is out and the well is shut in. If an explosive was used, we'll be able to tell you."

"Thank you; I'm heading out of town today." Alex showed him

around the office, pointing out memorable photos from years past. Bull recognized some of the famous oilmen and many of the locations where her company had been active. He noticed an old photo of her father.

"There aren't many men like him still around," he said.

"Thanks, I'm lucky." Alex gathered her things, putting papers in her briefcase.

Bull lifted an eyebrow. "Where are you going?"

"A fracking symposium in Dallas. I really shouldn't go at a time like this, but I committed to speak, and you and Wayne are in charge now," she said coyly. She could barely keep her eyes off the oil man as she showed him the invitation.

"You're on the fracking panel in Dallas?" he asked with surprise.

"Yes, this afternoon."

He grinned. "You want a ride?"

The question was confusing. "To the airport?"

"No," he said with a chuckle. "On my plane. I'm one of the guest speakers."

After several seconds while she processed the information, she answered, "That would be a huge help, thanks." Getting back sooner would allow her to be more available for the urgent situation. And the idea of spending more time with Bull Hawthorn was suddenly intriguing.

"The president of Meridian Oil, Riggs Austin, is giving the keynote speech." He was referring to one of the most notable men in the business and the grandfather of fracking.

"I've wanted to meet him for years." Alex was enthusiastic about meeting the legendary wildcatter, and she looked forward to participating in what would be an incendiary dialogue.

While fracking was an extremely controversial topic in parts of the U.S., in places like the Dakotas, where jobs were scarce and economic growth was anemic, oil and gas development and fracking were welcome. Residents believed the risks were far outweighed by the numerous job opportunities that came with the oil boom. In the Dallas/Fort Worth area, factions wanted to ban fracking in north Texas. As Schaeffer had discovered, the city of Denton had already voted to ban fracking. Millions of dollars were riding on the issue, and lawsuits and legislation were mounting.

"Wheels up at one-thirty. I can swing back to get you at one if you like?" Bull Hawthorn spoke as casually as an old friend, as if he had been her buddy forever. It was true they had many mutual friends and common ground, but Alex had known him personally for all of an hour, and now they were flying off to Dallas together.

He leaned over and brushed her cheek with his lips. What strange forces had brought them together in her office at seven in the morning? An out-of-control fire and a random speaking engagement had thrust them into the same orbit.

"I'll be downstairs at the main entry," she said. "I am truly indebted to you and your company."

He beamed down at her. "It's what we do."

She walked him to the elevator, and they chatted about the miserable performance of the Broncos, quarterback problems, and a bombing in Israel. As they parted company, a vibrant anticipation welled up inside her. She was completely distracted by this unexpected powerhouse of a visitor. The worst disaster that had ever been visited upon her company now seemed to have a velvet lining.

Alex returned to the reception desk to see if Fran had left anything important for her to review. There was a note from Schaeffer that an Angus Hawthorn would be coming by early in the morning.

Alex checked her texts. Another message alerting her to Hawthorn's appointment was there, but it must have come through after she fell asleep. It was a blessing and a curse that she had not seen it. If she had known the prominent oilman was coming early, she might have been nervous—but at least she would have been prepared for the meeting.

Alex thought he enjoyed catching her off guard at her desk. She smiled, remembering the boyish smile on his face. Life had served up a delicious surprise while reassuring her that her world would turn with or without Colt Forester.

CHAPTER 9

"**P**lease cancel today's Dallas flight," Alex told Fran, who arrived at Sheridan Enterprises just moments after Alex's early morning meeting with Hawthorn.

"Nancy Parker won't be happy if you are a no-show." Fran was referring to the powerful woman who was responsible for promoting the Dallas fracking symposium.

"I'm riding down on Bull Hawthorn's plane."

"Wow, that's convenient. Here are the notes for your presentation." Fran handed papers, neatly organized in a manila file folder, to Alex.

"Please get the 'Frack Baby Frack' tee shirts and put them with the other materials," Alex grinned. "This should be an epic event."

She watched as Fran fished a couple of the tee shirts out of the office closet. Alex smiled and hoped it might lighten up what had become a hot topic. The word "frack" itself had become volatile. It sounded on the edge of obscene, which was unfortunate for the industry.

She headed into the dressing room to work on her wardrobe, humming a tune.

Moments later, using a Bluetooth earpiece, she called Schaeffer. "We signed a deal with Wild Well, if you want to release the news."

"I'm on it," Schaeffer responded.

"Wayne can give you the details. I'll be in Dallas for the day."

"When do you leave?" Schaeffer asked.

"In a couple of hours." Alex opened a small case to carry what she would need for the trip. "Bull Hawthorn is picking me up at one."

"Be prepared for the press. They may ask some hard questions."

Alex paused. "Any suggestions?"

"Reiterate that the fire will be put out and direct them to Mr. Hawthorn—the best in the business—as a resource. Remind them of his success," Schaeffer added. "Don't let them drag you into the mud. 'No comment' is better than a foot in your mouth."

"Thanks, will do my best not to create more damage." Alex cracked a smile as she ended the call.

She dried and flat-ironed her hair and quickly applied a subtle eye shadow. On the radio, the NPR talk show host discussed the issue of tremors, small earthquakes that seemed to be cropping up in unexpected parts of the country where previously there had been no seismic activity. So far, there had been no tremors in the Thompson Divide area and, for that, Alex was thankful. She changed to the financial news that reported the stock market was down and oil was plummeting.

She considered several different outfits but, despite her lean body, nothing seemed to feel right. She tried on a suit and thought she looked too stiff, then a tailored dress—not right at all. She finally settled on slim black leggings, boots, and a fitted top. She surveyed the outfit and felt confident.

The door of a small safe behind a hidden wall in the closet swung open on the first try, and Alex picked up an envelope of cash and put on a pair of gold earrings. Her long black hair hung silky straight as she gathered a briefcase and walked out to meet Bull Hawthorn.

Fran intercepted her. "John Malone called."

The last thing she wanted to do was talk to the Rocky Mountain Bank president. "Please handle him." Alex looked at the clock; it was time to leave.

"He tricked me," Fran explained. "He asked if he could speak with you, and I admitted you were here. Then he said he was coming over right away."

"I'll slip out before he corners me." It was not the right time for a meeting with the banker.

"Sorry, I couldn't stop him," Fran said apologetically.

"It's okay. He's pushy," Alex offered, not wanting Fran to feel bad.

"You'd better read this." Fran handed her the morning paper. The headline read, "Moratorium on Drilling."

Drilling in parts of Oklahoma was being suspended. Alex skimmed the article before stuffing it in her tote bag.

"Glad you noticed this." Fran's attention to detail and her years of loyalty were invaluable. She was consistently one step ahead when it came to taking care of Alex and the business. Alex pulled out her cell phone.

The head of her Oklahoma operations answered on the first ring.

"Hey, Buck, what's going on down there?" Alex asked.

He was a salt-of-the-earth cowboy who rode bucking bulls until he shattered one too many parts.

"Good thing you sold those disposal wells." Buck's Oklahoma drawl was as rich as red dirt.

"Lucky timing," she agreed.

In the last year, unprecedented seismic activity had shattered Oklahoma. Hundreds of small earthquakes, seemingly coming from nowhere in a state with almost no history of tremors, was front-page news that frightened people. No empirical proof existed that tied the tremors to fracking but, in this case, the scapegoat was believed to be the fracking wastewater underground storage system. The drilling process used thousands of gallons of water, and the oil companies were required to dispose of it safely after use. It could be hauled away in trucks and later treated, but that was expensive. A system of storing it in old dead wells deep underground had been a revolutionary solution.

"Guess you saw the news about the quakes," Buck said.

Alex sighed. "We'll just wait and see what shakes out. In the meantime, if there is a fire sale, call me."

"I'll keep you in the loop."

Alex grabbed her iPad, briefcase, and the tee shirts and hurried out to the elevator. "Damnit." The light indicated it was twelve floors away. She turned and bolted toward the stairwell exit, shouldered hard against the heavy door and almost smashed John Malone in the face.

"Fancy meeting you here," the banker said, huffing from his stair climb. "Trying to keep up my cardio."

Alex looked at him blankly. He was the epitome of a banker in his dark suit, conservative tie, short-cropped hair, and wire rim glasses. He was buttoned up tight, she thought.

"I'm rushing to catch a plane." She tried to step into the doorway but he did not move.

"We need to talk, Alex."

"Fran will call to set something up." Alex tried to push past him, but he remained steadfast, his body blocking the passage.

"Everyone knows about the well and what it must be costing," he said flatly.

She stopped for a moment. "It's under control."

"Really? Alex, I am under pressure." He looked down at the floor.

"I can't be late, John." Again, she tried to move forward.

"Your collateral is insufficient," he blurted.

"There is nothing to be concerned about," Alex reassured him.

"The loan committee has called the loan."

She glared at him. "You have no cause."

"You are going to have to pay off the line of credit immediately." John Malone's shamed-child eyes darted anxiously, avoiding contact with Alex.

"We have never missed an interest payment." Her stomach tightened into a hard knot.

"You have never had a fire like this." He shifted his stance, still preventing her exit. "The board is uncomfortable."

"I'm one of your best customers, John." The reality of him calling the loan shocked her.

"It's a matter of regulations," he persisted.

Alex didn't miss the slight tremor in his voice. "Bullshit! Who's threatening you?"

"It's beyond my control." Sweat bubbled up on John's forehead as his face turned the color of a plum.

"Does Rutgers Johnson know about this?" she demanded.

"Yes, he is the one who asked me to call." The strategic call from his board chairman, Rutgers Johnson, had been the tipping point.

Alex knew the behind-the-scenes pressure would not let up on John. He answered to Johnson, who answered to the people with the money—the Sloane family.

"Don't try this tactic with me," Alex said boldly, as she retreated to the elevator. "I'm going to Dallas." Inside, she was quaking. John Malone's announcement was worrisome. Infuriated by the encounter, Alex was sure there was more going on than the banker admitted.

Down at street level, the dark Escalade idled at the curb. Bull Hawthorn waited for her inside. Briefcase in hand, Alex trotted to the vehicle. Bull beat her to the passenger door of the luxurious SUV to assist with her things.

"Thanks again for the ride," Alex said as he offered a hand up into the car.

"We should be able to take off soon." Once behind the wheel, he glanced in the rearview mirror and pulled out into the midday downtown Denver traffic, darting across 18th Street, past the Rockies stadium, and onto I-25.

"This is a great way to get to Dallas." She was grateful for the ride down on the private plane.

He smiled over at her. "Yes, and we'll be back in Denver this evening."

"Excuse me," she said after a moment. "I need to make a call."

Alex looked up the phone number for Great Western Bank, one of the biggest players in Denver oil and gas lending. They had been courting her for years, but she had been doggedly loyal to Rocky Mountain Bank and John Malone. The Boulder office of Great Western answered promptly and Alex asked for Tebo Stephens.

"May I tell him who is calling?" The woman sounded cool and efficient.

"Alex Sheridan; he knows me."

"Yes, Ms. Sheridan. One moment."

Bull Hawthorn's Bluetooth activated, but he declined the call, allowing Alex to conduct her conversation without the distraction.

Alex waited on hold for a few seconds.

"What a pleasant surprise! How are you?" Tebo Stephens asked with genuine warmth.

"I have a little fire we're trying to put out, but otherwise okay. I guess you heard about the well?"

"Lots of frustrated people up there," he said.

"Nothing like protesters," Alex said playfully.

"I'm sure you can diffuse it." She thought he sounded confident in her abilities, another reason she liked him.

"Do you have a minute?"

He chuckled. "Of course. Glad to hear from you and always interested in Sheridan Enterprises."

"That's good to hear," Alex said, "because I'm shopping for a new banker."

"When can we meet?" he asked, obviously pleased with the opportunity.

"I'll be back from Dallas tomorrow."

"Good," he said. "My assistant will text you to set up a time for us to meet."

Tebo Stephens was close to fifty and still well-known for his football days at the University of Colorado. A true local, he kept his money in the community. At one time, his interest in Alex had been more than professional. He asked her out a hundred different ways, but Alex had been so tied up with Colt, it never happened.

When the call ended, Bull commented, "Somebody must have crossed you the wrong way."

"I've been a loyal customer of Rocky Mountain Bank and John Malone for years. She glanced over at him. "Do you know him?"

"We've met." Bull sounded unimpressed.

"And?"

"He cheats at golf." Bull offered the information in a matter-of-fact way.

Alex laughed. "The bastard had the gall to come to my office this morning without an appointment, demanding we pay off a huge line of credit that we have faithfully serviced for years. I think the fire has his loan committee upset, but we have been loyal beyond a fault. I have never missed an interest payment. Screw him!"

"I have a close banking friend in Dallas if you want an introduction. He may be there this afternoon."

"Thank you. I'll take you up on that offer." She gathered her composure and temporarily parked her rage at the banker, and turned her attention to her host.

CHAPTER 10

L afayette stood out like a non-local as he ambled down Main Street in Carbondale. It was a small mountain community of mostly white and Hispanic residents. People stared, then looked away, trying not to gawk at the Goliath-looking man as if he was a living work of art. Everything about him was unique, beautiful and imposing—his stature, ebony skin, the dazzling twinkle in deep brown eyes, pink palms with lines etched like a treasure map, and tiny corkscrew hairs on his chin sculpted into a goatee.

The main drag was home to a mixture of secondhand shops and antique stores, a co-op grocery, a post office, and half a dozen watering holes. Lafayette walked past the small post office before arriving at the Black Nugget Bar, one of the town's oldest relics. He walked into the dark musty interior with its odor of stale cigarettes and beer. The lights were low, or not on at all, and an open door at the back of the bar let a slit of daylight sneak in across the floor. An empty stage near the front door waited for country and western singers to perform their tunes.

In the back of the room were several old pool tables, and some scruffy-looking young men playing eight-ball surrounded the second table. A woman who looked barely nineteen or twenty sat on a barstool watching the action. Stringy hair the color of turpentine hung to the middle of her back, and a blackish-green serpent was tattooed on her left shoulder. Holes, pins, and stains decorated the jeans she wore; a large rip revealed a knobby knee. She was apparently appealing to the group playing pool. One scrawny guy gave her an affectionate squeeze as he orbited the table in search of a good angle.

Lafayette, dressed in black, worked his way through the bar, his dark-chocolate-colored skin and clothing fading into the darkness.

The snaggle-toothed bartender, a craggy man in a Hawaiian shirt, studied the unusual guest. "You want something cold?" he asked, as he scrubbed the surface of the bar with a nasty-colored terrycloth towel.

"Maybe later, thanks," Lafayette declined the offer as he approached the serpent lady. He sized her up as a regular and figured she might know Colt, even if he hadn't been in recently. "Excuse me, I'm looking for a friend. You here often?" he inquired casually.

The serpent lady pulled out a pack of Marlboro Reds, shook one out, and lit it with a paper match. The match landed on the floor with the flame burning, and she stomped it out with a black biker's boot. Smoke poured from her mouth and nose.

Lafayette tapped the screen of his phone and selected the picture of Colt Alex had texted to him earlier. In the photo, a healthy-looking Colt had neatly cropped hair and an electric smile. "You know this guy? One of my partners."

"I don't think so." She studied the photo a second or two. "But he's real cute." She called to one of the young men. "Hey, Stick!" she said loudly. "You seen this guy?" She held up the phone for him to see, then she directed a comment to Lafayette. "Stick's in here all the time. Mind like an elephant."

Stick ignored the question and hit the cue ball deftly, knocking a stripe into the pocket. His dyed midnight blue-black hair made him look like a young version of Mick Jagger.

Lafayette waited patiently as Stick missed the next shot before walking over to the scrawny girl.

"Let me see." Not-quite Mick Jagger took a cigarette from the pack and lit it.

"Y'all go outside and smoke," yelled the bartender. No one moved.

The kid called Stick looked at Colt's picture. "Don't know him. Why, he done something?"

"No, I lost his cell number," Lafayette fibbed.

Lafayette left through the exit door at the back of the Black Nugget.

He worked his way down the street as the sun found its way to the fringe of the mountain peaks. Another bar hangout a few hundred yards away was his next target.

The Pour House, a locals' haunt, was one of the oldest establishments in Carbondale. Inside, the Pour House buzzed with patrons drinking and laughing. Lafayette entered the tavern and glanced around the room, trying to appear nonchalant. Gathered around the bar sat several men who had mortgages on the barstools. One man stood nearby, his hand resting on a guitar case, and another with broken teeth leaned on crutches. From nowhere, a heated argument about the well fire erupted.

"This is just like that well in the Gulf of Mexico," one of the men barked. "The oil companies are always cutting corners. They don't care who they hurt."

"Bullshit. It was arson!" Voices were raised as the debate escalated.

Lafayette eased up to the bar not too far away from the clique. "Can I have a large root beer float, please?" he asked the female server.

A female patron laughed at the giant man's order.

Lafayette removed his hat and leaned toward the bartender. "Hey, I'm looking for a friend." He flashed the Colgate-white twinkling smile that usually gave him an advantage.

The busty, overweight woman exuded warmth. Huge earlobes with heavy fake pearl earrings sagged almost to her shoulders. She studied the iPhoto picture, spread her fingers on the screen to get a close-up, and frowned.

"I don't think so. Hey, Gloria, come here," she yelled out to a harried waitress. The woman was scribbling orders, grabbing dirty plates, and refilling empty glasses. She looked worn down from a lifetime of work on her feet. She moved in their direction.

The bartender whispered to Lafayette, "Gloria's been here forever and knows everything—she's one of the fixtures." She straightened and held the phone out to Gloria. "Look at this photo. You seen this guy?"

Gloria squinted at the picture. "Sure, he used to come in here all the time. We had to call the police one night to get him to go home, but he was a pretty good guy."

Gloria filled up three beer mugs and scurried over to deliver them to a nearby table. Quick as a bat, she returned.

Lafayette felt slightly encouraged. "Has he been here recently?"

Her eyebrows furrowed together, creating huge crevasses in her forehead. "I haven't seen him lately. It's been a while."

"Thanks. Just trying to catch up with him." Lafayette looked around the Pour House.

Gloria cleared her throat. "There's a gal who used to come here…she lives in the trailer park on the other side of Highway 133. They seemed pretty close."

Lafayette turned back to her. "You remember a name?"

"Jenny something or other? I'm not sure." Gloria cleared her throat again. "She was in bad shape one night when the snow was blowing sideways. Your guy here," she gestured at the picture on the phone, "gave her a ride home." She thought some more. "She was real grateful. Jenny something? Not sure. She has a limp."

"Thanks a lot." Lafayette headed for the door and stepped out into the cool evening air. Now he had a lead.

He found the Crystal River Trailer Park a few blocks down Main Street on the other side of Highway 133.

Faded trailers filled the crowded park. Lafayette parked and went on foot to find the manager's trailer. A box for rent payments was attached to the front rail of the office, and potted plants filled with plastic flowers covered the porch. Twinkling white Christmas lights strung around a bent railing upgraded the atmosphere. Lafayette smelled the distinct weed odor that had become more common since legalization.

A dim light glowed in the window as he approached the door. A small sign indicated that the manager was on duty between 7:00 a.m. and 7:00 p.m. It was almost nine, so Lafayette knocked cautiously. The screen door squeaked open a bit as an old man with a scrawny ponytail, pink scalp visible through wispy strands, and bloodshot eyes peered out the door. He raised his sprawling eyebrows at the large man standing on his porch.

"Excuse me," Lafayette said politely. "I'm looking for someone, and I'm kinda lost."

"Can't you read?" The man pointed in the direction of the sign. A cigarette with a long ash dangled between his teeth and he had a shotgun in one hand.

"I'm sorry. It's just that I came from Denver to find a woman who lives here. There's been a death in the family," Lafayette improvised.

A suspicious look crossed the man's face. "What's her name?"

Lafayette spread his hands, trying to look helpless. "Jenny. She has a limp. The family asked me to come find her."

"You don't know her last name?" The old man arched an eyebrow doubtfully.

"Her maiden name was Anderson, but she married a couple of times, and we don't know what it is now. She lives here and has a limp," he repeated.

The manager pointed the barrel of the shotgun in the direction of the back of the trailer park. "Jenny lives in the back in the small trailer in the corner with the pink awning. You cause any trouble, I'll call the sheriff."

Slam! The sound of the screen door closing with force shattered the night.

Instinct told Lafayette this Jenny might know something. A few lights in the windows of the modest trailer homes allowed him to find his way. Creeping around a trailer park at night was risky, especially since he knew he was large and black and intimidating. But he strolled around the park, taking note of the various homes. Some of the matchbox structures looked so frail they might have been made of cardboard and tinfoil. It brought back memories of his own childhood, growing up with dirt floors in small shacks in the rural Arkansas Delta.

The pink awning was barely distinguishable in the darkness, but it was a landmark. No porch light was on, and the place looked quiet. For a moment, he pondered what his next step should be. He wanted to get answers, but it was after 9:30 p.m. and dark. Waiting was an option, but his goal was to obtain cooperation from Jenny, not scare her to death. After a few moments sizing up the layout, he pulled out a piece of paper, scribbled his number, placed the note between the screen and the door, and left.

"Carter, it's me." Lafayette was in his Lincoln driving away from the trailer park.

"What you got?" Carter queried.

Lafayette glanced back at the trailer park disappearing in his rearview mirror. "Think I found someone who knows Colt."

"Where?"

"In Carbondale, but I didn't want to get shot or thrown in jail for sneaking around in the middle of the night." Lafayette started looking for street signs. "Alex suggested the Comfort Inn, so I'll crash there tonight and get back to it tomorrow."

"Let me know what you find," Carter said. "I'm up to my ass in heroin smugglers."

"Be careful," Lafayette warned.

He drove to the motel. Once checked in, he went to the motel bar, ordered a Coke, and studied his notes. Hopefully, Jenny would call sooner rather than later.

When he took out his cell phone to check for emails, the picture of a young man with his arms around Lafayette popped up as his screen saver. Lafayette's eyes lingered on the picture of his son, then the screen went dark. He headed to his room.

CHAPTER 11

Bull pulled the black Escalade onto the tarmac at Denver International Airport next to a sleek Falcon 50, a private plane built by Dassault that was an aviator's dream. Alex collected her briefcase and left a tee shirt in the car for Bull. One of the young pilots greeted them politely; he assisted Alex with her things, and handed Bull a file. With his silver-white hair, tanned skin, and midnight navy suit, Alex decided Bull's looks rivaled George Clooney's.

Bull took Alex's elbow as they ascended the stairs into the plush cabin. It was an innocent gesture, but his touch was electric. In the cabin were eight tan glove-leather bucket seats, a bench seat, and television monitors to map the progress of the flight. Two uniformed pilots crewing the flight prepared for take-off.

"Would you like a drink?" he offered.

"Perrier, please."

Bull showed Alex the galley; the stocked bar had every beverage imaginable, as well as snacks for the short flight.

"Please, sit here." He indicated a seat across from his chair.

After securing her seatbelt, Alex checked a few emails and waited for take-off. Bull's phone chimed.

"Excuse me, Alex, I need to take this call." A bad-news frown spread across her companion's face, making him look sullen. Alex hoped the call wasn't about the fire in the Thompson Divide.

He stepped a few feet away to the rear of the plane, but there was no real privacy, and the yelling from the caller was clearly audible to Alex. She picked up the *Financial Times* and read the headlines, but the conversation was so loud that it was impossible not to hear.

"This is a horrific, no-win decision," Bull said, calmly. "I am sorry; there is no other choice."

Indistinguishable angry words came from the caller.

"It's time. I scheduled the transfer several days ago." His response was firm, but the diatribe continued.

"Forgive me, please." Alex heard more yelling before Bull said, "I am going to hang up now."

More angry words were hurled.

"Goodbye." Bull, looking a bit pale, put away his phone and buckled into his seat.

Alex focused on her notes and tried to disregard the personal conversation.

The Falcon taxied onto a runway. As soon as the pilots received clearance, they accelerated and the plane lifted off smoothly, yawing in the wind momentarily before finding calm air.

Bull smiled at Alex and adjusted the screen so they could watch the plane's flight path. The day had cleared, and there was little turbulence.

"I had a strange call today," he said, casually offering Alex a snack.

She looked up. "Strange how?"

"Some large offshore company tried to hire us off your job. Never really had that come up before."

"What did you tell them?" Alex put her phone down to give him her full attention.

"No, of course. But they offered a huge fee. Very tempting." He flashed his devilish smile.

Alex thought about everything that had happened during the last few days. The well looked like it might have been tampered with, but there was no proof yet. Colt was missing and maybe even in trouble, but there were no real clues. Once-loyal banker John Malone had turned from Jekyll to Hyde and made his cash call. She was no longer the bank's most important customer, but a sudden liability. Now, another company was trying to hire Wild Well Operations away from her. A riptide was pulling her into dangerous waters.

She expelled the breath she didn't know she'd been holding. "Thanks for keeping us on."

"I don't backstab. I don't care who they are." He lifted his chin. "If we are hired and committed to help put out a fire, that's what we do."

For a while, they sat silently as Bull studied the meeting notes and read emails.

"Can I interrupt?" Alex asked hesitantly.

"Shoot."

She paused for a minute before saying, "I think there is something nefarious going on in the Thompson Divide."

He lifted an eyebrow. "For instance?"

"The district attorney has asked the governor for a temporary moratorium on drilling. We leased the land from the federal government and have fulfilled every contractual obligation and then some. They have no legal right." Alex took a breath and went on. "The phone call you received is also out of order, and my banker showed up this morning looking as if he'd been thrown under a bus, suddenly calling our line of credit."

Bull shifted in his seat, his brow furrowed. "That's a truckload of coincidences."

"Maybe the government wants to run us off and take back the lands they leased to us and to the other oil and gas companies," Alex suggested.

"Maybe, but they get big royalties from those leases—twelve cents of every dollar of revenue that comes out of the ground, not to mention the upfront money for the lease." He shook his head. "The government can't get by without the oil and gas revenue."

Alex leaned forward. "What if they have realized there are trillions of cubic feet of gas and they want to take the leases back?"

"The protesters might be working for some extremist group or even for one of the other oil and gas companies. You'd better watch your back."

It was hard to imagine that one of her competitors might be involved with the mob of agitators. But why had the banker suddenly turned tail like a scared rabbit? And, as she reflected on the encounter, Malone had looked frightened.

From the cockpit, the pilot gave a weather update and announced they were half-way to Dallas. Alex found that focusing on the speech she was due to deliver was impossible as thoughts of Colt invaded her mind. What had been love had morphed into emotional trauma and abuse. It was likely that Colt was refusing her calls as a perverse form of punishment. A tight knot formed in her chest and she was unable to control the nagging anxiety brought on by his disappearance. She knew she had to let the professionals handle the investigation; she needed to get some distance.

Clouds raced past the sleek wings as they barreled toward Texas. They clipped the corner of Raton, New Mexico, and were crossing the Texas Panhandle when Bull reached over and took Alex's hand. "You seem anxious."

"That obvious?" She was wasting precious time. At this moment, she was with an incredible person on her way to an opportunity of a lifetime, and she was letting worry rob her of the pleasure.

"Are you afraid of flying?" he asked her, his face serious.

"Not at all...just a bit concerned."

"If you need help, just ask. There are some cutthroats in this business. It's not like it used to be when all that was needed was a handshake. You have to be on guard all the time now." Bull's indigo eyes locked on her like a laser.

Alex liked the way his skin felt and the touch of his hand. "You're helping already."

"Really, don't hesitate to ask. These fires have a way of rattling even the toughest guys in the business." He looked directly into her eyes, holding her attention—unblinking.

"I accept, with pleasure, but, as you know, our team is amazing." She smiled warmly, then looked away at her notes.

He gave her hand a squeeze, then let it go. "What's your topic for today?"

"The wells we fracked in the Barnett Shale in Texas." She offered him the outline Fran prepared. "We were one of the first ones there. And, of course, we will talk about seismic activity. Everyone's worried about the tremors in Oklahoma. What's your topic?"

"The oil rig explosion and how blowouts can be prevented." The explosion on an off-shore platform was devastating—numerous workers died and the oil spill devastated the Texas coast.

"Do you think there was negligence?" The conversation was helping to get her back on track.

"Drilling companies aren't in this business to lose money by blowing up rigs."

"Yes, but did they do something wrong?" Alex watched him as he read.

He finished reading and looked up at her again as he handed the outline back. "Mistakes happen, and it is incredibly dangerous, even when everything works according to plan. Maybe the operators were careless, and that may be too strong a word. Human error is always a factor, but it was on their watch and it's their responsibility," he said with finality. The environmental and human disasters were among the worst in the history of the energy business.

"Yeah," Alex agreed. "I wonder if someone made a mistake at our well."

"We'll see."

As they talked, Alex felt Bull's penetrating look all over her, and she liked it. She knew the subtle difference between admiration and ogling and, in truth, she took it as a compliment that he found her appealing.

Bull pointed at an article he had been reading earlier that was critical of the owner of the Cowboys. "What's Jerry Jones going to do?"

"They can't rush their way out of a paper bag," Alex retorted. She had lived in Dallas for years and was a serious fan of the football team. They both laughed.

Bull told several funny stories, then brushed her knee after making a joke and touched her hand flirtatiously. The temperature between them was rising as they sat inches apart in the seats. Their eyes locked and Bull's sharp gaze sliced through her like a hot knife in butter. At just the right moment, he leaned forward and kissed her on the edge of her mouth.

"I've been dying to do that all day."

"Aren't you full of surprises?" Alex smiled, and turned toward the window, trying not to reveal her roiling emotions. A ripple of heat ran down her spine. She hoped she did not look as flushed as she felt.

The Dallas Fort Worth International Airport, an airport complex larger than the island of Manhattan, was visible through the starboard window. She could see a drilling rig sandwiched in between runways. Oil and gas formations had been discovered on the property, and they were now producing revenue for the airport, which was partially owned by both municipalities.

"Are we landing here?" she asked.

"No, we're coming in to Love Field."

A few minutes passed before the landing gear came down and they began their descent. As the sleek plane skirted Bachman Lake, it looked as if they might hit the water but, in moments, the large private jet touched down at Love Field, the smaller airport located minutes from downtown.

The pilot came back to speak to Bull. "The car is waiting."

"Nice landing," Bull told him. The two men shook hands.

"See you this evening," said the pilot.

"We'll text when we're leaving the event. It could be late."

Bull followed Alex down the steps to the tarmac, where a driver in a dark suit waited.

The driver took one of Bull's briefcases and Alex's extra tote. They followed him a few steps across the tarmac and into Signature Air, the private airport terminal.

A member of the ground crew approached them. "Welcome back, Mr. Hawthorn," he said, then added, "We may be getting some weather later."

Bull nodded. "Thanks. Please keep me updated."

A black Town Car idled at the curb as Bull and Alex walked out.

Suffocating heat hit Alex like a slab of concrete. As Bull opened the car door and slid in after her, their bodies touched naturally. His hand brushed her knee in the back of the cool dark car and, suddenly, she felt as if they were traveling as a couple. It was a weird feeling she instantly quashed—the last thing she needed was another distraction. Attending the high-profile symposium and making a successful presentation was now much more important than at the time of the invitation. Sheridan Enterprises was under attack on multiple fronts. This speaking engagement had turned into a crucial media opportunity for the company. It was vital that the world see that she and the company were in control and that the fire was not a threat.

"I can't wait to hear your talk," Bull said genuinely.

Alex smiled. "I'll try not to bore you."

"You'll be a star. These old men get so stale."

As they exited the airport, the majestic buildings of Dallas appeared out of the flatlands. The driver headed east on Mockingbird Lane toward the North Dallas toll road to downtown. Architectural wonders created a unique skyline—the city's manmade Rocky Mountains, Alex reflected.

"Glad to have you back in Big D," the driver said to Hawthorn. "The Hyatt Regency?"

Bull answered, "Yes, please."

They headed in the direction of the large hotel topped with a glass sphere. Its incredible revolving restaurant with its world-class chef made it a popular destination for travelers from all over the world. The hotel of glass, concrete, and steel had been developed by one of Texas's most prominent oilmen, a descendent of the notorious H.L. Hunt, who was synonymous with oil, Texas, and women. At night, the hotel's Reunion Tower dominated the evening sky with its flashing light show.

As they inched along Mockingbird Lane, a lump settled in Alex's heart. How many times had she exited there on her way back to the mansion-sized home in which she had once lived? Ice flowed through her veins as she remembered the cold and powerful Steve Blake, the husband from whom she had barely escaped.

They exited the freeway, driving past the grassy knoll where Kennedy was shot, then turned into the hotel complex. They got out of the car and headed toward the main doors.

A beautiful woman surrounded by a team of people stood at the main entrance to the hotel, rattling orders.

"I guess you know Nancy Parker?" Bull asked.

Alex's eyes were drawn to the tableau in front of the hotel. "Not personally, but she invited me to speak."

"You won't ever forget her." He cracked a smile.

"What do you mean?" Alex asked curiously.

"You'll see."

ॐ

The public relations firm of Nancy Parker had been retained to guarantee the success of the fracking symposium. She and her team walked into the Hyatt Regency ballroom for a final check of the set-up and to assure every detail was perfect. Three Jumbotron closed-circuit television screens were strategically located to stream the speakers.

The banquet room, designed to accommodate hundreds of guests, was like a small football stadium. More than twelve hundred people were expected for the oversubscribed event: politicians, bankers, and all who had a vested interest in the industry. Expensive tickets for what was one of the hottest events on the industry had sold out in thirty-six hours.

"Sound test!" Nancy called to one of the technicians. "The lights need to be angled lower," she advised one of the crew. She had attracted big corporate money to make the event a success, and her clients would be showcased front and center. The lights and sound system were checked and rechecked as she adjusted one of the sponsor's signs.

Nancy was a calculating woman on the edge of fading beauty. Her experience showed. On an IPad, she reviewed a seating chart with names of attendees, patrons, VIPs, and members of the media. It was imperative that the important people be seated close to the stage and next to peers so no one was offended.

Nancy spoke into her cell phone. "People are arriving. Yes, it looks elegant," she said impatiently to her staffer. "Make sure the VIP area is perfect." An exclusive reception for the elite of the elite was scheduled to take place in an adjacent room.

"The flowers and tables look magnificent," the voice on the other end reported.

"Good. I'm waiting for the governor." Nancy stood at the room's entrance, awaiting the guests. Several security officers flanked the doors.

A slight man in wire rim glasses approached the reception table.

"Your name, sir?" asked the woman at the VIP check-in table.

"Ferrell Brandt, Nancy Parker's guest." He was given a nametag and a place at Nancy's personal table. Nancy brokered power in the major oil cities, including Dallas, Fort Worth, Houston, and Denver. Anyone who needed to get something done used her for almost every kind of influence-peddling.

A warm smile spread across Nancy's face when she noticed Ferrell.

She gave him a quick embrace.

"You got the check?" Ferrell Brandt had paid Nancy hundreds of thousands in consulting fees just in the last few months. She had been instrumental in helping him with a variety of projects in Texas and, more recently, in Colorado. She was on the payroll of some of the most influential people in the industry, who hired her for incredibly high retainers "to control damage" or "to consult." Most were in politics or the oil and gas business. After that, her job description was murky. It might entail getting a vote through a city council or securing influence from a county commissioner for whatever important project was under consideration. No one wanted to know the specifics because she was paid to run a covert operation. If she wasn't hired, she could make sure a project was shelved or stalled into oblivion. Those who needed extra help obtaining a development permit, a drilling permit, or a building permit, or securing the support of political leaders, relied on Nancy. At the same time, politicians depended on her to secure the contributions that fueled their campaigns. Everyone wanted her on his or her side. Ferrell paid to make sure he was her top priority.

Nancy squeezed Ferrell's sweaty hand, and then fluttered off to manage the other important guests. She left the large symposium room and headed to the VIP lounge. As she entered the elevator, she encountered a large, olive-skinned woman who gave Nancy a polite hug and said, "Thanks for the Cowboys tickets." The important councilwoman wore a stylish suit and bright red lipstick. Over the years, Nancy had called in favors from this powerful politician.

"Glad you could make the VIP reception."

Nancy used a considerable portion of her huge fees to grease palms. Always discreet, she accomplished her clients' goals seamlessly and quietly, never leaving a trail.

Alex stood outside the lobby entrance of the towering hotel. Her phone rang, and she stepped aside so Bull could continue on ahead of her.

She glanced down at the phone before answering. Sheriff Dan Salido came up on the caller ID.

"Hi, Sheriff. Any news?" Alex inquired anxiously.

"Not what you want to hear, I expect."

"Give me details," she told him.

"One of the local bartenders said your friend Mr. Forrester was a regular in his place," he said.

Alex figured Salido had filtered through the rumors that were being passed around like an STD. "Said he drank like a fish and got pretty sloppy some of the time."

"That was a long time ago." It was a defensive, knee-jerk response. Alex watched as people flowed into the symposium.

Salido sighed. "Not what I heard." Fact or fiction, the stories coming from the barbershop, the post office, and the Village Smithy breakfast joint were not flattering.

"He's been sober for years!" she retorted. Damn it, she thought, why was she defending him? The important thing was that the truth was unknown—Colt was missing and they had an out-of-control fire!

"And maybe not," the sheriff commented in a calm voice.

Alex fumed. "What if he was abducted?" This was what she feared. Colt's past might be the noose around his neck.

"There isn't enough evidence to suggest that," Salido said.

"Colt could be in desperate trouble!" Alex insisted.

"Has it occurred to you he doesn't want to be found?" Salido queried.

Alex bit her lip. "No one has heard from him since the explosion."

"Exactly," the sheriff agreed. "And, if we find him, he will have to do a lot of explaining."

Alex was enraged, but it was more than just the sheriff's attitude. She was angry about the well and even more infuriated about the cash call. And then there was Colt.

"I know you're concerned..." the sheriff began.

"I am a lot more than *concerned*, Sheriff Salido." Her tone was like a rusty knife blade. She didn't trust the sheriff.

There was silence on the line for a moment before he said, "We are doing all we can, Ms. Sheridan. Is there any other evidence you can provide us?"

"Such as?" As Alex stood in the 102-degree heat outside the Dallas Hyatt Regency building, her hair and makeup slowly melted.

He pressed further. "Is there anything missing or strange at his office? If you can provide some other clues, it could help. We don't have anything to go on. We don't have cause to issue a search warrant."

"We're not too far from proving that the well was sabotaged," Alex spat out the words, "and, when our well fire experts are finished, you will have a big problem on your hands."

"I don't like your tone." He sounded defensive and offended.

"And I don't like your conclusions," she shot back.

He was in way over his pay grade, she thought. Unfortunately, the FBI had left the investigation in the hands of the local sheriff's department. Salido's department wasn't really prepared or equipped for this type of investigation. What on earth did a sheriff in Carbondale know about sabotage and missing persons?

Alex hung up on Salido and went into the grand hotel, looking forward to meeting Riggs Austin, one of the most famous icons in oil and gas.

CHAPTER 12

The Colorado governor's office at Boettcher Mansion was quiet. An unusually thin, young female aide with strawberry blonde hair sat at an ornate period desk. The telephone on the desk buzzed. "Governor's office. Hello, Ms. Parker. Nice to speak with you again." She listened to Nancy Parker for about thirty seconds. "I will tell him; thank you for the generous contribution. Yes, he is preparing a statement about the well fire now."

After concluding the call, the aide hit speed dial to reach the governor in the back of a dark sedan.

Aaron Jeffries fingered the scar that ran down his neck, an unconscious habit. He waited patiently in the cabin, out of sight, pleased that everything was going as planned.

A man driving an old pickup truck parked in the back drive. Aaron peered out the window and recognized the truck as belonging to the Scott brothers.

Beaver Scott entered the cabin.

"Did you see the latest report?" Aaron opened the morning paper and waved it excitedly at Beaver. "The district attorney has ordered a review of drilling permits in the area and has called on the governor to help with the issue."

"We have them running for cover," Beaver said.

Aaron looked behind the other man. "Where's Jason?"

"Tending the plants. You know he doesn't like to be around people." A known recluse, Jason had not been seen for some time.

The brothers were an odd lot. They had been farmers, but now had one of the few legal marijuana growing operations and dispensaries in Carbondale. Ardent supporters of the anti-drilling movement, they had been eager to help. They attended most of the meetings in town and were instrumental in keeping the protesters agitated.

Aaron was happy to help the unsophisticated brothers. "Now we just need to lie low and let the politicians work their magic."

"Jason and I don't trust the politicians. They're worse than the oil companies," Beaver said with disdain. Long before fracking technology had been refined, a smooth-talking land man employed by one of the big oil companies had weaseled the brothers out of their families' mineral rights. Beaver and Jason still wore their bitterness like a purple heart.

"Nancy Parker is on board," Aaron said.

"She's okay." Beaver tossed some chocolate pot edibles on the table. "Brought you a treat."

Aaron had helped the Scott brothers secure the special agricultural permits needed to grow and sell marijuana in the area. Few permits were granted and, thanks to Nancy Parker's backroom lobbying, the Scotts received one of the only special use permits issued in the county.

He looked down at the marijuana product. "I'll save these for later."

"Careful; they're super strong," Beaver gloated.

"How is the cannabis business?"

"Jason's working on the fourth new greenhouse now," Beaver said. The greenhouses allowed them to cultivate their cash crop year-round to supply the retail shops. The brothers were for all things green, especially marijuana.

"No trouble with the locals?" Aaron asked.

"We're spreading the wealth, thanks to you." They were indebted to Aaron. He had appeared in their lives like a white knight, helping them maneuver through the maze of legal issues around the marijuana business.

"You've got the corner on this market," Aaron remarked, pleased that he had been an instrumental part of their success. Every county and municipality made its own rules about where and when and how pot could be cultivated, distributed, and sold, and where it could be smoked. The authorities were their friends. In return, Aaron had the brothers' support. It was easy to get them excited about the plan to stop drilling in the area.

"How did you get so many people to show up for the protest?" he continued.

The Scott brothers enjoyed their role—inciting the locals amused them, and it was a simple way to help Aaron.

"You have your secrets; I have mine," Beaver said.

The men shook hands before the pot baron left the cabin.

"He doesn't have a clue," Beaver mumbled to himself, masking his hostility. He was pumped up on steroids and too much testosterone. The few scraps of hair on his head were orange red, and his skin was freckled from ages in the sun. He was pleased with himself and with the latest developments. No one's going to know a thing, he thought with arrogant pleasure.

He spat in the dirt like a baseball pitcher and climbed into his dirty pickup truck. The bumper sticker on the back read: "Preserve the Thompson Divide. NO FRACKING."

CHAPTER 13

Just as the morning sun bled the sky pink, Lafayette rolled over, groping for the phone. "This is Lafayette."

A female voice said, "Hi. It's Jenny. You left a note?"

"Thank you for calling," he said, amazed that she called so soon.

"Happy to meet a friend of Colt's," she chirped.

"A waitress in town said you knew him." Lafayette rubbed his eyes, noticing a small spider hanging from a silky thread above the bed.

"He has been kind to me." The words were whispered in a sad way that sounded as if kindness was a rare commodity.

"Can I come talk with you?" he asked, hoping he'd have time for at least a cup of coffee.

"About?" Jenny sounded wary.

"I think Colt might need some help."

She paused for a long moment. "I haven't talked to him recently."

"That's okay—maybe you can give me some idea how to find him?"

"I'll be at work at the Red Rocks Diner on 133 if you want to drop by." She looked at the time and squealed, "Oh, no, I'm going to be late!"

"You need a ride?" Lafayette offered. He hadn't seen a car near her little trailer.

"Sure, that would save time." The offer seemed to lift her spirits a little.

"Ten minutes? I'm a large black man. You can't miss me." His levity broke the ice.

"Well, I'm a scrawny woman with a limp; can't miss me, either," she laughed. She remembered Colt speaking fondly of Lafayette.

"See you in a few."

Careful not to nick his goatee, Lafayette quickly shaved his head and face, then dressed. As he walked to his vehicle, a text came through on his cell phone.

No news yet.

The search for his son's ex-girlfriend was failing. She was probably trashed in a crack house in the seediest part of Denver. Actually, he didn't want to find her. He wanted to find the baby. He texted back:

Keep looking.

Blinding sunshine poured through the windshield as Lafayette drove slowly to the trailer park. Pickups with working people, trailers hauling cattle, and all sorts of service vehicles made a tiny traffic jam in the one-stoplight town. In the daylight, the entrance of the trailer park was much less ominous, and getting shot seemed less likely, but the unkempt parts of the community were more pronounced without the mask of dark.

Dented garbage cans, a few old cars, bare telephone poles, and a flea-bitten wreck of a dog greeted him as he pulled into the development. The pink awning was easy to find this time. Jenny waited on the porch, sucking on a cigarette, wiry thin as if she smoked more than she ate. She tossed the butt to the ground and crushed it in the dirt before limping over to the car where Lafayette held the door.

"Hi, thanks for meeting," he said, offering her his giant mitt of a hand.

"No problem." She shook his hand, then slid into the car.

Lafayette looked over at her for a moment before returning his attention to the road. "How do you know each other?"

Jenny looked a little nervous and her vague answer confirmed her trepidation. "We have some mutual friends," she hedged.

"Would that be AA? Colt was real open with me about his sobriety."

She nodded, gripping her hands tightly in her lap. We're not supposed to talk about people or what we talk about." She looked down at her hands. "I see him at meetings, and he helps a lot of people."

"We think something might have happened to him," Lafayette said gently.

"Like what?" Jenny asked as sincerely as possible.

"Not sure, but he hasn't been heard from in days, and his partner is worried."

He drove through the trailer park and onto the highway.

"That must be Alex. He really loves her," she said wistfully. "I can ask around." She bit her nails nervously while staring off into the distance.

"That would help." Lafayette said. "Is this the entrance to the diner?"

"Yep. You can drop me here." She pointed to a side entrance. Opening the truck door, she slid out. "Thanks for the lift."

"See you inside. I'm meeting a friend for breakfast," Lafayette said, waving goodbye.

"I'll come by your table when I can."

The Red Rocks Diner sat on the edge of Highway 133 at the entrance to Carbondale. Its retro building design with neon tube lights screamed 1950s. The only thing missing was Olivia Newton-John in a poodle skirt. The décor included black-and-white checkered floors, lots of stainless steel, and pink Formica counters. Buddy Holly crooned from the jukebox.

Jenny checked in with her boss and then went into the ladies room to wash her hands. She could not stop trembling. How and when was it all going to end?

She had told so many lies that she almost believed them, till now. After gathering her composure, she reentered the restaurant, where she saw Lafayette sitting in a booth. Another man sat in the booth opposite Lafayette, a service dog by his side. She headed to the kitchen.

After a few, minutes Jenny re-appeared, carrying coffee cups. She placed them on the Formica table.

"I'm Jenny," she said shyly.

"This is the nice lady I told you about," Lafayette offered.

She held up a dog biscuit. "Is it okay to give him a treat?" She couldn't help but notice the other man's handsome features. In her simple white tee shirt and jeans, she felt so plain.

Brutus's ears perked up as Jenny slid in beside him. The big dog wore a service harness and sat in the booth like a regular.

"He'll eat anything. I'm Trey and this is Brutus." Trey smiled at Jenny before beaming proudly at Brutus. Jowls and wrinkles drooped like draperies around the dog's face, and his lower jaw protruded, revealing two sharp fangs. The dog's eyes twinkled.

Just then, one of Jenny's co-workers showed up at the table carrying a load of steaming dishes and a dog bowl. She placed the stack of hotcakes in front of Trey and a bowl filled with scrambled eggs with diced bacon on the table for Brutus.

"When was the last time you saw Colt?" Lafayette inquired in a matter-of-fact tone.

"Last week maybe?" she said. "He was worried about work. No, maybe it was ten days." She rolled her eyes in the air and counted on her fingers. "Said there were a lot of people around here he didn't trust." Jenny took a sip of coffee.

"You from around here?" Trey asked.

"Tried to get away, but I always come back. I went to California for a while, but it was too expensive," she said with a small smile. She noticed Trey watching her intently. "Then I got hooked on the opioids they gave me for this hip, and I had to come back home to get clean."

"Family here?" Trey probed.

"Not anymore," she mumbled and stood. "My shift is starting. I'll call if I hear anything." She patted Brutus, who had finished the scrambled eggs and was taking a catnap.

Trey fished out a business card and handed it to Jenny. "I'm up here a lot flying for the oil company, if I can ever help."

"Thanks," she said, rewarding him with a soft smile. "I gotta punch in." She waved goodbye to the strange trio: Trey, the long-haired helicopter pilot; Lafayette, the giant southern black man who stood out like an ambulance siren; and Brutus, the rescued English bulldog.

She stopped to add, "I am here most days if you want to drop by."

"Call if you think of anything," Lafayette chimed in.

"I will, and thank you for the ride." Jenny limped away, ducked inside the restroom, locked the door, and retched.

"Will you follow up with her?" Lafayette asked Trey. "We have to find out where Colt is."

"No problem. How did she get that limp?" Trey asked with a resentful voice. He clenched his fist and glared at Lafayette.

"There was a record of a domestic assault, no charges filed, but I will find out more facts." Lafayette was a wiz at research and could find out most anything on the internet.

"I better not meet the ass hole who did that to her." His heart pounded. He wanted to scoop her up like a fallen sparrow. He hadn't felt these feelings in years, maybe not since the Gulf War. He liked her shape and her knobby hipbones that protruded through her faded jeans. She wasn't anorexic, just lean, and he had noticed her beautiful delicate hands. In Trey's eyes, she was an angel.

The inside of Sheriff Salido's truck cab was filled with fast food trash. He was just getting ready to go into the diner for a hot meal when his phone vibrated. "Salido here."

"Mike Carter from Denver."

"Alex mentioned you might call." The sheriff fidgeted as he waited for Alex's private detective to explain the purpose of the call.

"I worked homicide for years with the Denver Police," Carter said, hoping to create a common connection.

"Yes, I read about you," the sheriff offered, casually recognizing the toll that murder took on an investigator. "I worked homicide in Chicago before I came here." Salido had googled the detective. There was extensive data about his illustrious career as head of homicide in Denver, and even more information about him breaking the mysterious murder case of Denver business woman Christine Welbourne.

"Hope it wasn't too bad," Carter said lightheartedly.

Salido laughed. "I read what you did to help Alex capture and prosecute the man who murdered her partner. Big deal case."

"Jeff Ashton was a bad guy. He worked for Christine and Alex and no one suspected he was responsible for hiring the hit man." Solving the case and prosecuting Jeff Ashton was a source of immense pride for Carter.

He and Alex were the subject of numerous articles, and both of their testimonies—which put the murderer, Jeff Ashton, in prison—were available on the internet.

Salido had seen more than most. After too much blood, he found his way to the Western Slope, joined the Wildland Firefighters, became a fire jumper, then ran for sheriff. The Windy City was a distant memory.

The two men spoke familiarly as members of a universal fraternity.

"You know why I'm calling. We're trying to locate Colt Forester and figure out what happened at the well." Carter explained his role as a private investigator.

"Have you been to his house or talked to the bank to see if there are any strange transactions?" the sheriff asked. The question was Investigation 101 material and he already knew the answer.

"Yeah, nothing. Everything looks normal at his house in Denver. No signs of packing for a trip. But there have been no credit card transactions since the day the well blew up."

"I'll ask around here and get my guys to see what they can find." The fraternity tended to help its own, and Salido was willing to assist a fellow officer as long as he didn't interfere.

Carter sighed. "That will really help."

"Heard he was a boozer," Salido commented. It was a baited statement.

"Not lately," Carter defended, but he wasn't fully convinced Colt was still on the wagon.

"You never know," Salido countered. "He could be on a beach in Mexico. In Margaritaville."

They both chuckled.

"Thanks for checking things out. Let me know if I can help." Carter ended the conversation.

CHAPTER 14

Outside the Dallas Hyatt Regency, the official host hotel for the fracking symposium, a huge crowd had metastasized since earlier in the day. Alongside the protesters, pro-drilling supporters and oilfield workers waved signs favoring the industry: ENERGY INDEPENDENCE! NO MORE FOREIGN OIL! OIL = JOBS!

Bumper-to-bumper traffic clogged the roads leading to the hotel, and the shrill sounds of honking horns and police whistles directing motorists filled the air. Police helped manage the situation, separating the pro-business factions from those concerned about every facet of the energy business, especially the recurring earthquakes in the area.

At the main entrance, a woman with a bullhorn yelled: "Big oil kills! Stop the fracking!" Nearby, a local TV reporter, followed by a cameraman, interviewed arriving guests.

Some factions wanted the industry to fail. Ironically, these same concerned groups were against the United States being held hostage by dependence on foreign oil imports. Drilling and fracking were blamed as the possible cause of tainted groundwater, environmental pollution, and earthquakes. But the energy industry also fueled the economy and created high-paying job opportunities. A controversial proposed pipeline from Canada to the Gulf of Mexico was also under attack. While some swore it was a dangerous hazard, others were desperate for work, and the oil and gas industry offered real employment opportunity.

The media made sure no one would forget the BP oil spill in the

Gulf of Mexico and the Exxon Valdez in Alaska—two of the worst environmental disasters in modern history. Lately, environmental advocates pointed to the plumes of smoke pouring from Alex Sheridan's well into the pristine Colorado sky with a clear, "We told you so."

The day's special guests gathered at a reception in a private suite where they could mingle with one another. Riggs Austin, the billionaire oilman, stood in a corner holding court, surrounded by members of the press and other dignitaries, while the mayor of Dallas posed for photos with the speakers. A small line of guests waited for a photo with the business celebrity.

Nancy Parker skillfully managed all the details as she surveyed the room.

"May I have your attention, please?" she announced through collagen-filled lips. "Everyone, a special guest has arrived."

From the rear of the building, the governor appeared like a bottle rocket. Flanked by his handlers, he smiled and slapped backs as he worked the crowd en route to the microphone.

"Thank you all for coming." The imposing man addressed the group. "Our state is indebted to you, the leaders of the oil and gas industry. You are the risk-takers that make it all possible, and you are responsible for our tremendous prosperity and for the jobs in our great state." Applause broke out. "Thank you to Nancy Parker and to the Energy Business Council for hosting this event."

More applause greeted the prominent politician, and attendees pressed closer, all trying to get photos taken with the charismatic governor.

Nancy Parker positioned Alex next to the governor, then slipped between them for a quick photo. The moderator for the event, one of the top national news anchors, arrived and was immediately swamped by attendees and press.

Eager for information on the burning well, several members of the media cornered Alex. "When will the fire be out?"

"Our people are working on it twenty-four seven," she answered.

"But you would admit it is a colossal disaster?"

"Bull Hawthorn is on board; it will be contained," Alex insisted. "Please excuse us."

114

Alex sidestepped any more questions, then made her way over to Riggs Austin, the undisputed grandfather of shale oil and gas exploration and one of the leaders of the fracking revolution.

"Mr. Austin, Alex Sheridan, with…"

"I know who you are. It's a pleasure." The large commanding man shook her hand warmly.

Alex blushed. "The honor is mine."

"You know, we're buyers, when you want to sell some of those leases…"

"We aren't selling," she said with a smile, "but I'll keep you in mind."

"Please do; I would like you to look at some of our deals." His eyes twinkled like he had a secret.

"My partner, Christine, was fond of you," Alex said, blinking away sudden tears.

"Wish she was here to see this oil boom," Riggs said.

"She knew that shale would one day be the biggest play the United States would ever see." Alex's admiration for her former partner was unmistakable.

"Have you been to Williston?" Riggs asked, referring to the latest boomtown in North Dakota.

"We have several leases up there in the Bakken," Alex responded. "Can't find enough guys to work or a place to put them."

Riggs nodded sagely. "We had to build our own man camp."

Williston, North Dakota, was home to the vast Bakken shale formation. Men flooded to the area in pursuit of the American dream. Man camps were built as quickly as possible, and the sleepy little town exploded with activity. A shortage of workers, housing, and infrastructure attracted thousands, and it turned into a boomtown overnight. Wages and property values soared to unrealistic levels, and massive amounts of oil were discovered, tipping the supply scale and turning North America into the premier source of hydrocarbons. Energy independence had arrived.

A bell tolled, announcing the official start to the symposium.

"They're herding us in there," Riggs commented, placing a large weathered hand on Alex's back, moving her with him to the door.

"Let's go give them something to talk about," Alex flashed a smile.

She handed Riggs a tee shirt and he laughed, reading, "Frack Baby Frack." He was cut from the same cloth as Red Adair and other industry heroes, courageous men undaunted by mountainous odds. Their determination to find black gold from deep inside the earth in areas others had forsaken proved them to be a breed apart.

Alex was suddenly jostled by a man she didn't know. He had a perfectly formed bald head, rodent-like features, and thick glass lenses distorting his eyes. "Excuse me," he apologized. "Sorry. I am such a klutz."

"No problem. Alex Sheridan," she said, introducing herself.

"Ferrell Brandt. My pleasure."

Alex thought he looked out of place. He did not strike her as an oilman but, then again, she didn't look like the typical driller either. Must be a numbers guy, she surmised.

The mayor took the stage. He was a wiry man with a magnetic presence and scalpel-sharp mind.

"Welcome to all of you who are responsible for this incredible event," he said. "The importance of oil and gas to our city and state can't be overstated. We would also like to recognize Nancy Parker for her monumental effort in making tonight such a success. Nancy, where are you?"

Nancy Parker gave a royal wave from her seat at a nearby table.

The mayor pointed her out. "There you are."

He led the crowd in polite applause. Cameras flashed as the mayor continued.

"We are also indebted to the sponsors of this event. It could not happen without the support of all the corporate patrons." He mentioned some key names, including Petro Bank, one of the biggest oil and gas lenders in the business and the lead underwriter of the symposium, then stepped down so the symposium could begin.

A distinguished engineer and geologist made the first presentation to the crowd. He was a large man from Western Colorado who had studied at the Colorado School of Mines. He commanded the full attention of the crowd as he presented the science and techniques of the fracking process.

When the engineer finished his remarks, the mayor turned to the stage, saying, "And now, it is my pleasure to introduce one of the industry's most successful independent producers, a wildcatter and a lady who has drilled more wells than most of us put together, Alex Sheridan."

The audience cheered as Alex walked to the microphone. "I'll keep this short and to the point so we can get on to the star of the show." She turned and smiled at Riggs, who tipped his hat to the crowd.

Alex explained the history of fracking. "Most of you know there is nothing new about fracking. It has been around since the late 1800s in some form or another. Originally, they used crude explosives, but today we are much more sophisticated, and it is only in recent years that the public has latched onto the word 'fracking,' probably because it is so quotable."

Using a huge screen, she showed the audience how a drill bit cut into the earth way below the water table, and how the fracking system worked in a variety of different formations and zones miles below the surface.

After a few questions from the audience, Alex headed back to her seat as the next speaker was introduced.

Novak Energy, headquartered near Houston, operated one of the few export terminals for LNG, or liquefied natural gas. Its CEO was a self-made billionaire and one of the most popular men in the business. Blinding lights made it difficult to see the audience, so he stepped to the side of the podium, put on Ray-Ban sunglasses and a Novak hard hat, then stepped back to the microphone. "That's better. Now I can see."

The crowd roared. His remarks centered on LNG and his belief in its potential for fueling the world. He explained the process of cooling the predominantly methane gas to a solid and how it could be loaded on huge tankers that transported it around the globe. When it reached its destination, it was converted back to a gas and sent through lines to provide energy for lights and homes and industry. Several tanker companies were part of the portfolio, and Novak was competing for another highly sought-after permit to export LNG.

Ferrell Brandt listened intently.

"Thank you for the invitation," he whispered into Nancy Parker's ear. At Nancy's request, a special invitation was issued to Mack Sloane, but Brandt was sent in her place. Of course, Brandt had written six-figure checks to Nancy, too, so the paybacks revolved. "I hope the governor is well?" he inquired.

"The governor is so supportive," Nancy replied. She knew he was referring to her call and the contribution to the governor, who was beholden to them.

During a brief intermission, Brandt scoured the room and worked the crowd. He shook hands and handed out cards before returning to his seat. Most knew he was a conduit to the Sloanes.

The moderator stepped to the microphone. "And now we are honored to introduce the man who knows more about fracking than just about anyone, Mr. Riggs Austin."

In the dark room, hundreds of guests cheered and applauded the hero. Riggs's advancing age had not extinguished the passion that gleamed in his eyes. He was one of the entrepreneurs who had almost bankrupted his company on a quest to prove there was a way to extract the oil and gas from shale. Most of the other companies had given up, moving on to targets outside of the United States to prevent the world from running out of oil. Only a few years before, the world was concerned about what was believed to be the inevitable global shortage. Now, because of fracking, the United States had the largest reserves on the planet, and more formations were discovered daily.

The large Texan dwarfed the podium. He pushed the microphone aside, as his booming voice needed no amplification. Loved by many and despised by some, his controversial reputation attracted many in the audience. The terrain of his life involved courage, risk, and determination. Having started dirt poor, he had gambled and lost and gambled again, so many times, until eventually he hit pay dirt.

"Thanks, y'all, for having me today." Loud applause again filled the room. "You know, being here is a bit ironic. Twenty-five years ago, I was asked to attend a meeting here, but I didn't have two nickels," he began, smiling, "So I slept in my car in the underground garage, but the security guard found me and threw me out. I'll be staying inside the hotel tonight." He raised his hand to quiet a quick flutter of applause and laughter. "Now, let's talk about that god-awful word: *Fracking.*"

Bang! Out of the nowhere, an explosion shattered the room. Sparks flew as a man ran toward the stage. "You're a lying thief."

Bang! Bang! More shots were fired. Confused and frightened people jumped from their seats and dove for cover. Screams rang out. Startled, the shocked security guards in the back moved toward the commotion.

Riggs collapsed onto the stage. More screams sounded, followed by chaos.

Bull Hawthorn jumped from his chair and charged the shooter. Another man joined Bull to tackle and wrestle the flailing shooter to the floor. They pulled the pistol from the man's grip and grappled with him until he was subdued. Bull held the assailant down while two policemen handcuffed him.

People scurried for the exits.

Alex rushed to aid Riggs, who lay on the stage by the podium. Alex took him by the arm to help him struggle to his knees, but he could not get up. Blood gushed through his fingers as he held his shoulder.

"Don't move!" she told Riggs firmly. Alex called out to one of the event staff. "Call an ambulance, urgent!"

Riggs tried to move, struggling to get to his feet.

"Stay still!" she ordered, removing her jacket to sop up blood and apply pressure to the wound as they waited for an ambulance. "Paramedics are on the way," she said encouragingly, but Riggs looked pale and shocked. She knew he needed immediate treatment. Keeping pressure on the wound, Alex called out impatiently to one of Nancy Parker's event aides, "Where is the paramedic?"

As they waited for the emergency medical team, Bull ran onto the stage. "You okay?" he asked Alex.

For the first time, she felt the pain in her side. "I'm fine." In the distance, a faint siren whined.

Bull removed his own jacket and then took off his cotton shirt and handed it to Alex to apply to Riggs' bleeding wound.

"Are you hurt?" He pointed to a red stain on her shirt.

Alex looked down, stunned to see blood soaking her blouse.

"I'm okay," she insisted, oblivious to the wound.

"Let me see." He raised her shirt, revealing a nasty wound where a bullet had torn her flesh just below the ribcage. "Get some towels," he ordered one of the support staff. "And call the ambulance again, now!"

He turned back to Alex. "You've been shot."

Alex was distracted by the crisis and focused on Riggs. "I'll be fine."

Riggs, big and strapping, was in his late seventies. The shot had ripped through the lower shoulder area and done some real damage, leaving an ugly exit wound. "It's just a flesh wound," he said as the EMTs arrived. "I've had worse accidents in the oil fields."

News crews covering the event recorded all the mayhem as more police and media arrived. Attendees with cell phones uploaded the scene on social media. When gawkers tried to get in, police blocked the doors; no one in, no one out.

"Who was that man?" Alex asked no one in particular, ignoring the throbbing ache in her side.

"A disgruntled landowner," Riggs said.

The attacker seemed more than disgruntled, Alex thought. There had to be more to the story.

The police led the shooter, bent and broken, out of the ballroom in handcuffs. To Alex, he looked like a sad old man with nothing left to lose.

The emergency medical team arrived, checked Riggs's vital signs, started an IV, and wrapped his shoulder before placing him on a gurney.

"Where are you taking me?" he asked as they strapped him down.

The woman EMT smiled down at him reassuringly. "Parkland Hospital. We'll get you all fixed up." The new state-of-the-art county hospital was the best choice for any kind of gunshot wound and only minutes away.

"I hate hospitals." His eyes locked on Alex and, for a moment, the powerful man looked frail and frightened. Alex moved to his side and, as they wheeled the gurney away with Riggs protesting, Alex promised, "I'll check on you. Here's my number." She slipped him her business card.

Another EMT examined Alex and cleaned her wound. "You're going to need a few stitches when you get to the ER."

"Please," Alex pleaded. "Can't you just do it in the ambulance? I'm not going to the hospital." Her voice was kind but firm. "I'll do anything not to go to the emergency room," she begged, knowing it would take all night if she was admitted.

The EMT gave her a look, then led Alex to the ambulance, stitched her side, applied a bandage, and returned her to Bull.

"You'll need to keep it clean, and check the sutures to make sure there isn't any swelling or redness," the EMT instructed Alex, then directed a stern look at Bull, who hovered like a mother.

As calm was restored, Alex felt chilled. Her hands trembled from shock, and she was drained by the trauma.

A large man in a uniform presented credentials and introduced himself as Sergeant Ortiz. "Can I ask a few questions?"

She nodded. "Yes, of course."

"You were on the stage?"

"Yes, but the glare from the lights was blinding." She pointed to the spotlight still focused on the spot where Riggs had stood. "I could barely see the audience."

"Did you recognize the shooter?" Ortiz showed her a photo on his iPad.

"No, I only saw the flash from the gun. I have never seen him before."

Ortiz collected her contact information and offered his business card. "Call if you think of anything. You are in good hands."

The media milled about in the lobby of the Hyatt Regency Hotel, waiting for more of the story, but Alex managed to slip outside with Bull. The large sphere of Reunion Tower blinked bright lights in the twilight.

"Looks like we may have a big one," Bull commented as a tornado warning siren sounded in the distance and the sky swirled black and blue. A gust of wind almost knocked them over as Alex grabbed a hand rail, then they ran through pelting rain into the waiting Town Car.

Bull read a message on his phone. "We won't be flying any time soon," he declared.

"What about the fire?" Alex asked anxiously. "I have to get back."

"We will, once it's safe. Take us to the Melrose Hotel," he instructed the driver. "I've arranged for some rooms."

"Thank you." Alex knew safety was their top priority, but she couldn't control her anxious desire to return to the crisis at the burning well.

As the reality of the terrifying shooting sank in, Alex worried about Riggs. Everyone had rushed into the fray to stop the attacker while she helped Riggs but, in truth, he could have died. She avoided thinking about her own close call. With the adrenaline wearing off, she wanted a drink and some rest.

As the limousine pulled under the porte-cochère, a uniformed man stepped forward to open the car door. The historic Warwick Melrose Hotel, with its magnificent dark wood bar and old-world charm, was a perfect haven for the night, and possibly out of sight of snooping reporters.

"Welcome back, Mr. Hawthorn."

"Thanks, Sam. Good to see you again." Bull slipped some bills into the porter's palm.

A seasoned reporter and cameraman materialized from thin air. "Can I ask you some questions about the shooting, Ms. Sheridan?" he asked as his associate snapped a photo. The shooting was the top trending story, and scavengers were looking for a juicy piece of gossip. "How did the man infiltrate the event?" the reporter fired questions. "Why did he shoot Riggs Austin?"

"No comment," Alex responded.

"You saved Riggs Austin's life," the reporter persisted. "How does it feel to be a hero?" The click of the camera was audible.

"Anyone else close by would have done the same." She kept moving. "I was just trying to help."

"Do you have medical experience?"

Alex lowered her head, refusing eye contact. "Excuse me, I have to go."

The manager skillfully pulled them away from the pesky reporter. "Welcome back. Your suite is ready," he said to Bull as he escorted them to the top of the red-carpeted stairs. Less high-profile than the Hyatt, the Melrose was iconic and refined, and it was only minutes from downtown.

"May I take your briefcase?" asked the manager.

"Thank you for the last-minute accommodations." Bull shook his hand. "This is Alex Sheridan."

"Welcome, Ms. Sheridan. You are all over the local news." He showed her a Twitter feed that confirmed it.

"Thank you for the rooms," Alex responded, feeling slightly awkward. "I need to call the hospital."

"Bad luck on the weather," the manager commiserated, "but we are glad to have you with us."

Alex nodded, grasping the key the manager provided. She just needed a room, a phone and a bed, in that order, so she could try to make sense of the world around her.

CHAPTER 15

The 911 call center in the small town of Rifle routed an emergency call to the Garfield County Sheriff's Office in Glenwood Springs.

"We have a distress call about two missing hikers somewhere up on the Divide," he said, referring to the Thompson Divide, a popular hiking destination in the area.

"Lost?" asked the young officer on duty. Lost hikers and injured climbers were a regular occurrence in the Rockies, and the sheriff's office responded to numerous emergency situations. A broken leg or ankle meant emergency aid would be sent, or a helicopter would be dispatched, depending on the location.

The 911 operator confirmed the information. "Yes. It sounds like they are in the restricted area, back side, near the area of the fire."

"Do you have any coordinates?" the deputy asked, writing rapidly.

"Just their sign-in at the trailhead yesterday. They never returned after the day hike," the operator told him.

The deputy ripped the note off his pad in exasperation. "These vacation season tourists don't understand the risks. Have you called Mountain Rescue?"

"En route as we speak." Professionally trained volunteers from Mountain Rescue assisted most search parties.

Deputy JP Green updated Sheriff Salido on the emergency, handing him the note.

The sheriff shuffled a few papers, then picked up his hat and went out to lead the search party. "I thought the area was closed because of the fire," he remarked as they walked to the vehicle.

"Not closed soon enough?" the young deputy suggested. Green had joined the sheriff's office almost a year before and, since that time, he had helped with numerous rescue missions. He was one of the best young detectives in the county.

The mountain road curved and snaked as the sheriff and deputy headed in the direction of where the missing hikers were thought to be. As the crow flies, it wasn't far from the burning well but, on the rugged backside of the divide, it was difficult to access.

"We need to find them before dark," Salido said. He knew a cold night of exposure could be deadly. The firefighters were still combing the vast mountain space and putting out hot spots in the area that was on high alert.

Green pointed off to their right. "We're not too far from the trailhead."

"Let's leave the truck and go on foot," Salido suggested. "How many volunteers?"

"Five or six, hopefully. The trails up here are like a maze." A network of thousands of miles of trailheads crossed the national forests. Locating the young hikers would be a challenge.

At the trailhead, the experienced Mountain Rescue volunteers awaited assignments. Their skilled search-and-rescue methods were an invaluable help to the sheriff's office. Every imaginable piece of emergency gear, including packs filled with first aid items, flashlights, shovels, and blankets were brought to the search site. Dark clouds above created a threatening sky as a few large drops pelted down.

The two men, now in rain gear and followed by the volunteers, hiked up the path. Bullet-hard pellets rained down, instantly forming rivers in the path and driving the searchers to the refuge of a large conifer. They waited there for the hail to pass before continuing their ascent into the forest.

The path followed the downstream flow of a small tributary filled with fallen logs and large boulders.

Soon they entered a scorched and blackened area of the forest, the latest victim of the well fire. In silence, the search party headed toward the rendezvous point where cell phone service was nonexistent. A young marmot darted across the path, startling Green, who jumped in surprise.

Eventually, they arrived at the small campground, where other volunteers waited. In the distance, smoke from the burning well fire smudged the sky.

"Fan out in teams and search the area," Salido directed.

Green distributed radios and whistles to the experienced team of volunteers, and the hunt began.

The deputy trudged toward a high mountain lake, accompanied by several of the volunteers. Other volunteers fanned out in different directions while Salido settled in at the campground, managing radio communications. As the temperature dropped, the sheriff fielded updates from team leaders. Each minute that passed worked against them. Night transformed the mountains into a cruel and dangerous place when temperatures plummeted to hypothermic levels.

The tedious wait gave Salido time to reflect on his tenuous marital situation. His wife begged that she needed time and space, and he was doing all in his power to honor her wishes. Inside, his anger boiled. She was selfish to abandon her family. How could she leave their daughter? And where was she hiding? Part of him wanted to track her down and file for divorce, but that wouldn't be good for his precious Cathy. He was torn.

Green and his group walked a path through the forest until they approached a clear, high mountain lake, whose perimeter was surrounded by a rocky path. The team members shouted and blew shrill whistles with the hope of alerting the missing people. The narrow trail, covered with needles and leaves, was mushy from the rain, and a rock field spilled treacherously off to the right. Near a steep drop-off on the lake side of the path, one of the volunteers slipped, almost tumbling down the rocks. Green grabbed him just in time, pulling him to safety.

"Stop!" Green froze in the path, listening intently. "I heard something." He blew a loud shrill whistle.

Still as statues, everyone waited for a response. An answering whistle sounded, and they headed in the direction of the sound. It came again, and they continued toward it, maneuvering around a bend at the bottom of the rock fall where they saw movement. The two missing hikers, wet and frightened, huddled in yellow rain gear in a crevasse in a ravine.

"Over here. Down here!" a woman screamed, as she scurried over the rocks like a spider, making her way toward Green. "Thank God." She threw her arms around Green. "Thank God you found us." She pulled at his sleeve desperately. "Seth is in trouble. His leg is broken."

Deputy Green radioed the sheriff. "We found them." He looked down toward the fallen hiker.

The deputy moved carefully over the rocks toward the male hiker, who had a blood-soaked tee shirt wrapped around a leg.

"Do you need backup?" Salido asked over the radio.

"Yes, " Green responded as soon as he checked the wound. "One has a compound fracture. Bone sticking out of his ankle."

"I'll send some guys in with a stretcher and call for the chopper."

Green motioned to two of the rescuers with him to help stabilize the wounded man. "We'll move him to an open area where they can land the helicopter."

The lost hikers looked exhausted and worried. Introductions were made quickly, and they learned the young man was a graduate student from the University of Colorado. His girlfriend, Lucy, was a bright-eyed undergraduate.

"I fell off a boulder and snapped my leg," said Seth, wincing in agony. Deputy Green could see that the ugly wound needed immediate attention; excruciating pain was evident in the male hiker's eyes. One of the mountain rescue volunteers gave him some sedatives and fluids while they spoke.

"You know this area is closed because of the fire?" Green asked the novice hikers in a serious voice.

Seth moaned, then said, "The trails were open on the other side. Didn't know it was closed."

"We were looking for water." Lucy looked in the direction of the lake. They were on the hike that lead up to the Thompson Divide Plateau at the back of the disputed drilling area.

Green examined the ghastly wound and did what he could to help Seth as they waited for a stretcher.

Sheriff Salido's radio crackled with static as he provided an update on the rescue. "The chopper is on its way."

"Got it," Salido heard Green's choppy reply confirming the message.

The radio crackled again, and a guttural scream came across the radio.

"What's that?" Green yelled.

"I'll get back to you." Salido turned his attention to the desperate cry. He bolted in the direction of the scream while several other workers followed. The charred remains of conifers filled the once-beautiful green forest.

"Over here!" a volunteer beckoned. In a burned-out section of the forest, not far from the back of the well fire, another volunteer was doubled over, gagging.

"Are you hurt?" Salido asked, panting hard in the thin mountain air. He put his hand gently on her shoulder, trying to identify a problem. "Can you breathe?"

Her head shook back and forth, and she vomited. "Look over there!" She pointed to a low spot underneath the side of a large boulder.

Salido patted her on the back. "Back away and find a spot to rest."

She nodded affirmatively, already moving.

Like a man walking on broken glass, Salido approached the scene. He circled the perimeter of the tree and boulder. Several curious volunteers appeared. "No one come any closer," he warned, holding his hand up to bar their advance. What had been an arm was burned to a nub, and the charred remains of a body were partially visible.

He turned on the radio. "I need some backup here."

Salido gingerly approached the corpse. He took a good look around the area, then retraced his steps, careful not to step on any evidence or otherwise disturb the crime scene. He thought the body had been exposed for some time, but he didn't have the expertise to evaluate the blackened, barely human remains.

He keyed his radio again. "Find the coroner, ASAP."

Salido backed away, then approached the volunteers. "Sorry you had to see this." He tried to soothe the woman who had discovered the body. "Probably got trapped in the wildfire." Salido knew of many cases of people being trapped by raging fires.

"Should we try to move the body?" a young man in camo gear asked.

The sheriff shook his head vigorously. "No. No one touch anything... don't come any closer and be careful where you walk."

Another female volunteer asked, "Should we call the paramedics?"

"Too late for paramedics. Y'all go on back and please don't discuss this until we speak with the coroner."

Other volunteers gawked at the remains.

"I'll let you know if we need help," Salido barked. The newly-elected county coroner would need to get the remains to the morgue in Glenwood Springs, and then to the forensic pathologist in Grand Junction, who would determine what happened to the body.

But Salido had a gut feeling he already knew who they'd just found.

CHAPTER 16

Alex, aching and exhausted, waited impatiently for Bull in the lobby of the Melrose Hotel in Dallas. The high ornate ceilings and antique furnishings in the foyer created an elegant ambience. A member of the Dallas Mavericks basketball team dwarfed the concierge desk, as his entourage hovered nearby. Tall as a redwood and with a thick foreign accent, the player stood out like a neon sign.

Waiters and service staff hurried about as lively patrons filed into the dark, oaky bar, one of many vogue watering holes in the trendy area. A jazz trio played a low-key tune as the guests laughed and talked, oblivious to news of the nightmarish shooting.

Alex, having discarded her bloody shirt and now wearing a "Frack Baby Frack" tee shirt, went to find a drink. The bartender, a man in his late thirties with neat hair, greeted her warmly.

"What's your pleasure?"

She didn't hesitate. "Very dry, dirty Martini, straight up, three small olives, thanks."

He picked up a glass, then looked at her. "Vodka preference?"

"Anything potent will do." She scanned the room and noticed the press photographer at a back corner table.

"Nice shirt."

Alex picked up the drink he set in front of her. "Thanks."

An inviting club chair with overstuffed cushions beckoned. She wandered over to it, and slouched into its arms, ready to take the edge off the harrowing day. How many times had she sipped cocktails with old friends in this place?

Like a warning siren, the vision of her former husband slipped into the present. A master performer, he had fooled everyone in Dallas and beyond, including Alex, with his charm and intellect. But he turned from Dr. Jekyll to Mr. Hyde once he was behind closed doors, his dark, angry and controlling manner boiling forth in violent rage.

Seconds later, her phone lit up with Wayne Decker's name on the caller ID.

"Are you getting along okay?" she asked. She was grateful for his efforts and hoped for positive news.

"Bull Hawthorn's guys are real pros. It's all going to be fine. Just expensive!" Wayne said in the most reassuring tone she had heard since the crisis began. Alex listened to the quick update. The Wild Well people were managing the situation and, although the fire was still burning, a plan to extinguish the blaze was being implemented. The recent rains had helped the forestry service douse the worst of the surrounding blaze, and the winds had subsided, creating a moment of hope and calm.

"Thanks, I'll check in tomorrow." It was a relief that the crisis seemed to be abating.

"Get some rest. This is under control for now." Wayne's reassuring tone lowered Alex's stress meter several notches. Fortunately, Wayne had picked up the broken pieces of the job. He had worked for both Alex and Colt on so many joint ventures that the team respected his experience and leadership.

Bull entered the dark bar as she ended the call. In the shadows of flickering candlelight, he looked racehorse-handsome.

"Shall we go to the suite?" he asked, picking up the martini glass. "I'm pooped."

"Thanks for helping with the arrangements, but maybe I should speak to the front desk about my room. I need some rest," Alex objected.

"There are several rooms, so I think you'll find the suite accommodations acceptable...but, if you aren't happy, we'll get you another," he said in a neutral tone.

"I'm exhausted," she said, slightly embarrassed that she thought he might be putting her in a compromising situation. Alex guarded her privacy and, as much as she enjoyed Bull's company, she felt half-dead.

"Me, too! And no one shot me. Shall we go?" He escorted her to the suite, which was comprised of two large king bedrooms, a bar, and elegant living area. Moments after he shut the door behind them, the doorbell rang.

"Your toiletries." A polished young porter handed a package to Bull, who slipped him a tip. "And pajamas."

Bull showed Alex to a stylish bedroom decorated with reproduction antiques and a four-poster bed made up with a down comforter and a nest of inviting pillows.

"There's a robe and pajamas." He handed her a toothbrush kit.

Alex entered the marble bathroom, washed her hands and face, peeled off her clothes, and put on the white robe that was lying on the bed. She returned, at least knowing she looked refreshed and almost exactly as he had found her that morning.

They collapsed onto the sofa, and Bull pulled her into his arms. He held her gently for a long time before saying, "Thank God you're okay."

In the fully stocked bar, he found a double old-fashioned glass and some single malt whisky. He indicated the martini he'd carried up from the bar for her. "Hell of a way to get to know someone." He smiled at her, taking a sip of the soothing amber liquid.

Alex picked out one of the olives from her martini glass, nibbled, and then put the pit on the napkin.

"You take all your colleagues to a shoot-out?" she teased. "I can't believe this actually happened." She was just beginning to process the reality of the afternoon's events.

"It's a first," Bull agreed, as he kicked off his boots.

"I was shot at an oil and gas symposium in Texas," she pretended to explain, as if giving an interview. For the first time since the assault, she smiled.

He toasted her with his glass. "No one would believe it in a million years."

"Couldn't make it up. Want to see my scar?" she joked playfully before taking a sip of her martini.

"You're certainly taking this all in stride," Bull told her. "I like that resilient streak."

She blushed at the comment. "We should check on Riggs." She googled the hospital and found the main number.

The receptionist at Parkland Hospital Emergency Room answered immediately.

"Riggs Austin, please," she said. "He was taken to emergency a few hours ago."

"May I ask who is calling?"

"A close friend," Alex said.

"You can speak with him after he's assigned to a room."

The attendant refused to give out any other information, and Alex had no energy to push back. She sagged back against the cushions.

Bull gently took her hand. "I'm starving."

"Me, too."

He located the room service menu and, after reviewing the offerings, handed it to Alex. After she made her selection, she ordered the food and, while they waited for the meal to arrive, he gazed at her raptly.

On the plane, the sensual energy was electric, but preparation for the business symposium kept their feelings in check. Now, alone together and bonded by a tragedy that would forever cement their story, a survivors' friendship was born. Bull had fearlessly jumped on the shooter while she bolted into action, doing all in her power to save Riggs's life, and they had worked together to stop the bleeding.

"Your sutures need to be checked," Bull reminded her.

She shook her head, not ready for that. "I'm fine."

The stern paramedic had cautioned them both to make sure there wasn't more bleeding or redness around the wound. "Stop arguing and lie down." He opened half of her robe, revealing the wound and her finely curved body.

Alex put her hand on his. "Be careful."

The wound looked clean, no swelling or redness; her close call could have been much more serious. For just an extra second, his eyes lingered on her shape. Then their eyes met, igniting a smile.

"Nice stitches."

She fastened her robe as Bull leaned over and kissed her, at first gently, then more sensuously. He smothered her in warm kisses, moving from her ears, down her neck, and back to her mouth. She did not protest as powerful emotions spilled out like water from a ruptured vessel.

She responded to his affection, kissing him deeply and passionately, then gently touching his mouth with her lips, tracing them with her tongue. She could feel herself falling off the edge of a cliff into a nowhere place. Her heart pounded like a runaway train.

Bull kissed her feverishly, and she welcomed his intensity. Alex had been restrained for too long, ever the responsible one, trying to be a stable force for Colt when he couldn't be there for himself. But tectonic plates were shifting.

Because of the fire, she met Bull Hawthorn. No, she had not met him; he had materialized in her life like a phantom to help her save her business. It felt as if they had been friends forever. A simple comfort and trust rested between them like a warm blanket. It was a feeling she had almost forgotten.

At this moment, for just this time, she felt safe. In the recent years with Colt, trust and comfort had been washed away, and her life had been an exercise of walking on hot embers. With Bull, the tempo had changed. Their worlds collided, and he took responsibility for the raging fire, and held her at the end of this harrowing day.

Her phone rang, interrupting them. She pulled away and fumbled for her cell phone. "Alex, this is Riggs."

Breathless, Alex suppressed her emotions. "How's your shoulder?"

"I've had worse." His voice sounded weak. "Just wanted to thank you for helping me and to see if you're okay,"

"A bit tired from the excitement. Thought you were going to bleed out on me," she said lightheartedly. It was easy to joke now that the icon was safely out of harm's way. But only a few hours before, she had fought for his life, and that reminded her of so many other painful, senseless losses.

"When I get out of this place, please accept an invitation to Houston and we'll have lunch at the Petroleum Club."

"Do I need a bulletproof vest?" she teased.

"Let's hope not," he said with a pained chuckle. "But I owe you one, big time."

"Take care of that wound," Alex ordered. "I'll check on you tomorrow."

"As soon as I escape from this place."

The new friends said goodbye and, after she ended the call, she put her phone back on the coffee table. "What a nice man," she remarked.

Bull picked up his drink. "Yes, but not without controversy."

"What do you mean?"

"He didn't get where he is by being a choir boy." His tone was strained, and he took a drink before setting his glass back down.

"And?"

He gave her a direct look. "He plays hardball. The man that shot him was wrong, but what Riggs did was ruthless. Riggs had enough power to force the lender to foreclose on the man's ranch, knowing he could pick up the land for nothing. It wasn't illegal, but it was heartless. He assumed the loan and the property for almost nothing, and that man lost a ranch that had been in his family for generations." Bull sighed. "Then Riggs drilled for oil and made millions."

Alex felt defensive for her new friend Riggs. "It's a cutthroat business."

"In my book, it was criminal. But there's no statute for meanness."

"Sounds pretty ruthless." Still, Alex knew there were two sides to most stories.

Bull leaned back, his eyes gazing into the distance. "Riggs could have made a fortune by keeping most of the mineral rights. He could have helped the man by guaranteeing his loan and giving him a small override...but that isn't how it happened."

In the middle of their conversation, the doorbell buzzed and Bull walked across the room and opened the door to welcome the waiter. A smorgasbord of delicious food was wheeled in: filo dough stuffed with cheese and mushrooms, steaming pasta, sliders and salad, along with a large basket of fries.

"Can I have another one of these?" she asked, gesturing with the martini glass. "The bartender should remember, dirty with three olives."

"Right away." The cork popped as the waiter opened a bottle of Pinot Noir, leaving it to breathe on the table. Bull deftly slipped the server some cash as he backed out the door.

While the picnic was devoured, they listened to local news, which was all about the shooting at the prestigious Hyatt Regency. A reporter fired a barrage of questions at Nancy Parker, who was trying to mitigate the crisis. "Was there adequate security? How did the man get into the building with a gun?"

The face of the shooter flashed across the screen, followed by a stock photo of Riggs Austin. "Why weren't there metal detectors?"

Then the camera cut to footage of Alex on the symposium stage helping Austin. "Oil wildcatter, Alex Sheridan, was pivotal in saving the life of the great Riggs Austin."

In a matter of minutes, a fresh martini arrived, heralding the national news version of the shooting. Experts on opposite sides of the gun debate offered opinions freely, with one man arguing that the shooting was a prime example of why guns needed to be banned. A Texan with a rifle in the back of his truck cab and an NRA sticker on the bumper eagerly stated his position: "We're not about to let some crazy rogue shooter erode our Second Amendment right to bear arms."

When most of the food was finished and the wine and martini had worked their magic, Angus turned off the noise.

"Let me hold you?" He kissed her gently and took her by the hand to lead her to her bedroom.

"If you'll behave," she teased.

"I'll try my best."

Alex watched as he removed his shirt, revealing magnificent shoulders.

He led her to the four-poster bed as if he were taking her onto the dance floor, carefully climbing up next to her. Silently, he lay gazing at Alex.

"What?" she said, aware of his penetrating stare.

"Just want to look at you."

Alex laughed. "I must look exhausted." The magical effects of the martini, coupled with fatigue from the excitement of the shooting, left her ravaged.

Bull took in every line and curve, making her uncomfortable.

Finally, he spoke. "You are quite the puzzle."

"How so?"

Bull shook his head, looking uncertain. "Just not like the rest of the guys in the oil patch."

"It is kind of a good ol' boys club." A coy smile spread across her face.

"But they let you play?" he asked, his face more serious than his question.

"Yeah, most of the time. They trust me." She smiled like a woman with a big secret.

"Because?"

Alex shrugged. "I deliver...and no BS, I guess."

He brushed a stray hair away from her face. "You sure are a lot prettier than the other guys."

"Thank you but, as you saw earlier, it doesn't matter to the bankers and insurance people or investors...it's all about the money." She tried not to sound bitter.

He moved closer, softly placing a calloused hand on her torso just below her breastbone. His large worn hands—covered in small nicks and scars—were gentle to the touch, turning Alex's insides to Jell-O. Resting on one elbow, silently studying her, he stared as if she was a treasure map. He inched closer, burrowing against her body with his mouth close to her ear.

His lips brushed her skin and he kissed her gently, rolling her to him and wandering inside the robe. In slow motion, he kissed and caressed her. Pulling her hips toward him, he worked his way around her breasts, staying away from the wound. Light as a feather, he caressed and nuzzled her until she couldn't stand the ache inside, wanting to let her mind and heart be lost in him. The desire to ride the wave of the serendipitous moment was powerful. They were so close to making love and letting it all go, but she paused.

"I'm pretty sore. Can I just hold you till I fall asleep?" she asked.

"I would love that," he said.

They lay together, quietly enjoying the feel of their skin and the warm closeness.

"Every part of me is aching. I need to rest," she said, not sure which of them she was trying to convince.

Bull shifted to look down at her. "Should I move?"

"No."

"I don't want to accidentally hurt you," he said softly. "Push me away if you need to."

"You'll know if I want you to move," she whispered in a sleepy voice. His breath was warm against her neck, and it felt good as she fell asleep.

Late in the night, the throbbing wound awakened her. She was pressed against a soundly sleeping Bull, whose silver hair spilled across his face like threads of mercury. Her nose was buried in his chest fur. In the silent shadows, his chest rose and fell with each breath.

A sense of comfort and safety surrounded her. Careful not to disturb Bull, Alex slipped out of bed, noticing a deep scar that ran the length of the inside of his forearm.

In the living area, she located her handbag. In the bottom of her purse was a bottle of Tylenol. She washed down three capsules easily. Against her good judgment, she checked her text messages and felt a small, sad pang. There was nothing from Colt. With the lights of downtown filtering into the room like moonbeams, she wondered how life and time had brought her to this beautiful place and to this man. It was probably best not to dissect the magic. Fairytales had a beginning, and this was the once-upon-a-time moment of a story yet to be written.

Sheriff Salido guarded the body, protecting the area as he waited for the coroner. Most of the volunteers had left with the rescued hikers, and something felt creepy. There were no obvious clues.

The coroner, the always jolly Frank Kellogg, arrived as if he were at a political rally, with lots of smiles, hand shaking, and small talk. Then he went to work, surveying the vicinity while taking photos from every angle and perspective.

"Hey, help me roll it over." Kellogg pulled on heavy gloves.

Salido beckoned Deputy Green. "Give us a hand."

Green approached deliberately. The deadweight required all three men to roll it onto the tarp. Charred black skin and a gruesome chest wound revealed the body cavity and organs, possibly foraged by an animal. JP Green's face looked like the belly of a dead catfish. "Ugh."

"Didn't teach you this at the police academy?" the coroner chuckled.

JP ignored the comment, looking away from the remains.

A former EMT and a retired firefighter, Frank Kellogg had chosen dealing with the dead as his way of life. A dense man with thick fingers and a neck like a telephone pole, Salido thought he looked like a rugby player. His heavy job responsibilities appeared to be an easy chore.

"Grab the body bag. Can you believe that idiot trade the Broncos made?" No one responded to the insensitive question.

Wrestling the remains inside the bag required more heaving by all three men.

After the body was in the bag and arranged on the stretcher, they loaded it into Kellogg's waiting vehicle, dubbed the "Death-mobile," an old Ford Expedition that Salido refused to ride in on social occasions.

He looked it over with distaste. "Why don't you get this thing detailed?" Old blood—and who knew what else—stained the carpets and upholstery.

"My clients don't complain," Frank said, chuckling.

"Don't *you* care?" Salido knew it was Frank's only car and that others were subject to riding with him on occasion. The interior had been sprayed with a disinfectant and the pungent odor of scented air freshener did not camouflage the deathly, old-corpse aroma.

"I'll call the Fish and see if he can examine him right away," Kellogg said, ignoring Salido's comments. "The Fish" was their behind-the-back nickname for Dr. Fischer.

"Let me know ASAP," Salido ordered.

The sheriff knew Frank Kellogg relished collaborating with the medical examiner and forensic pathologist, Dr. Carl Fischer, who was all about the forensic details. Both men possessed an ability to marvel at the forensic science while searching for truth, completely divorcing the soul and life of the victim from the exercise.

One last search by Salido's team revealed no clues. The scorching hot fire had burned everything away in the area.

"You have any missing persons?" Kellogg asked Salido.

"Nothing official."

Kellogg closed the back of his vehicle and made his way to the driver's door. "It may take a while to determine cause of death and make an identification. We'll probably need dental records."

"How long?" Salido pressed.

"I'll let you know as soon as I talk to Fish. This body is a mess, for sure."

They shook hands and Kellogg climbed into the truck. He would drive the corpse to Dr. Fischer's, which was adjacent to the body farm in Grand Junction, one of the few body farms in the country and a place Salido avoided. Decomposing bodies were left outside in various stages of decay, to be studied by investigators and forensic specialists. It was a stomach-turning place.

Glenwood Springs didn't have a proper morgue, just a couple of lockers for emergencies. In Grand Junction, Dr. Fischer had a complete exam room to perform autopsies. He received bodies from all over the state. His state-of-the-art exam room wasn't like a city morgue with its backlog of bodies and a waiting list for an autopsy. Fischer was responsive when it came to the few murders that occurred in his jurisdiction.

Reluctantly, Sheriff Salido called Mike Carter.

"You got a minute?"

"Sure. How can I help?" Carter asked.

"Off the record?" Salido wasn't sure of the best way to make use of the private investigator's expertise. Carter was a friend of Colt's and on Alex Sheridan's payroll—she could turn into a suspect. But they also might have valuable clues. The situation was delicate.

"You have my word."

Salido decided to trust the other man; after all, he'd been a cop, too. "We have an unidentified body up here, burned in the fire."

"Where?" Carter swallowed hard.

"Near the Divide. But not a word to anybody, especially the press or any officials, okay?"

"I understand," Carter said. "Any clues on the body?"

"Don't know much else but, if you want to get me some dental records from your missing guy, we can save some time and possibly eliminate him." Salido did not want to admit that their missing friend was his only lead.

"We'll find his dentist. Can I send one of our men over to look at the body and see if we can give you an ID?" Carter offered.

Salido paused while he thought about the request. "There's really not much to see, but okay," he agreed. If the charred body was Colt Forrester, then Carter could be invaluable.

"He'll be coming from Carbondale," Carter said before ending the call.

CHAPTER 17

Lafayette answered the phone on the third ring. "Yeah?"

"They found a body." Carter explained the situation and where the body was discovered.

"Is it Colt?"

"I doubt it," Carter told him, "but can you go look, just to make sure it's not him?"

"As soon as I leave the community meeting."

Lafayette was on his way to one of the Carbondale town council meetings about the fracking issue, hoping to meet someone who might offer new information about Colt or the burning well.

"The body will be with the forensic pathologist," Carter continued.

"Where's the morgue?" Lafayette grabbed a pen.

"Grand Junction. Ask for Dr. Carl Fischer. He's doing the autopsy."

"By the way, I met with the girl, Jenny, this morning," Lafayette added. "She knows Colt but hasn't seen him recently."

"Keep digging," Carter said.

"I've got Trey helping with her. They hit it off, and she might talk to him."

"About what?"

"Just a hunch," Lafayette said. "She's holding her cards too close to her chest."

"Stay on it."

Lafayette hung up, his mind troubled. The chances of the corpse being Colt were slim. People turned up dead all the time.

After a few wrong turns, Lafayette located the community meeting in the social room of St. Mary of the Crown Catholic Church in Carbondale. The landmark church stood on a hill overlooking Main Street, its spire towering over the iconic mountain village.

As he entered, Lafayette tried to look inconspicuous.

Gathered in the social room were diverse community members, activists, and protesters waiting to hear the status of the burning well. Many believed the fire was the result of a careless mistake made by the well operators. It looked much like the BP explosion in the Gulf of Mexico and was, to them, a good reason to permanently stop the drilling the governor had temporarily halted. The possibility that someone might have intentionally set it on fire was something no one wanted to hear.

A young woman moved to the front of the room. "Please take your seats. We don't want to be here all day."

Beaver Scott, looking redder and stouter than usual, moved to the front row of folding chairs that filled the room in neat rows. He studied scrawled notes and prepared questions while the volunteers gossiped and grew restless. Behind the podium, a copy of the Golden Rule was prominently displayed.

"The governor has signed the temporary ban on drilling," announced a man from the back of the room. Cheers followed.

Beaver moved to the podium. "We can't get complacent now," he warned.

Lafayette, leaning against the back wall of the room, surreptitiously studied the small group and took note of a man, watching from the back, who wore a nondescript work jacket with the collar turned up. A baseball cap pulled low over his forehead hid most of his face, but it did not hide a long, jagged scar. Lafayette cringed inside. From another time in hell on earth, he knew about homemade prison knives that cut deep into the skin and inflicted similar injuries.

"This is just a temporary restraining order," Beaver explained. "We need to stay focused and make sure our representatives in Washington support our cause."

Lafayette, observing every detail, felt uneasy. He felt the escalating tension from these activists, and his reconnaissance had unearthed information about Beaver Scott and a few others whose names were brought up repeatedly.

After the meeting, Lafayette approached the man with the scar, who was talking with Beaver.

"How do I get on board?" Lafayette inquired.

"We're kind of winding things down." Aaron Jeffries glared at Lafayette like he was a potential terrorist. "Where are you from?"

"Worked on a wind farm in West Texas," Lafayette fabricated.

"Wind is the future," Aaron agreed as they shook hands.

Lafayette nodded. "Yeah, the oil companies have to be stopped."

"We're trying."

"Just moved here. Still trying to find a good place to rent." Lafayette was convincing with his casual, matter-of-fact style.

Beaver stared at the big black man before saying, "Give us your contact info."

Lafayette scribbled down a special email and pay-as-you-go phone number he used during investigations, and handed the details to Beaver. He managed to get their names and one phone number as well without arousing their concern. Then he headed to the parking lot.

Alone in his sedan, he sent a text to Carter, typing with his large fingers:

Here is a contact number for the protesters. Going to morgue now.

As he drove toward the pathologist's office, he shuddered at the thought of the bodies he had seen at the Tucker Prison morgue. He had been another man in another reality, almost like a dream, when he did hard time for an accidental murder. Days went by when he would almost forget that part of his past, but certain scenes were seared into his memory.

Lafayette hesitated in the parking lot of Dr. Fischer's morgue in Grand Junction, anticipating the smell of chemicals and death. Then he walked inside.

"Dr. Fischer is expecting me. I'm Lafayette Boudreaux," he told the receptionist, who led him back to a room of body lockers. Two custodians pulled the body out of the refrigerated unit and unzipped the bag, revealing the blackened remains.

Lafayette, completely unprepared for what lay before him, cringed and looked away. The body was burned beyond recognition.

"I'm Dr. Carl Fischer. Salido said you would be coming," the doctor said, offering a feeble smile and a gloved hand.

"Lafayette Boudreaux."

Lafayette extended his catcher's mitt of a hand.

The doctor nodded. "Thank you for coming."

Wearing a white lab coat, Dr. Fischer was cadaver pale from too much time spent under bright lights looking at lifeless flesh. The attendants placed the body on an autopsy table with a drain at one end.

"Do you recognize the body?" Fischer inquired.

"I can't tell for sure," Lafayette stammered.

Nothing resembled the bright human being he had known as Colt Forester. Lafayette had witnessed brutality and too much blood in his life, but this burned body tore at his heart.

He shook his head. He had watched Alex and Colt find each other, come together, and slowly unravel. After Alex lost her best friend Christine, he feared she'd be unable to come to terms with losing Colt, if this was really him.

"We will get dental records, and the autopsy will reveal more, of course. Come here, please." Dr. Fischer, a willowy figure, directed Lafayette to a stainless steel table where he showed him a blackened watch. He took tongs and disconnected the latch. He laid the timepiece upside down and flat so Lafayette could view it.

For long minutes, Lafayette stared at the metal tray and the watch. A small audible whimper, like the faint cry of an injured puppy, came from the heart of the large man.

CHAPTER 18

B ull Hawthorn emerged fresh and wet from the shower like a Greek god rising from the sea. He combed his silver hair straight back and secured a white towel around his lean waist. In the mirror, he watched the razor as it glided across his face and pondered how to explain his life circumstances to Alex.

Moments later, he discovered her sleeping on the sofa in the living room of the Melrose Hotel suite, softly breathing. The soothing sound was peaceful. After making coffee, he poured a cup and placed it on the table next to Alex, who opened sleepy eyes and saw him standing over her.

"Good morning, Sleeping Beauty," he said.

She reached up and tugged at the tail of the towel.

"Oops." She smiled playfully.

The towel dropped to the floor, revealing a body that was hard and tan from labor rather than the gym. He had a neat carpet of fine, dark hair on his chest that trailed down his torso to below his belly button and beyond.

"Be careful," he teased, bending over to pick up the towel. Another ragged pink scar was visible on his hip. As he refastened the towel, he placed a sweet kiss on her mouth. "Were you uncomfortable last night?" he asked, walking to the bathroom. He returned in a plush terrycloth robe, sat close, and kissed her forehead.

"A little restless," she murmured. "But I found some Tylenol and that helped."

"How about breakfast?"

Alex noticed the time. She looked at her phone and frowned. Multiple missed calls, several from Carter, and who knew how many emails showed up on her phone, but she decided they could wait a few more minutes.

Then her phone rang, and John Malone's name popped up on her caller ID. The disloyal banker would have to wait. She knew what he wanted—money. Bull started to move away so she could have some privacy.

She turned the phone over on the table. "I could eat something."

"We should be cleared for take-off by midday," he told her."

He walked to the kitchen to refill her cup, and placed an order for room service.

"So, what are we going to do until then?" Alex asked when he returned, looking innocent.

"I will try to entertain you." A provocative smile spread across his face. He pulled a bottle of champagne from the refrigerator and set it with two flutes on an end table. He entered the marble bath, and turned on the hot water.

She spoke loudly from the other room. "What are you doing?"

"Running your bath. We can talk in here." He came back into the living room.

Pop! A champagne cork rocketed across the room.

Alex looked up at him doubtfully. "I'd better not get these stitches wet. Rain check?"

"Promises, promises."

"Besides, we'll never get back to Denver if we get in that tub." She laughed, and Bull went to turn off the water.

"Next time," he said. "Besides, I promised myself I'd be a gentleman."

Sitting on the sofa as they sipped champagne, Bull rubbed her shoulders and kissed her neck.

"I have something we should discuss," he said, just as the doorbell chimed, interrupting his thought.

A room service waiter appeared with a feast of eggs, fruit, and pastries, and another pot of steaming coffee. Alex moved to the table to survey the beautiful breakfast spread.

After eating a modest portion, she looked at the clock and pushed back from the table. Several more texts had vibrated on her phone.

"Excuse me, I need to make a quick call." She moved away.

"No problem," he said, turning to the news on his iPad. One of the news feeds showed a fire burning in Oklahoma.

Alex returned to the breakfast table set with linen and silver. Even exhausted, she was incredibly happy.

The excursion to Dallas had blindsided Alex with pleasure, creating a new curiosity about the fire-fighting oil man. Suddenly, she wanted to know more about his private life.

She pressed Carter's number and waited. After several rings, he answered. "Hey, there!"

"Is everything okay?" she asked.

"Did you listen to my messages?"

Alex picked up her coffee cup. "No, I've been busy. The symposium was incredible."

"Were you a star?"

"Yes." Her heart was light for the first time since the well fire and the fight with Colt. In fact, she was ready to let Colt go. It was time to find a new drilling partner.

"Did you see the news?" she asked, hoping Carter wasn't worried about the shooting.

He said, "I haven't seen anything."

"There was a shooting. Some crazy guy shot the keynote speaker— Riggs Austin. I got caught in the crossfire."

Alarm made his voice louder. "Oh, God! Are you okay?"

"It's nothing," she said, smiling at Bull with a finger over her mouth, making sure he didn't giggle and give them away.

"Where are you?" Carter inquired, hearing her lightness.

"Dallas. Weather grounded the plane, but we should be back later today." Her eyes caught Bull's gaze confirming the departure plans, and he reached over to squeeze her hand.

"Can I pick you up?" Carter offered, his tone almost too casual.

Alex knew Carter like her own fingerprints. "What's going on?" she demanded. "I want to know, now."

Seconds passed like minutes as a heavy cloak of silence hung between them.

Finally, he said, "They found a body."

"Where?" She could barely force the word out.

"In the Divide."

Alex sucked in a breath. "Near the well?" The Thompson Divide encompassed thousands of acres.

Carter confirmed her suspicions. "Not too far."

"You have an ID?" Her fingers tightened on the phone for a second. It couldn't be Colt.

"Not yet; it was badly burned," he said, and she could tell he was trying to ease the pain of the news.

"But you think it's Colt!" The words, barely a whisper, fluttered out like moths as her hand trembled.

"Possibly. It could be Colt, but we are trying to ID the body by process of elimination."

A week had passed since Colt disappeared. She had not allowed the possibility of death to take root in her consciousness. She imagined him hurt, in rehab, even drunk somewhere. Maybe in bed with a woman, but not dead. She had even entertained the possibility that he had sabotaged the well for some sick drunken reason…but not dead.

Suddenly, the suite turned surreal, and she felt as if she were watching herself in a wicked play. The stage was the hotel room, and the Dallas skyline looming outside was the set. Bull Hawthorn stood stage right, but she was disembodied as she watched herself with phone in hand, speaking to Carter. She wasn't really present. Her body was in the room while her consciousness hovered, observing the insane events.

"The body is at the pathologist's office now," Carter continued, his tone solemn, "and Lafayette is there to see if he can help."

A sound somewhere between a cry and a groan came from Alex's mouth. She bent over in a fetal curl, face in her hands. "Oh, God, no."

Carter spoke into the silence. "I'm sorry, but we don't have any facts yet."

She gulped for air before asking, "When will they know for sure?"

"Dental records will be needed." Carter's voice echoed as if from a canyon far away.

The taste of bile rose in Alex's throat. "I'll be back as soon as possible."

"There's nothing to do now."

Alex cried, "I want to see him."

"I don't think that's a good idea." Carter told her. "Just call me when you get in."

Bludgeoned by the news, Alex sat motionless. Far inside herself, she processed the words. Small bits and pieces of her soul space imploded, crumbling in slow motion as she processed the likely reality that Colt was dead.

She couldn't cry or make a sound.

Bull put his hand on her shoulder, but she went rigid, gently pulling away.

"Bad news," he said, stating the obvious.

"They found a body." Her speech halted and jerked. "Near the well." Her face fell into her clammy hands as she took several deep breaths.

"A friend?"

The word was wrenched out of her chest. "Yes."

He knelt next to her, not touching her. "I'm so sorry. You were close?"

"Yes, very." Her voice caught in her throat, but she went on. "My best friend and drilling partner has been missing for days."

"And they think it's him?"

"Not officially, but yes. They will have to get dental records to be certain, but his truck was abandoned at the well and we found some of his personal things nearby." She paused. "Colt and I have been everything at one point or another. I loved him. It's impossible to explain."

"Maybe it's not him," Bull said, sympathy in his voice.

"Maybe," she said flatly. "But everything went silent, his cell phone has not been used, and there are no credit card charges and no other transactions. He disappeared—it doesn't look good." There were so many clues pointing in the wrong direction, she reflected. Something bad had happened at the well site. She had been certain of that when she dragged the sheriff into the burning forest.

The bloody handkerchief was an omen.

There were no adequate words, not for this kind of loss. Colt held a vast space in her universe, and the void of him being gone was instant and infinite. They had made mistakes, broken promises, and forgiven. They had hurt each other, but they had also loved each other, even as they had ripped apart and mended.

Alex labored to breathe normally, but it felt like a shard of glass pierced her heart. She willed herself to exhale.

"I need to go home," she whispered. It was a simple statement, like saying, *there are no more stars*. She looked around for her clothes.

"I'll call the pilot." Bull rummaged in his bag and found a clean tee shirt for Alex, which she took before heading into her room.

"We'll be checking out in a few minutes," she heard Bull inform the concierge on the phone.

Alex finished dressing and went back into the main suite. She saw Bull organizing his briefcase. His packed bags waited by the door.

"I'm ready," she said.

"The car will be here in twenty minutes," he told her.

"I'll be in the lobby," she said, gathering her briefcase and purse. She turned and left the suite without speaking.

The drive to Love Field Airport felt like the journey to an execution. Once in the powerful jet, Alex and Bull rode in silence. There was no solace to offer and no words to relieve the emptiness. Alex stared out the window as they headed to Denver, propelled by a strong tail wind.

"We've started our descent," the pilot announced as Bull reached over and gave Alex a warm embrace.

"You know I am here to help."

"Put the fire out, and that will be a miracle." She tried to smile.

Denver loomed in the distance.

"God, I don't know how to do this," Alex suddenly exclaimed. The death of her former partner and best friend had been a crippling loss, and those old feelings roared back now and mixed with the pain of Colt's possible death.

She remembered walking into her former office years before, elated with good news she anxiously wanted to share with Christine. She ran down the hall and into their office. She burst through the door, calling Chris's name. The vivid memory burst into the present. Rigid in death, Chris sat stone-like in the chair. A bullet had ripped through her head. Blood covered the floor and splattered the windows. Alex willed her mind to push the memory back down.

"I wish I could do something," Bull told her. There were no Cliff

Notes for grief. "There is only one way through it."

"I know."

The plane taxied to a stop, and Alex gathered her belongings and exited the plane ahead of Bull. On the tarmac, she turned and offered her hand.

"I am grateful for the ride."

Out of the corner of her eye, she saw Lafayette, bigger than life in a long overcoat and a black bowler hat, waiting on the tarmac. Alex ran to him and hugged her giant angel friend.

"How did you know to be here?"

"Carter gave me your arrival details," Lafayette explained. It had not been difficult for Carter to find the tail number of the plane, then he asked Lafayette to follow her on flight tracker.

"Thank you for coming." Tears poured down her cheeks. She held on tight to Lafayette as she swiped at the tears.

When Bull approached, she turned back to him. "This is Bull Hawthorn. Bull, Lafayette Boudreaux, one of my best friends."

The men shook hands, then Alex gave Bull a kiss on the cheek. "Thank you again for the ride."

"Please let me know how you are and how I can help," he reiterated.

"I will, I promise."

With Lafayette's hand on her shoulder, she climbed into the front seat of his immaculate car.

"Tell me the truth," she demanded as he got in on the driver's side.

"Colt's gone." His words were abrupt.

"You're sure it's him?" Some small specks of hope and denial forced her to ask the question.

"He was wearing the engraved watch you gave him. I never saw him without it." He showed her the photo of the watch that he had taken at the morgue.

Alex eyes widened like saucers as she studied the photo. "He had the watch on the last time I saw him." She pushed the phone away. "I want to see the body."

Lafayette put his phone back in his pocket. "Alex, Colt is gone."

"You're certain?"

He gently took her hand as he spoke. "The body was badly burned

151

in the fire."

"I need to see him so I don't have any doubt. I can't be wondering if there is a chance."

"The dental records will be the official confirmation." He took her by the shoulder and looked into her eyes. "He's gone, and you don't want to see the remains." His words were like a slamming door.

Alex looked out the window at nothing, then back at Lafayette. "Thank you for going." She could tell he'd been affected by what he'd seen, and she hated that no one had been there to be with him. It must have been horrible, but a small part of her felt relief that she'd been spared the sight of Colt's burned body.

"Let's go to the Brown Palace. I'm hungry, and you should eat." Lafayette put the car in drive and headed toward downtown. Food was his comfort.

CHAPTER 19

The front page of the *Glenwood Springs Post Independent* reported that a charred body was found near the well fire site. Channel 9 covered the story, and *The Denver Post* picked it up and alluded to foul play.

Every fifteen years or so, a sensational murder occurred in the Aspen Valley. The death of Olympic skier Spider Sabich had occupied the Aspen media for years, as had the Nancy Pfister murder, whose victim, a member of a beloved local family, was found bludgeoned in her closet. But a murder in Carbondale was rare.

Rumors spread through the oil patch and the corner bars like fire in a high wind. The sheriff's office tried to control the circulation of conjecture, but word of a murder was delectable, and truth was far less vital than sensational speculation. A barrage of media calls pummeled the sheriff's office.

"Hi, Bev," said a reporter from the local paper, who happened to be an old friend of the sheriff's receptionist.

"You shouldn't call me here," said Beverly, mumbling under her breath. As the sheriff's gatekeeper, she was under scrutiny.

"Any new information?" the reporter asked.

She glanced around the office, trying to keep her voice down. "I really can't talk. The sheriff is watching everyone."

"How's Bobby?" the caller asked, turning the conversation personal. They occasionally met for coffee at Bonfire, a trendy café, to discuss their children, who had been classmates.

"Better these days. He has a part-time job." Beverly's only son, Bobby, was a habitual pot smoker who had littered the years with disappointment. "I really have to go."

A corpse was big news in the small community. Everyone near and around the event whispered about it. The janitor in the morgue drank with a group at the Black Nugget, and Beverly Doyle thrived on being a powerful source of inside information. Desperate to keep the details of the case under wraps, the sheriff called everyone into his office.

The reporter made one last attempt before hanging up. "Let me know if anything comes up."

"I gotta go!" Beverly waddled in last, wearing a large muumuu-style top that did not hide her bulk.

"You know this is a highly confidential and potentially explosive case. If I hear a word around town about the details, people will be fired." Salido glared at each one of them. "Is that clear?"

They all mumbled, "Yes."

But speculation was already out of control, especially after the sheriff released a statement to the press asking for information from anyone who may have been in the vicinity of the well before the fire started. Calls and false leads poured in—most were crackpots, but each lead had to be investigated, just in case it held a shred of truth.

Sheriff Salido sat at his desk drinking cold coffee, looking frustrated and overwhelmed. Beverly knew he was upset about missing another of his daughter's games.

A diligent reporter had discovered the information about the watch and the location of the body. It had also been confirmed that an explosive device was the probable cause of the well fire. It wasn't hard to fill in the gaps and infer that the body was Colt Forester's. Within twenty-four hours, the story had reached gigantic proportions.

Bev was tired of fielding the incessant calls from the writers for the *Aspen Daily Papers*. They ran photos of Colt with stories about the charred body and the burning well. Many in town knew Colt. The latest round of gossip escalated to a gruesome version that had Colt being devoured by a bear. Another tale suggested an angry protester was responsible. Salido wasn't any closer to identifying a perpetrator. And no dental records had arrived.

Until something broke, Beverly had nothing to tell the news hounds.

❧

Back in Denver, Carter set up mission control in one of the empty offices of Sheridan Enterprises. He helped respond to the deluge of calls, hoping a clue might come in, and he quarterbacked the investigation for Alex.

Lafayette called in. "Did you check on those names I texted? Something didn't sit right with me about these guys."

Carter had immediately called the number from Lafayette's text, but had reached a recording: *"The number you have dialed is not a working number."*

"We're doing a background check now," Carter told Lafayette.

"Need that ASAP."

❧

Sheriff Salido's name came up on Alex's caller ID as she shuffled through a pile of financial papers in her office.

"Hi, Sheriff. Any news?"

His voice sounded tired. "Trying to make some sense of this. Any person you can think of that would have wanted Forester dead?"

Alex thought for a moment. "No. I am completely baffled."

"Did he piss off anyone?"

"Not really. He was pretty well liked all around."

"Financial trouble?" the sheriff pressed.

"No more than anyone else." Colt was a laissez-faire guy with lots of casual friends and no enemies that came to mind. "Finances were a regular challenge, but he paid his debts. Mystery to me." Inside Alex felt herself crumbling.

"Call if you think of anything. I'll get back with you soon." He hung up abruptly.

❧

Schaeffer was also at Sheridan Enterprises helping Fran manage the torrent of calls.

A large rotund man with only a few wisps of hair remaining on a pink scalp entered the main office area. "I'm here to see Alex Sheridan," he announced, handing Fran a business card.

"May I help you?" Schaeffer offered, stepping forward to run interference. "Alex is swamped." And trying to keep from drowning under the pressure of losing a loved one and possibly losing her company, Schaeffer reflected.

He extended a soft, squishy hand toward Schaeffer. "I'm Robert Tetley, with Boyle & Boyle Insurance." He handed her another business card.

Schaeffer took it and slid it into her skirt pocket without looking at it. "I will ask her to call."

"I need to speak with her now." He was a sphinx.

Schaeffer turned her back to the man and walked to Alex's office. The formidable woman, her dear friend, had an ominous look in her eyes, a heaviness that even the darkest moments in the past had not produced.

Alex glanced up as Schaeffer entered her office.

"Do you want to speak with a Robert Tetley?" Schaeffer asked.

"Who is he?"

Schaeffer handed her the business card. "He says it's urgent."

Alex nodded and walked into the outer office. "Alex Sheridan." She smiled politely.

"Robert Tetley. I handle Mr. Forester's insurance."

Alex was familiar with the well-established Denver insurance firm that had been in business for more than fifty years.

"How can I help?" Alex inquired in a friendly tone. Behind her and a few feet away, Carter stood in the doorjamb observing.

"You are aware of Colt Forester's life insurance policy?"

"Not specifically. I know he had an umbrella policy for the business."

He frowned at Alex, as if he thought she was bluffing. Alex waited patiently for Tetley to get to the point.

"Did he have another policy?" Tetley asked with obvious irritation.

"I only drilled wells with him. I don't know about his personal business." Alex had intentionally distanced herself from Colt's personal business affairs, especially as his life had grown messy. One day, the business was in disarray and the next it would be running on all

156

cylinders. Many times, they had argued about details that affected both their companies. She kept as far away as she could from his turbulent management style and fiscal house of cards.

"And you don't know about his personal policies?" He arched an eyebrow, still sounding skeptical.

"I don't know anything about his insurance. I told you, he had a business policy that covered our projects, but that's all I know," Alex said, not disguising her frustration. There were hundreds of brushfires on her plate and the last thing that she needed was a persnickety insurance agent.

"You are unaware of being the beneficiary of his life insurance policy?" he asked with unmistakable sarcasm. His face wrinkled with disbelief. He placed a paper policy on the desk for her to see. His doubt was palpable.

"Beneficiary? He never told me anything." She was emphatic. She picked up the policy and skimmed the pages.

"He bought a ten-million-dollar term life insurance policy payable to you upon his death." He took the policy from Alex and showed her a page signed with Colt's distinctive flourish. "It was purchased just over four months ago."

The news silenced Alex and brought Carter into the inner office. He had been listening to every word.

"You are also his emergency contact," the man continued, wiping his brow with a white monogrammed handkerchief. "You don't know that either, I suppose?"

She thrust the paper back at him, her nerves frayed to the breaking point. "No, but that isn't surprising."

Alex leaned against the desk next to her. Could Colt have felt threatened in some way? She was aware he had been updating the business insurance, but news of his personal coverage came as a shock, and naming her as beneficiary was a fact he had kept secret. Alex could hear the argument now, as she would have told him it was a total waste of money.

"Ten million dollars?" She looked at her friends in dismay.

Tetley shuffled the paper back into the stack he held. "We will investigate the cause of death."

"Sheriff Salido is in charge of the investigation," Alex said defensively.

"We will be looking into this closely, Ms. Sheridan, very closely."

Alex's head was spinning as she motioned to Carter. "Please show Mr. Tetley to the elevator."

Carter returned from showing Tetley out and took a chair across from Alex at her desk. He noticed gray-blue circles under her eyes.

"Wow, that is shocking," Carter exclaimed. "It's staggering."

Alex looked dazed. "He bought a policy a couple of months ago and didn't tell me about it!"

"You said he was always short on details," Carter reminded her.

"He knew I would have protested."

Carter's phone rang. Salido came up on the caller ID.

The sheriff barely waited for him to answer. "Hey, Salido here."

"Yeah, any news?" Carter inquired.

"Just a courtesy," Salido said gruffly. "The insurance people read the news."

"They found us. Cause of death?"

Salido paused, then said softly, "We're not releasing any details yet, because we don't want the killer or any witnesses hearing rumors."

"Let me know what you can; I want to help," Carter said.

"Only the murderer would know how he died," Salido observed. "By the way, the insurance man told me about the policy benefitting Ms. Sheridan. I am going to have to speak with her soon," he said in a foreboding tone.

"Total shock to Alex."

"Is she willing to cooperate?"

"What do you mean?" Carter knew what the sheriff meant, but he wanted to hear it, if only because it was so unbelievable.

"She has motive." Salido sighed.

"It's a rabbit trail, Salido. Look somewhere else."

"Have her here tomorrow."

Carter hung up and looked at Alex. His face was as readable as the front page of the newspaper.

"They want me for questioning?" she guessed.

"It's just a formality." Carter minimized the threat, but he was concerned. An avalanche of coincidences was careening down on his friend.

"Bullshit." Alex knew the insurance policy was nitroglycerin. With ten million dollars on the table, she had just become the prime suspect in Colt's murder. She had been in Carbondale when they were looking for Colt, and she had stayed at the Comfort Inn, with no way to prove what she had been doing all night and in the initial days of Colt's disappearance. The insurance benefit created motive.

"They always look at the family," Carter said, trying to make it seem routine.

"Or those closest to the victim, right?" Alex said. Fear and anger filled the room.

"It's just procedure."

Alex slapped her desk, making him jump. "It is common knowledge that we were up and down in our personal life. Christ, we fought like cats and dogs! But we would have died for each other."

"I know that."

"The sheriff doesn't," Alex said flatly.

"You might want a lawyer. Just in case." He tried not to make it like an order.

After Carter excused himself, Schaeffer entered the office.

"Fran, please hold all calls." Alex closed the door to her office, and they moved to the comfortable chairs looking out at the majestic view. Schaeffer was her most trusted confidant.

"I'm sorry about Colt; I don't even know what to say." No consolation was adequate at a time like this.

Alex put her face in her hands as the sobbing began. These were the first of many tears that would have to fall. "I am so angry," she blurted. "I just thought he was drinking again." Tears streamed down her face.

"He might have been." Schaeffer waited for Alex to speak.

"We had a huge fight before he left. He was blowing off our well project." More sobs. "We never spoke again," she cried.

159

Schaeffer pulled Alex into a hug. The two women had been friends through almost every obstacle life had offered. "You tried to call him—repeatedly."

"I was so hurt and furious." Alex didn't know how to deal with the emotions flooding through her. It would need time—time she didn't have if the sheriff, or anyone else, really believed she would murder her lover for money.

"He knew you loved him," Schaeffer murmured.

"But I was going to end it! I was sick of the chaos and not knowing where he was."

"You didn't do anything wrong."

Schaeffer tried to console her, but Alex needed to vent. Her emotions needed to run their course. "And now he's dead. Do you know how many nights in the past I lay awake wondering if Colt was dead or alive or drunk? But this time I didn't even consider he might be dead—and now he is!"

Schaeffer offered a box of tissues. "Why don't we call it a day?" she suggested. "We can start over in the morning."

Alex nodded.

Schaeffer spoke on the intercom, "Fran, we're going on radio silence for the rest of the day."

"Got it." No explanation was needed. Fran knew to take messages and respond to emails until otherwise instructed. She proudly fulfilled a trusted and important role in the company and in Alex's life.

Schaeffer retrieved a chilled bottle of Pinot Grigio from the refrigerator, poured two glasses, and sat down.

"I don't believe this is happening. I feel like part of me has evaporated." Tears poured down Alex's face while she tried to catch her breath. "And I am terrified that in some way I am to blame. Maybe he was going up there to try and make it right after our fight? No one knows what happened to him, but he was there." She looked at her friend in horror. "What if the people who did this were looking for me? Oh, God." She sobbed harder.

Schaeffer handed a blotchy-faced Alex a glass of the wine, along with a wad of tissues, and waited. Finally, the stream of tears slowed. Alex took a deep breath and a sip of wine.

"I can't believe what happened in Dallas," Schaeffer remarked.

Alex blinked away tears. The shooting at the fracking symposium had been overshadowed by the discovery of Colt's body. She showed her friend the wound that was just beginning to heal. "I was so frightened by the shooting, I didn't even feel the bullet graze me."

Schaeffer looked appalled. "It was a close call."

Memories of trying to stop the flow of blood from Riggs snapped sharply into place. "The place was insane. The gun fired from nowhere. Everything was dark, people fled screaming, and the man kept shooting."

"Thank God you're okay."

Alex leaned back and expelled a breath. "Riggs Austin could have died. You know, I really wanted to meet him."

"What an introduction!"

"Yeah, he's tough. I think we will be friends."

Alex stared off into the horizon, crying quietly. Schaeffer sat patiently, waiting for the wave of pain to pass.

"I stayed with…" Alex sobbed and dry heaved. "I spent the night with Bull Hawthorn." Her crying intensified.

"You made love to him?" Schaeffer didn't intend to react with surprise.

"No, but I wanted to, and I was really happy. I didn't feel bad about Colt at all," Alex admitted honestly. "And then Carter called. Oh, my God." A new wave of tears burst forth, fueled by guilt and remorse.

Schaeffer patted her knee. "You deserve to be happy."

"Then Carter dropped the nuclear bomb that they found the body," Alex murmured. "It's unbelievable. I haven't been able to get my head around the situation. Never once did I think he was dead…never."

"Why would you? He disappeared all the time."

"And I was tired of it," Alex confessed, "finished with the hide and seek."

They sipped on wine and commiserated until something made them both laugh, relieving a tiny bit of pressure.

"Should you contact Colt's family?" Schaffer asked, beginning to think about the responsibilities of dealing with a death.

Alex sat her glass down and shook her head. "He didn't really have any. Fran is trying to track down a second cousin."

"I can let some of his friends know," Schaeffer said.

"That would be nice." Alex sighed. Mascara streaks added to the dark circles. "Thank God Bull is on board to help with the well. I don't know what we would do without him."

Her friend nodded. "It's one of those miracles."

"So, do you know anything about Hawthorn?"

"Just public stuff, never met him."

"But?" Alex could tell by Schaeffer's slightly furrowed brow that she was holding something back.

"You know about the accident?" Schaeffer asked, assuming Alex was familiar with Bull's story.

"What do you mean?" Alex asked.

"I thought everyone knew." Schaeffer hesitated.

"What?" Alex sat up, curiosity piqued.

"It's difficult," Schaeffer hedged.

"Can't be harder than losing Colt." Alex poured more wine in her glass.

"It's from the papers and secondhand word in the industry." Schaeffer looked skeptical.

"Go ahead." Alex lifted her chin, ready for almost anything.

"There was a horrible accident. His wife was left severely injured."

"His wife?" Alex bolted out of the chair. "He didn't tell me he was married."

Schaeffer raised her hands in a calming gesture. "Hear me out. The word is that she is in a coma."

Alex settled back down a bit. "So, he has a sick wife, and he's sleeping around."

"That's not fair."

"I feel blindsided. He acted as if he really cared for me."

"I am sure he will explain. It must be very painful."

"No," Alex reassured her. "I deserve the truth."

"Yes, but I'm not sure about the facts. It's a tragic situation. Only a matter of time, I heard."

"I don't need to be a part of this," Alex said coldly. "I can't believe he didn't say anything."

Inside she was sad, but it was a muddied, murky sadness. Her feelings were all tangled. The investigators wanted to speak with her, the well was burning out of control, cash flow was drying up, and important investors weren't going to stay with her company. She needed to hold tight to the rudder of this floundering enterprise and leave Bull to put out the fire.

"It's not something you need to think about right now," Schaeffer said. "It's complicated."

"I don't need complicated! I am up to my ass in complicated, if you know what I mean."

"Colt was special," Schaeffer remarked, .

"There is no way to explain Colt with words," Alex added, knowing that Schaeffer understood.

"But he was complicated," Schaeffer said, and they both smiled.

"Bingo."

They clinked glasses and, for the moment, Alex could almost think clearly. "Here's to simplification."

"You'd be bored in under ten minutes. Colt kept you guessing."

"Do you remember that time we flew out to Marfa for dinner at the Blue Tortilla?" Alex reminisced about a trip to the small eclectic West Texas town.

"The restaurant owner had to go to the liquor store to get more booze."

"God, he could make a dust storm fun." Silence settled in between them for a moment. "What am I going to do?" Alex asked forlornly.

"One foot in front of the other is all you can do," Schaeffer said sagely.

"I know you're right, but I feel…alone." Many of the people in Alex's life had come and gone. Her mother died when she was just eleven, and later she had lost her partner.

"I'm staying till we clear things up."

"Thank you." She and Schaeffer loved each other like sisters and had always shared the good and tough moments in life. Time and distance were irrelevant. They were in each other's lives for the long haul.

CHAPTER 20

D r. Carl Fischer stood over the stainless steel worktable, continuing his examination of the remains of Colt Forester, a project that had occupied most of the day. The condition of the corpse made establishing the time of death almost impossible. Several wounds caused by foraging animals complicated matters further.

Sheriff Salido entered the exam room wearing a white mask over his mouth and nose and booties on his feet. "Too bad we only get together like this."

Dr. Fischer's eyes were trained on the torso. "It will take a while to get the liver results." Tools were scattered next to the table, including a pair of large shears used to cut through the ribcage.

"What have you found?" the sheriff asked, leaning toward the body.

"Too desiccated for fluids," the pathologist reported.

"Speak English."

"The body is too charred and dried for us to be able to retrieve body fluids. But we are testing liver and bone samples."

"And?" The sheriff was ready for a list of information, but Fischer liked to let details trickle out like molasses.

"Look here," he said, pointing to the interior of the body cavity.

"Can't you just tell me?" Salido looked the other way.

Fischer proceeded as if he were teaching a forensics class. He was oblivious to the fact that Salido was not interested in a close inspection of the corpse.

"He was shot in the chest, here. It did a lot of damage, and that was probably the cause of death." Fischer moved the sheet back to show Salido his work.

"I believe you." Salido averted his eyes.

"This is where the bullet went in. " Fischer gestured. "It transected the aortic arch. He would have died almost instantly. Lots of blood."

Salido's face turned greenish.

Dr. Fischer held up a bullet with stainless steel tweezers. "We have something for ballistics!" He was pleased to find the bullet that might help the investigation if they ever located a gun. "It was lodged in the chest cavity."

"Let me look at it." Salido looked carefully.

"Nine-millimeter," stated the doctor. "I did my job; now you need to find the gun."

"You're certain?"

Dr. Fischer looked offended. "Yes, and he burned after he died. But these are details you might want to keep close to your chest."

The sheriff nodded and moved away, looking relieved. "Let me know what else you find."

"You'll be the first." Fischer held up a plastic bag containing the watch. "This is inscribed, 'From Alex'." He showed Salido the engraved inscription. "Lafayette Boudreaux said it was a gift to Colt Forester from Alex Sheridan."

"I'm getting her statement later. And, yes, mum's the word," Salido reiterated as he wiped sweat from his forehead .

"When are you going to get used to the autopsy lab?" Dr. Fischer asked with a big grin. "You look kinda green."

Salido ignored the jibe and exited quickly.

After escaping from the morgue, Salido drove to the district attorney's office. A body was something rare for Garfield County, and now they had a confirmed homicide.

The DA's office was deathly quiet. Now in his second term, Robert Portland was immersed in the goings-on of the county. A workaholic, he kept oppressive hours. Even though it was well after 5:00 p.m. on a

Friday, he welcomed Salido.

"Where you been?" the attorney asked, anxious for information.

"Trying to put this case together." Salido took the seat the DA offered, sinking into soft leather.

Portland's wife had left him after the last closely contested race. While the votes were still being counted, she packed his bags, refusing to be married to a politician and prosecutor one more season.

"Any news?" Portland asked.

Salido shook his head. "Fish is still working on the body."

"But you said there is a bullet wound?"

"Yeah, and we expect the dental records will match Colt Forester's. His engraved watch was on the body." Salido lowered his voice and made sure the door was closed. He didn't want anyone to overhear their conversation. "He was shot at close range, in the chest. Hard to tell what else Fish will find. The body was fried."

Portland flinched. "Smoke inhalation?"

"No. Bled to death from the gunshot before the smoke got to him." There was no one within earshot, but Salido's eyes darted around as if he thought he was being watched.

"When you make a statement to the papers, don't give up any information about the cause of death. We don't want anything to mess up this case," the DA cautioned.

"I'm trying to keep this case quiet," Salido said, "but it's not going to be easy."

"Any suspects?"

"The most obvious is Alex Sheridan, the woman who owns the well. They were lovers. Money and sex make for lots of friction."

"The media love her, but what's the motive?" Portland asked.

"Well, there's a ten-million-dollar life insurance policy that the victim bought not long ago—she's the beneficiary and they were in a very combustible relationship. Love and war."

Information about Colt and Alex had not been difficult to uncover. Salido interviewed some of the men at the well site, and Colt's friends painted the tumultuous picture.

Portland whistled. He stood up and combed his fingers through his hair, trying to contain his excitement. "That's enough motive for anyone."

"I can't figure out how she did it without help." The sheriff shifted in the chair. "There is no way she could handle a large dead body alone. And why leave him up in the woods? Why leave evidence near the well?"

"Was he cheating on her?" the attorney asked.

Salido shrugged. "Who knows? That could explain the rage and sloppiness. I'll keep looking."

"Of course, she could have hired someone."

"Maybe," the sheriff said doubtfully. "She's rich enough. But the first day of the fire, she seemed genuinely frantic to find him."

The DA looked interested. "Good actress?"

"Perhaps. But we certainly don't want to get distracted by circumstantial evidence and miss the real killer," Salido warned.

"Well, it's a strong motive, especially if his negligence caused the fire."

"We need more information about the explosion." Salido was frustrated with the lack of information on the cause of the blaze.

"What do you think they'll find?" Portland asked.

Salido frowned, perplexed. "Wayne Decker swears it's sabotage, but there is no official report yet."

"Maybe she caught him in the act of blowing up the well. They fought; she shot him trying to prevent the fire?"

"We have no evidence." The sheriff knew that a case depended on facts, not hypothesis.

Portland nodded. "Any other facts?"

"Hearsay. I spoke to several petroleum engineers—this gas well was producing and it would not explode spontaneously—something caused the explosion."

"I can go to the grand jury now if you want."

The sheriff shook his head. "Hold off until I get more facts."

"Don't let it drag on. I want to nail Alex Sheridan." Portland seemed jacked up by the news, ready to attack like a rabid hyena.

Salido stood up, shook the DA's hand, and left. He was exhausted and for days he had barely seen his daughter, who was staying most of the time with their kindly next-door neighbor. There was still no word from his absent wife. Maybe she was really gone this time.

❧

Robert Portland closed the door after the sheriff stepped out into the night, then he hurried back to his desk and picked up the phone. "Ferrell Brandt, please."

"One moment." The receptionist recognized Portland's voice. She didn't ask the nature of the call.

"What's up?" Ferrell Brandt did not mask his impatience.

"I just had a visit from the sheriff. The evidence is pointing toward Alex Sheridan."

"How soon can we get an indictment?"

Portland backpedaled. "We need facts first."

"Put a nail in her coffin if you have to!" Brandt snarled as he abruptly ended the call.

Robert Portland's blood boiled. It was the first time in his career, in his life, that he had fantasized about killing someone. If he could get away with it, he would dispose of Brandt with pleasure.

Steaming, he walked out of the office and headed to his car. Since his wife had excommunicated him from their home and her life, he had lived alone in a small cabin on the Crystal River some miles outside of town. His winning a second term in office had come at a high cost.

After parking the car beside the cabin, he picked up an ax and proceeded to attack a pile of logs. He stood the first large piece on edge and swung the ax skillfully, splitting the log down the center. He imagined Brandt's head rolling as he swung again and again. He checked his watch to make sure he had enough time. After an hour, he had worked through the pile of wood and his rage. Brandt was safe.

Just after stepping out of the shower, Portland heard a familiar *rap, rap, rap* on the door. His heart pattered as he walked toward it.

A beautiful young woman with honey-colored hair jumped in his arms.

"You sure you weren't followed?" he asked, lines creasing his forehead.

The woman gave him a sly smile. "I don't think so. I drove around the block several times before leaving town, like you told me."

They kissed passionately.

Bob Portland was taking a risk. There were any number of women he could tryst with who would offer far fewer complications than the sheriff's wife, but the attraction to Susie Salido was too powerful. He had not been able to turn her away, and she filled the lonely, raw hole left in his life after his wife's desertion.

"Where are you staying?" he asked, pulling her in and slamming the door behind her.

"I found an extended-stay hotel in Glenwood near the doctor. He says I will be just fine once I confront the situation. He says it's all stress." She headed toward the back of the cabin.

Portland followed her to the bedroom, unbuttoning his shirt. "I'm glad you're here." He grabbed her hand, knowing it was selfish of him to prey on the vulnerabilities of a broken woman. She had shown up at his office pleading for help, and it had been impossible to say no. She was a damsel in distress and he had come to her rescue, providing some cash and a used car that enabled her to stay in the area undetected.

Soon they were in bed together in his cabin.

CHAPTER 21

The headline on the front page read: "Body of Missing Oilman Found Near Burning Well."

A less-than-flattering photo of Colt, similar to a mug shot, accompanied the story. The newspapers were frustrated with the gag order issued by the DA. No one was talking, but everyone was whispering. The victim's name had been released and an official statement was made, but there were no new details other than that it was being investigated.

At the Red Rocks Diner, Jenny read the story in the *Aspen Daily News* during one of her breaks. Chronic nervousness had turned into an acid burn in her stomach, and her fingers trembled uncontrollably. She went outside into the parking lot to smoke a cigarette. The cool blue morning had turned warm, making it a perfect Colorado day. She continued to hope that her new friends, Trey and Brutus, would come back to the diner, but no one but locals turned up. Trey had seemed like a nice man, the kind of man she dreamed of, nothing like the string of losers from her past.

She unzipped a small pocket in her purse where she had saved his card. She fingered the card, staring at his name. Maybe she should call.

"Hey, Jenny, hustle up," her manager called from the door.

It wasn't until later that day, as she walked home along Highway 133, that she thought about Trey again. She was afraid of flying, but the fantasy of flying off with him and away from Carbondale was like a siren's song. She limped through the trailer park, chewing her lip and

170

wondering what to do. Was telling a lie better than breaking a confidence? Was lying to save her life acceptable?

She felt cornered by the frightening truth, and she had lied so often that sometimes she wasn't certain of anything. Her friendship with Colt had turned into a nightmare.

Back in her little trailer, she fixed an iced tea and thought about her predicament. She was too scared to go to the police.

After vacillating some more, she finally picked up the phone. She dialed the number with trembling hands and waited as the phone rolled to voicemail. "This is Trey, leave a number."

She hung up without leaving a message.

Aaron Jeffries sat in the Pour House restaurant.

"You want breakfast?" a waitress asked.

"Just coffee for now."

He opened the paper and practically dropped it when he saw the front page. He read the startling lead story—a body had been discovered. The investigators would not give any specific information about where it was located. The story speculated that the deceased was the well operator Colt Forester, a name he recognized. Stunned and in shock from the news, Aaron sat stone still. The article reported that the body of a man had been found in the national forest, but not exactly where. It was being treated as a homicide. This was not what he had signed on for—he had never wanted attention like this. The protesters seemed to be getting out of control.

Beaver Scott approached the table. "Running late; sorry."

Jeffries slid the paper across the table without saying a word.

"Bad news for that guy," Beaver said casually, as if he had heard that the Broncos had lost.

"It's a homicide investigation," Aaron said in a dire tone. The investigation would bring scrutiny, something he meticulously avoided. Anger swelled inside him. Rage ratcheted into fear. But he had to contain his feelings and move carefully.

Beaver shrugged. "Guess he won't be drilling any new wells in the Divide. What luck."

Aaron thought he saw Beaver smile.

Bull Hawthorn sat at an elegant desk in his state-of-the-art Denver office. He watched the well fire from a remote camera and communicated with his team, which was making final preparations to extinguish the fire.

The well was burning from the wellhead, fueled by the gas coming up the well pipe. They could use explosives to suck all the oxygen out of the air and quickly cap the wellhead. This involved great risk. Any small spark and another explosion could follow, worse than the burn they were fighting. Their equipment, made from special bronze that would not spark and cause a secondary explosion, had arrived, and now they just had to wait for the right conditions.

Bull picked up the phone and called Alex's number. Her assistant answered.

"I've been trying to reach Ms. Sheridan."

"She's in a meeting. Can I give her a message?" Fran asked.

"Yes, from Bull Hawthorn," he muttered. "Not good news. High winds again."

"I'll let her know."

"Please ask her to call." Bull hung up, worried about Alex, the well, and her dead friend. They were going to have to wait while the men worked tirelessly to contain the blaze. He was disappointed about the delay, but this business demanded patience. Every detail had to be handled perfectly to save lives and wells.

Fran interrupted Schaeffer and Alex. "Mr. Hawthorn asked you to call."

"Thank you." Alex, confused about her feelings for Bull and their delicate situation, turned to Schaeffer.

"Should I call him back?"

Schaeffer shrugged. "Give him a chance…see what he has to tell you."

"I'll call later. Thanks, Fran."

"Wait and see how you're feeling tomorrow," Schaeffer suggested.

"I need to prepare to meet the sheriff." The words sounded like a slamming door.

Schaeffer went back to her work, leaving Alex in the privacy of her office with nothing but her own thoughts.

Alex squared her shoulders. She would focus on her business and pressing matters at hand as a way of avoiding the situation with Bull and her feelings for him; they were just stuffed in a closed compartment. For now, at least.

Numb from worry and fear, Jenny felt almost drugged as she watched television and tried not to think about the truth. She should never have called the number on that paper and met with the big man, Lafayette. That had led her to meeting Trey, and now people knew she was a friend of Colt's. If the police were any good, they would put them together, too.

She didn't want any attention. Her safety depended on staying under the little rock of a life she had created. She didn't want anything to happen that might lead the man with the baseball bat back into her life. He had moved on to fresher victims and didn't care where she was as long as she kept her mouth shut. This belief allowed her to sleep some nights.

The ringing phone startled her out of the worried daydream. Trey's number showed on caller ID and, for a moment, she hesitated. But something about Trey made her feel safe. She barely knew him, but instinct drove her to trust him. Maybe he would understand and she wouldn't have to talk to the police.

"Hello, this is Jenny."

"I was happy to see you called," Trey said.

Seconds passed, and there was an awkward silence between them as if they were teenagers trying to figure out what to say next. Then Trey spoke again, softly. "I was hoping I'd hear from you."

"Thanks. I just…" She paused.

"I have to fly over there tomorrow. Are you free?" he asked. "Alex has a meeting with the sheriff so I will be on call, but should have plenty of time to see you."

Jenny held the phone tightly to her ear. "I get off work early afternoon."

"Can I take you to dinner?" he asked.

"That would be nice." On the inside, she smiled.

"And Alex may want to stay over and go to the well site. Should know more in a few hours."

"She was mentioned in the paper." Jenny's words were soft whispers.

"I'll call you after we land in Glenwood."

Jenny murmured, "Thanks."

"Brutus will be excited."

"He's all about the eggs and bacon," she said in a lighthearted tone before she hung up.

Trey was elated to hear her happiness. In his small downtown loft apartment, he jumped up and gave Brutus a huge hug.

"She likes us!" he said, and Brutus seemed to understand.

A blinding purple-pink sunrise and a splitting headache jolted Alex into reality. After Schaeffer left the last evening, she had tossed and turned all night, thinking about Colt, dreaming about fire, and wrestling with the idea of calling Bull Hawthorn. She looked at a favorite photo of Colt resting on the credenza. Even now, she could imagine his touch and the way he felt lying next to her. A magical chemistry had bound them through the years. She closed her eyes and, in her mind, felt the touch of his hand. Then, as visceral as stepping on a landmine, she felt the pain of his angry leaving. He had lied and left one too many times.

With a strong coffee in hand and the mountains in the distance, she meditated on the chain of events. A powerful force had sewn the tapestry of her life. She needed to trust her intuition, even amid a maelstrom. The phone rang, interrupting her thoughts.

"Good morning." Bull's voice was warm and inviting. "How are you feeling?"

"A bit fractured," Alex said.

"Sorry to hear that. Heard the news about Colt."

"I can't believe he is gone." She still couldn't believe the words as they came out of her mouth.

"Can I help?"

Alex wiped her eyes. "Not now. I have a meeting with the sheriff and the DA. They want to ask me some questions. Apparently, Colt took out a ten-million-dollar life insurance policy and named me the beneficiary."

Bull's tone sharpened. "You have an attorney?"

"I don't think that's necessary yet. Do you?"

"Someone left you ten million dollars," he snorted. "That would sound like motive to anyone."

"They can look at my finances. I don't need the money," she insisted.

"Investigators live in a different reality," he argued. "Do you know what ten million means to most people? There are people who would barter their children for much less than that."

Alex took a deep breath. "I need to go. The sheriff wants me for questioning as soon as I can get over there." She was a bit annoyed by his advice. Just because he was a world-renowned expert on oil well fires did not make him legal counsel.

"Let me know if I can help," he said. "There are several matters I'd like to discuss."

"I have to run. Let's talk later." She hung up before the conversation could go any further.

With a look of concern on her face, Fran entered Alex's office from the reception area. "Mr. Malone is in the lobby."

Fran waited patiently for direction. The banker was an unwelcome guest. This could not be good news.

"Ask him to make an appointment," Alex suggested.

"He says it's urgent."

Alex grimaced. "I'm sure it is."

"He was insistent." Fran waited for guidance.

"Give me five," Alex relented but, just as she said this, John Malone shoved Fran aside and burst into her office.

The psychological chokehold tightened around Alex's neck. He tried to shake her hand, but she refused the gesture.

"John, I'll be out there in a minute!" She glared at the pushy banker.

"It is import—"

"I'll speak with you in a minute," she said abruptly.

The banker retreated with Fran while Alex took a few minutes to review their financial agreement. She entered the reception area looking determined and cold, like polished marble. "Please come in."

He followed her into her office and took the seat she indicated. "This is a difficult time," he began. "How is the well?"

"I assume this is about the loan." Alex had many labels, but one of them was not "coward." Getting to the point was vital.

"They are calling your loan," he blurted out, then sheepishly looked away.

She would make him look her in the eye to deliver the pathetic news. "Who the hell are *they?*" she demanded. As if *they* were some super power! Even so, she was certain he was powerless over some malignant force, which was the only reason she didn't verbally rip him apart.

"The board," he lied.

Alex was disgusted. "You don't want more collateral?" she asked sarcastically.

The answer was clear. The loan was being called because someone way over Malone's head had cut her off at the knees. The well was burning money by the day, and she had valuable leases all over the area, strategic properties that she might now be forced to dump in a fire sale to raise more capital. But this was the wrong time to sell. Someone had her in their sights.

Malone refused to look at her. "They want this paid off. Maybe after the fire is out…"

The hollow words turned her stomach. "There's no maybe."

"I just wanted to tell you personally how much your business means—"

Alex interrupted. "John, save it for someone else!"

"This is regrettable." His eyes studied the floor.

She glared at him. "This is no way to treat a loyal customer. You will have your money, and our business is over."

With nothing left to say, she indicated the way to the door, and he slipped out with his head bowed.

Chris would have been furious with Malone's tactics. Alex smiled. Chris would have liked the way she handled the man. This was one of the many moments when she missed their partnership. She and Christine would have schemed at their partners' desk, had a good laugh, and hatched another plan. It was as if they played their own personal chess game. If a pawn was taken, so what? Make another move and take a rook, or a queen.

What would Chris and she have come up with?
Alex pondered her next move.

CHAPTER 22

Bull Hawthorn, crisp and sleek in starched, faded jeans and Italian loafers, walked into Sheridan Enterprises. He bumped into a woman hurrying through the reception area and almost spilled his coffee.

"Bull Hawthorn," he said, offering his hand.

"Bull? Heard lots about you from Alex. I'm Schaeffer London." She studied his eyes as she accepted his firm, warm handshake.

"Ah, the damage-control guru." He smiled. Alex had proudly told him about Schaeffer's expertise in handling all sorts of business emergencies and media situations.

"I put out fires. Not your type, but they are fires nonetheless." Schaeffer smiled, studying him.

"Is Alex free?" He motioned in the direction of her office.

"Yes. But I don't think she's slept since y'all got back from Dallas. What a day that was!"

Bull nodded. "Glad it wasn't worse."

Schaeffer handed him a business card. "I'm late. Excuse me for rushing." Her husband was waiting at the Brown Palace Hotel. He had flown in for a few nights to be supportive.

"Thanks." Bull put her card in his wallet and walked to Alex's office. He tapped gently on the door. She smiled and gestured for him to come in and sit anywhere as she concluded a call and waved the *Denver Post* in his direction. The front-page story detailed the discovery of the body and the suspected murder, and it mentioned Bull's participation in the burning well. He glanced at the paper as she fielded calls.

৵

"I understand your position, but I can assure you that your investment is safe." Alex stood behind her desk while she talked on the phone. She listened for a moment, but lines were embedded in her forehead. "I understand."

News of the fire rattled even Alex's most savvy investors. Many who had sent deposits begging to be part of future deals were now scared. Calls demanding refunds for future projects poured into the offices of Sheridan Enterprises. Her assurances did nothing to stop the tumbling dominoes.

She held up a finger in his direction before she dialed another number. "Hi, Tebo. This is Alex. Please call so we can set up that meeting." She was frustrated that the banker had not returned her calls. Her attempts to set up an appointment with Great Western Bank had all failed. After courting her for years, Tebo Stephens, who once said he would do anything for her business, was silent.

After she hung up, Bull walked around the desk and gave her a warm kiss on the forehead. "Thought you could use a break. Come on; let's get some coffee."

Alex looked at her desk covered in files, needing her attention. Each investor needed a personal call and assurance that the company would not fail.

"I can't. Look at this." She gestured at the orderly mess, but he sensed her hesitation was much more than just the business.

"It will wait."

Alex wasn't accustomed to having anyone tell her where and when she should work. Besides, she was beginning to wonder about Bull after hearing Schaeffer's story about his marriage.

"I really need to talk with you about something," Bull said.

Alex was preoccupied. "I can't do anything now except call my investors and find an attorney. A potential lawyer is supposed to call back in a few minutes."

"I have a source who might be able to help." He smiled.

"Really?" Alex brightened. "Who is it? Would I recognize the name?" For a moment, she was hopeful. It seemed like the first positive news of the day, if having a criminal attorney on the payroll could be considered a positive development.

"I'll just go outside and make a call." Bull stepped into an unoccupied office while Alex stood at her desk, continuing to place calls. She rarely sat, having a life-long habit of pacing in front of the windows as she managed her business affairs.

In a matter of minutes, Bull popped back in. "We're meeting around the corner on Larimer Street in twenty minutes."

"With…?" She raised an eyebrow.

He smiled wider. "A lawyer."

Alex stopped pacing, looking surprised. "How did you manage that?"

"I have my methods," he answered playfully. His smile was magnetic. "Thank you."

"Mr. Brandt is supposed to be as good as it gets if you need a criminal attorney." He came closer, put his hands on her shoulders, and kissed her deeply. His touch took her away, if only for a moment.

Sheriff Salido sat in his office, raking through the details of the Colt Forester missing person-turned-murder case. File folders were stacked on the credenza behind his desk.

Several photos of his young daughter at various ages were displayed around the office. Cathy's resemblance to Salido was undeniable. Still AWOL, her mother had left him in an impossible predicament. He did not know how to be two parents to the precious angel left in his care. He had placed discreet calls to all their closest friends and the family doctor, looking for his wife, with no luck.

Orders were given to his investigators to compile a list of protestors and people around town who had been vocal against the drilling program. Salido had attended a plethora of town council meetings and community hearings. The core group of ringleaders interested him. The Scott brothers, hardworking men, might be able to help connect the missing links in the mystery. He couldn't help but think there was a connection between the well fire and the murder.

He picked up his phone and dialed. "Beaver? This is Sheriff Salido."

"Guess you've been busy?" Beaver said casually.

"You know some of the protesters?" Salido could match Beaver's casual and then some.

"Yes, good folks trying to protect our land."

Salido kept his voice calm. "Anything or anyone you think could be trouble?"

"You know everyone as well as I do," Beaver snickered. "Only odd duck is that Jeffries guy from Marble. He's kind of a weird loner."

"Didn't he help you with permitting?"

"A little, at first," Beaver said, blurring the truth, "but when we tried to check him out, it is like he doesn't exist."

"Okay, thanks. If you think of anything else, call me."

"You'll be the first to know. I'll ask Jason, too," he said in a cooperative tone.

"Thanks for your help. You have a number for that Jeffries guy?" Salido asked as an afterthought.

"I'll send it to you. Glad to help."

Beaver's brother Jason had suffered from developmental problems as a child, and he was a shy introvert who rarely spoke. Everyone in town accepted that Beaver did the talking. If someone got too close to Jason, he became so nervous that spittle would leak out of the edges of his mouth. He had mouse-brown hair and medium-brown eyes, and was nondescript in every way. He was rarely seen in public, and the people of Carbondale knew to leave him alone. Beaver protected him like a mother lion.

Salido thought about several individuals who should be brought in for questioning. His head began to pound. He was deep in thought when a knock on the door startled him, causing him to spill a Diet Coke down his shirtfront.

"Shit!" He tried to catch the can and spilled more.

A stranger stood in the doorway, wearing a fleece vest and khaki pants. "Sorry about that."

"Can I help you?" Salido wiped at the spill.

"Mike Carter, from Denver."

"What are you doing here?" The sheriff was surprised. As much as he shared the bond of law enforcement brotherhood with Carter, he really didn't want anyone invading his office like this.

The other man stepped toward him, offering a hand. "Just thought I would introduce myself."

They shook hands.

Salido studied Carter like a map. "I'm really busy; what's up?"

"You want to speak with Alex?" Carter asked.

"We have questions."

"She's not your killer," Carter said bluntly.

"That's for me to decide." Salido stood up, towering over Carter.

"She loved Colt Forester; they were…very close."

"Love can be lethal," Salido countered.

"I hear you," Carter said, trying to get them back on the same side.

"I have my guys working every lead. We are talking to all the locals. This is a small town, and people talk."

Carter cleared his throat. "I thought I would hang around for a few days, see if there is anything I can do to help Alex—and you, of course."

"Just stay off my turf. We don't need any confusion." Salido stood strong, hands on hips, dwarfing the room.

"I understand. Any more information from the pathologist?" Carter pried.

"Nothing for the public. Look, you know how this is done. We don't give out the details. We are keeping this quiet." The sheriff motioned toward the door and ushered Carter out.

Carter's next stop was the Village Smithy for coffee and snooping. It was a quaint frame-and-brick building on the edge of Main Street and a favorite local hangout. As he read the story about the fire and the protestors, a large woman with tattoos on both arms came to the table.

"What will you have, hon?" the waitress asked, flesh wiggling on the backs of her arms.

He glanced down at the menu. "Breakfast Special."

"Coffee?"

Carter nodded. "Black. Hey, I'm looking for a local guy, Aaron Jeffries. Would you know him?"

"Don't know names." She pointed toward a man at a corner table. "He might. He works for the city council." A pile of hotcakes and bacon sat before the man while he devoured a large buttermilk biscuit.

"Looks hungry," Carter observed. "Thanks." He waited a few minutes to give the man time to consume most of the food, then walked over to the table.

"Excuse me, I'm doing a story on the successful protest," he fabricated. "Would you know who to speak to about the Thompson Divide?"

"Sure, try the Scott brothers," the city councilor said. "They're involved."

"Great. Do you have a number?" he asked.

The other man wrote a number on a napkin and gave it to Carter. "Jason and Beaver are their names," he said. "Who do you work for?"

"One of the wire services," Carter lied. "Heard of a man named Jeffries?" he asked as if it were an afterthought.

The man nodded, forking up the last of the hotcakes. "Yeah, I think the Scotts know him."

Carter thanked the man and returned to his own table. He waited a few minutes before pulling out his computer to check video footage and news coverage.

Carter dialed the number on the napkin.

"Jason Scott," Beaver answered.

"Hi, Jason. My name is Mike Smith, and I'm writing a story on the drilling business in this area. I heard you're one of the organizers against the drilling?"

"We want to preserve the National Forest," Beaver said proudly.

"I see," Carter said. "Anyone else you might suggest we interview? Isn't there another local who has been involved in organizing the protestors?

"You should call a man named Aaron Jeffries."

"Would you have a contact number for him?"

Beaver laughed. "Sure, but I'll warn you, he's kind of reclusive."

"What do you mean?"

Beaver's tone flattened. "Nothin', just kinda weird."

"Thanks for the warning."

Still sitting in the back of the Village Smithy, Carter dialed the number for Aaron Jeffries. The phone rang six or seven times. Just before he gave up on the call, a man answered.

"Hello."

"Hi, this is Mike Smith calling. I'm writing a story on the effort to stop drilling in the Thompson Divide." Someone had answered, but the line went dead or the call dropped.

Carter called back, but there was no answer. He pondered his options and decided to reach out to a trusted contact. He decided to call a friend who had taken over in the Denver homicide office, a master at unearthing buried pasts. He picked up his phone.

The phone was answered on the first ring.

"Hey, Blue, it's me," Carter said. "Can you do me a favor?"

"Just because I like you. What's the scoop?" Blue Davies, a powerful homicide investigator, had deep connections.

Carter lowered his voice, looking around to make sure no one could hear him. "I need to know the back story about a man named Aaron Jeffries."

Blue's keyboard clicked in Carter's ear. "What's the angle?"

"Not sure how he's connected but he's one of the protestors at that burning oil well," Carter explained. "We need to find out every detail about these locals. If the well was sabotaged, it's a felony, possibly with intent to kill."

"I'm on it."

Carter smiled. The homicide detective loved a hunt.

Back in Carbondale, a line of people stood outside, waiting for a seat at the Village Smithy. While Salido waited, he noticed Mike Carter at a corner table with an extra seat.

"You found your way around pretty fast," Salido said as he towered over Carter.

"Best breakfast in town, I'm told."

"That's for sure. Mind if I sit?" Salido removed his uniform hat and sat it on the corner of the table.

"Please. Hey, have you checked out this Jeffries guy?" Carter queried.

Salido lowered himself into the chair opposite the other man. "He hasn't caused any problems."

"Seems like the ringleader."

"Peaceful protestor as far as I know." The sheriff didn't want any interference in his investigation. He wanted Mike Carter to stop asking questions.

"I asked a friend for a background check. I'll let you know if we find anything suspicious."

"Carter, this is my investigation."

"But it's my client's oil well!" Carter shot back. "Millions are at stake. Colt Forester was working on it before the explosion, and now it looks like he's dead."

"It's *my* investigation!"

"Someone wanted this well destroyed, Sheriff Salido. Someone murdered Colt, and someone is trying to profit from the crisis."

The sheriff pushed back from the table, the legs of the chair screeching violently. "Like Alex Sheridan."

"It's a setup!" Carter argued.

"Stay out of my way." Salido wasn't about to have some Denver P.I. insert himself into Salido's jurisdiction.

Salido knew Carter had been on the law enforcement side during a host of investigations. He knew it was paramount that the sheriff guard the facts of the case and prevent all leaks. People could not be permitted to go around pushing their views and prejudice into the investigation.

But Carter was working the other side now, and his job was to protect Alex and find the truth. As a private investigator, he wasn't bound by the rules and procedures that hampered the police and county officials. He could look into any lead that might help prove Alex's innocence and find the real murderer.

And that made Carter a wild card. Salido didn't like wild cards.

CHAPTER 23

The 16th Street shuttle ran from lower downtown to Larimer Street, the heart of downtown Denver. Alex and Bull elbowed their way onto the bloated shuttle, crammed with businesspeople hanging onto straps and rails, as it passed bars and restaurants overflowing with chatty patrons.

She wondered when Bull was going to tell her the truth about his private life. But that was dwarfed by worry about meeting the lawyer and her upcoming interview with the sheriff.

They hopped off the shuttle and entered a quiet French bistro. Soft light enveloped them, French music played in the background, and the aroma of fresh baked baguettes filled the room. A young French girl in a starched white apron escorted them to a corner table with three chairs.

"Coffee?" she asked, looking at Alex, who nodded.

"Black, no sugar."

"Double espresso, please," Bull ordered.

Almost instantly, steaming cups arrived.

A few minutes later, a slight man in a dark suit approached their table. "Hello, Bull," he said, calling Bull by his nickname.

"This is Alex Sheridan. Alex, Ferrell Brandt, the attorney I mentioned." The handshakes were brief.

"I remember you." It took only seconds before Alex recalled their brief conversation at the fracking symposium, then Riggs Austin was shot and everyone scattered. "We met in Dallas," Alex remarked.

"What a coincidence," Brandt said with surprise, his eyes blinking double-time.

"Nancy Parker suggested Ferrell might be a candidate to help your situation," Bull suggested.

"You specialize in energy law?" Alex inquired, feeling slightly confused. She needed a criminal attorney who also understood the complexities of oil and gas law.

"I do anything related to energy law, including criminal issues around oil and gas." The little man sat in the empty chair, and signaled for the waitress. "Bull explained the well explosion and the possibility of sabotage to me, and he mentioned your dead colleague. The case is right in my wheelhouse."

Alex took a deep breath. "His body was discovered in the vicinity."

"Had he been missing for some time?" Brandt paused for a moment to order his drink, then turned his attention back to her.

"Not exactly sure," Alex told him, "but I had not been able to reach him for a week or so."

"And he had an insurance policy with you named as the beneficiary?" Brandt verified the facts without taking notes.

"I just found out about the policy," Alex said defensively.

He looked up as the waitress delivered his drink. "How can I help?"

"The criminal investigator from Glenwood Springs, Sheriff Salido, wants to question me immediately."

"You must have counsel present," Brandt said sternly.

Alex took a sip of water and sighed. "Colt and I were very close."

"The less you say the better." The lawyer's eyes darted to the watch on his wrist as he checked a message.

"Can you go with me to meet the sheriff?" she asked.

"Of course. You won't have to answer any questions."

"But I want to help," she said emphatically. "I had nothing to do with his disappearance or murder and I want to find out who did this."

"There are certain questions that should not be asked and others that should not be answered." His tone was authoritative.

Alex nodded. "But if I want to answer?"

"I will advise you." Brandt set his cup down with a thump. "We will decide how you will proceed. What time do you need to be there?"

"Later today is best if you can free up your schedule."

"Let me see." He looked at his phone and quickly checked his calendar.

Alex felt like some of the weight she'd been carrying had been lifted. "I appreciate you meeting at such short notice."

Brandt tapped his phone a few times. "I can move some appointments."

His professionalism was admirable, Alex thought, and she was grateful for the introduction.

The young waitress interrupted. "More coffee?"

"No thanks. Check please," Bull said.

"The helicopter pad is on top of my building, and we can leave from there," Alex told Brandt.

"I'd like to come along and check out the well, if there's room?" Bull inquired.

Alex nodded. "Our pilot will email the flight departure details as soon as I get back to the office. He will need your legal names and birthdates for the insurance company."

Alex felt the tumultuous events closing in like a vice. She was absorbing the reality of Colt's death like a series of deep bruises. While her mind knew he was dead, her heart had not been able to accept that he was gone. Despite all the hurtful episodes of recent years, there in the restaurant, with the interview with the sheriff looming, she yearned for his presence.

"Alex?" Bull interrupted her thoughts.

She glanced at him. "Sorry."

"Are you okay?" he asked.

"Yes, I need to go." She wanted to go home to her office and be alone for a few hours to mentally prepare for the meeting with Salido. "This has all been difficult."

Ferrell Brandt stood up. "I will be available in a few hours."

As he shook hands with Bull, Alex noticed that his eyelids blinked incessantly and he had a nervous twitch that wrinkled his nose as if he were sniffing.

"See you then," he said and, like a puff of smoke, he disappeared from the bar.

As soon as he was gone, Alex said, "What a coincidence meeting

Brandt again."

Bull grinned. "I knew Nancy would give us good advice."

"She shows up everywhere."

"She knows everybody in the industry, but if you aren't comfortable…"

"I don't have time to find someone else." The day was escaping. "Thank you for the introduction. I'm grateful for the help."

But Alex felt like she had fallen down a mine shaft. Mourning Colt wasn't simple, and her feelings for Bull only added complications. It would have been easy to feel angry and outraged about the information or misinformation Schaeffer had given her about Bull Hawthorn's wife, but Alex wasn't. His demeanor and kindness left her feeling incredibly attracted, and she welcomed his consolation. He had his own tragedy to deal with and, regardless of the rumors, there was a truth she hoped he would one day share with her.

They left the restaurant and he put his arm around her as they walked toward her office. Busy passersby made their way through LODO.

"I am so sorry for your loss, Alex." His voice held sorrow. "There are absolutely no words to capture the depth of love and loss between two people."

"Feels like having my lungs ripped out." Alex tried to hold back the tears, but without warning, they began to stream from her eyes in an uncontrollable torrent. She sank into a chair at a small outside table on the street as the walls holding back her grief crumbled.

Bull offered her a handkerchief, then he went inside the restaurant and returned with water and paper napkins. They sat in silence at the little sidewalk table while the river of emotion flowed out of her heart. A server materialized, offering a beverage, but Bull gently waved him away.

After a few awkward moments, Alex finally caught her breath.

"Wow, I guess that was overdue." Her face was flushed and blotchy.

He brushed a tear away and leaned down to give her a soft, reassuring kiss on the forehead. They were still on Larimer Street with its charming shops, restaurants, and bars. People hurried past, busy with their lives, all unaware that, for Alex, the brightest star in her hemisphere had fallen from the sky.

"Crying cleanses the soul," Bull said.

"Mine needs some mending." She smiled.

"You have a strong spirit, Alex. It will all work out." He gave her hand a reassuring squeeze.

"Has it all worked out for you?" Her eyes bore into his as the words jumped out of her mouth. She awaited a response.

"There have been landmines." He looked away, avoiding her eyes.

Alex felt her heart sink. "I understand you are married?" she blurted, then added, "With a desperately ill wife?"

His expression melted like hot wax. "I wanted to find the right time to talk to you." And, for a moment, he looked exhausted and sad.

"But you didn't," Alex persisted.

"I couldn't find the right moment." He sighed. "I saw your anguish and it is clear that you loved Colt deeply, and I didn't want to bring up my own traumatic issues and make matters worse."

She had no idea what he was going through. "So you booked us into a hotel suite together and slept in my bed? And what, chat about it later?"

"That was not planned!" he said defensively, referring to their night in Dallas.

Her voice was as sharp as a serrated knife. She felt violated. "You should have told me," Alex snapped, unable to push away the feeling of violation. She wondered if she was the only person close to the situation who did not know he was married.

"There is no good excuse," he said. "I was afraid."

"That I might not sleep with you?" She felt duped.

"No, Alex, that you might not understand."

Her anger pushed her on. "So you just deceived me."

"No. Riggs Austin was shot, you were hurt, and the situation cascaded out of control."

Alex got up. "It's late."

Bull rose with her, his face saddened. "I was a coward for not talking to you sooner."

"You set me up. It was a conscious decision when you booked a suite with connecting rooms." Alex started walking.

Bull followed. "I want to explain the circumstances."

She didn't even pause her stride. "You had time."

"There is more to it."

"Not now. I must go prepare to meet the inquisition; maybe later."

In awkward silence, Bull walked her to the main entrance of her building.

"I'll see you later."

Bull gave her one more tortured glance, then vanished into the crowded streets of Denver.

Inside her building, Alex stepped into the elevator. She had stayed in Carbondale at the beginning of the fire and had worked around the clock ever since. A wave of relief rippled through her as she entered her office sanctuary. She inhaled the silence, thankful for the solitude.

The drive home felt like a prison sentence to Bull. He listened to the BBC World News report on the satellite radio, which had the latest on the radical ISIS terrorists. A journalist was beheaded, and the U.S. coalition was dropping bombs. Bull switched the radio off and embraced the silence. His mind swirled with confusion and possibilities. How could he have such a heavy heart and fluttery butterflies in his stomach at the same moment? He should have explained everything to Alex. He had let her down.

As if on autopilot, the car wound its way through the streets of downtown toward Cherry Creek, eventually arriving in the drive of an imposing limestone house. The beautifully landscaped lawn was trimmed like a putting green. Flowerbeds were mulched, with not a weed in sight. Two large French olive jars filled with coral red geraniums braced the front porch.

As he approached, the front door opened and a mature woman in a white and pink uniform welcomed him.

"Hello, Mr. Hawthorn," she said in a soft Hispanic accent. She stepped back so he could get in.

"How is she?" he asked as he entered the foyer.

"The same. She is comfortable."

Bull gave her a half-hearted smile. "Thank you. I'll be in my office for a while."

The nurse excused herself. She filled a vital role as the primary caregiver for Hawthorn's wife, Laura, who was brain-dead and in a coma. The woman tended to all of Laura's physical needs, including bathing her, changing her diapers, and turning her to prevent bedsores. Sadly, Laura's body was alive, but that was all that remained of her once-vital person.

The imposing home office was beautifully decorated and served as his Denver base when he wasn't in Houston or onsite at fires. Bull stood still, unsure of his next move. High ceilings, bookshelves, and antique carpets made the office feel like a library. On a desk, a pair of computer terminals provided a link to all of Bull's well projects.

Minutes passed as he waited for the computer to come to life. Distraught, he put his face in his hands and again read the weeks-old letter that was in his top drawer.

Dr. William Thomas
Chief of Neurology

Dear Bull,

This is a disheartening situation. Laura's life ended months ago. You have made the right decision, even if it is difficult. I have notified the staff to expect the transfer. I am here if you have any other questions.

William

Eight months had passed since reality shifted. Bull and Laura were driving home from a well site. The road was like a hundred other winding mountain roads, full of twists and turns. The car gripped the road firmly as it sped through the canyon. A bighorn sheep jumped in front of the car. Bull swerved and lost control. The car flipped and rolled, coming to a stop on the edge of a ravine. Sam, their golden retriever, was killed instantly. Laura's window was smashed and her head was severely injured.

Bull tried desperately to dislodge Laura from the wreck, sustaining deep gashes from the broken window glass. The jagged wounds bled profusely and left permanent scars on his legs and forearms. He called for help, and the car had sent an instant warning through the GPS. Eventually, an emergency medical team located them, and a fire truck followed. When the emergency workers arrived, they skillfully removed

Laura from the tangled wreckage. But, by the time she was airlifted to Denver, the damage was pervasive and her injuries were almost fatal.

Almost. The doctor patiently explained the situation until there were no more words. Laura's head injuries were irreparable. She underwent emergency surgery to stop the bleeding in her brain, but she never regained consciousness. Brain scans showed she was brain-dead. Only a flat line was left.

The words on William Thomas's letter stared back at Bull. He had come to trust Dr. Thomas, and thought of him as a friend. With his support, Bull had finally worked up the courage to disconnect the ventilator that kept Laura breathing, against the wishes of Laura's sister. After months of agony, the final exam was scheduled.

Bull pulled up the doctor's email and sent a reply.

Dear William,

Thank you for arranging for the transportation to the hospital and the final brain scan. If there is no brain activity, I will follow your advice. We will go ahead with disconnecting the ventilator.

Thank you for all your kind support over these last months. I don't know what I would do without your help and guidance.

Sincerely,

Angus "Bull" Hawthorn

The final scan had been scheduled more than once, but Laura's sister refused to support the decision. Her acceptance never came and, finally, Bull was forced to move ahead without her consent.

Bull walked out of his home office and down the hall into a beautiful room with pale yellow walls covered with exquisite impressionist paintings. Finely arranged fresh flowers were everywhere, and classical music played softly. Every detail had been carefully arranged to make the room peaceful. Laura lay in a hospital bed connected to breathing tube and feeding tubes. Bull approached, knelt by the bed, and watched silently, without hope. He had been told some eye movement under her lids was normal. He held her hand, but the cool, limp fingers did not respond.

"I love you, and I'm sorry." He squeezed her hand and kissed her forehead.

CHAPTER 24

Lafayette sat in the bar in the Comfort Inn in Carbondale, hoping he might learn something about Colt's movements before he died. The Comfort Inn was his base camp for the project. He had checked with the front desk clerk, who confirmed that Colt had been there just one night and had not checked out of his room. The credit card that was on file was charged, and Carter confirmed that it was the last transaction that was processed.

Lafayette spoke with the girls who cleaned the rooms, but they knew nothing. Chatting with the woman who was responsible for coffee and continental breakfast had been easy. She vaguely remembered Colt, but she did not recall a conversation or any helpful details.

Eventually, the bartender arrived. Lafayette stood and approached him slowly. "Coke, please," he ordered.

"You from out of town?" the bartender asked while he filled a glass with ice and stared at Lafayette. The young man of mixed race had dark hair, light tan skin, and almond eyes. No one else sat in the bar on this late afternoon.

Lafayette settled on a barstool. "Over from Denver."

"You heard about the murder?" The bartender pointed to the front-page story in *The Aspen Times* laying on the bar. It was the subject of the day. "Everyone is discussing Colt Forester's death."

"Just a little. Who was the guy?"

"He stayed here!" the bartender said with an edge of excitement in his voice, sliding the Coke in front of his guest. "He was here late one night."

Lafayette tried not to show too much interest. "When was that?"

"Last week."

"Did you get to talk to him?" Lafayette asked, almost as if he were inquiring about a celebrity.

The bartender picked up a towel and began to wipe down the bar. "Yeah, just shot the breeze. He drank a lot, I remember that much. He could really knock 'em back."

Lafayette took a sip of his drink, drawing it out, then asked, "I guess you're part of the investigation?"

"Not really. I don't know anything." He sounded slightly dejected. He busied himself washing out a few glasses in the sink underneath the counter.

"Was he by himself?"

"Yeah, he talked with some guys, then they left."

"Locals, I guess?" Lafayette led the conversation. "Everyone here seems so friendly."

"Yep, our local marijuana kings. But the guy was drunk, and they didn't want to listen to him rant about the toxins in marijuana."

"What do you mean?" Lafayette asked, playing ignorant.

"The Scott brothers own the pot shops and the growing operations here. They're on their way to being millionaires. They didn't find Colt Forester amusing." The words spilled out effortlessly. It was what he did—poured drinks and spread gossip, and this was one of the most exciting things to happen in Carbondale since he'd been on the job.

"It's a pretty good place to drink if you're staying here and don't want to drive." Lafayette burrowed in, hoping the bartender might offer something more.

"Yeah, after the guys left, it was just the two of us. I was worried about serving him more, but then some lady came in and dragged him out of here. Must have been his wife." He snickered. "She was *not* happy."

"I had that happen once. Embarrassing!"

"She could barely walk, but she managed to drag him to his room."

"What do you mean, she could barely walk?" Lafayette asked. "Was she soused, too?"

"No, she had a limp."

"Do you remember anything else about her?" Lafayette continued to probe.

"No, it was really late. We didn't speak. You aren't a reporter, are you?" The young bartender suddenly seemed concerned.

Lafayette gave him a disarming smile, raising his glass. "No, just curious. Have you talked with the investigators?"

"Not yet. Guess they'll get to me eventually." He sounded a bit hurt and ignored.

Just then, Lafayette saw Sheriff Salido walk into the lobby outside of the bar, accompanied by a young uniformed woman. He moved to a strategic table near the door so he could watch without being seen.

Salido got right to the point. "Can I speak with the manager?"

The receptionist disappeared to the back, then returned quickly.

"She's coming."

"Hi, Dan." The manager was an older woman with short gray hair and piles of wrinkles. Her smile was electric, and her eyes were bright and welcoming. "I got your message."

"This is Officer Brown. She's helping me today. Can I see the room?" he asked.

The two women nodded and exchanged smiles. "Haven't let anyone in there since you called," the manager said.

Lafayette tried to look preoccupied with reading the newspaper as he eavesdropped.

The young woman with Salido took out a small notebook and pen. "Who cleaned the room?"

"Lourdes. She thought it was strange that he left his things. He was a regular, so we saved them."

"He never called or came back?"

The manager shook her head. "No."

"Had he left his things like that before?"

"I don't think so, but we can ask the girls."

He nodded, seeming satisfied with her answers. "You have the bag?"

"Yes, in my office."

After several minutes, they returned from the back with Salido carrying a clear bag full of clothes that he handed to the young female investigator. "We need to get this to the lab."

"The room is this way." The manager beckoned Salido to follow.

She led Salido through the lobby and down the hall to Colt's hotel room.

The hotel room looked like it had been cleaned long before anyone knew Colt was missing. Salido looked around thoughtfully, but the room was spotless, not what he wanted. Gingerly, like a man with a stiff back, Salido got down on his knees, searching under the bed. Nothing.

He pulled the bedside tables back to look behind them, then moved the bed away from the wall to search behind the headboard. A business card on the floor caught his attention. Colt's business information was printed on one side. A phone number in ink was on the back of the card.

Salido put the card in a plastic bag and looked around a little more. The young investigator came in and took a few photos.

"I think that's it."

They walked back to the lobby. The hotel had that old, institutional odor that new carpet and paint could not completely hide. Salido peered into the bar and noticed the large black man talking to the bartender.

"Thanks for your help," Salido said to the hotel manager. They had known each other casually for some time. "Please don't discuss the case or details with anyone," he repeated the warning.

The manager nodded assent.

"If you think of something, or if anything happens that could be of interest, call me." Salido handed her a card.

She tucked it in her pocket. "He was a nice man. I hope you find the killer."

"I'll just go speak to the bartender." Salido hitched up his pants, revealing the 9mm Glock on his hip, and entered the bar with several large strides.

"Sheriff Salido." He stuck out his hand.

"I'm Stump." The young bartender beamed with enthusiasm.

"Can you please answers some questions about the murder investigation?"

The young man straightened his back, suddenly serious. "Sure."

"What's your name?" Salido asked.

"My real name is Fred Broken Hawk, but everyone calls me Stump. My dad is Native American."

Salido showed him a photo of Colt Forester. "You served Colt Forester one night?"

"He was here." Stump pointed and said, "In that very chair."

"Let's go sit where we can speak privately." Salido looked at Lafayette as if he were in the way. Lafayette did not move.

Stump smiled proudly as he followed Salido to a corner booth. The young female investigator joined them for the interview, and Stump regurgitated the story with excitement.

"You say he drank a lot? How many drinks?" Salido methodically asked the questions.

"Maybe four or five."

"He was alone?"

"Yes, at first. But these two guys, Beaver and Jason Scott, came by for one drink."

Salido exchanged a look with his investigator, then asked, "Do you remember what they talked about?"

"Kinda argued about the fracking stuff and the legal pot issue, but Forester was pretty sloppy. They got irritated."

"How irritated?" Maybe he really pissed them off, Salido speculated.

"They stormed out," Stump said with relish. "Pretty soon, this lady arrived. She was angry, too."

"What did she look like?"

"Nothing special. She came right up to Colt and ordered him to leave."

"Details, if you can." The sheriff listened while his assistant scribbled notes. "Tall, short?"

Stump cocked his head to one side. "She was thin, and she had a bad limp."

"Hair?" Salido asked.

"Brown. There was nothing distinctive except the way she walked."

The sheriff looked around the bar as if he could rewind the night Colt had spent there in his head. "They left together?"

"As far as I could tell, she took him to his room. She was pissed."

"What did she say?" Salido asked.

"She told me he couldn't have any more to drink. She was like a drill sergeant, and she yelled at him."

"Can you remember exactly what she said?" the sheriff persisted.

"Not exactly, but he was ranting about some bitch. Then she said, 'You're coming with me!' He did," Stump laughed.

"So, she must have known him?"

Stump nodded. "For sure. He acted like a little kid in trouble with his mom."

Salido slid his business card across the table. "If you think of anything else, please call and don't discuss the case with anyone."

Inside the sparse cabin in Marble, Aaron Jeffries worked like a fiend, ripping posters off the walls of what had been his home for most of the last six months. The phone call from the reporter was more than a warning. A large bonfire roared in the backyard, and Aaron, like a scared rabbit, ran out back to feed it everything that would burn. Small pieces of furniture, chairs, boxes, loose papers, old newspapers, old clothes—all went into the flames. He opened a new burner phone and tossed the old one in the fire. Again, he picked up the newspaper story about the dead man, his hands shaking uncontrollably. Then, he dialed Beaver's number for the fifth time within the last hours. The deranged man refused to answer, he believed.

Aaron put cash for future rent in an envelope and stuffed it into a duffle bag. Everything else—clothing, personal items, and records from the protest—had to be burned. He scrubbed the bathroom with bleach and stripped the bed, burning the sheets in the fire pit. He loaded his computer and the duffle bag into his old Jeep, removed the license plate and screwed on a new Colorado plate, placing the old one under the seat. He could be in Crested Butte or anywhere else in few hours, he thought.

A final search around the cabin assured him everything was clean. He walked toward the door as a loud knock sounded. He stopped abruptly.

Another knock came, harder.

No one ever came to the cabin; in fact, he could not think of anyone who knew where he stayed. A tick in his eye twitched.

"Aaron Jeffries?" called an official voice.

He cracked the door wide enough to a man in a forest green uniform.

"Hi, I'm Deputy Green with the sheriff's office." He flashed a badge.

"How can I help you?" Jeffries stepped outside, pulling the door closed behind him.

Green pointed toward the woods around them. "I guess you've heard about the murder investigation."

"The one in the papers?" Aaron asked, pretending to be uninterested.

"Yep. We're questioning anyone who has been involved in the protests. Couldn't find a number for you. Someone said you lived up here in Marble." Marble was miles into the high mountains above Redstone and Carbondale.

"Yeah, been trying to write a book, but I'm blocked."

The deputy surveyed the outside of the cabin. He smelled the fire and noticed the smoke billowing up behind the cabin.

"Real quiet up here," Green commented.

"Yeah, it is. Any leads?" Jeffries inquired casually.

Green coughed. "Some. Did you know him?"

"Only saw him around. It's a small town."

Green stared at him. "But you were up at the well protesting?"

"I was curious—a lot of people were." Jeffries knew he sounded defensive.

"You know if Forrester had any enemies?"

Jeffries shrugged. "No one likes the drilling."

Green's gaze sharpened on him. "Anyone angry enough to kill him?"

"The people who want to keep the forest safe for their families aren't violent," Jeffries said confidently.

"When was the last time you saw him?" Green asked.

"I don't remember, uh—didn't know him personally—a lot of people came to the meetings and protests." The questions seemed to agitate Jeffries, Green observed.

"Weren't you kinda in charge?" Green probed.

"Just a bystander."

The smell of smoke was pungent. Green asked, "What's burning?"

"Trash. It's legal up here," Jeffries declared.

"Better watch that open flame," Green warned.

"Always do. We want to protect the forest."

"If you think of anything, give me a call." Green studied him for another minute, making Jeffries more nervous. Finally, he turned away.

"Sure will," Jeffries agreed.

"So, do you have a number?" Green asked, turning back.

"I lost my phone. Do you have a card in case I think of something?" he offered, wanting to sound helpful.

Deputy Green handed him a card, looking over Jeffries' shoulder at the cabin.

"Okay if I take a look inside?"

"Another time would be better. I'm kinda busy." Aaron stood his ground, blocking the door.

Green gave him another probing look. "Let us know if you're leaving the area, okay?"

"Of course." Jeffries made a show of putting the card in his shirt pocket, patting it as if to make sure it was secure. "No clues?"

"Nothing definitive."

Aaron waited until the officer got in his truck and drove away before he began to shake. He went inside and studied a map for a few minutes, long enough to make sure Green was really gone. After checking the fire again, he went through the cabin one last time before leaving.

With fear gnawing at his insides, he started the engine of his Jeep and drove into the tiny hamlet of Marble. A few cabins and a general store made up the entire settlement, which was defined by an old marble quarry.

He waited in his car in front of the general store until he was certain he wasn't being tailed, then dropped the rent money into a lockbox outside the store. He circled back to the cabin to make sure the officer had not returned, then he headed out of Marble.

CHAPTER 25

Trey waited with Ferrell Brandt on the helipad on top of Alex's office building in downtown Denver. Alex appeared, looking serious. Brandt, with the chronic nose twitch, nervously studied the helicopter.

"Where's Bull?" Alex asked, obviously agitated. It was getting late.

"A conflict came up," Brandt said.

"Then we'll take off now," she said flatly, tossing her things into the back of the copter.

She climbed into the pilot's seat and knocked fists with Trey, who said, "You're getting pretty good at this."

"You're flying?" the lawyer asked nervously. A fresh glow of sweat appeared on Brandt's shiny bald head as he waited outside the chopper.

"Trey is here for backup," she said smiling, but Brandt did not laugh.

Angus's no-show did not surprise Alex after she had called him on the carpet for not telling her he was married. Still, she felt weirdly disappointed he had not come.

Alex glanced around as if she expected Bull to appear out of thin air. After a moment, her phone pinged with a text from Bull:

> Sorry I can't make it; will explain when we
> can talk. Please give me a chance.

She did not reply.

Alex directed Brandt into the back of the chopper and showed him how to buckle the safety harness. The lawyer carelessly dropped his briefcase on the adjacent seat, bumping Brutus, who sat up and snorted.

"Oh, shit!" Brandt jumped as if he'd stepped on a snake.

"Be careful!" Alex ordered harshly. "You startled him," she said with a concerned frown.

"I didn't see it." Brandt looked at Brutus as if he carried the plague.

"It's okay, Brutus, he won't hurt you." Alex patted the bulldog on the head. The big dog curled back onto his cushion, moving as far away from Brandt as he could.

"He doesn't bite?" Brandt looked revolted.

"Not often," Alex said, flashing a devilish grin. Brutus made a low, grumbling growl.

While Alex buckled into the co-pilot's seat and put on her headset, Trey lifted the sleek black chopper into the air, hovering over the city of Denver and on into the Front Range. Then Alex took the yoke and steered the chopper through the ragged mountains, following a route along the Colorado River. Even from high above, white and frothy rapids were visible. A group of rafters paddled through the churning water of Glenwood Canyon. Alex could just make out Hanging Lake suspended above the river.

The river's course led them to Glenwood Springs, where the district attorney's and Salido's offices were located. Alex set the helicopter gently on the landing pad, unbuckled her safety belt, and then she and Ferrell Brandt jumped into a waiting rental sedan.

Trey and Brutus got into a large company pickup parked nearby. A few miles down the highway, Trey, with Brutus sleeping in the passenger seat, pulled over. With voice command, he said, "Call Jenny."

"I'm on my way," he told her when she answered the phone.

"Come to my place in about thirty or forty minutes," she said. "I'm just finishing up at work."

Then, he continued on the short drive to Carbondale.

Jenny didn't want to be seen with Trey at the diner, where her co-workers thrived on gossip. She wanted to keep him to herself. She thought Trey was incredibly handsome in a hand-hewn sort of way and she loved his sandy grey hair pulled back in a neat pony tail and his incredibly muscular physique.

Jenny cleaned her last table in the packed diner and removed her apron. She was anxious and happy about seeing Trey again, but she was still extremely nervous about the case. She glanced at an old-fashioned wall clock. Ten more minutes before she could leave, so she looked for things to occupy her. She emptied the trash and filled the salt shakers.

More details of the murder had been reported in the paper. She looked at her phone again, feeling like a schoolgirl waiting for a first date. It was worrisome that she liked Trey so much. Finally, she walked over to her manager.

"I'm leaving in a sec."

"See you tomorrow." The manager was a mature woman who had worked at the diner for years and a constant reminder to Jenny of what her future might be if she could not escape sleepy Carbondale.

Jenny ducked into the bathroom to check her makeup and remove her apron. She spread foundation over her acne scars and applied lipstick. Then she stepped out the door of the ladies' room and came to a full stop.

Sheriff Salido stood in the entry, looking directly at her. A large lump formed in her throat.

He walked straight toward her, offering his hand in a friendly gesture. "Jenny? Can I ask you some questions?" He handed her his business card but did not flash his badge.

"Why?" Jenny clutched her handbag and tried to gather her composure.

"I found your name and phone number on the back of Colt Forester's business card." He held up the plastic bag with the card inside. "You're Jenny Cartwright?"

Jenny trembled, but she hoped he wouldn't notice. "Yes. We were friends." She tried to sound casual and her eyes looked toward the floor.

"Let's sit over there." He slid into a booth with worn, red leather seats and motioned for her to join him.

The girl who shared Jenny's shift came over to offer coffee and a flirtatious smile. "Hi, Sheriff. Hope you catch the murderer. Can I make you something special?"

"An iced tea, please." Salido removed his hat, ignoring the server.

"Excuse me, I'm going to wash up."

Jenny, nervous and scared, waited and speculated.

When Salido returned to their table, Jenny tried but failed to appear relaxed. She signaled to her coworker to let them talk alone. She looked around at the few people in the diner. It wasn't unusual for the guys in the sheriff's office to eat breakfast and hang out there. Maybe their meeting would go unnoticed.

"Were you at the hotel last week?" the sheriff asked, picking up his cup.

Jenny nodded. "Yes, Colt called me to help him."

"Help with what?"

"He had a slip...and was drinking."

"How did you know him?" the sheriff asked.

Jenny put her hands out of sight beneath the table top, twisting them together in the removed apron she nervously clenched. "We both went to AA."

"And you came to the bar?"

"Yes, and I took him to his hotel room to sober up."

He leaned toward her, his eyes intent on her face. "Were you romantically involved with him?"

"No!" Even to herself, she sounded defensive.

The sheriff did not appear convinced.

She continued, "I got us some strong iced tea and stayed in his room until he fell asleep. Then I went home." It was a small white lie.

"I have to ask again—you were not involved in a romantic relationship with Colt Forrester?" the sheriff asked, his look razor-sharp.

"Absolutely not!" she blurted out.

"Where do you live?" Salido asked.

"At the Crystal River Trailer Park." She gestured in its general direction.

"And did you see him after?"

"No, I didn't see him again."

He raised an eyebrow. "Did you think that was strange?"

"No. He wasn't here that often." Jenny did her best not to think about all the lies she told. She just had to get through this so she could get out of here and see Trey.

"He didn't call you?" Salido pressed.

"No, I never saw him again." Jenny chewed her cuticles as they spoke. Part of her statement was true.

"The bartender said there were two other men at the bar."

She frowned, trying to remember that night. "There was no one there when I arrived."

He pulled a small notebook from his pocket and consulted it. "Two brothers, one called Beaver?"

"No one was there." She hoped he couldn't see the fear in her eyes.

"You know Beaver?" he probed.

"Wish I didn't." She looked away, embarrassed.

"You went out some?"

She shook her head, hair falling down to hide her blushing cheeks. "Not for long. A while back."

The sheriff seemed to know she and Beaver had briefly been an item. It wouldn't have been difficult to find records showing that Jenny had been hospitalized with a fractured hip, but no charges were pressed. She speculated that several of Beaver's female friends had come into the emergency room with injuries, so the sheriff would have been notified. Secrets were impossible to keep in a small town, but this was just gossip and not important to the case, she reflected.

"Can I go now?" she asked. "A friend is waiting for me." She looked at the time on her phone.

"You call me if you think or hear of anything."

"I will." Her slim, sweaty thighs stuck to the faux leather seat as she slid toward the edge of the booth.

"Jenny, call if you need help, okay?" Salido sounded sincerely concerned and, for a moment, Jenny trusted him. An awkward silence fell between them as she waited to be dismissed, but Salido's eyes were locked on her. Finally he added, "My stepfather terrorized my mother and our family. I don't tolerate abusers," he said firmly.

The GPS directed Trey along Highway 82 until the road intersected with Highway 133. He turned right, crossed the Roaring Fork River, and entered Carbondale. He was almost giddy with anticipation. Jenny had captured his imagination.

Brutus, sitting on the front seat watching the world go by, looked large and fearless.

After almost missing the turn, Trey pulled into the trailer park and looked for the trailer with the pink awning. Jenny had provided detailed, accurate directions. She waited on the porch, looking like the angel he remembered. Trey stepped out of the car and walked up onto the porch with Brutus.

A bowl of clean water and an iced tea waited for them. Trey gave Jenny an affectionate hug that lingered several seconds longer than a casual hello. It felt safe and warm.

She smiled up at him shyly. "Thanks for coming over."

"I'm glad to be here." He'd taken extra care to prepare for the meeting. He'd showered and shaved and wore his best pair of jeans and a long-sleeved polo. Weighty work boots made him taller than usual.

"I made some salad and chicken if you're hungry."

Trey frowned. "Wish you would let me take you somewhere nice for dinner."

"Next time."

Trey thought he saw her tremble. He took her by the shoulders, searching her eyes. "Are you okay?"

She tried to look away.

He put a finger under her chin and raised her face to his. "Jenny, what's going on?"

Quietly, like soft rain, tears spilled down her cheeks, running to her jawbone and dropping onto the floor, and she whispered, "Come inside, please."

Trey and Brutus followed her into the neat little living room of the small space, which was decorated with second-hand almost-antiques. Items were thoughtfully placed. A vase of daisies stood on the oval wooden coffee table.

He waited for her to compose herself.

"I knew Colt Forester," she choked out. "We were friends, and I let him down."

That got his attention. "What do you mean?"

"I didn't help him," she sobbed.

Trey put his arms around her, then led her to a small loveseat where he sat close, dwarfing her small form. She smelled of fresh soap and flowers. "You can trust me."

She nodded. "You can't tell anyone," she said fearfully.

"Okay." His heart contracted, but he meant it. He would keep her secret, no matter what.

Jenny shivered. "You have to promise. He'll kill me."

"Who?" Trey asked.

"I can't tell you."

"I'll protect you." He squeezed her arm warmly.

"This is a really bad man. He did this to me." She pointed to her hip.

"What did he do?" Trey felt anger stirring, desperately wanting to take the fear from her.

"He shattered my hip with a bat."

Trey had been in combat where he and his fellow Marines protected one another. Jenny's words rippled through him like electric current. Every part of him wanted to find whoever had done this to Jenny and show the guy what a bat could really do.

"He said he would kill me if I told the police," she continued.

"And he's here?"

"In the area," she groaned. "The sheriff came to see me and, when this guy finds that out, he'll kill me."

Trey held her. "I won't let that happen." Then he asked, "Why did the sheriff come see you?"

"The bartender told him I had been with Colt."

"When?"

She lowered her head, her cheeks pink. "The night at the hotel when he disappeared."

"So you were the last one who saw him alive?" Trey added up the days.

She nodded. "I tried to sober him up. I left, and...the well blew up early the next morning."

"And Colt was never seen again?"

"The killers obviously saw him," she said quietly.

Jenny served a simple dinner of salad and chicken while she explained how she had met Colt and why he called her for help. They had shared a common bond of sobriety, and sometimes, when he was in town, they talked over coffee. While she and Trey talked, she ate around the edges of her food, pushing the salad around the plate. She shared her chicken with Brutus.

When the meal was finished, they moved to the small loveseat where Trey held her and told her his story of flying in the Gulf War, days in brutal combat, and harsh desert heat. Soft country music played in the background and Jenny snuggled a little closer. He kept his arm protectively around her, desperately wanting to keep her safe.

Jenny noticed a silver chain around his neck. She examined the square-shaped cross on the end of the chain. "That's unusual."

"It's a Coptic cross that belonged to one of my buddies who died in the war."

"I like it." She studied it, noticing its similarity to the tattoo on his bulging arm.

Trey looked at the time as he tucked the cross back inside his shirt. "Damn. I have to make a run over to Denver, but I'll be back again soon." He kissed her goodbye, relishing her warm hugs.

"Hurry back," she murmured.

"You call me for anything."

The sheriff's office for Garfield County was in a new brick building on 8th Street in Glenwood Springs, just off Highway 82, not more than twelve miles from Carbondale. Glenwood Springs, the county seat, was home to the courthouse, jail, and sheriff's office, as well as other county buildings, all basically connected with the sheriff's office in the middle.

A grumpy woman with too many years behind a desk looked up at Alex and Brandt as they entered. Beverly Doyle had stiff hair and was overweight, with large bosoms that rested on the desk where she worked.

"Ferrell Brandt." He did not extend his hand. "We're here to meet with Sheriff Salido," the lawyer said authoritatively, transforming himself from a nervous-looking man to an intimidating advocate.

Alex was beginning to feel more confident now that she was represented by high-powered counsel.

"He'll be here in a minute." Beverly sat and stared at them until Sheriff Salido appeared.

He stuck out his hand. "Dan Salido."

"Ferrell Brandt."

Sheriff Salido turned to her. "Hello, Alex. Come this way."

They followed the sheriff back to the office. "I just want to ask a few questions, informally, of course," Salido said.

"I will advise her whether to answer or not," Brandt interjected confidently. In this venue, he oozed self-assurance, but there was something slick and oily about his presentation. The few strands of hair left on his head were slicked back and his dark banker's suit looked custom-tailored. If MGM had tried to typecast an actor to play the part of a criminal attorney for the oil and gas industry, they could not have created a more compelling character than the real Ferrell Brandt.

"I want to find out what happened as much as anyone," Alex said sincerely.

"Where were you last week when the well blew up?"

"Denver, in my office." Eight days had passed since the epic fight with Colt.

"Anyone able to vouch for you?" Salido asked.

"Not during the night. I sleep alone."

"And the night after the well exploded?" The sheriff was referring to his notes and calendar.

"In the Comfort Inn in Carbondale. My well manager, Wayne Decker, was there, too. I went to sleep about one a.m."

He looked up. "Alone again?"

"Alone."

"And when was the last time you saw Colt?"

"About a week before I received the emergency call about the well," Alex told him.

"And the last time you spoke?" the sheriff asked.

"In my office on Monday, a week before the fire."

"Did he say or do anything that would cause you to have concern?"

Alex raised her eyebrows. "Like what?"

"Was he upset? Did he act unusual? Anything out of character?"

Brandt jumped in. "You're trying to cross-examine my client. She isn't a mind reader."

Salido looked at Alex, who looked at Brandt. "Let me try to answer."

Brandt nodded his approval.

"He was his usual self. Nothing unusual stood out at the time." How could she possibly explain their combustible relationship? They fought and made up, they argued and they loved while at the same time they tried to work together. It was all in a day's work for them.

"And then, on Wednesday night, he was at the Comfort Inn?" Salido stared at a rudimentary timeline. "And the well explodes early Thursday morning?"

"We had all been trying to locate him."

"Why didn't you call the hotel?"

Alex fidgeted. "I called his cell repeatedly. I had no idea he was in the area."

"Wasn't he working on the well?" Salido didn't sound convinced.

"He had other projects. Ask Wayne Decker; no one could find him. We thought he was somewhere else. He had a project in West Texas." Alex crossed her legs, uncrossed them, then squirmed in her seat.

"He didn't answer his cell?"

"No, but that happens in this business."

Salido frowned. "Was he always hard to reach?"

"Sometimes."

"Strange way to operate a business," Salido remarked. "We will get a record of all cell phone calls."

"It was frustrating for all of us," Alex admitted.

"How frustrating?"

"Very!" she snapped. "Wayne Decker called the next morning, Thursday, and told me the well was on fire."

"Is my client a suspect? Because if she is, we are going to stop this right now," Brandt threatened.

Alex looked at Brandt and indicated she was okay.

"You are the beneficiary of his life insurance policy?" Salido asked.

"I did not know that until yesterday."

The sheriff studied his notes. "What is your financial situation? Could this burning well break your company?"

"I don't need his money, if that's what you're asking."

Brandt spoke into the momentary silence. "Ms. Sheridan is prepared to offer a financial statement of proof of her solvency. She is a wealthy person and the insurance money would not be a motive."

The sheriff ignored Brandt. "Ten million dollars is a lot of money—to anyone." Then he asked, "Is there any reason Colt would have for blowing up the well?"

"No!" Fear crept up Alex's spine. Schaeffer knew about the fight, but that was their secret. She had told Carter, but he kept everything between them in confidence. Could Colt have been vengeful enough or drunk enough to blow up the well? A shade of doubt existed.

"Sometimes he was hot-headed," she admitted.

"Who would have wanted him dead?"

"Who wanted to destroy the well?" Alex shot back. "That might help you find the person who killed him."

"We are questioning everyone who was interested in or close to the project," the sheriff said.

She glared at the big man. "There were some nut jobs out there who almost rolled my truck."

Salido leaned back in his chair. "We are interviewing anyone who had any contact with the project."

"What about the protesters? They were angry and extreme."

"They are being questioned. You'll be staying in the area?" the sheriff asked, making it sound like an order.

"In my Denver office or around here."

"Good. Let me know if anything changes. This is an active murder investigation." He opened a manila file and looked at the contents. "You were in good standing with Mr. Forester?"

"We fought like cats and dogs, but we loved each other. I would have died for him."

Or killed him? Salido wondered silently.

"You said he carried a gun?" Salido inquired.

"Always. Did you find anything in the truck?"

"No. Do you know what kind of pistol he carried?"

"A nine-millimeter, I'm sure, but I'm not certain of the manufacturer. A Browning, I think."

He made another note. "They dusted the truck for prints, but nothing came up in our database."

"Other people used his truck." Including her, on occasion, she thought.

"Would you be willing to be fingerprinted?"

Alex clenched her fists. "Yes, but I was in his truck all the time, if that's what you're getting at. And in his office and his apartment, for that matter. We were very close."

"Thank you for cooperating."

"If you have more questions, don't hesitate to call." Brandt handed him a card.

Shaken and speechless, Alex walked with Brandt to the rental car. He got in the driver's seat and started the engine.

"Let's stop at the diner so we can talk," she suggested.

Alex listened to a message and answered several texts and emails at a stop light. Her heart sank—there was nothing from Bull. She regretted having been so hard on him. How had she managed to let her feelings get wrapped around this man?

The Red Rocks Diner on 133 was crowded, but they found a space in a back corner booth. Brandt's eyes darted around the room that was filled with men in heavy work clothes.

"So, how bad does it look?" Alex asked, bringing his attention back to her.

"Ugly. We need to tighten up your alibi." The dark-suited lawyer stood out among the manual laborers and farm hands.

"I wasn't anywhere near the area where they found him," Alex said.

"That doesn't matter. It's all circumstantial."

She picked up a menu out of habit. "What do you think I should do?"

"Put out that fire! That's the first thing. I know what a well fire of that magnitude costs. It will bleed money, and the lawsuits haven't even begun, and there *will* be lawsuits!"

"But Forester was the operator," she said weakly. The argument was not a very good one, and she knew it. She was familiar with lawsuits around other well explosions. Everyone close to the project was sued. Anyone that had an affiliation and money was named. This could be a financial bloodbath, and that made insurance money look like a motive.

"He's dead and left all his money to you."

She slapped the menu back down on the table. "Someone murdered him!"

"And you are the prime suspect. It's not going to be difficult to find out you had a volatile relationship."

"How did you know that?" Alex didn't like the idea of her love life being part of any discussion.

"Pretty obvious. It will all come out in the investigation, so you better get thick-skinned real fast."

"I am not afraid of the truth."

Brandt grimaced. "It's not about the truth. Motive, opportunity and suspicion are the weapons we face. The questions will get ugly."

Alex sat up straight. "I have nothing to hide."

"They will bury you in slander. Where and when and how often did you sleep with him? They will hire private investigators to uncover other liaisons and possible lovers, his and yours. Were you having an affair with someone else who might have been jealous? Are there any indiscretions I should know about?"

"No!"

"I don't like surprises. If they dig someone up, photos will be slapped all over the internet and probably go viral. They will try to make you look like an angry, vengeful woman or a cheap whore." Brandt seemed to want to show her how tough a murder investigation could be.

"I did nothing."

"Were you seeing anyone else?"

"No!"

"I believe you, but they will ask, Alex. Their goal is to try this on social media and make you look guilty."

Alex felt a tightening in her throat.

His next question cut her to the quick. "Has the bank called your loans?"

"How did you know about that?" she almost screamed.

"Just guessing. They will look under every rock, and it will be incredibly expensive." He looked satisfied, she thought.

"This is unreal. I only wanted to help find him."

"Angry lover threatens to blow up the well. You send someone to stop him and he winds up dead." Brandt painted a compelling picture.

Alex looked around, lowering her voice. "That did not happen!"

"Fran told me Colt stormed out of your office in a blind rage."

"When did you talk to Fran?" she demanded.

"On the way to the chopper. I told her she had to tell the truth to help you. It's my job to know the facts so I can protect you."

The unravelling of her privacy enraged Alex.

Brandt continued. "I need to be a step ahead. If a grand jury is convened, and I believe that will be the next step, they will present a strong case, a believable story, with plenty of motive."

"Oh, my God."

Brandt was throwing cold reality in her face. "Alex, my advice is to stop the financial bleeding and show them a strong financial statement. If you have to sell some assets, do it, and establish that you have absolutely no financial motive for the insurance money. I can help you if that is the direction you choose to take." His voice sounded sincere.

"I see your logic. Yes, I have some leases I can sell. Will you represent me?" She had to trust someone to help extract her from this situation that felt like dark matter surrounding her. And he had come well recommended.

"If that is what you want. You need representation on several fronts. I suggest we bring in a criminal attorney to handle the homicide," he suggested smoothly. "I can help quarterback the case and guide you with the financials and dissolution of assets. I will oversee everything, including the investigation into the well sabotage."

"I'm not about to start dismantling my company," she stated defiantly. In her heart, she was a heavyweight fighter and her instincts drove her to start punching. She felt cornered, and her only option was to aggressively fight for her life. She would do whatever it took to defend her business and the people that made up the family at Sheridan Enterprises.

Cash was a major challenge in her business. A crisis like the burning well altered everything. Her other assets were valuable only as long as she could afford to hold on to them.

Brandt took her hand in his and looked in her eyes. "I can help you review the options, determine the most desirable tracts to sell to raise money, and shore up your situation."

"I know you're giving me wise advice, but I am not going to lose my company."

"That is why I am here, to help protect you and your business. This is what I do, troubleshoot. Strategize and problem-solve." He patted her hand in an almost fatherly gesture. "I can handle this for you."

"Do I need to sign something?"

Brandt smiled. "Yes, at some point. My retainer is one hundred thousand dollars."

The district attorney anxiously waited for Salido. He jumped up from his chair when the sheriff entered his meager office.

"Any news?" Robert Portland asked, hungry for facts. His tie was loose and his suit jacket hung on the back of a chair.

"Sheridan is hiding something," the sheriff said, taking the chair Portland offered. "I interviewed some of her guys that work up at the well site. One of them said she and Colt had a huge fight over the project when he went to work on another job."

"People have fights," the district attorney said, playing devil's advocate.

"They were lovers and business partners on a lot of deals. They have a fight, the well blows up, and he turns up dead?"

"Strange coincidence. An accident?" mused Portland.

"Murder for hire?" Salido hypothesized.

"Where's the evidence?"

The sheriff shrugged. "If she knew about the insurance policy, then I would say it is a high probability that she's involved."

"But she didn't know," the DA stated.

"That's her story," Salido said. "I spoke with the insurance guy. She played dumb with him, too. He was hard-pressed to believe she was completely in the dark about the life insurance policy."

"Is it really believable that they were sleeping together and doing business together and she didn't know about the policy?" Portland rolled his eyes.

"Unlikely."

"I'm ready to take it to the grand jury!" Portland blurted.

"Not yet," the sheriff cautioned. "We don't have enough facts. Let me follow her a little first and see what she does."

Portland knew Salido. He would turn over every stone and build a tight case to ensure they would get an indictment. And the DA was just fine with that.

Mike Carter sat in the Village Smithy, pondering the mystery of Colt's murder. Despite the sad circumstances, he relished being reunited with Alex. The small restaurant buzzed with patrons. Servers had to squeeze between the tables and the hungry customers.

Carter waved his hand, trying to get the attention of the server. Lafayette walked in and joined Carter in the corner, where they spoke in low voices to avoid eavesdroppers.

"I think something happened after Colt went to his hotel room," Lafayette surmised.

"Yeah, but we have to connect the dots, and there are a bunch of missing pieces."

A waitress appeared with order pad in hand.

"An extra-large stack of pancakes, please." Lafayette requested as he studied the menu. "And a side of bacon."

"Coffee?"

He gave her a brilliant smile. "Please."

Carter reviewed hundreds of scribbles on a legal pad. Something about the well fire and Colt's disappearance did not fit. They were connected, but vital parts were overlooked or missing. His cell phone rang. The caller ID read, BLUE.

"Thanks for getting back to me," Carter said. "Did you find anything on Aaron Jeffries?"

"Still working on it," said Blue Davies. Their friendship dated back to the early days on the Denver police force. Now Davies was head of homicide. He and Carter had collaborated on numerous cases over the years.

"We need to know who this guy is, where he came from, and what he was doing before he got to Carbondale and Marble."

Davies talked over the sound of rustling paper. "I ran several background checks and nothing came up. This disturbs me."

"Nothing on my searches, either. It's like he materialized out of thin air."

"Someone has covered his tracks," Davies said ominously. "But I'm working up the food chain. There are only a few departments who can create a clean sweep like this."

CHAPTER 26

After returning from the meeting with Alex and the sheriff, Ferrell Brandt walked through the streets of downtown Denver. There was a lightness in his step—he could almost taste the payoff. A pure money man, he worshipped at the altar of the Green God. It was the lens through which he viewed the world. Money made him happy.

Brandt was extremely pleased with the progress he had made with Alex. He rounded a corner and approached a rust-colored brownstone building. He loved coming home to the historic Brown Palace, his hotel. A feeling of power pulsed through him as he pushed through the revolving door into the enormous lobby.

The wonderful old building had an open atrium stretching up to the sky. Period furnishings and elaborate décor filled the impressive reception area. Brandt entered the elevator that rumbled slowly up to his suite. He had lived at the Brown Palace for some years now. Its famous bar was a popular meeting place for his business associates, and the kitchen willingly prepared anything he desired.

Several hotel rooms, renovated by one of Denver's leading designers, had been converted into a palatial apartment with sweeping vistas overlooking the city. Brandt walked into the luxurious suite, dropped his briefcase, and loosened his tie. Millions of dollars and just as many lies had fueled his exotic lifestyle over the years.

The phone rang as he poured a glass of Chablis. He put the phone on speaker and turned to revel in his majestic view.

"I need the rest of my money," the harsh voice said desperately.

"A dead man wasn't part of our arrangement," Brandt said coldly.

"I had nothing to do with the murder."

Brandt chuckled, an unpleasant sound. "Who will believe that?"

"I fulfilled my contract!" the man screamed.

Ferrell Brandt's voice was bloodless and frigid. "You've left a mob of investigators circling like sharks."

"You got your protest. Now I want my money and documents!" the man demanded.

"Lie low till I call you," Brandt snarled.

"I want out, now."

"You leave now and there will be a manhunt. You don't want the sheriff speculating. You have an alibi, so just stay put until we tell you it's okay."

Brandt hung up the phone, knowing the situation would have to be dealt with soon.

The Denver Hospital was antiseptic and cold. Staff in light blue scrubs rushed about, treating urgent needs. The neurosurgeon greeted Bull warmly. Dr. William Thomas was a stout, engaging man with gray hair and an unparalleled intellect. He had a worldwide reputation as an exceptional neurosurgeon, and his empathy for Bull was heartfelt. "Come this way."

"I know this is best," said Bull, but his anxiety and doubt were evident.

"This is the right choice," the doctor said, patting him on the back.

Bull, exhausted from thinking and rethinking his decision, choked back tears. His wife's circumstances were hopeless, and numerous EEGs had confirmed her condition. Contemplating pulling the plug on her life support made him shudder, but the prospect of letting her body waste away in a bed that was a prison was equally disturbing. Her brain-dead existence in the house was slowly killing them both.

"The documents are in here." The doctor led him into an office where a witness waited for them to sign some papers. The doctor and the witness patiently watched the agitated man review the orders to disconnect life support.

Bull breathed hard. Life was precious, and he had never been a part of a decision like this. He was known for saving lives. None of his men had been lost in all his years of fighting fires.

He picked up the pen with trembling fingers. He read the fine print again. Minutes passed as they waited in silence.

The door to the room flew open, and a woman with wild hair and bloodshot eyes burst in.

"You murderer!" she screamed. "You didn't kill her the first time, so now you're going to finish the job." Laura's sister, Frances, spat the venomous words toward Bull. Her bipolar rage and sorrow were unrelenting—moods swung between intense anger and tearful grief.

"Please stop." The nauseating accusations and diatribes had been repeated many times.

"You never loved her," she cried, tugging at his lapels. "It was always about the money."

"Frances, it's time to let go," the doctor intervened. "Laura has been gone a long time."

Dr. Thomas took Laura's sister in his arms and held her. "This is the right thing to do." He signaled to one of his physician assistants to take Frances out of the room.

"She is my only sister," she wailed.

"And she loved you." The doctor's calming reassurance mitigated her rage and, after a few minutes, she docilely left the room.

Bull scribbled his signature and the witness signed. Just like that, the legal papers were executed.

Dr. Thomas gave Bull a sympathetic look. "Let me know when you're ready. You can wait in my office for as long as you need."

"Let's go now." Bull followed the doctor as they walked down the hall to end Laura's tragedy. He wondered how long it would take him to cross the bridge from guilt to forgiveness.

Laura lay peacefully in the hospital bed as the life support systems were disconnected. If she were to live, it would have to be without a feeding tube and ventilator. Bull leaned against the wall for support as his head whirled.

The doctor stayed with him as she slowly slipped away. After what seemed like an excruciating length of time, the heart monitor went flat.

Laura was officially gone, and his world was changed.

In the foyer of the hospital, Bull stood with Dr. Thomas.

"What do I do now?" he asked.

A vast wasteland of emptiness descended upon him. He was consumed with responsibility, guilt, and remorse.

"It's time to start living again," said the doctor. "Let's go have a drink."

"I don't know…"

"I'm buying." He gave Bull no choice.

The two men walked outside where the doctor's car waited.

At home for the first time in many nights, Sheriff Salido tucked his baby girl into bed. She would always be his baby, even though she was beginning to grow and change. They talked briefly about her mom, and he tried to explain that she was sick, but all Cathy understood was that her mom wasn't there.

After saying goodnight, he entered the modest master bathroom and looked in the mirror. Little was left in his emotional reserves, and worry about his daughter showed on his face. His wife was nowhere to be found. How would Cathy make it without a mom? Part of him would be relieved if the emotional merry-go-round would stop and he could get on with his life, but his daughter would never understand being abandoned.

Meanwhile, the murder investigation had become more demanding. He was responsible for managing all the different support personnel for the forest fire. Tabloids around the country were angling for a story—anything to sell papers to their readers. A recent headline was one of the more sensational ones: "Oil Tycoon Alex Sheridan Last One to See Dead Lover."

Then, as a skeleton crew worked the late shift at his office, Salido tried to get a few hours of sleep.

In the early morning hours, the sheriff's office settled down to manageable chaos. The calls from anonymous leads had abated, but there was still a heavy load of emergencies, complaints, and false alarms that came from throughout sprawling Garfield County. Bears foraging for food were reported to the animal control unit, a mountain lion was spotted in Basalt, and several DUIs were brought in and booked. Some climbers were rescued from a rock ledge somewhere out in the vast national playground. Each twenty-four hours passed with dramatic crises that would challenge even the most experienced professionals.

Deputy JP Green's patrol car eased up one of the remote mountain roads off Highway 82 near the gravel pit. He was relieved to be out of the office and in the peace of his patrol car. The murder investigation was an exhausting, new experience for him, and he was half-pumped with the excitement from a real murder case while frayed from the stress.

Green wound his way up a dirt road that bisected large open pastures. Fortunately, the radio was unusually quiet, and no new incidents interrupted his late-night solitude. It was an especially dark night with the moon obscured behind clouds as he patrolled the remote area that was mostly home to pastures and horse operations.

Small distant beads of light moving in the darkness caught his attention. Curious, he slowed down and put the car in park, letting the black silence wash over him.

He watched for a moment. Could be headlights, but they were out of place in an open field, he thought. They soon disappeared and all was deep blackness again. He turned off his headlights and got out of the car. In a few minutes, his eyes adjusted to the dark and he could just make out some large shapes in the distance—they looked like buildings with white canvas tops. He felt for his pistol and inched in the direction of where the lights had been. Movement of some kind was barely visible, and another faint light moved in the shadows. Perhaps it was a flashlight? He had been around long enough to recognize a fishy situation, so he returned to his patrol car and radioed dispatch:

"Possible breaking and entering off County Road Ninety. I'm going in to investigate."

He worked his way on foot along the dirt road until he made out the shapes of large structures that looked like huge permanent tents. These must be the marijuana greenhouses everyone in town had been arguing about, he thought.

Crouching in the dark, he approached cautiously. Soon he could make out a large windowless van parked outside the structures. It was large enough to move furniture. Someone shifted in the driver's seat. He heard a clonking sound and saw two figures by the doors to one of the buildings wielding what looked like a crowbar. As he observed, they broke a lock on a large chain that secured the double doors. The vehicle's engine started and the lights came on.

Green held back and hid in the shadows.

"Shut off the lights, you idiot," a voice called in the darkness.

The lights went off, and the van backed closer to the double doors. Deputy Green activated his body camera, turned on his iPhone, and started to shoot video. The doors to the back of the truck swung open.

"This is the mother lode," one man said, ogling the plants inside the greenhouse. He was skinny as a beanpole and had dyed blue-black hair.

JP texted dispatch:

> I need back up. Up Farm Road 90 near some
> greenhouses. No sirens. No lights.

He ducked down, hiding behind a pile of debris by a fence leading into the greenhouse compound.

Unable to sleep, the sheriff had returned to his office. Seated at his desk in the wee morning hours, an exhausted Salido gnawed on a slice of day-old pizza. He found the half-eaten pie in a box in the break room and had seized the opportunity. He was pondering the situation at the well and the evidence Alex had discovered. People dropped things all the time, and finding someone's personal belongings near where they worked meant nothing.

Alex identified the bandana as belonging to Colt, but she could easily have known about it if she was involved in the arson. For that matter, she could have planted it. The body was found on the back side of the Divide not far from the well, but how did it get there?

The allegation that someone might have blown up the well was another matter. That would be arson, and Salido was suspicious. It could be a convenient excuse by an oil company to avoid culpability. It had already cost millions in damage, and the fire still burned.

Alex willingly answered his questions, and she seemed to be genuine, but the life insurance policy was a huge red flag. Could it be a motive? Alex was the only one who was directly linked to both the well and Colt. The protesters were against the drilling, but there had never been violence against an oil company. In Salido's mind, activists blowing up a well made no sense. It would only cause more damage to the pristine forest they wanted to protect.

All roads led to Alex...she was the likely suspect. She had access to the entire area. The equipment belonged to her and it would be easy for her to stage an explosion, especially if she wanted a body to burn. It was the link with Forester's death that was puzzling. He had been shot, but no murder weapon had been recovered. And Alex claimed Colt's pistol was missing.

Could she have shot him with his own gun and ditched the weapon, then sabotaged the well? And how had the body gotten to where it was found? Did she have an accomplice, and why would they help her? Forester's truck was at the site and had no blood in it.

Salido had to put Alex in the area or find the murder weapon and link it to her.

An urgent knock on the door interrupted Salido's thoughts.

"Yeah!" he growled through pepperoni and dough.

"Deputy Green called. Burglary in progress," the duty officer reported.

"Where is it?"

"Up the county road above the gravel pit."

JP waited and watched and videoed. He was outnumbered, but he was also running out of time. Soon the thieves would try to speed away, but he knew it would be best to wait for support from the other officers.

"Start loading." The two young men ducked into the greenhouse and came out carrying a large plant. They placed it in the back of the van.

The thieves carried out the plants one by one and secured them inside the van. JP counted the seconds.

Next came the grow lights. They removed several of the special lights and placed them in the back of the van.

Finally, the backup detective who was trying to locate Green texted:

Where are you? I see your patrol vehicle.

JP texted back:

Near the white tent-looking buildings. Be quiet and come on foot.

The backup detective replied:

Roger. On way.

JP warned:

Sneak along the road toward the greenhouses.
Don't let anyone see you. ASAP!

The thieves worked like carpenter ants.

"There's no more room," said one man. The skinny man with blue-black hair walked back into the greenhouse carrying a red gas can. He poured out the flammable contents and stepped back to light a joint. He took a big hit before passing it to his buddy.

JP jumped out from his shadowy hiding place, gun drawn and leveled at the thieves. "Freeze! Freeze! On the ground! Now!"

He fired twice, shooting holes in two tires of the van. The shots sounded like cannon fire in the silence.

"Now! On the dirt," he ordered as he pointed the gun at the two young men.

The skinny man hit the dirt, dropping his joint in the seeping gasoline.

JP stomped on his hand and kicked the joint out of the way, but the gas—and the thief—caught fire. The other man bolted into the darkness.

The driver put the van into drive, and the night filled with the sound of the revving engine and the muted roar of growing flames.

"*Stop!*" JP shot at the tires again, ripping into the rubber.

Flames erupted as the greenhouse ignited. The skinny man rolled in the dirt, trying to smother the flames.

"Out of the car!" JP bellowed at the driver. "Out! Now!"

The driver didn't move.

Headlights raced from the road and light flooded the area. A back-up officer chased the man who was running across the open field. He caught up to him and wrestled him to the ground. Sirens came on and a second patrol car followed. Tires screeched as they skidded in behind the van. Sheriff Salido jumped out, charged to the van, and pulled out the driver, a young woman with ashen white skin and serpent tattoos.

Sheriff Salido took the woman over to his SUV, handcuffed her, and put her in the back seat. These punks, petit thieves, were known around town.

The frame of the greenhouse burned ferociously, threatening to spread flames to the other greenhouses. Salido spied a fire extinguisher and sprayed, trying to salvage the structure. Another officer ran up behind him with a second extinguisher and helped put out the fire. The sheriff walked into the greenhouse when the fire was out and located the lights. A powerful stench filled the building.

They surveyed the damage inside. "The owners aren't going to be happy."

Salido asked, "Who owns this place anyway?"

"Beaver Scott, I think," one of the officers said.

"No one wanted them growing weed up here," JP observed.

"It was a hard fight at city council to get the permit," another officer commented.

"This is only the beginning," Salido speculated. They all knew he was not a proponent of legal weed. "This weed means cash, which is hard to trace and account for. There will be ugly consequences. Canvas the area and check everything out carefully," he told the officers.

The men entered the greenhouse. The smell was overpowering. They walked up and down the aisles between what had been rows of plants. Another officer took photos of the contraband in the back of the van.

"I'm wondering about evidence," Salido told JP. "I don't want to impound a van full of valuable plants that will be dead in days, increasing damages for the victims. Best to get the Scott brothers involved, I think."

Jason and Beaver Scott owned a modest house in Carbondale. It sat a couple of streets off Main and had a second building attached on the back that served as their retail pot shop. JP called the number they had on file and let it ring until he got voice mail. Then he hung up and called again.

"Who the hell is this?" Beaver Scott growled into the phone. "And it'd better be good."

"Mr. Scott, this is Deputy Anthony Green." JP described the situation.

"Shit," Beaver said. "I'm on the way."

While they waited for Beaver to arrive, Sheriff Salido and Deputy Green split up and worked their way around the greenhouse, surveying the damage. Water lines had been cut and lights were broken. Part of the roof had burned. The damage was extensive.

JP walked to the rear of the greenhouse past a pile of fertilizer. An old refrigerator sat in the corner, and he wondered if it might contain some bottled water. Thirsty, he opened the door and looked inside. His jaw dropped.

"Hey, come over here," he called to Salido, but his boss didn't even look around. The deputy hurried over to get his boss's attention. He pulled Salido by the sleeve, dragging him back to the rear of the building.

"Open it," JP said, pointing to the old fridge's door.

"Why?"

"Just look." JP's eyes were wide as saucers as he opened the door.

The sheriff's mouth dropped open and he whistled. "That's something you don't see every day."

Stacks of Ziploc bags filled with money filled the interior, more than Green or Salido had ever seen in their lifetimes.

Beaver Scott pulled up to the chaos of vehicles surrounding the van. JP glanced at the grower over Salido's shoulder and saw fear on the man's face as he surveyed his violated kingdom. He tapped Salido on the shoulder and indicated the new arrival, then closed the refrigerator door quietly.

"What's going on?" Beaver demanded.

An officer was loading the three young thieves into a police car, so another officer walked over to Beaver.

"Looks like they were getting ready to haul everything off," the officer replied.

Beaver shook the officer's hand. "Caught 'em in the act?"

"Yes. Are you the owner?"

"Yeah, it's our place." Beaver seemed calm.

Sheriff Salido walked out of the greenhouse with JP right behind him. They approached Beaver.

"Can we put these back in the greenhouse before they're ruined?"

Beaver asked. "They're expensive plants."

"We'll get to the plants in a minute. Glad they located you," the sheriff said, extending a hand to Beaver.

JP nodded a silent hello. He remembered meeting the Scotts at some community event. Before legalization, they were rumored to be illicit suppliers, but catching them in the act of dealing had been impossible. They always managed to stay just one shade away from the law.

The elusive pair had been seen with the other protesters near the well, too, and they were on the list to be questioned.

"I came right away," Beaver said.

Salido indicated the greenhouse behind them. "They did a lot of damage."

An officer was recording the scene, taking pictures of the plants in the back of the truck.

"Follow me." Salido led Beaver into the greenhouse, walking slowly through the destruction. Green had his hand on his weapon.

The sheriff turned and quickly opened the refrigerator door.

"And what about this?" He pointed to the cash.

The officer taking video of the entire scene had finally reached the back of the greenhouse and had his camera pointed at the old appliance and the money inside.

"We deal in cash," Beaver explained. "It's legal." But his face turned reddish purple.

Doubt flitted across the sheriff's face. "That's a lot of money."

"The banks and credit card companies won't work with the pot business yet. It's illegal federally."

No clear proof of wrongdoing was obvious, but experience told JP there was something amiss. There was too much cash.

The sheriff started to walk away.

"What about my plants?" Beaver demanded.

"Put them back in the greenhouse, but you have to come in tomorrow and answer questions."

Salido drove away with the three young punks in the back of his car. It wasn't their first arrest, but maybe this time the charges would stick, JP thought as he walked back to find his vehicle.

Later that morning, operating on caffeine and little sleep, Sheriff Salido and Deputy Green sat in the sheriff's office. JP's eyes were bloodshot and puffy. Salido wore the same rumpled shirt he had been in the night before.

"Did you separate those punks last night?" He took a sip of coffee and grimaced.

"Yeah. The girl hasn't stopped crying," JP reported.

"You ask them about the Scotts and the murder?"

His deputy nodded. "They all said the same thing. Stick swears he knows nothing about the murder, just wanted the plants."

"Guess it's time to let them make their phone calls."

"How do you drink that stuff?" JP asked, referring to the stale coffee brewed in the office. He sipped on a Starbucks cup.

"It's free."

"When are the Scotts coming in?" JP asked.

"In about an hour." Salido cracked a smile. "Beaver was pissed."

Beaver and his attorney, a local Glenwood man whom few liked, arrived at the sheriff's office at about 11:00 a.m.

Beverly Doyle, enjoying the action, greeted the guests like a hostess for a cocktail party.

"Hi, Beaver, y'all want coffee?"

Beaver squinted his little red eyes and managed to grunt. "Sure."

She peered behind him. "Where's Jason?"

"Somebody's gotta work, and you know he gets rattled easily. I'll take it black."

Beverly brought him a small black coffee.

Salido walked in and directed Beaver and his attorney to the conference room. The attorney was a hired gun known for taking high-profile cases and charging huge fees. "I have some questions about the Forester murder."

The small conference room was clean and bare. There were no photos; it was just a place to do business without distractions. Deputy Green joined them for the questioning.

Salido began the inquisition. "You and Jason were at the Comfort Inn and spoke with Colt Forester the same night the well exploded?"

"We stopped by for a drink. He happened to be there."

"What did you talk about?"

"Nothing. We just shot the shit."

"I heard you argued," Salido said.

"Friendly debate," Beaver clarified. "He said they were going to drill more wells."

"You are against drilling in the Divide?"

"That's no secret. And it's no crime. What does this have to do with those thieves destroying *my* greenhouses?" Beaver demanded.

Salido smiled. He could tell his questions were getting to Beaver. "Nothing. Where did you go afterward?"

"Home. It was late."

"You went home?"

Beaver's jaw jutted out. "That's what I said."

"Did anyone else come in to speak with Colt while you were there?"

"No. He was alone."

"You know Jenny Cartwright?" Salido probed.

"What does she have to do with anything?" Beaver asked defensively.

"Did you see her?"

"No!"

"But you know her?" Salido pressed, letting Beaver know he was aware of the rumors about the grower and Jenny.

"Who cares?" Beaver's eyes turned empty and hollow like a dead man's gaze when he was mad and, at this moment, he was seething.

The sheriff changed the subject, hoping to disorient Beaver. "How did you know Aaron Jeffries?"

"He was one of the protesters."

"You didn't know him before that?"

"No, he was the guy who organized the protest up at the well. It's still legal in this country to protest." Beaver stood up. He wasn't about to tell the sheriff, or even his attorney, about his entanglements and favors from Jeffries.

His attorney stood as well, and picked up his iPad. "Salido, my clients are the victims. What are you doing about those punks who destroyed their property?"

"They are in jail," Salido told him.

"And my clients are finished." The voluntary part of the interview was over.

"I have to clean up the mess at the greenhouses and meet the insurance people," Beaver said, putting on a dirty green baseball cap.

The sheriff let them go, but the Scotts were on his radar screen, and Beaver knew it.

On the way to the parking area, Beaver's attorney asked, "Why would he be asking about Jenny?"

"She's a bitch." Beaver spat out the words, disgust dripping off each syllable as he remembered her rejection.

CHAPTER 27

Schaeffer walked into Alex's office looking sleek as a jaguar. It was the weekend and quiet but, not surprisingly, she found Alex at her desk, coffee in hand, poring over financial documents.

"Have you seen this?" Schaeffer handed a section of the morning paper to Alex.

"I haven't seen anything but red," Alex said, referring to the company's negative cash flow. The well was burning through cash in a way she had never seen before. "I don't know where to raise the money." Her voice had a desperate edge to it.

"Read that." Schaeffer pointed to a feature in the local obituary section.

A large flattering photo of Laura Hawthorn and her obituary were prominently positioned in the paper. It described her as a beautiful woman in the prime of life from an old Denver ranching family. After an injury that left her in a coma for many months, she had passed away, leaving behind one sister, Frances, and a husband, Bull Hawthorn. She was a well-respected citizen who had been an active philanthropist, contributing large sums to the Denver Art Museum and to St. Jude Children's Research Hospital.

Alex read the obituary in stunned silence. "Why didn't he tell me? Oh, God, I was so hard on him."

"Ask him."

"The service is in a couple of hours," Alex murmured.

"It would be nice of you to go," Schaeffer advised.

Alex struggled with the suggestion. "I didn't know her."

"Be supportive of him. He was there for you last week in Dallas."

"It's his wife." Alex debated the wisdom of attending the funeral service. But she felt a pull to go. The closeness she felt for Bull was impossible to articulate. They were connected.

"Trust me, you should show up."

"Will you go with me?"

"Of course," Schaeffer said.

"I'll change."

Alex ducked into her changing room and tried on various ensembles. She wanted to be conservative and understated, yet pretty and attractive, and she cursed herself for feeling that she was dressing for Bull. She cared about what he thought of her, and that was frustrating. She hated feeling so vulnerable. And muddled among those feelings were powerful pangs of guilt. She was not supposed to be thinking about another man, not now, not days after Colt was found dead in the forest. How could she be so callous?

Detective Carter walked into one of Carbondale's dives and went to a booth in the back where Salido was eating refried beans and drinking a beer.

"What's so urgent?" the sheriff asked through a mouthful of chips and salsa.

"This is confidential." Carter produced a printed report and plopped it triumphantly in front of Salido. "Aaron Jeffries is your man." He gloated with the satisfaction of having solved the mystery.

Salido scanned the report while he ate. "Where did you get this information?"

"Friend high up in law enforcement who owed me a favor. It is totally off the record. This information does not exist in any database, and it can't be used as evidence."

"So this guy…"

"Jeff Ashton," Carter interrupted.

"Changed his name to Aaron Jeffries after he got out of prison?"

"It was really hard finding the tracks."

Salido wiped his mouth on his napkin and reached for his beer. "What was he in for?"

"Murder. But the slate has been wiped clean. Pardoned and then buried in the federal witness protection program. Jeff Ashton does not exist. He changed everything: name, hair, even had plastic surgery. But he didn't change his fingerprints."

"So what's the motive?" Salido asked.

"Jeff Ashton murdered Alex's partner, Christine Welbourne."

"What else?" Salido continued to probe as he read the history.

"Rage, anger, resentment...revenge," Carter speculated. "Pick one."

"Wow..." Salido processed the information. "So he gets out of prison after murdering Alex's partner, Chris Welbourne? And now he just happens to be in the area?"

Carter grinned like the Cheshire cat. "More than a coincidence! It was Alex's testimony that nailed him and sent him to prison."

"What do you think, Carter? He blows up the well to get even?" Salido took a huge forkful of beans.

"Or maybe to kill Colt. That would have been the ultimate revenge. Kill her lover and destroy her business." Carter, brimming with excitement, built the case around motive.

"Someone had to help him with a new identity. Why would they do that?" Salido was skeptical, chewing slowly as he considered Carter's suggestion. "And how could he mastermind the plan from prison?"

Carter scoffed. "Money can buy almost anything. He had access to a lot of money and power then."

A waitress came over and Carter ordered a beer.

"But why would he risk going back to prison?" Salido questioned Carter's hypothesis.

"He's a murderer," Carter said. "You can't expect him to be rational, or maybe he owes someone?"

"There is no evidence connecting him to Colt's murder," the sheriff pointed out.

"Jeffries was virtually leading the protesters. He could have easily sabotaged the well and murdered Colt."

Salido shook his head, taking another drink of beer. "But still, no evidence linking him to Forester."

"Revenge is motive! He would want to frame and destroy Alex," Carter reiterated.

The waitress appeared with his beer, and he lifted the mug in a salute.

"You don't want to see it, Carter, but your client has just as much motive, if not more."

"She loved Colt." Carter didn't understand how the sheriff couldn't see Jeffries was their man. It all made perfect sense when he put it together.

"She's about to get ten million dollars because he's dead."

"Just look at this guy," Carter pleaded.

"Jeffries, who may have nothing to do with your fabricated, off-the-record story, was trying to live a quiet life up in Marble. And none of this is evidence—what am I supposed to do? Show this paper? It is all off-record."

"Just look at him. Alex's testimony sent him to prison!" Carter knew he had to convince Salido to be open to a possibility other than Alex being the murderer.

"It isn't a crime to be against drilling."

But Carter could tell Salido was considering the new information. "My people are doing a bit more digging behind the scenes," Carter offered, trying to sound helpful.

"Just don't jimmy with my case." The sheriff gave Carter a stern look, somewhat spoiled by the beans smudged around his mouth.

"You'll be the first to know, and here is the file on the Christine Welbourne murder case and the sentencing of Jeff Ashton—late night reading," Carter said, handing over a hardcopy file before he left.

After looking through the file Carter gave him, the sheriff took a big swig of beer and called the office. "Where's Green?"

The receptionist connected him to Deputy Green.

"Bring Aaron Jeffries in to answer some questions," Salido said.

Jeffries, if he was really Jeff Ashton, as Carter proposed, could have been out for revenge against Alex, but that didn't mean he had anything to do with Colt Forester's murder. The fire and murder seemed connected, but maybe it was just coincidence. Salido was grateful for the new information, but he was concerned about Carter interfering in the investigation and possibly clouding the evidence. Besides, Carter had an agenda. He worked for Alex.

And Alex was at the top of Salido's suspect list.

Ferrell Brandt sipped on a cappuccino in the dining room of the Brown Palace Hotel in Denver. The table was elegantly set with crystal and china. He ate fresh fruit and read *The Denver Post*. He was pleased with the developments in his plan. Alex had agreed it would be wise to raise some cash, and she agreed to sell some of her properties once a reasonable offer was presented. He had reviewed the valuable assets the Sloane family coveted and felt confident he would be able to manipulate the arrangement to suit them. His fee for successfully executing the deal would make him another fortune, and he would make even more under the table.

An impeccably dressed waiter came to the table. "More coffee, Mr. Brandt?"

"No, and put this on my account, please." He tipped the man and stood up from the table, a large manila envelope marked 'confidential photos, DO NOT BEND' in his hand. At the concierge desk, he said, "Please have these hand delivered to this gentleman, no one else, only to the recipient. Immediately, please."

The concierge said, "Of course, Mr. Brandt. I will take care of it personally." Brandt handed him two hundred dollars in cash.

Moments later, Brandt was in the elevator with its ornate brass-and-wood trim, vestiges of a bygone era. He pressed the button for the 12th floor. He stepped out of the elevator and walked down the beautiful hallway to his suite's entrance with its large brass lion head knocker and massive doors imported from England. The personal finishes and upgrades had been added when he moved into the suite. He felt for his keychain and inserted the key in the lock.

A hard poke in his back caught him by surprise. He froze in place as a gloved hand clamped over his mouth.

"Let's go inside," said the assailant. "Quietly!" The gun jammed in his ribs kept Brandt quiet. The hot breath on his ear made him shudder. "Not a sound," the gravelly voice ordered.

The key turned the bolt and the door opened. The assailant shoved Brandt inside and closed the door behind them.

The man released Brandt and they stared at each other.

"What are you doing here, Mr. Ashton...excuse my faux pas. I mean, Jeffries?" Brandt demanded sarcastically.

"Collecting for my part of the agreement. I want my money and passport."

"We play by my rules, remember," Brandt sneered.

"The rules have changed." Aaron's grip on the pistol would have choked a dog.

"You would still be in that hellhole of a prison being raped for sport if it weren't for me."

The other man's hand wavered for just an instant. "Your debt's been paid."

"Don't forget that I financed your new name and face."

Jeff Ashton, now Aaron Jeffries, had once worked for a powerful U.S. senator, Bill Bridgeforth, and they had often taken surreptitious actions on behalf of the influential Sloane family. When Ashton was tried for murder, it was Brandt who had secretly overseen the defense case. Later, Ashton paid Brandt millions to manipulate the system and purchase his freedom and new identity. Thanks to Brandt's contributions to the governor and other powerful players, Ashton had been mysteriously paroled and pardoned and had his identity changed. Jeff Ashton virtually disappeared as he was given a new life, becoming Aaron Jeffries.

Jeffries snorted. "You can tell Mack Sloane we're even."

Brandt knew the prison inmates had not been kind to Jeffries. He had been left with scars on the outside and inside. There had been more than one trip to the prison hospital to sew up his body cavities and face.

"The Sloanes won't be happy," Brandt said threateningly. With Brandt, obligations were never-ending. Brandt blackmailed Jeffries into participating in the well fire protest scheme, which was part of a major plan to enable the Sloanes to acquire valuable assets owned by Alex Sheridan's company. Jeffries was forced to agitate the protesters and create the diversion in the Thompson Divide, jeopardizing his new identity.

"That is your issue. We are finished!"

"No one wanted a dead man," Brandt pointed out.

"Especially me," Jeffries retorted. "I've done my time for murder. And now, this is your problem."

"If you disappear now, it won't look good." Brandt's tone was slightly less edgy.

"That is no longer your concern." Jeffries pointed the gun at Brandt. His anger had festered into a tumorous rage. He had risked everything to regain his freedom, and he was not going to be permanently chained to the ruthless lawyer.

"It would be best if I don't ever see or hear from you again," Brandt suggested as he moved toward the large safe.

"We agree on something." Jeffries had no intention of interacting with the lawyer again. Their ugly partnership was over.

"Your money, then." Brandt opened the safe.

"Careful," Jeffries warned as Brandt reached inside. The lawyer tried to make sure the other man couldn't see the neat stacks of gold bars inside the safe as he handed him several packages of cash.

"Now my passport."

Brandt handed him a new passport with the name Aaron Jeffries. "That should conclude our business."

Jeffries left Brandt's office. He kept his head down as a bellman wheeled a room service cart down the hallway. He darted into the elevator, made sure it was empty, and took it to the ground floor. He slipped out the side door of the Brown Palace Hotel into the alley where his truck was parked.

He drove into a seedy part of Denver and found a used car lot. A weathered man with oily hands walked out to make a sale. After selecting a car, Aaron gave him the keys to his truck and some cash. He moved his things into the back of his new vehicle and drove away.

When he found an empty alley, he exchanged the license plates. Then he drove into the wealthy Cherry Creek neighborhood to pass some time and formulate a plan.

The parking garage of the Cherry Creek shopping mall, an easy place to hide, was about half full. He wandered around the mall, biding his time until his next move, seething over Brandt. Even though he had his money, there was no reason to trust that Brandt was out of his life and every reason to believe Brandt would never let him go.

Impatient and now a bit worried that Mike Carter might be correct in his allegations, Sheriff Salido paced in his office. He watched the clock like a boiling pot as he waited for Deputy Green, who had gone to Marble, a thirty-eight-mile drive up the Crystal River, to find Aaron Jeffries.

While he waited, Salido made a call to check on his daughter. "How are you getting on?" he asked the neighbor who was watching Cathy.

"Playing and having fun—don't worry."

"Thanks again," he told her. "I'll be home later."

As the sheriff ended the call, JP walked in looking dejected.

"Did you find him?" Salido asked anxiously.

"He's gone. Not a trace." JP looked around. "The cabin was spotless, scoured clean."

"Damn it."

"Smelled like bleach," JP said.

Salido slammed his fist on his desk. "I'll put out a blast for Jeffries as a person of interest in the case."

"Burned a bunch of stuff in a fire pit behind the cabin," the deputy told him. "Fire was still smoldering."

"Find this guy before he evaporates."

"My money says he's not coming back."

A few hours later, there was still no news of Jeffries. The sheriff worried that he might have slipped out of reach. Anyone who had the resources to escape a murder sentence and create a new identity would be hard to find. It threatened his ego that Carter could be right. But, at this point, they had no cause for arrest, and they could not use Jeffries' past against him in court. There was no murder weapon, no evidence, and zero witnesses.

CHAPTER 28

S chaeffer and Alex arrived at the cemetery, a place filled with exquisitely aged granite monuments and headstones, their patina wrought from rain, wind, and time. The clock read 1:50 p.m., just ten minutes before the graveside service for Laura Hawthorn was scheduled to begin. Expensive sedans and a few trucks filled the parking lot.

Alex gripped the steering wheel, turning her knuckles white. She chewed ferociously at her bottom lip. After locating a parking spot, she opened the vanity mirror to check her makeup and hair, making sure all was in order. She added lip color and then blotted it away.

"Come on, Alex, you look fine," Schaeffer prodded. "Smile."

They locked the car and followed the small crowd that was moving in the direction of the burial site. A man in scrubs, talking into thin air with a Bluetooth piece in his ear, walked in the same direction. He stood out in the crowd of dark tailored suits.

A large white tent was erected by the grave, and chairs slipcovered in burgundy velvet were lined up in neat rows. Pots of mums decorated the area, and a wooden cross stood on a linen-skirted table. A priest dressed in vestments shook the hands of the guests. He had a warm round face and a few strands of hair, and he could have been Friar Tuck's twin. The thought made Alex smile. The priest stood close to Bull, who bore tracks of fatigue on his face. Hollow, blank eyes revealed that his spirit had been bludgeoned. The doctor who had arrived when they did walked over, shook Bull's hand, and embraced him for a brief moment.

Alex and Schaeffer, observing the gatherers, stood back from the area in the shadow of a large oak tree, waiting for the mourners to take their seats. A man stared in their direction. Alex noted several mourners, hands cupped over their mouths whispering and looking their way.

The self-conscious feeling that she did not belong nagged at Alex. The sun was shining and she wore dark glasses to conceal her own emotional erosion. This was the first burial she had attended since the death of her partner, Christine. The memories were vivid reruns in her head that replayed out of control.

The coffin, covered in a blanket of white and pink roses, was positioned at the front of the tent next to a newly dug grave, the cold destination. A violinist softly played a familiar hymn, but Alex could not recall the words.

Schaeffer whispered under her breath to an acquaintance who had joined them in the shade as they waited for the service to begin.

A vibration alerted Alex, and she stepped off to the side to glance at an incoming text message. While looking at her phone, she felt a gentle hand on her shoulder.

"Thank you for coming." Bull placed a polite kiss on her cheek, as his eyes bored deeply into hers.

"Of course. I'm so sorry." Alex was profoundly moved by his loss, but it was more than just sympathy. It was a bone-deep commiseration for the pain that follows when love is ripped away prematurely. Laura's death, like Colt's, was out of sequence.

"Let's talk after the service." Bull squeezed her hand and glided away. His motions were fluid and elegant.

The priest in his formal vestments gathered the attention of those assembled. "Please find a seat." An aura of warmth radiated from him. He beckoned people to move to the front row.

"I won't bite. Over here, there are more seats up front." Smiles broke out. For a fleeting moment, the heavy fog of sadness lifted.

"Come closer." He laced his fingers together in front of his round abdomen, patiently waiting until the silence was almost awkward. The last guests took their places. One young man stood and offered his seat to a thick-waisted dowager wearing a magnificent black-plumed hat. Blood-red lipstick and rouge recalled a more formal era.

After giving thanks to all in attendance, the priest began his personal remarks.

"Laura Hawthorn was an incredible woman who will be missed by all. Her generosity will live on forever." Prayers and blessings were offered. After the final reading, the priest turned to Bull.

"Would you like to say a few words?"

Bull stood to face the crowd, shifting awkwardly. His eyes searched the familiar faces as everyone waited. He swallowed again and again to force the lump in his throat to move.

Finally, after a painful silence, the widower spoke. "Laura would be so pleased you are here with us today. All of you are friends."

In the front row, Laura's sister Frances cried quietly. An older man hacked and coughed.

Bull continued his attempt to speak. "This has been a difficult time. The last eight months have been excruciating. So many of you came to the house, wrote notes, and sent flowers. Thank you." He paused. "It means a great deal to us that you are here." Bull's voice cracked. He used the word "us" as if Laura were still there. "Most of you know that Laura and I had an incredibly close relationship. We were blessed…" He halted, unable to finish.

The gatherers waited as the silence mushroomed. "…blessed beyond measure." The words lodged in his throat as tears gathered behind his eyelids. "Thank you."

A heavy cloud of finality hung over him. They were not celebrating a life lived out to its natural conclusion. This life, their life together, had been cut short, and he felt responsible for his wife's early death.

The priest stepped in and offered the final blessing.

"For you were made from dust and to dust you will return," the priest uttered the familiar words.

As the coffin descended into the grave, a Marine offered an a cappella rendition of the classic hymn *Amazing Grace*. His soulful baritone voice riveted the guests.

Amazing Grace! How sweet the sound
That saved a wretch like me!
I once was lost, but now am found;
Was blind, but now I see.

When we've been here ten thousand years,
Bright shining as the sun,
We've no less days to sing God's praise
Than when we'd first begun.

The haunting words destroyed the remains of Bull's composure as the coffin disappeared. The tide could not be contained.

Alex cried, too. Fat, salty drops spilled like water from a spring. Deep-seated feelings for Colt and Chris and all the people she loved burst forth from her heart as she listened to the moving lyrics. She had forgotten a tissue. "Who goes to a burial service without Kleenex?" she whispered.

Schaeffer produced a paper napkin from her purse.

A modest pyramid of fresh dirt was piled on the ground next to the grave. The priest signaled to Bull, who picked up a handful of soil and sprinkled it down onto the coffin. Tears ran down his cheeks in small streams. He pulled out a handkerchief to wipe his eyes.

Laura's sister followed immediately behind him and softly dropped a dusting of small earth particles. She was quiet today, calmed by Valium. Bull took her arm and escorted her gently to the waiting car. The chauffeur, a tall, thin man in sunglasses, held the door for her.

Bull returned to the remaining guests, forcing himself to linger, speaking with close friends, chatting as if he were in a play. He looked as if he was in a painful dream. People patted and hugged him and offered words of encouragement.

When the dowager spoke, everyone listened. "The service would have made Laura happy." She pronounced her approval with authority.

A simple "thank you" was the mechanical response from Bull.

"You did everything you could." She squeezed his hand.

The wind suddenly picked up, blowing leaves in the air. It ruffled Bull's silver hair, and Alex thought he looked beautiful and wild. He reminded her of the mustangs that ranged free in the west.

"Think we should go?" Schaeffer asked.

"I guess," Alex said, "good call that we came."

"He needs time with family and friends."

Just as they were moving away from the remaining guests, Bull approached. "Thank you for coming."

"I'm sorry about how I spoke to you before," Alex said sincerely.

"No apology needed." He leaned over, kissed her politely on the cheek, then shook Schaeffer's hand.

"Please call when you feel like talking." Alex didn't know what else to say.

"People are coming by the house if you want to drop by?" The hopeful tone in his voice was inviting, but Alex didn't feel right about going to the house. The gathering would be for personal friends and family, and her relationship with Bull was new and murky.

One part of her felt deceptive and cheap. She was the woman who had slept with the husband of the dead woman. She hadn't made love with him but, in some strange way, their night together had been more intimate than sex. They had shared the terror of the shooting; they had opened their hearts to each other. There was nothing casual or superficial about the encounter or their feelings. In his presence, she could feel the powerful attraction drawing them closer.

How do you know Bull and Laura? Alex imagined guests asking.

I spent the night with Bull last week, she imagined as her hypothetical response. And she remembered the bubble bath invitation. If it had not been for the gunshot wound, who knew what would have happened?

Alex was usually deliberate and slow to get close to someone. After saving Riggs and surviving her own near miss, with Bull supporting her, their intimacy had followed an unchartered course. In the span of one long day, they became closer than many friends ever do. She had welcomed his warmth and affection during a vulnerable moment. If she had known he was married, she would never have allowed herself to be in that situation. And the fact that Bull had managed not to mention his wife, sick or not, still bothered her. All these thoughts ricocheted through her mind as she stood with Bull.

"Let's talk when things have settled down," Alex suggested.

"I'll be ready for company." Bull smiled at her with a look that could melt stone.

The doctor walked over as Schaeffer and Alex were saying goodbye.

"William, this is my friend Alex. Remember, I told you about the fire in the Thompson Divide," Bull said, introducing Alex and then Schaeffer.

"William Thomas." The doctor's eyes lingered for just an extra second.

"I heard about the fire and all the related drama." The doctor looked warmly at Alex. "He's going to need some friends." The doctor's smile made Alex wonder what he knew about their friendship.

As Alex and Schaeffer drove through the narrow lanes of the cemetery, a quiet mist hung over the moving car. The tombstones seemed to follow them with their haunting stone faces. Alex heard the minister's voice in her head talking about dust. More and more dust, she thought.

A siren in the distance whined into the infinite.

Alex felt as if she had lost control of her soul. It had taken leave of her body and journeyed to where it needed to go to try to heal and make sense of the blankness. All she could think about during the service was *the end*, like the end of a movie. But she wasn't sure what was over. *The end* of her business? *The end* of her life with Colt? It all swelled in her head and her heart until she couldn't feel anything else. She felt carved out like an old tree trunk, left on the bank of a river. Surely Bull must be feeling the same way, in space but floating, wondering what the world offered now.

As the mountainous buildings of downtown came into view, Alex's phone rang. It was an unidentified caller. She did not want to answer, but so much of her business was in urgent mode.

"Hello," she answered in a guarded tone.

"Hi, Alex, this is Tebo," the banker said.

"What a pleasant surprise."

"Sorry it took so long to get back to you."

"Thought you had forgotten me," she told him.

"It's not good news. I've been trying to convince my loan committee to take on your account, but they're afraid of potential lawsuits. If this is anything like some of the other well disasters, it could bankrupt you." There was honor in his voice. At least he had the courage to call and tell her the truth.

Alex was disappointed. "I had hoped you would come through."

"If it were my choice alone, we would. I have pledged my word and tried every way possible to convince them you are good for it." Deep disappointment edged his words.

"Thanks for trying."

"Don't give up on me yet. I just don't want you waiting on Great Western."

After ending the call, Alex turned to Schaeffer. "Great Western is out. We may have to sell some of the prime leases."

"There's got to be another choice," Schaeffer said. Dismembering the company would be devastating.

"We're running out of options." Still, Alex was determined to pull out of the mess. She had been in tight spots before. This wasn't her first cash call and it would certainly not be her last. Big risks were part of the oil business.

She called Ferrell Brandt, who answered immediately.

"Let's talk about liquidating," Alex said reluctantly. She was going to have to trust his guidance, raise cash, and retrench.

"Sorry this has to happen, but I have some clients who might be interested in buying." Brandt's concerned tone conveyed sincere empathy for her dire situation.

"Talk to them. We are burning through cash, and I need money."

"I'm sure a deal can be arranged."

"Bring me some options," Alex said. It was one step backward but, in her mind, there would certainly be two steps forward after she got past this problem.

When the call ended, an ebullient Brandt stood up at his desk and swung his fist, pumping it in the air. This was the chess move he had set up. Soon it would be checkmate, he thought. He put his phone on speaker mode and hit the speed dial. "Mack Sloane, please." He waited for a few seconds until the powerful woman came on the line.

"What do you know?" she demanded harshly.

"Alex Sheridan is ready to sell," he pronounced with pleasure. Ferrell's eyes blinked and his nose twitched with excitement.

"What about the murder investigation?" Mack Sloane growled, skipping over the positive news.

"It will all work out."

Her voice became threatening. "It better not come near us."

Brandt knew there was force behind her threat. If mistakes were made, the unscrupulous matriarch was merciless. "Yes, I understand."

"I don't tolerate sloppy."

Many of Mack's opponents had mysteriously disappeared over the years. Brandt had seen the lives of politicians and powerful business leaders destroyed, as he himself had helped to release vicious, life-eviscerating lies that ruined many of their enemies. Their threats alone had caused a powerful attorney in Washington to kill himself.

Ferrell Brandt swallowed hard and cursed her silently. He was painfully aware of Mack Sloane's terrifying power.

CHAPTER 29

Two enormous file boxes filled with documents were wheeled into Alex's office on a dolly, followed by Ferrell Brandt.

"Here are the offers for the leases we discussed. These are the contracts and proposals for their acquisition."

Only forty-eight hours had passed before offers materialized and, with uncanny efficiency, the necessary documents had already been generated. He slapped a thick stack of contracts triumphantly on her desk. The signature pages were highlighted with brightly colored sticky notes.

Alex, pale with concern, knew she was facing tough decisions. "Let's go over the details," she said, knowing the gravity of the consequences she might face.

"They are fair offers but, with the short fuse, not the highest price."

Alex reviewed one of the offers.

"This is rape!" She slammed the contract onto the desk and papers scattered across the floor. As she bent to pick them up, Brandt rushed to help put them back in order.

"You can't think this is acceptable for my company," Alex said.

"Time is not your friend," Brandt reminded her. "You're bleeding cash." He reorganized the contracts back into neat piles.

"But it's your job to protect me!"

"Word on the street's that you're in a jam." He gnawed on a thumbnail, his eyes blinking faster. "And everyone's talking about the fire."

"This would be the end of my company!" Alex paced like a caged tiger while her mind churned for a solution. She glared at Ferrell Brandt.

"I am looking out for you." His voice dripped with concern. "You must trust that I am here for you."

"It doesn't feel like it!" The barometer in her gut fired an alarm.

"Everyone knows you're in trouble. It's a time bomb," he told her.

"There has to be another way." Alex paused in front of the windows, staring at some faraway place on the horizon. She stood defiantly on long slim legs in black riding boots, masquerading as a *Vogue* rodeo model. But she had a Fortune 500 heart and a brain wired like Warren Buffett.

"If you don't sell, you're going to fail," Brandt said, pushing for her cooperation.

She turned around to face him. "That is not an option. I've spent years accumulating these leases. And we finally have the technology and the ability to extract the oil and gas!"

"You'll be able to acquire other properties after this crisis is behind you."

"Not like this!" The purchase offers he was presenting were way below anything Alex had envisioned and would do little to shore up her balance sheet.

"You need to cut your losses."

"I don't quit!" Alex raised her voice forcefully. She had not reached the pinnacle of success by giving up at the first or second roadblock. She knew the sale of the valuable assets of her company would devalue the business and then she would have less borrowing power. It would be a death spiral.

Brandt kept the pressure on. "If you will just sign where the highlighted stickers are, I can take care of the rest."

A knot tightened in her stomach. She hadn't been able to slow the cash burn or raise new capital. It looked like she might need the ten million dollars in life insurance after all.

"I need time to consider my options."

"Alex, TIME is running out!" Brandt warned.

"You're my lawyer. *Stall!*" Alex fired back. He was pressing too hard, and the offers were unacceptable. She didn't like being pushed, especially by her own counsel.

"The sheriff is hungry for motive," he reminded her. "We have to improve your financial story."

"Don't pressure me, Ferrell." Even though he had a point, Alex was as stubborn and dangerous as a mother bear when it came to fighting for her business.

"I'll do what I can to stall." Brandt retreated, surprising her.

"I'll get back to you," Alex said abruptly. An internal alarm was sounding, and she could not determine its origin. She also knew that a time bomb was ticking. A few more large cash withdrawals and there would be no choice.

After showing Brandt to the door, she returned to her office to review the offers. They were all unreasonable, she thought, throwing the papers back in the file box. And Brandt had managed to produce the contracts too quickly, she reflected.

She needed to think carefully about the next crucial step, which could save her company or take it down. She settled into a chair overlooking the mountains, stilling her mind. Chris came into her thoughts. Her friendship and counsel was missed, but she knew how Chris thought. What would she do?

After some time, a plan began to crystallize. She made a list to deal with the most urgent matters. The Forestry Service had requested a meeting, the insurance company had called repeatedly, and a dozen similar requests had come in from other individuals and agencies. She needed to respond to them all, and there was an urgent need for a new financial plan. She left a message for the CPA who was preparing a cash flow projection.

She also needed to plan the details for Colt's memorial service and meet with his attorney. Colt's will left everything to her—his house, his business, and his prized Harley-Davidson. It all hung over her head.

A knock at the door interrupted her planning.

"Who is it?" she asked, walking to the door. She opened the door, and then exclaimed, "Jake!"

Jake reached down to encircle her in a huge hug.

"Where have you been?" Alex asked, perplexed by his absence and silence but happy to see her old friend.

He looked down at her, his face sympathetic. "Out of town. I just heard the news about Colt."

"It's devastating." She moved away, motioning him to join her near the windows.

"I'm so sorry."

Alex wasn't convinced. He was sorry, but he had never been a fan of Colt's. He had always wanted her to make a different choice, but he was her friend and she was thankful for his presence.

"I'm numb."

"Thought you might need some moral support." He sat down on the sofa.

"I need a banker!" she told him.

He leaned back. "The fire must be eating your lunch."

"Everyone's bailing. I'm going to have to sell."

"Drilling in that area wasn't meant to be," Jake added in an *I told you so* tone.

"For Christ's sake, Jake! We were sabotaged!"

"You're going against the tide."

"This wasn't some act of divine intervention!" she volleyed back, not concealing her frustration.

They had argued before—Jake for the land preservation side and Alex for the resource development side—and were destined to disagree. It felt as if Jake was gloating over the debacle in the Thompson Divide. He and the environmental lobby were ardently opposed to drilling in that area.

"Maybe just no drilling in that area," he repeated.

"Jake, this is not the time. I am going out of my mind trying to keep my company afloat, and Colt just died."

"Sorry." He got up and moved over to give her a warm kiss on the cheek. "How can I help?"

"I'm a bit stressed."

"Let me take care of you." Jake wrapped his arms around her.

Alex looked around the cluttered office with its quicksand of projects crying for attention. "I'm swamped."

"Dinner at my house tonight?" He had a disarming and loving way that tended to melt stress.

Alex shook her head. "I wish I could—there is so much hanging over me."

"It can wait." Jake lifted her chin to smile at her.

"A break would be appealing."

"You can kick back and relax for a few hours."

Fond memories of the incredible times they had shared in his house perched on the side of Sunshine Canyon popped back into her mind. The house was nestled in the foothills above Boulder where the sky, mountains, and plains ran together like sea and sand.

"A change of venue might be good," she admitted. She had missed spending time with Jake because of the issue of Colt's smoldering jealousy. It had been easier to avoid their friendship than to deal with Colt's anger.

He moved to look out the window. "What are you in the mood for?"

"Anything that doesn't involve money," she said with only a touch of sarcasm.

"Good," he said, "I'm buying."

Alex smiled. "I can't remember when I've last eaten a meal."

"I'll make something scrumptious." He put his hands on her shoulders and pulled her closer. "Bring your jammies and we'll have a sleepover."

"As soon as I can break out of here." The drive to Boulder was about an hour away, but she wasn't sure that spending the night was a good idea. Besides, a hundred different projects needed her attention.

"See you tonight."

Jake put on his Stetson and left Alex to the unrelenting financial crisis.

One of Brandt's contract offers caught her eye. It was a thick document that would take hours to review. Not now, she decided. There had to be another solution. When in doubt, *pause*. It had proved to be a useful philosophy.

She changed into her running clothes, strapped her iPhone to her arm, and crammed earbuds in her ears. She scampered down the stairs on to Broadway, then loped through the bustling streets past the Holy Ghost Catholic Church. The classic steeple was constructed with ancient gray stone. A tired woman in worn clothes walked with a little girl in a matching pink hat and coat toward the back of the church hall. Alex could see the parishioners gathered for a morning service.

She veered off course and ran down the stairs of the church. A tin can for donations sat at the edge of the welcome table. Alex took twenty dollars out of her running shorts and put it in the contributions can, making a mental note to send more later. One of the volunteers thanked her as she spoke with several of the homeless patrons. After offering a quiet prayer of gratitude for her own good fortune, she went back to pound the streets.

Alex listened to The Band and some raucous country rock, then a rotation of fast music. When she reached a nice pace, she cranked up Aretha Franklin. For close to an hour, she ran through the streets, no destination, no prescribed route, just running.

She paused when her cell phone sounded. "What are you doing?" Bull asked.

"Trying to run into a solution." Her breath was labored.

"For?"

She stopped and bent over to catch her breath. "Cash crunch. You okay?"

"Tired, but sure could use your company."

"I'm by the Starbucks in Cherry Creek."

"My house is around the corner. Can I come get you?" His voice was warm and inviting.

"I'm soaking wet."

"All the better."

For a second she hesitated. "I'll jog over."

He gave her the address and best route through the wide, tree-lined streets. Expensive cars were parked in the driveways of stately homes. A nanny with a stroller and a Labrador retriever blocked the sidewalk and Alex ran around them, searching the street numbers. Jogging toward the house, Alex saw Bull waiting on the front porch, looking like he belonged in a Ralph Lauren catalog. As she approached, he reached out to give her a warm hug.

Alex stepped back, holding her hands up in the air. "I'm a sweaty mess." In her Lulu leggings and a fitted halter-top, she knew she looked great.

"I don't care."

He pulled her to him, holding her gently with a caring that penetrated her heart, then led her into the house.

"What an excruciating time you've been through," Alex said.

Bull's dark eyes held traces of pain, not pain that comes from an outward event, but aching sorrow from the inside, working its way out through the eyes in a slow, seeping exit.

The exquisite décor of the home was noteworthy. Weathered wide plank floors covered with antique carpets gave the room warmth. Flower arrangements were on almost every surface, and personal memorabilia filled the ornate bookshelves. Several riding trophies were scattered among the books and statuary, and a large portrait of Laura rested on an easel. Laura was stitched in all the seams of his life.

"I should have told you." Bull sounded embarrassed about his deception.

Alex noticed a picture of Bull and Laura on a sideboard in the living room. Other photos of the handsome couple were placed around the room.

"It was complicated." Her words were a gracious offering.

"I was blindsided by my feelings for you." His explanation was sincere. "I loved my wife. Love." He shook his head. "And I miss her. But I need to feel alive, and I haven't felt that way since the accident. Until I met you."

She put a hand on his arm, hoping he could see that she understood his pain. "I can't imagine the trauma of your decision."

Bull covered her hand with his. "Alex, the decision to disconnect life support was made long before we met."

Gabriella, the housekeeper, appeared in the living room, looking through Alex as if she weren't there. "Do you need anything else, Mr. Hawthorn?" She pronounced his name with a slight lisp.

"No, thank you. Please take the rest of the day off."

She left without another word. Gabriella was in mourning. The entire purpose of her life for the last eight months had disappeared. Alex realized Laura's death had affected all the people around her.

"Laura's sister has been a handful." Bull looked a bit lost in the large room. "I don't know where to begin."

"It must be daunting."

Bull offered Alex a bottle of water as he led them outside where more flowers filled the back patio.

"You mean a lot to me." Bull slipped in the comment.

"It has been a roller coaster of emotions." Alex wasn't just referring to Bull's situation. Colt's death was a festering wound, overshadowed by the looming murder investigation. The insurance people were looking to find fault or fraud and, at the same time, the sheriff was seriously considering an indictment.

"You're a bright spot for me."

"Some kind of timing," Alex remarked. She could really use a bright spot on her own horizon. "Ferrell Brandt wants me to liquidate my most valuable assets," she said, admitting her dire circumstances.

Bull looked at her with alarm. "Is there no other option?"

"We'll see. I'm running out of choices."

"Sorry it has gotten so out of control." He moved closer to Alex and rubbed her shoulders.

Alex sipped on the bottled water, absorbing the beauty of the tranquil garden. The warm feeling of his hands on her skin was familiar, as if her skin had known his touch forever.

"Wayne and I spoke. We plan to try to extinguish the fire tomorrow," Bull said, offering something positive.

"I didn't come here to talk about my business. I just wanted to see if you needed an ear."

"I need a kiss." His lips tenderly brushed her mouth.

Just then her phone rang. It was a 713 area code—Houston.

"Excuse me."

Bull inclined his head graciously. "Go ahead."

She moved away from him.

"This is Alex." There was a pause. Her face lit up. "Riggs Austin! What a surprise." Alex broke into a broad smile, pleased to hear from her new old friend. She put the phone on speaker for Bull to hear.

"Hope you're okay?" Riggs inquired.

"Sitting here with your other buddy, Bull Hawthorn." The two men exchanged greetings.

"How's that shoulder?" Bull inquired.

"Hardly feel it," Riggs chuckled. "It'll take more than this to do me in." Riggs was tough as boot leather, even though he was nearing eighty years.

They all laughed.

"So, what can I do for you?" Alex knew he must have something on his mind.

"Just wanted to see how things are going up there. Heard you might be in a pickle." Riggs's voice dropped an octave, becoming more serious and to the point.

"From?" Alex asked with surprise.

"One of my oil and gas cronies. This is a small club we're in." His voice was rich and jolly. He was right. They operated in the thin-air world of independent oil and gas wildcatters.

"Yeah, I may have to fire-sale some assets." Alex took a deep breath. "The lawyer is pressing me to raise cash."

"Who's that?"

"Ferrell Brandt."

"That rattlesnake! I heard he was trying to railroad you!" His anger was palpable through the phone. "Alex, I don't want to get in your business, but I am going to do it anyway! That man should be in jail."

She looked over at Bull. "He brought offers to buy my leases."

"Steal is the word! He works under the table for powerful people like the Sloanes, and he's swindled and blackmailed more people than I can count."

The words hit her like a flamethrower. "The Sloane family?" Stories of the hard-dealing tactics of the Sloane machine were legendary.

Riggs snorted. "Brandt's setting you up so he can broker your assets and pocket the money. I bet someone is paying him double what he is offering you—that I would bet my life on."

Rage rose in Alex like mercury as the reality of her situation came into focus. A patchwork of blotches erupted on her neck. "Why would Nancy Parker recommend him?"

"Money. She's as sketchy as Brandt. And who knows? Brandt could have her on his payroll, too."

"That is a huge conflict of interest." She paced back and forth on the flagstone deck.

"He's a snake." Riggs's anger was powerful.

"He is supposed to be my advocate. I retained him."

"You can't trust him," Riggs told her.

"Thanks for the warning. What do you suggest?"

"You haven't signed anything?" Riggs sounded worried, but he had arrived like the Light Brigade.

"No, but he pushed hard to persuade me to." Alex continued to pace in Bull's garden. "Wait until he gets my suit. We'll have his hide."

"Don't sign a thing. Tell him you're getting a second opinion, and tell him nothing else."

"I'd like to see him skewered," she said, venom in her words.

Riggs chuckled. "Me, too. Let's see what we can do."

"I'm still in a vise with the cash call," Alex said, almost as an afterthought, reminding him of the underlying problem.

"Maybe I can help."

Alex smiled for the first time since she'd picked up the call. "I welcome any solutions."

He sounded invigorated, ready to help her take on the world. "When can you meet?"

"Any time. You tell me," she said.

"Denver Petroleum Club at 1:30 p.m. today?"

Alex looked at the time. "Didn't realize you were here."

"On the way to the hangar now. See you in a couple hours. You saved my life, Alex. I owe you one." Riggs Austin's deep voice was genuine.

"I'll be there."

She disconnected and turned to face her host.

"Did you hear what he said about Ferrell Brandt?" she asked Bull.

Bull looked stricken. "I'm so sorry I connected you to him. He sure fooled me and he came highly recommended from Nancy Parker."

"You were trying to help." She gave him an affectionate hug and silently wondered about Nancy Parker.

"What will you do about a lawyer?"

"I don't know, but Brandt won't get away with this! I have to go meet Riggs now." Alex slid her phone back into place and picked up her earphones.

Bull looked like a lost child. "Can I drive you home?"

"That would help a lot." He guided her through the house to the garage.

"Would you like to come over sometime soon?" Alex inquired as they drove through town.

"That would be my dream," he said, but his eyes were hollow.

In minutes, they were at the curb in front of her majestic office building.

He leaned over and put his lips on hers, lingering for a few precious moments. Alex liked the way she felt velvety soft inside when he kissed her.

"I gotta go." She left him to go up to her office, taking the stairs so she could think about what was about to happen.

It was such a challenge being female and at the same time being an entrepreneur, risk-taker, dealmaker, and all-in-one kind of business person. There were so many compartments to manage. Sometimes a compartment division leaked like a sieve, making her life messier than she wanted it to be.

Men didn't seem to face the same challenge. People and issues could be neatly filed away and then retrieved again at will. She, on the other hand, was both emotional and intense. One part of her was love-struck over Bull, and the other part of her was ready to skin Brandt alive with a rusty paring knife while they discussed conflict of interest.

Ferrell Brandt was supposed to be working for her and, if Riggs Austin was correct, he was really working for the Sloanes or himself and trying to steal the very life out of her company. Thanks to Riggs, she now knew the truth about Brandt. Alex boiled as she thought of the deceit. One signature and she might have lost the core holdings of her business. She hauled the stairwell door open on her office floor and strode into her office.

But the momentum had changed. Now, the truth gave her the upper hand and Brandt was still in the dark, not knowing she had discovered his plot. She intended to bide her time and strike back at the crooked lawyer when the moment was right.

CHAPTER 30

The Denver Petroleum Club lobby was appointed with fine antiques and dark leather furniture. Alex arrived, poured into a smart black suit. Her long shiny hair and chic attire made a billion-dollar presentation.

After taking the elevator to the restaurant, she found Riggs Austin waiting in an oversized club chair. His blazer and Western hat could have been borrowed from a John Wayne movie set. He dwarfed Alex as he stood to give her a one-armed bear hug. His other arm was still in a black sling.

"You sure you're an oilman?" Riggs teased.

"Just one of the guys." She placed a kiss on his cheek, then they followed the maître d' to a window table set with fine linen and delicate crystal.

"I took the liberty of asking my banker to join us," Riggs told her. "He has several business deals up here."

In seconds, a man in a brown suit arrived at their table.

Riggs made the introductions. "This is Ms. Sheridan. I would like you to meet Charlie Maxwell of Pentacle Bank in Texas."

"Nice to meet you. Riggs had only nice things to say, which I assure you is not the norm." He smiled and shook Alex's hand firmly. His genuine demeanor was comforting and sincere.

"My pleasure," Alex said.

"I think we have a mutual friend, Bull Hawthorn," the banker stated.

"Yes, Bull, is working on our well as we speak."

"He is a long-time client of ours." He smiled encouragingly at Alex, who was legend in their business.

She returned the smile. "Fire should be out soon."

"His wife just died, very sad situation."

"A tragedy," Alex concurred, wondering if the banker was trying to telegraph a message. He certainly seemed to know significant details about Bull Hawthorn.

A well-dressed waiter approached the table, offering to take their orders. "Nice to have you back, Ms. Sheridan."

"Scotch and soda here," said Riggs. "You want a drink, some wine?"

"Iced tea, please," Alex requested.

Riggs looked disappointed. "Come on; we're celebrating. Get something more interesting than tea."

"Glass of champagne," she conceded, changing her order. "Is there more information about Brandt?" She asked, not quite sure about the nature of the celebration; she still felt mired in quicksand.

Charlie ordered a gin and tonic.

Riggs smiled. "Charlie's going to arrange for whatever cash you need, and I'm going to co-sign the personal line of credit, if that works for you?"

"I can have the e-documents sent for your review," the banker said, patting the slim leather briefcase he'd brought with him.

Alex looked shocked. "I am overwhelmed and not sure what to say."

"You're worth the risk, and I'll make some money on the backend if we are successful." Riggs smiled with glee. "I refuse to let that rat Brandt try and steal your business."

"What's the interest rate?" asked Alex. This deal seemed too good to be true.

Charlie looked at some notes lying on the table. "One percent below prime."

"That the best you can do, Charlie?" Riggs teased, and chuckled. It was a dream rate, way below market, and the open line of credit would be a lifeline for the company.

After serving the drinks, the waiter retreated.

"Charlie needs your signature, but I'll just take a hug and a handshake," Riggs said proudly. "I respect your business prowess and, more important, I've seen how you react under fire." During the pandemonium at the oil and gas conference, while many were running for cover, Alex had calmly applied pressure to his bleeding gunshot wound. She stayed by his side in the line of fire, called for the paramedics, and made sure he was attended to.

Alex asked, "Any other terms?"

"Pay it back when you can." Riggs raised his glass. Alex and Charlie joined him in the toast and they all clinked glasses.

"You can count on it."

"You're a safe bet," said Riggs. They clinked glasses again.

"How did you know I was in trouble?" Alex asked, wanting to know what he had heard about her financial squeeze.

Riggs grinned. "Ferrell Brandt was trying to broker a big tract of land, some of it titled to your company."

Alex's jaw dropped open and her eyes widened. "What a weasel." Anger reignited and her rage burned.

"You told me in Dallas that you didn't want to sell. I smelled a rat."

Alex picked up her cell phone, then paused. "He won't get away with this!" Her mind raced. The lawyer was a thief.

"Fire his ass!" Riggs exclaimed.

The lunch arrived.

"I'm going to call Brandt and tell him our business is over," Alex said with satisfaction. "But that doesn't change the case the sheriff has against me."

"In fact, will you let me have the honors?" Riggs asked with a devilish glint in his eyes. "We'll deal with the sheriff after."

Alex looked surprised. "That's the least I can do."

"It will bring this old man a great deal of late-in-life happiness, if you don't mind."

"No time like the present." Alex dialed the number on her cell phone and placed it on speaker mode.

Brandt answered immediately.

"Alex, are you ready to sign?" The lawyer's anticipation vibrated through the phone.

"Not just yet. I'm having second thoughts."

"You have to sell to save your company," he said frantically. "You could go to jail."

"You are on speaker. I have someone here who wants to speak with you."

Riggs oozed confidence. "This is Riggs Austin."

The connection went silent. A few long seconds ticked by.

"What do you want?" Brandt hissed.

"Alex won't be needing your help anymore." Riggs sported a wide grin.

"Stay out of my business!" Hostility oozed from the lawyer's tone. "I'm her lawyer."

"I will have you disbarred!" Alex interrupted.

"You're my client!" Brandt howled.

"Not anymore," Alex said firmly. "You're fired."

"Go fuck yourself." Riggs disconnected the call with a satisfied smile. "Please excuse my French, but he only understands one language." They all laughed.

"I guess you've run into him before," Alex commented with a big smile.

"Not our first rodeo," he said.

Alex and Riggs toasted again and shook hands and, for the first time in weeks, she felt a sense of stability.

Driving Riggs to the airport gave Alex a few extra minutes to go over their financial arrangements and to thank him for the incredibly generous offer to provide a cash lifeline of credit for her company.

"I'm sorry you have to leave."

The older man tipped his hat to her. "I'll be back soon. Besides, there are some interesting deals we should consider."

"Like?"

"I want you involved in some of my developments if you agree. I think we could be good partners." He waved goodbye.

She pulled away, with just enough time to return to her office before heading to Boulder. Riggs Austin's help had turned the tide in her favor.

Back at Sheridan Enterprises, Alex hummed a tune and organized a few things in preparation for the drive to Boulder. With a smile, she picked up Ferrell Brandt's contracts and placed them on the shredder.

Now she could relax and enjoy the evening with Jake. The financial crisis had turned into a golden opportunity to do business with Riggs Austin. She was elated by the conversation and a bit in shock as the frightening consideration of having to sell her company turned into an association with Riggs. They could make a formidable team.

Fran, who never seemed to need to go home, called to Alex. "Carter's on the back line. He says it's urgent."

"I'll be right there." With the weight of the financial crisis lifted, Alex's voice was cheery and light. She picked up the landline. "Hi, Carter. Things are looking up."

"Are you sitting down?" Carter asked seriously.

"No, why?" A sense of foreboding smacked her cheeriness right in the face.

"I've been trying to reach you for hours."

"I have great news! I've been with Riggs Austin. He's going to back the company." The financial lifeboat that Riggs provided would allow her to survive the well fire and return money to fearful investors. Even if the well failed, her company would make it. "And we may do some deals together. It's amazing."

"I got some news from Glenwood." Carter sounded like a drowning man.

"What?" Alex felt the ominous weight in Carter's voice.

"You haven't spoken with Salido?" His voice was more somber.

"No, why?"

"Damn it! He told me he would call."

"He's not on our team, if you haven't noticed."

"The district attorney, Robert Portland, is going to bring the case against you to a grand jury."

Alex froze in place like a statue as the news sunk in. A red blotch broke out on her neck. Just moments before, she was reveling in fantastic news, but now she was looking at a possible murder charge. Apparently, it didn't matter that there was insufficient evidence to go forward with a case. The accusation alone would be damning, and her reputation could be destroyed. What investor would trust her with a murder charge hanging over her head? Riggs would probably change his mind about loaning her money.

"There's no evidence," she cried in disbelief.

"I know. There is no weapon, and they don't even know where he was killed."

"Did they get the dental records?"

His tone got even more serious. "No, it's a stab in the dark. Don't get scared."

"I'm screwed."

"They don't have enough evidence."

"Clearly that's not important," she said sarcastically.

"I don't understand why they are pressing so fast." Carter sounded perplexed. It seemed a rash action on the part of the DA. "Unless they have something we don't know about."

"I need a criminal lawyer," Alex said flatly.

"What about Brandt?"

"Turns out he's a crook," she muttered. "Who's the best defense attorney in Denver?"

"I'll ask Blue Davies. He's head of homicide and will know who to call."

"Thanks."

Carter paused, then added, "There won't be any defense or cross-examination in the grand jury hearing. The prosecutor presents the case alone. The jurors decide whether there is enough evidence to go forward with an indictment."

"So I can't even defend myself?" she asked, recognizing the fear in her voice.

"Not at this stage. It's all up to the DA to prove he has a case. I think he's fishing."

"Salido threw me under the bus." Alex believed Salido had sacrificed her because he had no other leads. It was easier to accuse her than to look for the real killer.

"There is another clue that might help your case," Carter said cautiously.

"What's that?"

"One of the protesters might have motive to sabotage the well."

Alex perked up. "How?'

"We're checking out a suspicious guy named Aaron Jeffries."

"He was at the well one day," Alex remembered.

Carter hesitated. "What I'm about to tell you is totally off-record and confidential."

"Why?" she asked, curious about his tone.

"You can't tell anyone."

"I promise."

"My friend Blue Davies at homicide broke every rule to get a background check," he said.

"I'm listening."

"Aaron Jeffries is Jeff Ashton."

"Jeff Ashton!" she shrieked in astonishment. "I saw his face—it can't be! Ashton is in jail."

"Somehow he bought his way out and was paroled with a new identity…he is a free man."

Alex began to pace. The news was lethal.

"It can't be him. He looks totally different."

"Surgery."

Jeff Ashton had murdered Christine Welbourne in cold blood, and he would have gotten away with the crime had it not been for Alex's testimony and Carter's tenacity. His venomous hatred following his murder trial and sentencing was directed at Alex. He promised he would one day kill her. If Carter was correct, if it was true that he had a new identity and was free, then Colt's death and the well explosion made sense. Ashton was ruthless, and no one was safe.

She took a couple of deep breaths to steady her heart rate. "You're sure?"

"I trust the source."

"I'll call Lafayette."

"I already let him know."

The news from Carter pounded in her head. She had hundreds of questions that probably couldn't be answered. One thing was certain—if anyone was capable of pulling off the stunt Carter described, it was Jeff Ashton. He had managed to fool Christine, a shrewd woman and great judge of character. He was not someone to be underestimated.

After saying goodbye to Carter, she started to call Salido. Fear and anger hit her like a poison dart. For a moment, she was the eleven-year-old girl hearing the news that her mother had died in a plane crash and would not be coming home. The feelings returned like a fever. Alex wanted to rip Salido apart for not having the decency to at least let her know what was coming down. But then she decided she'd better keep her mouth shut. She needed a lawyer before she spoke to anyone.

A huge lump formed in her throat, and the fragile part of her wanted to curl into a fetal position. Jeff Ashton had murdered her best friend in a cold and brutal execution in their office, effectively imploding their world. The loss left her untethered and afraid. She made sure he paid for the crime. She remembered vividly every word of her testimony, as well as his vicious promise of revenge. Knowing he was locked away was her only promise of safety, but he was not in jail, and she was not safe.

A different call had to be made. Alex reluctantly dialed Jake's number.

"Hi, it's me," she said, dreading the conversation.

"You on the way?"

"No, still in Denver," she told him.

"You'd better hurry. I have big fat steaks marinating."

"So sorry, Jake, something happened. I can't make it."

She could feel Jake's shoulders crumple through the phone but, before she could explain, he went on the offensive. "I'm not surprised. You don't know how to be a friend." The hurt in his voice stung her.

"I've had an unavoidable emergency, Jake." Alex wanted to tell him about Jeff Ashton, but she had promised Carter to keep it in confidence and she could not afford to say anything that might compromise her case. And only Carter and Lafayette would truly understand the depth of her fear. Carter knew that Ashton was fueled by a vendetta toward Alex.

"That sounds familiar." Bitterness dripped from his words.

"I should never have agreed to come. There is too much going on here."

"Your priorities are obvious."

Alex refused to engage and take the bait. She was not going to tell him about the call from Carter or her desperate need for a new lawyer, and it was becoming clear that any effort at friendship would be like trying to bottle the wind. Jake didn't want a friendship; he wanted her love and devotion.

"I treasure you, Jake, but I don't make you happy." She did not like making decisions under pressure but, if he wanted to force her hand, she would go ahead. Time had passed them by, and the elements that once brought them together were too painful.

"Good luck, Alex." It was a harsh goodbye.

"We'll talk soon."

The call ended like a slamming door, and a strange relief flooded through her like warm vodka. She felt a weight lift off her mind and heart. She needed to be safe in her lair, in her home, wherever that was, she thought. Home was a vaporous thing. Sometimes it was out on a well site. Other times, it was a modest, bare-essentials motel that felt like home. Tonight, it was her office.

Certainly it was a heart place rather than a locale, and tonight her restless heart was distracted by memories of lying in bed next to Bull Hawthorn.

CHAPTER 31

District Attorney Robert Portland perched at his desk, eating a prepackaged turkey sandwich from the mini-mart and reading the local papers. He still seethed over the controlling Ferrell Brandt. Surrounded by disheveled files, he scanned the Drudge Report on a tablet.

Slam! The door banged open and Sheriff Salido burst in with a raging glare and palpable anger filled the room. A picture fell from the wall, crashing to the floor.

"What the hell are you doing?" the sheriff demanded.

"What?" Portland looked baffled.

"You're taking the case against Alex Sheridan to the grand jury?" Salido yelled. The news had traveled like heroin through the departments and eventually reached the ears of Beverly Doyle, who was pleased to deliver the rumor to Salido.

Portland shrugged and walked over to pick up the fallen frame. "I think she's guilty."

"You should have had the decency to tell me first." Salido slammed his fist on Portland's desk.

"Thought it might piss you off, and I was right."

The sheriff fixed him with a baleful glare. "You can't prove it. We don't even have the dental records or a weapon."

"That's my problem." Portland turned his attention to his tablet to avoid the sheriff's rancor.

"This is wrong!" Salido argued.

"I don't see it that way."

"You're gonna lose."

"If they fail to indict, it's my issue." Portland looked smug, like he had secret information.

"I don't understand. Why are you rushing this?" The sheriff raked his hands through his hair in exasperation.

Portland produced a manila envelope that he opened slowly. Carefully he removed some photos. They were pictures of Alex Sheridan and Bull Hawthorn, partially dressed, in a hotel room.

"What is this?" Salido gawked.

"They were taken at the oil and gas symposium after Colt Forester went missing and the explosion. Alex hired this guy to help with the fire but it sure looks like they are more than friends."

"How did you get these?" the sheriff demanded.

"I have my sources. But this will play really bad for Alex Sheridan. No grieving lover here."

Salido said, "Maybe you're right…"

"You call me if there is any new evidence." Portland stood, indicating the debate was over.

Salido stormed out of the office.

Portland let out a breath and reached for his phone.

The call was picked up almost immediately. "I am presenting a case against Alex Sheridan to the grand jury."

"Good work. I'll let Ms. Sloane know." Brandt assured him the message would be delivered.

"I don't expect them to return an indictment." Robert Portland knew the weak case would probably be no-billed, but that was irrelevant—his assignment was to put pressure on and smear Alex Sheridan.

"A grand jury hearing followed by negative press will be a devastating blow."

"Rumors about Alex Sheridan will spread like a plague, regardless of the facts." Portland hoped this would be his final payback for taking the sticky money.

℘

Aaron Jeffries drove south on Interstate 25, the major freeway that serves as the north-south artery up and down the Front Range. The switched plates on the car he purchased in Denver allowed him to travel undetected. Even so, he watched his rearview mirror, sweating nervously as he drove through Colorado Springs. Pikes Peak loomed in the distance as he barreled toward Raton, New Mexico. Raton, with its plateaus and stark mountain vistas, would be an easy place to lie low if it became necessary, he thought. All he really wanted to do was disappear. He had negotiated with Brandt in his own currency. Blood and money had bought him a new start with a new identity. It was only a matter of hours and miles before his new life would finally begin. As he listened to music, he tried to relax.

From out of nowhere, flashing lights appeared in the rearview mirror, and the sound of a siren ignited fear in Jeffries. Adrenaline pumped through every cell, but he tried to stay composed.

Against his will, sweat formed on his brow and a volcano of bile rose in his stomach as he pulled over to the shoulder. The ferocious-looking squad car strobing red and blue parked behind him while he waited. An officer with the face of a boy walked up to his window. No more than twenty, maybe twenty-two years-old, he was armed and stern. His hand rested on the holster on his hip as he unsnapped the safety strap on his pistol.

"May I see your driver's license?"

"Yes, sir. How are you?" Trying not to tremble, Aaron Jeffries handed over the license. He watched the officer walk back to his squad car to run the details.

Jeffries considered his options. He could kill the man, but murdering a cop meant a death sentence. *Run! Run! Run!* His reptilian brain went into flight syndrome, but he suppressed the impulse. He had done nothing.

That didn't mean the sheriff in Carbondale hadn't put out an all-points bulletin for his arrest. The deputy had come to his cabin, and he feared they might be trying to connect him to the murder. Jeffries cursed Brandt and the Scott brothers. He had exchanged favors with them, an eye for an eye. In exchange for inflaming the protesters, the Scott brothers had received help with their permits from Nancy Parker—all part of Aaron's obligation to Brandt. Unfortunately, the project had blown out of control, leaving each one of them in a compromising situation.

But Aaron's circumstances were far more precarious than those of the others. No one had wanted a forest fire and the negative media attention, and no one was supposed to be dead. Fear riddled his mind.

Aaron wiped his brow and neck, nervously fingering his scar as he waited in the car on the edge of the busy highway with cars blowing by. If the cop moved to arrest him, he would have to act. On the seat, by his side and under a jacket, was a scalpel-sharp, deer-skinning knife. Part of the stainless steel blade was serrated. It was a frightening weapon he had learned to use with proficiency in prison, where there had been no alternative.

Minutes went by as he caressed the knife with sweaty fingers. He could remember with clarity the way the blade slid smoothly through flesh and bone. It was a weapon that offered a swift and silent solution. He moved the knife closer and held tightly to the grip under the jacket.

Looking in his rearview mirror, he saw the young officer step out of his squad car. Aaron prepared to lunge.

The officer appeared at Aaron's window. Aaron held his breath.

"Mr. Jeffries, you have a broken taillight," he said as he returned the driver's license.

Aaron felt the blood drain from his head. The whiff of terror slipped away as he tried to look calm and his grip relaxed. Silently, he cursed the jerk who had sold him the old car. He should have checked the vehicle more carefully. Anxiety had robbed him of his measured, disciplined ways.

"I'll get it fixed right away, sir."

The officer leaned down to look around the interior of the car for a moment. "Where you going?"

"Raton. I have a sick aunt there." His lies were as natural as breathing.

"That's too bad."

"I try to check on her." Aaron put the license back in the wallet.

The officer handed him a warning slip. "There's an Auto Zone in Raton."

"Thank you for the warning." He had to make it to the border with Mexico with his money and passport. Every day, hundreds of desperate illegal aliens risked their lives trying to cross into the United States.

Surely sneaking out would be easier.

He drove away knowing he had barely escaped detection.

In Raton, he pulled off the highway and evaluated his situation. He shook like a cold dog. Now there was a record of his location. He abandoned the car in front of a dollar store and called for a cab that took him to the bus station.

On Main Street in Carbondale, pedestrians walked dogs and window-shopped. JP Green rode in the official Garfield County SUV with Salido.

"Still no sign of Jeffries," Green remarked.

"Keep looking. He didn't evaporate," the sheriff said bitingly. Finding Jeffries was an urgent priority. His frustration over Portland's actions could not be contained, and he was furious that the DA had decided to proceed with the grand jury hearing against Alex Sheridan. It would make his department look inept if they went forward with half-baked evidence. Money and resources would be wasted, and they would all look like idiots.

Salido strode into the Black Nugget, where Carter and Lafayette waited in a booth in the back with large frosted margaritas.

"We can't find Jeffries." Salido reluctantly admitted the embarrassing situation. But he was so angry with the DA that he was willing to take help from anyone, including Carter.

"Where would he go?" Lafayette asked.

"I'd leave the country," Carter speculated, sipping from the salted glass.

"We have put out word with all the agencies and the southern border patrol."

"What's the DA in such a hurry for?" Carter asked casually.

"Damned if I know. Get me one of those." Salido pointed to the margarita as the waitress passed by.

"I can put the word out on my end," Carter offered.

"I'll let you know."

The front page of the morning newspaper boldly featured the district attorney's decision to proceed with presentation of evidence against Alex Sheridan to the grand jury. The other lead story was that Aaron Jeffries was now a "person of interest" in the Colt Forester murder case. The article emphasized that he was not wanted for anything, just a person who might have information about the murder. Salido knew that all the details provided by Carter had to be kept in confidence. Regardless, Aaron Jeffries was bombshell news feeding the hungry media.

Beaver Scott, reeking of cannabis and looking disheveled, sat reading the newspaper in the Comfort Inn bar in Carbondale. The story about Aaron Jeffries stared back at him.

"This is good news," he thought with relief.

He waited for the bartender to show up. It was late morning, and no one was drinking yet. Stump, the young bartender, arrived carrying a small stack of newspapers.

"A beer," Beaver ordered as he watched the news on the television mounted over the bar. The local station reported that one of the protesters, Aaron Jeffries, was wanted for questioning in connection to the sensational murder.

"Did the sheriff ever speak with you?" Beaver trolled Stump for new information.

"Yeah," Stump said proudly, standing a bit more erect. Being part of the investigation made him feel important. "He asked about the night Forester was in here." Stump confirmed what Beaver already knew.

"He ask about us?"

"Not too much. Just if you were here." Stump arranged glasses and tidied the bar as they spoke. "But I'm not supposed to talk to anyone."

"And?"

"I said yes."

The news station was now covering the well fire and the plans to put it out today since the forest fire was under control.

"Anything else interesting?" Beaver tried not to act overly curious. He slurped beer, wiping the leftovers on the back of a hairy hand.

"He asked a lot about that girl, but I didn't know much, and she wasn't here too long."

"Kind of late for a woman to come in alone?" He fingered his eyebrow hairs as he spoke.

"She dragged Forester out of here," Stump said with a smile.

Beaver downed the beer and placed twenty dollars on the bar.

"I'll get your change." Stump picked up the twenty.

"Keep it."

Jenny arrived early to work. The Red Rocks Diner was quiet and clean. She made coffee and wiped the counter tops, readying the restaurant for the day. The free local papers were delivered and stacked up in the entry to the diner. After pouring a coffee, she picked up the *Aspen Daily News*, which reported on anything eventful in the Roaring Fork Valley. There was a new person of interest in Colt's murder case.

Jenny could read between the lines. She knew that a person of interest was more than just a curiosity…there was something terribly wrong. Even more concerning was the story about Alex and the grand jury hearing. Jenny winced. She thought about running and hiding. Something had to be done.

First, her boss arrived, then several other employees showed up for work. The construction workers arrived like bats coming home to a cave. Shaking and distracted, she dropped a plate of food and forgot several orders.

"Are you okay?" a co-worker asked.

"Bad night."

The other girl put a hand on her shoulder. "I can cover for you if you need a break."

"Thanks."

Jenny smoked as she waited for the bus. The situation left her with no good choice. She stamped out her cigarette, berating herself for the nasty habit. She had tried and failed to stop on several occasions. She finally pulled out the business card and made a call.

"Sheriff's office," said Beverly Doyle, the doughy receptionist.

"Can I speak with Sheriff Salido?"

"Who's calling?" Beverly had been with the sheriff's office since time began, and everyone in town knew her. Several different sheriffs had come and gone during her tenure, but she had endured.

"Jenny Cartwright." Jenny was trembling. Her anxiety had become unbearable.

"Just a minute, please."

Jenny could picture where Beverly sat, right outside Salido's office, making her privy to most of the intimate details of what took place in his world.

"This is Sheriff Salido." His voice sounded gruff.

"Sheriff, I really need to talk to you. I forgot something when we spoke. Can we meet?" Jenny asked.

"Yes, I can meet you. Tell me where," he said.

Salido looked at his watch. It was late morning, and the tremor in Jenny's voice was concerning. He walked out to Beverly's desk. Her dependability and efficiency and, more important, her kindness toward Cathy, had been invaluable to Salido.

"Do we have anything to eat around here?" Salido asked, knowing Beverly usually brought sugary treats to the office.

"Homemade pumpkin bread." She presented the heaping platter to the sheriff as she beamed with pride.

"You know that's my favorite." He picked up two slices and took a large bite. He relished her baking skills.

"What did Jenny want?" Beverly asked innocently.

"She forgot to tell me something."

"What could that be?"

"Something about Beaver Scott. I'll find out."

She set the platter back down and looked up at him. "Do I need to pick up Cathy after school?"

He'd almost forgotten. "Oh, my God, yes. Can you go to the house after work?"

"Of course. I'll fix dinner for her and leave some for you in the oven."

"You're an angel." Salido said through a mouthful of bread. "This is amazing."

Jenny went home to her little trailer with the pink awning. With just a little time before she was due to meet the sheriff, she cleaned out her handbag and fidgeted. Finally, she picked up her phone.

"Hi, Trey, this is Jenny." Her voice quivered.

"How are you?" Trey inquired, his voice warm.

"I'm fine," she said, the way people say "fine" when they mean something else—usually terrible or not good, but definitely, not "fine."

"When are you coming back?" she asked, hoping he would return to Carbondale soon.

"You must be psychic." Trey chuckled. "Sometime later today, possibly. Not exactly sure of the time."

"I'm scared." She didn't know what else to say, willing him to understand how hard it was for her to admit it to him.

"Can you tell me what's going on?"

She took a deep breath. "No, but I am meeting with the sheriff in a while."

"I'll be there as soon as possible, and Jenny, you can trust me."

Beverly Doyle waited nervously at her desk in the sheriff's office. She shuffled papers, and organized and reorganized the drawer. She checked office supplies and the kitchen inventory. She answered emails. She checked the time obsessively as she anxiously awaited Salido's departure.

Salido finally picked up his hat and jacket.

"Bev, thanks a lot for helping out with Cath." He stopped by her desk on his way out.

"She's a joy," Beverly said, smiling.

She waited two minutes before making a call. Sweat formed in her arm pits as she delivered the alert: "Beaver, Jenny called, and she's meeting with the sheriff."

Beverly had known the Scott brothers for years, and her son had done manual jobs for them up at the greenhouses. They had been decent to her boy and had given him work when there were no other jobs. Enabling her son had been a pattern for years. The fact that he could not stop smoking pot was part of the reason he rarely held a job. He lived in the back of her house when he came home and was basically a bum except for the part-time work he did grooming marijuana plants.

Jenny, looking particularly gaunt, sat on a picnic table on a small side street by a taqueria in Carbondale. The inconspicuous table was under a bushy tree off an alley. While she waited for Salido, she smoked nervously. She thought about what she knew and what she had seen, and all the vows and promises and pretenses. She searched the area but saw no cars. She sipped a Diet Coke and worried about how much to tell the sheriff. Again, she carefully surveyed the area, hoping the random meeting would go unnoticed.

Sheriff Salido turned his squad car off Highway 82 and onto Highway 133, the main route in and out of Carbondale.

Beaver spotted the squad car from his look-out at the Valero gas station. He eased into the lane to trail him, following Salido onto Main. He passed the Black Nugget and went down to 3rd Street and turned left. Beaver watched the car pull up in front of the taqueria, following just close enough to observe the meeting. Salido slid out of the squad car and went over to the table.

Beaver spotted Jenny, and his left eye began to twitch as his face turned purple-red. He raised his binoculars and watched Salido sit down and talk with Jenny. The magnification allowed him to see the nervous twitches on the waitress's face but he could not hear what she said.

After about twenty minutes, Jenny got in the squad car with Salido and they drove away. Beaver followed in the shadows and saw Salido drop Jenny off at the diner.

The sheriff drove away, and Beaver watched Jenny hurry back into the diner, clutching her purse and waving to the other waitress as she headed to the back. He didn't know what she'd told Salido, but he knew it had to do with him, and he knew she should know better.

CHAPTER 32

As the sun crept over the eastern Colorado horizon, Alex woke up with Bull lodged in her mind. She had deflected his call the night before, but now she was anxious to hear his voice. She texted a flirtatious good morning note:

You kept me awake all night.

In seconds Aretha belted out a tune from her phone.

"Good morning," Bull said. "I woke up thinking about you, too, and it was so nice." There was a sleepy, seductive tone to his morning voice.

"Are you bringing coffee?" she asked coyly.

"Starbucks at your command."

"Just kidding," she said, laughing. "I'm over my caffeine limit already."

"Just spoke with the team; we're going to have the fire out today," he said confidently. "If everything cooperates."

"I'll be there."

There was a short pause before Bull said, "I don't usually come to these, but thought I might ride over with you?"

"I'll set it up with Trey." Alex's heart tap-danced to the news. "We will probably stay over. I want to spend some time with Wayne and the team."

"I'm with you."

"They've been working around the clock." Alex slipped out of bed and headed toward the bathroom, already thinking about what she needed to take.

"My guys could use some appreciation. It will be nice to surprise them," he said.

The prospect of putting an end to the well fire lightened Alex's heart. If the well could be capped, they had a chance of salvaging the project.

Moments later, she was on the phone with her pilot.

"Trey, what's the weather like?"

He sounded like he'd already been up for hours. "Just checked—we can pick our way around the clouds."

"Let's leave as soon as possible." She turned on the shower and grabbed a large gray towel.

"I'll be ready in twenty-five minutes," Trey said.

"Cross your fingers. This might be the day we put the fire out."

"Let's hope it works."

Trey texted the flight schedule and news of his arrival to Jenny's cell phone, which vibrated with the incoming message.

She responded within a minute:

I would feel safer if you and Brutus stayed at my place tonight.

Trey almost danced a jig. His heart pounded with delight. She wanted them to stay.

He replied:

Will do.

Lafayette drove into an ugly section of North Denver. He had returned from Carbondale to handle an urgent personal matter, responding to the call no one wants to get. His would-be daughter-in-law had overdosed on heroin and was in critical condition in the city hospital. The prognosis was poor. That was bad news—but worse, she had a little girl, his son's daughter, and the baby had been left with someone in a crack house where she had been staying.

279

Lafayette parked the sedan and studied the building with its busted windows. He was intimidating in his bowler hat and long black trench coat. He walked with purpose, ignoring the graffiti, dirt, plastic bottles, and weeds that made the place a wasteland. Street gutters were filled with broken beer bottles and cigarette butts. It was only ten or fifteen minutes from Alex's office, but it felt like a third-world country war zone. The sadness and anger on the soulless faces of people lying in doorways or leaning against buildings tore at his heart. He had one thing in mind, one mission, and that was to find the little girl and keep her until her mother could recover.

He beat on a door, but no one answered. He knocked again, more forcefully. Finally, a young black man in a Broncos cap opened it a sliver.

"What you want?"

Lafayette straightened to his full, impressive height. "I'm looking for my grandbaby. They took the mother to the hospital."

Slits that were almost eyes failed to focus. "Man, I don't know." His eyes rolled in his head.

Carrying a long metal pipe in his left hand, Lafayette pushed past him and walked down a low-ceilinged, narrow hallway. Half-conscious bodies were in rooms in different stages of delirium. The smell of urine and hopelessness permeated the building. He opened a door, interrupting a couple having sex, and the man yelled at him to get out.

In the back room of the dilapidated building, an emaciated woman sat listing at a Formica table. Pint bottles of cheap vodka were her companions.

"I'm looking for Tashiba's baby," Lafayette said in a commanding tone.

"Tashiba's not here." The words slurred out. Long bony fingers gripped a bottle. Lafayette snatched it away.

He slammed his hand on the table. "Where's the baby?" he demanded.

The woman's pupils were dilated as she swayed in the chair. "Try next door." She spit brown liquid in a cup.

He burst out the back door and past a mangled chain link fence with no gate. Trash bins overflowed with debris, giving off a putrid odor. He entered the adjacent building, moving cautiously. A young girl was passed out on a sofa. Her eyes popped open in terror as he shook her.

"Where's the baby? Tashiba's baby?" he demanded.

Just then, he heard a whimper.

The sound led him to a room off the kitchen where a man lay in a fetal position on a dirty blanket on the floor. Lafayette closed the door as another whimper sounded. He opened a door leading into a pantry filled with trash. On the floor in the middle of the garbage, the baby, about ten months old, played with a Coke can. When she saw Lafayette, a large smile spread across her face.

Lafayette grabbed the baby and lifted her up to him like a doll. His son had fathered the little girl before he died in the crossfire of a drug bust. The mother, an addict, was now on the edge of purgatory. Lafayette had not seen the young woman since his son died, but then he had heard about Samantha, the baby. He recognized his face in hers...she had his eyes and smile.

"Come on, sweet girl, let's get out of here." Her innocence and loving eyes were heart-piercing. Together they ascended out of the hellhole.

Later that day, Lafayette sat at the computer in a spare office at Sheridan Enterprises. Papers surrounded him. Articles were pinned to the wall, making a storyboard. His theory about the case had been incubating for some time and pieces of the puzzle were now falling into place.

Samantha, in a clean jumper and blue hair bow, played on the floor under the desk. Toys and a few stuffed animals kept her happily occupied.

Carter erupted into the office and stopped short. "Who's that?" he asked in surprise.

"Her mother's in the hospital...drugs."

"But who is she? Where's her family?"

Lafayette looked down at the little girl, smiling proudly. "I'm her family. She's Jeremiah's child."

Carter was painfully close to the tragic loss of Lafayette's son Jerry, who had been buried in late winter just seven months before. Lafayette had tried to be a role model to his only son, but his years away in prison had made it difficult.

Carter leaned in the doorway. "What are you going to do with her?"

"I don't know." Lafayette smiled a big wide grin. "Guess she's on the team."

"If you say so." Carter smiled. "Just remember, I can barely take care of Tom, my tom cat; little girls are way beyond my pay grade."

Carter looked at the photos and papers that Lafayette had organized in the office. "What's all this?"

Lafayette motioned him over. "Thought you might find this interesting."

Ferrell Brandt's picture and name were everywhere. Exhaustive research had unearthed a patchwork of information of Brandt's undercover life. He had crossed paths with everyone from Aaron Jeffries to Nancy Parker, to the powerful Senator Bill Bridgeforth, Christine Welbourne's former lover. His tracks were neatly disguised inside LLCs and shell corporations, but they incriminated the lawyer.

"Wow!" Carter exclaimed.

Lafayette handed him a list of contributions made by Brandt.

"He's in bed with some incredibly powerful people," Carter said.

"Alex said he had a conflict of interest and, of course, she was so angry she turned purple. You know that look." They laughed.

"So I thought I would dig deeper." Lafayette continued to explain his theory.

Lafayette had dredged up many sordid details on Brandt. References to him working with the consultant Nancy Parker were unearthed, links to the governor and, coincidentally, it all circled back to entities controlled by the Sloane family.

Alex stuck her head in the office. "I'm heading out with Trey. Wish us luck."

"Y'all will get it out," Carter said encouragingly.

Abruptly, she stopped. "What's this?" She was looking at a photo of Brandt.

Looking around the war room, she saw the plethora of data on the sleazy lawyer. She stared in awe at the documents, devouring the information. Brandt had been named in numerous suits, but his legal prowess and unlimited cash had enabled him to weasel out of every indictment. "What a crook."

"He's the front for some scary, powerful people." Lafayette found mention of companies owned by the Sloanes and, in every one, Brandt was either an officer or the manager of the LLC.

"I'll see him in jail if it kills me," she pledged defiantly.

Lafayette saw the first blotch erupt on her neck.

"Go put out the fire. We'll take care of Brandt."

Just then, Alex noticed the beautiful little girl under the desk. Samantha looked at her with big dark eyes and raised her hands, gesturing to be picked up.

"Who are you, pretty girl?" Alex asked, bending over to pick up a smiling Samantha.

"That's Sam. I'm...well...she's my granddaughter. She's mine." Then a smile as broad as West Texas spread across Lafayette's face. He was so proud he felt almost embarrassed. How could the instinct to love and protect be so instant and deep, he wondered?

Fran poked her head in the room. "The hospital is on the phone for you, Lafayette."

Lafayette felt the cryptic news immediately. He took the phone and listened.

"Her mother is dead," he announced after the call ended. His face was somber.

Alex turned to her assistant. "Fran, please make sure we have everything Lafayette needs. We can set up a nursery in an extra office, if that's okay with you?"

Alex handed Samantha back to Lafayette, who put her back to play with her toys. "Let's use the empty one down near your office."

"God, I hope they let me keep her."

"We will all make sure that happens," Alex said forcefully.

"This will be fun," Fran said, kneeling to say hello to Samantha. The friends at Sheridan Enterprises were a close-knit team that knew prosperity and adversity. They knew how to form an impenetrable line of defense. "You're going to learn all about drilling oil wells."

Alex took Lafayette by the hand, leading him out into the hall.

"When we get this fire out, we will need to find Jeffries." The seriousness in her voice was unmistakable.

"I'm on it."

"The police may not find evidence, but I know he's dangerous." The words stuck in her throat and Lafayette heard fear.

"We'll find him."

She nodded. "I'm off to the well."

Lafayette joined Carter back in the war room. Carter picked up an article about Mack Sloane and the Sloane family. Ferrell Brandt was quoted in it.

"This is great work!"

Lafayette said, "I read something in the paper that this Brandt guy was working for some high-powered oil people. But you told me he was supposed to be defending Alex. Well, I started digging. He also did work for the deceased senator, Bill Bridgeforth, as did Jeff Ashton, now Aaron Jeffries, who murdered Chris. Sure seems like a lot more than coincidence." There were lines connecting all the people, and they all intersected at Ferrell Brandt.

"You're a genius." Carter looked impressed by the organization of the information Lafayette had unearthed. "Brandt is dangerous."

"I think we should pay him a surprise visit," Lafayette suggested. "He probably knows where Jeffries is hiding."

Carter looked up. "Where is he?"

"He lives and operates from a suite at the Brown Palace Hotel, but there's no answer when I call."

Lafayette had developed into a first-class investigator. His sense about people was uncanny. He had studied human behavior for years in Tucker Prison, and he had observed thousands of people that had come in and out of the Brown Palace during his days as the head doorman. Few details escaped him.

"What are we waiting for?" Carter asked with an impish smile. "Let's go have a drink at the Brown Palace."

Carter and Lafayette left Samantha safely perched on Fran's lap.

CHAPTER 33

The streets of Denver were filled with casually dressed business people coming and going from work. Carter and Lafayette made their way in silence to the landmark Brown Palace Hotel. It brought warm memories and a smile to Lafayette's face.

"Been a while since I held the door here." It was his job as the doorman of the Brown Palace that had brought his life into Alex Sheridan's orbit. They had been connected ever since.

The two men walked into the inviting, elegant lobby of the 19th-century hotel where patrons relaxed on period furniture.

Entering the ancient elevator that ferried them to the 12th floor, they approached the massive doors and knocked at the suite where Ferrell Brandt ran his empire.

Lafayette knocked harder, but there was no answer. Calls to Brandt's phone continued to go to voicemail. After they returned to the lobby, Carter called his friend at the Denver Police Department.

"Hey, Blue, I'm trying to surprise the suspect we discussed. Any luck with the warrant?"

His friend hesitated, then said, "I talked to the judge about Brandt."

Carter had already alerted Blue to the situation. Blue knew how to get a search warrant faster than any cop in the city, and he had a pipeline to a judge who signed his warrants.

Carter and Lafayette waited patiently in the lobby where a pair of older ladies with stiff-set hair sipped tea and ate biscuits. Businessmen came in and out like the tide.

Blue Davies and two uniformed cops soon arrived at the Brown. Blue was a large man with a shaved head and dark, neatly trimmed eyebrows. The men shook hands warmly and introductions were hastily made.

"The manager hasn't seen him all day," Carter explained.

"Okay, we'll look inside." Blue, search warrant in hand, led the way with a confident stride. He was a bold man, a veteran Special Forces Marine, and Carter trusted him. "But don't be surprised if he's gone. These types are slippery."

"We just want to ask him a few questions," Carter said.

"He's connected to the killing in some way?" Blue inquired.

"He's connected in a hundred ways, but there's still no hard evidence like prints or a gun."

The officers, Carter, Lafayette, and the hotel manager headed up in the ancient elevator.

Blue understood the circumstantial evidence as well as anyone. As a veteran homicide detective, he was intricately familiar with the ropes.

"Have they located that Jeffries guy yet?" he asked. His blue eyes were large and clear.

"The person of interest has disappeared."

"How convenient." Sarcasm dripped off every syllable.

Carter shot him a look. "Coincidence?"

"Funny how that happens."

"I think we were getting a bit too close for comfort and, in some way, I believe this lawyer is a link."

After exiting the elevator, they went to the entry of Brandt's suite and knocked forcefully.

"Mr. Brandt!" one of the officers called out. "Police, open the door."

Blue checked the door for scratches or signs of a forced entry, but there was no obvious evidence. The hotel manager used a master key to open the large double doors that swung in slowly. It was dark and quiet. Blue turned on a wall switch, illuminating the large reception area.

"Mr. Brandt, police!" he shouted into the void. "Mr. Brandt?"

After a few seconds he said, "Don't touch anything and watch where you walk." Blue ordered his colleagues to put on gloves and an officer to stand guard at the entrance. Nothing obviously sinister stood out.

A half-empty dark green champagne bottle rested on the coffee table with two glasses. Both glasses were partially filled and one had lipstick stains. A large faux fur throw was stretched out on the floor in front of the westward-facing windows, and the mountains stared back at them like silent voyeurs. Under the coffee table, a red thong with black lace lay on the floor. It was balled up inside out as if it had been removed quickly.

"Mr. Brandt?" Blue called again. Carter, Blue, and Lafayette walked through the office.

With care, they opened a door that led from the main sitting room into an ornate bedroom. A king-sized poster bed with scrolled carving dwarfed the chamber. Above the bed, the ceiling was covered with beveled mirrors. Trapeze cords dangled from the ceiling. Sex toys and paraphernalia rested on the bedside table.

Blue reached over and looked at the golden rope that was attached to pulleys in the ceiling. "Playtime."

The men snickered. The rumpled bed sheets had been well used, but nothing appeared sinister. In the bathroom, an open bottle of Viagra sat on the counter. Blue snapped a few photos and took notes. They opened drawers and examined closets, but nothing ominous appeared.

Back in the living room, another door led into a private office. They entered the dark room, and Blue felt for the lights.

At the desk, Brandt sat in his chair, slumped over the keyboard in front of the computer. He wore a navy velvet smoking jacket and his bald head stared back at them from a puddle of blood.

"Whoa!" Lafayette exclaimed as the lights came on.

A large, elegant letter opener was buried in the side of Brandt's neck. Only the handle, inlaid with semi-precious stones, was visible. The weapon had severed the carotid artery and Brandt had bled out in minutes.

Carter snapped a photo of the dagger and the bloody scene around the desk.

"Just about to get ripe." Blue covered his nose with a handkerchief. He called for a crime scene team.

"I can't smell anymore...too many murder cases." Numbness had been a blessing to Carter. The smell of death and body fluids was pungent, but Brandt had not been dead long enough to attract the neighbors.

"Don't touch anything," Blue reminded everyone, "and watch the blood."

"Must have pissed off the wrong guy," Carter mused as he studied the room. Accolades and framed awards were strategically arranged in the well-organized office. He took note that the safe door was closed. There was no apparent theft.

"Or woman. Don't forget those panties and gender equality," Blue reminded him. "Equal scrutiny for all." He chuckled at his own joke.

"Approached him from behind," Lafayette commented. "Very neat. There was no struggle."

"Like he never saw it coming," Blue added.

Lafayette had brought his own gloves and was searching for clues. He examined the papers lying on the desk and credenza, then those in an open file drawer. There were several files on the Sloane family.

Blue spoke into his phone. "Get the coroner over here," he ordered one of the officers.

Carter touched the computer mouse, bringing up Brandt's emails. He saw a message from Alex's email address. It was a scathing letter threatening to sue him for conflict of interest. Carter closed the screen and busied himself looking around the office.

"Carter, if you think this is part of the Colt Forester murder, it's Salido's case," Blue reminded him.

"But it's yours for now."

In moments, a team of professionals arrived. Carter shook hands with the coroner, a well-worn member of the homicide investigative family. Two officers were posted at the entrance to the apartment.

Carter and Lafayette watched as the coroner and his associate examined the body. The hands were bagged and hundreds of photos were taken. The officers took samples of everything while Blue made sure the crime scene wasn't compromised. Murder was his specialty, and managing a crime scene was his expertise. The body was eventually removed and the process of dusting for prints began. Luminal spray would reveal vital information. Finally, yellow tape was put across the door.

Lafayette looked at Carter. "This is tied to Colt."

"Yeah, but how?"

CHAPTER 34

The flight over to Glenwood Springs was bumpy and nauseating, but Trey avoided the worst turbulence and ensured a safe arrival. The chopper fluttered down to where Wayne Decker waved from a waiting truck. Decker had driven down early, anxious to take them to the well to see the team attempt to extinguish the fire.

After giving Alex a good-luck hug, Trey said goodbye. "I'll meet you up there later." He got into a truck and turned toward Carbondale and Jenny.

Trey sang along to a country rock tune as he drove up Highway 82. At the main entrance to Carbondale, he pulled off the highway and into the parking lot of the Red Rocks Diner. Even though she wouldn't get off until much later, he wanted to see Jenny. The diner was packed. Trey waited in the crowded entry until Jenny noticed him.

With a big smile, Trey reached to embrace her, but she stood soldier straight, looking formal and slightly embarrassed.

"Hi, Jenny."

"Hi. I don't get off for a while." She smiled at him. "Glad you're here." Her eyes darted around the room as they stood awkwardly in the entry.

"Can I leave Brutus at your place while I go back up to the well?"

Jenny nodded. "Sure. The key is under the pot by the front door. I'll check on him as soon as I get off."

Not wanting to further embarrass her, he slipped out quietly.

The sign to her community was modest. In the mobile home park, he found the key and entered the small trailer. After filling a dog bowl with water, he left Brutus sitting on the sofa. "I'll be back. You're in charge."

৩০

On the way to the well, Bull and Wayne discussed the strategy for the well. Smoke still billowed in the distance.

"Do you think it will work?" Alex asked with an edge to her voice. This was a monumental endeavor. If the fire could be extinguished, then the company could move in a positive direction. As long as it burned, they were in trouble with everyone.

"I am counting on it," Bull said casually. This path, he had walked many times. He was confident in his crew. His entire team had worked around the clock, waiting for the winds to die down. Now it was time.

At the well site, an army of men and equipment was assembled. Bull walked up to one burly man and gave him a huge bear hug. He shook hands and slapped backs. Several of the men gave him a brief tour of the site. Clearly, they were excited to have the owner at their project. It was an honor for them that he was present.

Bull spoke to each man and complimented him on the job.

A manager in a hard hat came over and reviewed the plan with Bull and Alex.

"You ready to shut this baby down?"

"We were waiting on you." He handed Bull a hard hat. Finally, it looked like all the pieces of the puzzle were in place.

Electric anticipation filled the air. Thousands of gallons of water continued to spray the well.

As everyone got into position, Alex and Wayne stood back and out of the way. At this moment, they were simply bystanders. Extra firefighters were there to watch, just in case there was some emergency. Alex put on ear protectors and a hard hat while they waited. Would they succeed?

At the last minute, Salido arrived. Alex had not seen him since she had heard about the DA's decision to call for a grand jury, but she ignored him.

A warning signal sounded. Bull's engineers had decided to use dynamite, which would blow out the fire by forcing the burning fuel and oxygen away from the fuel source. Explosives placed in fifty-five-gallon drums were surrounded by fire-retardant chemicals, and the drums were wrapped with insulating material. Off to the side was a horizontal crane that would be used to lower the drum filled with dynamite toward the wellhead. All the team members anxiously prepared for the explosion.

Bull stood off to the side, admiring the organization of his team. The biggest danger would come immediately following the charge. They had to cap the wellhead before a spark caused another, even greater fire. The fuel was extremely volatile.

As they anxiously observed, the crane lifted the drum above the fire. Everyone hoped the technique would succeed. Slowly, the drum was lowered as water sprayed the area. Closer and closer it moved into the fire.

A massive explosive charge went off, sucking the oxygen out of the air. Thousands of gallons of water were directed at the wellhead, and huge amounts of drilling mud were pumped below the surface into the pipe to alleviate the pressure and stop the flow of gas.

While water rained on the scene, men scurried to secure the well to prevent re-ignition. Equipment was moved away from the wellhead. It was an awe-inspiring moment.

They all waited, holding their breath. The fire was out. Cheers erupted as people jumped up and down.

After the well was stabilized, Bull came over to congratulate the team.

Alex focused on Wayne, who had been the constant stabilizing force during the crisis. When Bull's team was brought in to take over the crisis, Wayne had ably managed the situation and kept the men pulling in the same direction. All the men respected his wisdom and leadership. She gave Wayne a high five and a warm hug as many from the team shook hands and patted backs.

Sheriff Salido stood off to the side, clearly pleased that the disaster was ending. Alex didn't want to spoil the moment with a confrontation with Salido, who seemed to appreciate her position. Out of the corner of her eye, she saw Salido approaching, his Smoky the Bear hat in hand. "Congratulations on putting the fire out."

Alex looked toward Bull.

"Good men and a team effort," she responded.

Salido shuffled awkwardly from one foot to another. "Just for the record, I did not recommend taking your case to the Grand Jury."

"Just for the record, I don't believe you." Alex walked away.

He watched her leave, his shoulders slumped.

Alex and Wayne sat on the back of the pickup with Bull and some of his men. She leaned over and gave Bull a spontaneous hug and kiss.

Trey appeared, carrying a large cooler filled with cold beer.

"It's about time!" one of the men yelled. Two young hands jumped up, took the cooler from Trey, and started tossing bottles and cans to the men, who were ready to celebrate. They were hot, tired, and triumphant.

Darkness was winning the battle for the night sky, as the sunset became wild with pink and orange. Despite their diversity, they were united members of the same team. Several young guys were college graduates working to gain experience in the oil fields. Others were seasoned career laborers. Gustavo, a Hispanic jackhammer of a man, had been with Wayne and Alex for years.

Bull's men were the same kind of family of hardworking, tough, honorable men. Together they all drank beer, told stories, and reminisced about putting out fires. Smiles and relief animated their faces in the atmosphere that was thick with pride and honor.

This was their athletic field. They were a team, and putting out the fire was like winning the Super Bowl. The huge accomplishment reminded Alex of her father and the way she always felt on well sites. This was where she most belonged, where her heart and head and soul were connected. Her family was this group of hardworking men who understood one another, regardless of their origins.

"We're staying over tonight?" Trey clarified the plans with Alex.

"Yes, rooms are booked at the Comfort Inn."

"The chopper is secured." He pulled Alex off to the side. "Would you be willing to meet Jenny?" His face was creased in a deep frown.

"Sure; why?" Trey rarely asked Alex for anything. He was always available. Known for her devotion and loyalty to her business family, Alex welcomed an opportunity to help Trey.

"I think she knows something about Colt's murder, but she's frightened."

"Of what?" Alex's brows formed a frown. The murder case was serious, and she was in the sights of the sheriff and the district attorney. If Jenny knew anything about Colt or the case, she needed her help.

"She's been too scared to say, but she might talk to you."

"Okay, as soon as I say goodbye to the guys." Alex nodded and moved toward the large group of men, wanting to offer her personal thanks again for a job well done.

Alex offered a few more thanks to the men who were still celebrating the success. She thanked Wayne for all his help as she again congratulated the team from Wild Well and waved goodbye. Then she meandered over to Bull and pulled him aside.

"I need to go to town and tend to something."

"Y'all save a cold one for me. I'll be right back," Bull said to his elated group.

He walked her to the truck, squeezing her hand affectionately. "Will I see you later?"

"I hope so. I'll call when I'm on my way back to the motel. Thank you!" She kissed him warmly on the cheek.

Trey and Alex climbed in the truck and drove together out of the mountains. It was a tedious, bumpy ride until they reached the blacktop and turned onto the highway toward Carbondale. A low-slung moon rested lopsided in the evening sky.

CHAPTER 35

Just after eight that evening, Jenny returned home to the pink awning and Brutus snoring. Her legs ached from long hours serving hungry customers. She walked to the bathroom and turned on the hot water to run a bubble bath and freshen up in anticipation of Trey's arrival. An internal war raged throughout the long day until there was nothing left to fight. Every instinct urged her to run, but she finally overcame her terror. Her talk with the sheriff provided temporary relief. At least part of the truth was out and, more important, she was excited that Trey was coming to see her. It was a new friendship, but knowing that he cared had given her courage. A tiny bud of hope sprouted in her arid world.

A knock on the door made her jump. Trey was early! Quickly, she turned off the water.

"I'm coming. Just a sec." With excitement, she glanced in the mirror. There had not been time to clean up, but she was euphoric. She quickly sprayed on some perfume and put on fresh lip color. She patted Brutus, then moved to the door.

"I'm coming," she said again as she unlocked the deadbolt.

Slam! The door burst open and sent her sprawling against the wall. Beaver Scott stood in the door with a baseball bat in one hand and rage in his eyes. His face was purple-red, as if he were about to explode.

Jenny let out a guttural scream as Beaver swung the bat. She ducked and ran toward the back of the trailer. Beaver stepped in, bolting the door behind him. Brutus jumped up and growled as he followed Jenny into the bedroom.

Jenny bolted the door just before Beaver could force his way inside.

"Open this door!" Beaver roared.

She fumbled with the phone with shaking fingers and dialed Trey, but the call went to voicemail.

"Help me. Hurry!" She left the terrified message.

Crack! The bat crunched against the door. Beaver swung it again.

"What did you tell the sheriff?" he yelled. "I told you I'd kill you."

Jenny wedged the rubber doorstopper under the door. The small window in the bedroom had security bars on the outside, preventing any entry or escape.

The second swing cracked the thin wood veneer. Brutus growled and barked as Jenny pushed a dresser in front of the door. She reached in the back pocket of her jeans, retrieving the sheriff's card. Trembling, she dialed the number.

The next swing cracked through the top of the door. Jenny screamed as the sheriff answered.

"Help me!" Jenny screamed again. "My trailer!"

From his squad car, Salido radioed JP Green. "Meet me at the trailer park, pronto!" The siren blared with flashing lights as he raced toward Jenny's at breakneck speed. The tires of the squad car squealed onto the highway as he swerved past cars headed back toward Carbondale. A startled deer jumped onto the road. He swerved, barely missing the guardrail, then steered back onto the road and continued. He radioed to law enforcement officers in Carbondale, alerting them about the incident. Still minutes away, he prayed like hell that nothing happened to Jenny.

Trey and Alex drove along the road in front of the diner, heading toward Jenny's, when the delayed message from Jenny's cell came through to Trey's phone.

"Someone's after Jenny." Trey hit the gas, tires spinning and rubber burning, accelerating as fast as he could.

Orange construction cones blocked one lane on Highway 133. He stamped on the brakes hard, throwing Alex forward. Several trucks moved in slow motion while Trey honked the horn. He dodged around one car and bullied his way past a dawdling pickup as he maneuvered the truck at a dangerous speed down the shoulder.

The light was red at the main intersection. Cars and pedestrians meandered, almost motionless. He honked again, running the light. They raced down the road to the entry of the trailer park. The tires screeched as the truck took out a trashcan, swerving around to the trailer. In a back corner where few would notice, a worn pickup truck was parked off to the side. The front porch light was off at Jenny's, and it was pitch black.

Before the truck was all the way in park, Alex catapulted onto the front porch. The locked door wouldn't budge. Trey, right behind her, jerked at the knob, but the deadbolt refused to give. Suddenly, he remembered the pot. He kicked it over, but the key was gone.

"I'll go around back." Trey jumped off the porch, racing to the back entrance of the trailer.

A terrified scream came from inside the small home. Alex threw her shoulder against the front door, trying to force the knob. She desperately slammed against the door, to no avail. She had the heart of a warrior, but no brawn. She tried the front window, but it was locked. Finally, she dug in her bag and retrieved the Colt .45.

Beaver broke through the door to the bedroom. The dresser had done little to stop his assault. He raised the bat, swinging wildly at Jenny. The near-miss allowed her to scramble out of the way.

Brutus, the forceful tank, growled and ferociously bit Beaver's leg in his shark-like jaws. Beaver howled an agonizing scream. The bulldog snarled, holding on with razor-sharp fangs. Beaver raised the bat and brought it down hard on the dog's head. Brutus whined but bit down harder.

The bone-deep bite was excruciating. Beaver desperately tried to get the dog off his leg, which was spewing blood. In the split second that he looked down at Brutus, Jenny picked up a large glass vase filled with thousands of pennies. She swung the heavy vessel with mighty force, hitting Beaver square in the head. The glass shattered, coins flying everywhere.

As Beaver rocked back, dazed from the blow, blood spurted from a deep gash and ran down his face.

୨୦

On the front porch, Alex fired at the lock and broke through the front door. Terrified screams still came from the back of the dark house. She fumbled for a light switch as Trey burst through the back door. Alex ran into the bedroom with her gun drawn.

Beaver, still standing, with blood streaming down his face, managed to lift the bat high in the air and bring it down hard on Brutus, who whimpered and crumpled.

"Put it down," Alex ordered, gun trained on Beaver.

Beaver, startled at her command, raised the bat again, swinging at Alex. She stepped back just out of reach.

"Drop it or I'll shoot."

Beaver's nightmarish face looked like a vision from a chainsaw movie. Again, he swung the bat at Alex.

Alex fired. The shot hit Beaver in the upper torso, knocking him back. The bat fell to the floor. As he stumbled backward, Jenny grabbed the bat. She raised it overhead and hit him ferociously across the neck and back. She swung again, scoring a direct hit that took him to the ground. With determined anger in her eyes, Jenny raised the bat again.

Trey lunged forward, catching the bat in full swing. He pulled the bat out of Jenny's hand as she slumped to her knees, crying. Trey knelt to comfort her while Alex examined Brutus, who lay motionless on the floor with blood oozing from his nostrils.

A siren sounded and a deluge of officers and vehicles swarmed the house. Sheriff Salido and Deputy Green, flanked by the Carbondale police chief, burst into the small mobile home. They found Alex, Jenny, and Trey in the bedroom.

"He tried to kill Jenny," Alex blurted, breathing hard.

Beaver was bleeding from the nose and gunshot wound and had cuts on his head and face from the broken vase. Blood splatter peppered the room.

"You're under arrest for attempted murder," Salido announced.

"Bitch!" Beaver spat in the direction of Jenny.

"Call an ambulance and take him to the hospital, and then book him for attempted murder," Salido ordered one of his officers as the officer handcuffed the criminal. Beaver, bent and bleeding, staggered as he was led to the squad car.

Alex was on the floor with her face close to Brutus. "He's breathing." She wiped the oozing blood from his nostrils, but the huge English bulldog was down.

Trey kissed Jenny gently, then scooped up Brutus and hurried toward the door. "Where's the closest animal emergency room?"

"I know the way." JP took charge of the emergency transport. With sirens flashing, they pulled away from the trailer, Green alerting the doctor that they were on the way with a life-and-death case.

The squad car sprayed gravel everywhere as they raced to try to save Brutus, who lay deathly still in Trey's arms.

Alex and Jenny, who was crying softly, made their way into the small living room.

"Do you have something to drink?"

"There's some iced tea," Jenny offered.

After the supporting officers left, Salido sat down in a large club chair, patiently waiting for Jenny to talk. Alex poured three glasses of tea, bringing one to Jenny, who collapsed in a trembling heap onto the sofa. The terror and shock from the invasion and assault were taking their toll.

Alex set Jenny's tea on the end table. "Trey said he thought you might have information about Colt," Alex said.

Jenny nodded. "Let me catch my breath."

Salido sat up, attentive, but didn't pressure her.

No one said a word as Jenny, still shaking, composed herself.

"Do you think you can talk now?" Alex asked gently.

"I couldn't let anyone else get hurt because of Beaver," Jenny said. They watched and waited as she took several deep breaths. Jenny cradled a box of Kleenex as she settled on the sofa.

She took a deep breath. "Colt called me that night."

"When?" Salido jumped in anxiously.

"The night he died?" Alex clarified.

"Yes, from the hotel bar," Jenny explained.

"You went to meet him?" Salido asked.

"I found him in the bar, really drunk."

"I can't believe he started drinking again," Alex interjected, with obvious disappointment.

"He couldn't help it. He wanted to stop." Jenny raised her voice in defense of Colt. She looked at Alex. "The struggle was constant."

Alex thought about that for a moment, then asked, "You walked him to his room?"

"After dragging him out of the bar, I waited with him in the room to make sure he didn't get sick. Then he kinda passed out." Jenny pulled out a tissue and blew her nose, hard.

"And you went home?"

The waitress shook her head. "No, he had a bad habit of waking up and going back out to drink, so I stayed."

"You're a good friend," Alex declared.

"Not really." Jenny started to cry.

They waited, giving her time to find the right words. The truth and pain cascaded out of her.

"Colt woke up and said he was going to drive up to the well, but I had taken the keys. When I refused to let him drive, he got really mad." Jenny smiled proudly, relaying her moment of triumph when she had done the tough, right thing.

Salido's phone rang, interrupting Jenny's story. "What?" Salido demanded.

"Hi, Dan. This is Carter."

"We're in the middle of something here. Beaver Scott tried to kill Jenny Cartwright," Salido said impatiently.

"He's bad news," Carter stated, "but we have a development that might be tied to the case."

"I can't talk right now." Salido demanded curtly.

"We found Ferrell Brandt, the attorney."

"So?" Salido asked, irritated by the detective's continuing interruption.

"Murdered in his Denver office, a dagger buried in his neck."

"Whoa...let me get back to you when we finish." He ended the call, saying nothing to Alex. "Go ahead, Jenny."

Jenny stood up, stretching and rubbing her neck.

"Let's see. He woke up in a drunken rage. It was still the middle of the night." Alex and Salido listened intently. "He ranted about wanting to see the drilling progress and needing to protect the well."

"Protect it from what?"

"I don't know. He was still pretty messed up. He had just gotten back from the Permian Basin in West Texas and had not seen what was going on."

Jenny drank some tea. "Colt would not back down. I finally gave in and agreed to drive him up there. I didn't trust him or believe he wanted to go to the well. I thought he was trying to sneak out to get more booze. There was no way he could drive!"

"What time was it?" Sheriff Salido asked.

Jenny tilted her head to one side, thinking. "Maybe one-thirty? After we got in the truck, I stopped at the gas station for coffee."

"Where?"

"The Valero. It's open all night."

Salido scribbled details as Alex listened. "I'll check the video cameras," he said.

Jenny described the slow drive up to the well site. She tried to relay every detail of the night. It had been an overcast starless night, black like oil, as they rattled along the dirt road. Colt navigated and insisted he was fine to drive, but Jenny knew he was still legally drunk. She argued that it was stupid to be going up there in the middle of the night, but into the darkness and up the rocky unpaved road she drove. They slowed as the road steepened and pulled into the area of the well.

"When we arrived at the well, we immediately noticed a strange vehicle parked close to the well. Colt was really concerned. He told me to stay in the truck."

She paused. "There was a light on in the cab, and he knew no one belonged up there. He said no one leaves a truck up in the middle of the forest unless it breaks down. So he got his pistol from under the car seat."

Jenny continued, "I watched as Colt walked toward the vehicle. Just then, I saw two dark figures by the well machinery. One had a box of some kind and placed it by the well. It was hard to see," she explained to Alex. "But I saw Colt walk toward them, and I heard him yell out to the men. Then a flashlight came on."

"Could you make an ID?" Salido interrupted.

"I was hiding," she explained. "I peeked out the window to see what I could." She continued the story of their encounter. "There was a lot of yelling."

"Did you recognize the men?" Salido asked again, looking anxious to extract the truth.

"When I looked up again, I saw Beaver with the bat, and the men started fighting and yelling. I heard Beaver's voice. Then I heard a shot, and one man fell to the ground, I think it was Colt, but it was really dark. Beaver was screaming and cussing as he forced the other man into the pickup. I saw him use the bat again. He hit him hard enough that I heard the thud. Then Beaver dragged Colt's body into the back of the truck.

"I climbed in the back of Colt's truck bed and hid under a tarp, praying they didn't come back. The next thing I heard was a massive explosion. Then their truck engine started, and I heard them coming my way. They stopped right next to where I was hiding and their car door creaked open. I had been holding my breath, and my heart was about to explode. The tarp smelled of old paint, and I could barely breathe." Jenny sniffed, nose wrinkled in distaste. "After a few minutes, I heard the truck drive away. I waited, not knowing if they would come back, but the fumes and the heat were terrifying. I thought I might die."

Salido continued taking notes, but he'd had the presence of mind to turn on the recorder of his iPhone.

"After what seemed like hours, I crawled out. I could feel the heat of the fire. It was incredibly hot, and the blaze lit up the area like a floodlight."

"It's a miracle they didn't kill you," Alex exclaimed.

"I was paralyzed with fear." More tears escaped, running down Jenny's flushed cheeks. "I didn't fight them. I just hid like a coward," she cried.

"There is nothing you could have done."

"I wiped down anything I might have touched in the truck with a rag. The whole place was on fire," Jenny reflected.

"Do you remember their truck?" Salido asked.

"Yes, I know it was Beaver's. I saw the dent in the back," she said.

"Beaver's truck has a dent," Alex said, looking at Salido. She'd noticed the dent in the truck parked out front.

Sickened by the account, she put her face in her hands and moaned as Jenny recreated the events.

"How did you get back?" Salido asked.

"Walked to the blacktop and then hitchhiked," Jenny stated. "A trucker picked me up."

"That was a long way," Alex said, not mentioning her limp.

"There was no other choice." Jenny shrugged.

Salido asked, "Do you remember the name of the driver or the truck company?"

"I have his card somewhere."

Alex and Salido sat still, silently processing the details of the dreadful tale.

"He must have dumped Colt's body after the well explosion." Salido was piecing together the details.

"That man I read about in the paper, the person of interest, had nothing to do with Colt's murder, and then I read they were going to try to indict Alex. I couldn't let innocent people go to prison for Colt's murder. I was a coward not to go straight to the police...but Beaver would have killed me."

"I wonder why they wanted to blow up the well?" Alex pondered. "It makes no sense. They were in the marijuana business."

"Maybe Colt pissed them off in the bar," Salido speculated.

"They really hated the oil business," Jenny reminded them.

"The fire was a convenient way to get rid of the body. I'm sure they thought it would never be recognized," Alex proposed.

"We'll find the answers. Someone wanted that well destroyed." Salido stood up and adjusted his hip holster.

"I have to go question Beaver Scott. Will you be all right?" Salido asked.

"I'll stay," Alex offered.

Salido came over and gave Alex a quick hug. "Thank you for staying with Jenny." The headlights of Salido's truck shone through the front window as he pulled away.

"I have to ask you something," Alex said to Jenny.

"Anything."

"Colt and I had a huge fight, and I never saw him again." Tears tiptoed down her cheeks.

Jenny took her hand. "All I ever wanted was a man to love me the way Colt loved you. He talked about you all the time."

"I just don't understand what happened…"

"He wasn't himself when he drank. It made him sick. He regretted the pain he caused, and it tortured him. Alex, he never wanted to hurt you."

But doubt would linger with Alex for a long time. She hugged Jenny.

The two women sat talking on the sofa for hours, patching the wounded pieces of their lives.

CHAPTER 36

S alido glared as he marched into District Attorney Robert Portland's office.

"Making any progress?" Portland asked casually.

Salido relayed Jenny's story to Portland, who was riveted with the break in the case.

"You trust this Jenny woman?" Portland looked slightly pale.

"I am confident in her story."

"So Alex Sheridan had nothing to do with it, despite all the circumstantial evidence pointing her way."

Salido shared the off-the-record data Carter had uncovered on Aaron Jeffries, formerly Jeff Ashton, the convicted murderer.

"I guess that destroys our case against Sheridan," Portland conceded. "I won't present the evidence for the time being." His points had already been scored when he announced the grand jury proceedings against Alex Sheridan, and his debt to the Sloanes was paid.

"We have an eyewitness who will testify that Beaver Scott shot Colt Forrester."

"Sounds like you have your case against the Scotts," Portland said.

"We'll indict them both for the murder of Colt Forrester. Beaver will also be charged with the assault and attempted murder of Jenny Cartwright."

"You don't have anything on this Jeffries guy, even if he was in prison. You can't prove any connection to Forester. His slate is clean, and there is no new evidence." Bob Portland made a case for dropping the person of interest.

"I want to ask him questions about the well explosion, if we can ever find the son of a bitch."

Salido felt that Aaron Jeffries was more than a person of interest, but they had no proof, only Carter's insistence that he was a potential suspect. He was peripheral to the case at this point, Salido thought.

Salido's cell buzzed and he looked down. "Let me take this; it's the Fish."

Portland nodded.

Salido said, "Hi, I'm here with Portland now. We have an eyewitness who saw Beaver Scott kill Colt Forester."

"That's interesting, because I just received Colt Forester's dental records, and they don't match the burned corpse. I don't know who the hell this corpse is, and we have no prints."

"But the watch?" The shocking news hit Salido in the gut. His entire case was based on the burned remains being Colt Forester.

"It may be his watch, but the corpse is not Colt Forester." The news was an atomic bomb.

Salido ended the call. He turned to Portland. "The body is not Colt Forester," he told the DA, looking unconvinced. "If Jenny was telling the truth, and I believe she was, then she was mistaken. She saw Beaver, she heard gunfire, and she saw a body being put in the back of the pickup— but it was dark. She was there but what she saw was murky," Salido mused.

Suddenly, a flash of insight popped into Salido's brain. "I need to talk to Beaver Scott!" He rushed out of Portland's office and headed directly to the hospital where Beaver was being treated.

Aaron Jeffries arrived in the high-desert oasis of Marfa, Texas, and checked into the El Paisano Hotel. On the walls were photos of Rock Hudson, Elizabeth Taylor, and James Dean from the classic 1956 movie, *Giant*, the most famous oil movie ever made. The old adobe hotel had been home to the movie stars when the famous film was shot in what was truly the edge of nowhere.

He wandered into the bar and made small talk with one of the eccentric locals. Characters drifted through the town like tumbleweed. It was an easy place to melt into the West Texas dirt. The town had become a ghost town after the military moved out, and then had its renaissance as an art mecca. People from around the globe traveled there to enjoy the spectacular light and landscape as well as the imposing sculptures by Donald Judd. It was about as far west as one could go, like sailing to the edge of the sea where ships fall off the horizon.

Aaron knew he was at one of the last outposts, Presidio County, where outlaws and outliers escaped into the mountainous desert to disappear forever. Thirty-three miles from the Rio Grande and the Mexican border, it was a part of the world that even the border patrol could not protect. It was too remote and barren, a rugged edge of the world where drug runners and human smugglers ruled.

A weathered old-timer drank whiskey next to Aaron. "What you doing here in Marfa?" the man asked, studying Aaron's scar.

"I'm an artist."

"Everyone's an artist these days," the old man scoffed.

Aaron was safe. For now. He would move farther south when the time came.

Toot! Toot! A truck horn alerted Alex and Jenny, and they rushed to open the door for Trey.

"We were just talking about you," Alex smiled. Her face was blotchy from tears.

Trey carried Brutus, who had a bandage on his head. He was snoring peacefully. Jenny quickly arranged several cushions. She covered them with a cotton blanket, creating a nest for the patient.

"Is he going to be okay?"

"Fractured orbit and a couple stitches, but tough as nails." Trey smiled proudly. "The doc gave him meds and said to keep him real quiet."

Jenny stroked Brutus and gave him a kiss. "You saved me."

While waiting for Trey, the women had shared intimate details about their lives. Jenny confessed her feelings for Trey. She had a huge crush on the big man, which pleased Alex. They had found each other in the midst of a terrible tragedy. Life brought people together in strange ways.

"I'd better get back to the hotel," Alex said. It was time to leave the new lovers to recover alone. She hugged Trey. "Thank you for everything."

"You want me to drive you?"

"No, thanks. I'll take the truck. It's just down the road."

"I'll have the chopper ready whenever you want to go."

She looked from him to Jenny and smiled. "Let's all get some rest and touch base later tomorrow morning."

With his arm around Jenny, Trey walked Alex to the front porch. "I'll check in tomorrow."

Alex climbed into the truck with her backpack and gun. After waving goodbye, she drove slowly back toward the motel. A wave of fatigue rippled through her exhausted body. The fact that she had shot Beaver Scott was just beginning to register. She trembled at the memory of the shooting, thankful it was not fatal. He was a cruel and pathetic man, and she was relieved he would face the consequences within the legal system. A judge and jury would handle his punishment.

Bull waited anxiously in the lobby of the Comfort Inn. She watched a broad smile crease his face when he saw her enter the hotel. It was late, and she felt beyond exhaustion. She had called Bull from Jenny's and told him the high points of the attack by Beaver, and the truth from Jenny about witnessing Colt's murder.

Bull held her gently.

She sighed. "Jenny's settled down, and Trey is with her."

"How about a drink?"

Alex nodded against his chest. "That would be wonderful."

Stump was just about to close the bar, but he mixed double martinis before they retired to their rooms.

After taking a quick shower, Alex showed up in her pajamas at Bull's room. They discussed the gruesome day and Jenny's revelation about the Scott brothers.

"You won't go down for murder?" Bull teased.

"Not tonight anyway." Alex's lids fluttered like she might fall asleep.

Just then, a text from Carter beeped on Alex's phone.

"Oh, God." Alex stared at her phone screen with a troubled expression.

"What happened?"

"Ferrell Brandt has been murdered...found dead in his office. Carter said he would fill me in later when they have more news."

"It must be connected." Bull looked horrified.

"Who knows? Riggs said he had a lot of enemies."

"What a terrifying turn of events."

"I'm glad he's dead. I mean it. He was trying to set me up for murder and steal my company."

The second time Alex's eyelids fluttered, Bull reached over and led her to the bed. "Can we rest for a while? I want to hold you."

"Thanks for staying."

He nuzzled up next to her in the darkness, his strong arms around her and his hands on her skin. He kissed the back of her neck and pressed up against her as if they had been formed together. They slept until the wee hours of the morning.

Alex awoke and made coffee, then climbed back in bed. Bull lay facing her, and they talked more about Colt and the Scotts and the mysterious murder of Ferrell Brandt. Carter had texted her with the disappointing news that there were no real clues in the Ferrell Brandt killing. Blue was heading up the investigation in collaboration with Sheriff Salido, but it was a very professional murder. Aaron Jeffries had disappeared, frustrating Carter and Salido, and Alex was sure they would not find him. The well explosion was still a mystery.

This was the beginning of healing. They had the truth, or most of it. He took her cup and set it on the end table.

"Can we start over?" Bull gazed at her with eyes that begged for understanding.

"That's a good idea."

"Let me tell you exactly what happened." He shared all the details of the horrible accident that led to his wife's eventual death and his inability to be up front with Alex when they first met. It was all over now and she empathized with his loss.

He loved on Alex for the rest of the early morning, gently caressing her. She savored his skin and his touch. She loved him back, touching every part of his body, clamping herself around him and driving him wild with sensual pleasure. Finally, she let out a wilted cry of delight and curled up into him. He held her and moved into her again, letting her relish his strong force inside her. Then he moved back and forth, rocking her gently and moving her under him. His hands held her tight as she felt his intensity rising. He devoured her with his passion. He moved her, and she responded. She rolled him onto his back and kissed every part of him. Straddling him, she rhythmically rocked until every part of him shattered into bliss.

Sleep overtook them. Alex buried her face in his chest and rested peacefully for the first time in recent memory.

CHAPTER 37

Out of a dead sleep, Alex was startled by the cell phone ring. She groped for it.

"This is Alex."

"Sorry to disturb you."

She blinked, trying to clear the sleep from her eyes. "Sheriff Salido, is everything okay?"

"Not exactly," he said, "there is a new development."

"I'm listening." Alex was now sitting bolt upright in the bed. She pulled the sheet up to cover her bare breasts.

"The forensic pathologist has Colt's dental records. They don't match the burned body."

Alex felt like someone had just gut-punched her. "What do you mean?"

"The burned body we found is not Colt Forester."

Bull watched in silence as Alex turned pale and her eyes filled with fear. The phone connection was silent as Alex processed the ramifications. "Then who?"

"We are working on that now."

"But Jenny witnessed…" A clammy fever rippled through her body as she began to shake.

"Jenny saw shadows. She heard the gun, and she heard yelling, but she was hiding, and it was dark. She knows for sure that Colt walked over with his gun to confront the men, and she saw Beaver, but we don't know anything definitive about the other man or the burned body. The burned body could be anyone. It may be related or it could be a hiker who was caught in the fire."

"Oh, my God." The news spread through her bones. "Where's Colt?"

"Alex, I went back to Jenny's to go over the story several more times. She was absolutely certain that she saw Beaver wrestle the gun away from Colt, and she heard the gunfire. She saw Beaver swing the bat, hitting someone, and she saw Beaver load a body into the back of the truck."

He paused for a moment, then added, "I'll call when we know something more."

The news knocked Alex from all moorings. After a few moments, she called Carter with the shocking development, then sat frozen and motionless, staring into nothing.

"Can I get you something to drink or eat?" Bull offered.

She shook her head, declining the offer. Her world had just exploded.

Family Dental was a favorite dentist office for the locals of Carbondale. Sheriff Salido knew the dentist, who had taken care of his family. It took one call to get the needed records.

Salido called the Fish from his car. "Dr. Fischer, I have a hunch."

The doctor sounded interested. "What's that?"

"Some other dental records—I'll bet you a steak dinner they will match our burned guy."

"I'll take that bet," Fish said doubtfully.

"I'm heading that way."

In less than an hour, Salido walked into the pathologist's office.

"He's waiting for you." The receptionist pointed toward the back.

Salido walked in and slapped the dental records file into Dr. Fischer's hand. "Let's take a look."

Two sets of dental records were displayed on a lighted panel in Dr. Fischer's office, and the Fish's mouth gaped open.

"How did you know they'd match?" he asked.

"A strong hunch and process of elimination."

၈

Beaver sat with his attorney in an interrogation room. He was covered in bandages from the bullet wound and the gashes to his head. Salido walked in and glared at Beaver. After reminding him of his Miranda rights, Salido began. "How difficult are you going to make this?"

"My client is not talking," the lawyer announced boldly.

"We have an eyewitness who will testify against him."

"For what?"

Salido smiled. "First-degree murder in the death of his brother Jason, and we believe enough evidence to get a murder charge in the death of the missing Colt Forester. Along with eye witness testimony to attempted murder of Jenny Cartwright!"

"You don't have any proof!" Beaver yelled. Sweat droplets ran down his temples, and he swiped at them with nubby fingers.

"The pathologist has a match on your brother's dental records, and Jenny saw you fire the gun."

"I didn't shoot him!" Beaver jumped up, screaming. Salido had scored a direct hit. The officer behind them stepped forward and pressed Beaver back down into his chair.

His attorney interrupted. "I advise you not to answer."

"I advise you to start helping or you are going to be charged with capital murder," Salido countered.

Beaver, an impulsive bully, was out of his mind with rage and fear. "Colt pulled his gun on us!" His face was crimson and his eyes darted wildly.

"You were trying to blow up the well," Salido prompted.

"He was drunk!" Beaver began to weep and heave, the chains on his feet and ankles clinking. "He murdered Jason like a dog." Beaver's rage and sadness filled the room like fetid gas. But Salido wasn't buying the clever act.

"Why were you and Jason blowing up the well?"

"Don't answer," the attorney ordered.

An awkward silence filled the stuffy room.

"If you give us a statement, we will try to work out a deal," Salido offered, but he had no real interest in trying to assist this scum. He intended to take advantage of the situation and strike while Beaver was terrified and compliant. He did not believe for one moment that the shooting was an accident.

"He murdered Jason," Beaver wailed.

"You shot him, and you murdered Colt," Salido probed, hoping to get Beaver to make a slip.

"Don't answer!" The attorney tried to rein in his out-of-control client.

"You killed Colt Forester." Salido repeated the charge.

"He tried to shoot me."

"You dumped Jason's body where it would be burned."

"He murdered Jason," Beaver insisted, but Salido hoped he would crack.

"You tell us where Colt Forester is, and we will try to work with you."

"Don't answer," the attorney ordered.

"Where's Colt Forester?" Salido bellowed.

"I don't know. The son of a bitch murdered my brother." With his head in his hands, Beaver sobbed.

Salido pushed back from the table. "We'll take a break and I will come back. You better be prepared to tell the truth or this will get ugly."

"Stop trying to intimidate my client. You have no proof!" the attorney argued.

The sheriff gave him a level, confident look. "I can prove that he dumped a body."

"What if we can provide you with some facts about the well explosion?" the attorney negotiated.

"Besides the fact that your client sabotaged the well?"

"My client has to get a deal," the lawyer persisted.

The door slammed loudly as Salido left Beaver and the attorney squirming in the interrogation room.

Salido consulted with Bob Portland and devised a plan. Beaver was on the ropes, and they needed to extract the truth, not some story invented to buy Beaver's freedom. One man fell and another was bludgeoned with the bat. Which man he killed first was not really the issue. Both men were dead, and the last man standing was Beaver. They had Jason's burned body with the gunshot wound. Beaver had to know the location of Colt's body, and Salido wasn't letting him off until he had an answer.

After an excruciating break, Salido returned to the interrogation room. Several more grueling hours passed with oblique threats. With tears running down his face, Beaver finally imploded and told Salido what sounded like the truth.

Having gotten what he believed was an authentic confession, Salido retreated to his office to speak with JP Green.

"Did he crack?" Green asked enthusiastically.

"I hope so." Salido pulled out a map, spread it out on an empty desk, and pointed to a location. "I'll take some backup and go up to the Marble quarry. Let's hope it's not a wild goose chase." He peered at the map. "Mountain Rescue and the EMTs will help. It may be hard to find. Someone could get hurt." The Mountain Rescue teams were highly skilled volunteers who specialized in all types of dangerous rescues.

"I'll help organize the search," JP offered.

"And alert the chopper team in Gypsum in case we need the Blackhawk." Trained military pilots that responded when an emergency airlift was needed in the county flew Blackhawk helicopters.

"Will do," the deputy affirmed. "After Beaver gives us a sworn statement, I'll meet you there."

Salido's next call was to Alex's private detective, Mike Carter. He filled him in on the developments.

"Can you call Alex and tell her?" Salido asked, but it was more like an order.

"You want me to deliver this news to Alex?" Carter sounded incensed.

"It would help; you're her friend and I have to get up to the quarry." It was all Salido could handle right now. He just had one more question. "Any clues to who killed Brandt?"

"Not a print or a witness—nothing." Carter sounded exasperated.

Carter sat in his car, staring at his phone and trying to figure out how and what to say to Alex. His stomach churned. Finally, after several false starts, the call went through.

In the motel in Carbondale, Alex answered in a hollow voice. "Hi, Carter."

He paused. "There's been a development." Carter sounded cryptic.

"I already know the burned body is not Colt," Alex announced.

"They found dental records that match. Jason Scott, Beaver's brother, is the burned body."

"And no one knows anything about Colt. He could be anywhere." He heard her sobs through the phone.

"Beaver broke down and confessed," he told her.

"About?"

"Beaver may be lying." Carter wanted her to be prepared in case it turned out the bastard hadn't told the truth.

"Tell me."

He blurted, "He says he dumped Colt's body in the Marble quarry."

There was complete silence on Alex's end.

Carter continued, "Mountain Rescue is on their way now."

Alex said nothing.

CHAPTER 38

Alex accepted the news about Beaver's confession as if she were drugged. It was one in a series of shocking revelations. Moving like a zombie, she gathered her things and checked out of the motel. Bull insisted upon accompanying her to Marble on the circuitous drive to the quarry. It was a little more than an hour from the motel.

Alex's mind raced with possibilities. Could Colt be alive after more than a week out there? Surely not. No one knew. He might not even be where the brutal man said the body had been dumped. Alex tried not to let hope creep into her mind. What if he was alive?

She swatted the fantasy away and sat in silence as Bull drove the winding road toward the quarry. She had to recalculate everything. Inside, she churned as she shifted into high performance mode. This had to be treated like an out-of-control fire. Her wit and strength were required to help the team try to find Colt. And, if there was even one chance of him being alive, Alex would make sure every possible resource was deployed.

Then she looked at the date on her phone—eight days had passed since they believed the attack occurred. This was a body recovery mission. No one believed Colt was alive.

A squadron of official cars and emergency vehicles was parked around the entrance to the quarry, where search-and-recovery people with rock-climbing gear prepared to descend into the depths. The quarry was dug out of the side of a mountain above Marble, deep in the wilderness. Numerous volunteers showed up to assist in the endeavor. High up a treacherous mountain road, huge pieces of discarded marble the size of cars littered the area like bodies on a battlefield. Paramedics awaited instructions while Salido orchestrated the search. The hollowed-out quarry, hundreds of feet deep, was a cavernous dark hole in the belly of the mountain.

Alex approached Salido. He extended his hand in friendship, and she accepted.

"We finally got Beaver's confession. Sorry for this bad news and all the stress on you," the sheriff said.

"Aaron Jeffries is still a threat."

"He's not really a part of the case from what I can see."

"He wasn't here by accident." But Alex was determined not to argue with Salido. It would have to wait until after they found Colt's body.

"We're keeping an eye out for him," Salido told her.

"The well is totally under control. Bull and several of their experts will testify that it was sabotaged." Alex moved with him toward the knot of men who seemed to be directing things.

"Thanks; his expert testimony will help. Sorry, but we are only treating this as a rescue for today. After that we switch to a recovery mission...for the body. It's just been too long." The lines on his face deepened into sad crevasses.

She didn't want to utter Colt's name. While they spoke, the search-and-rescue team descended into the depths with flashlights. Alex and Bull and volunteers paced around the perimeter of the massive hole. Volunteers offered bottled water and snacks to the workers. They called out just in case Colt was alive, but there was no response. Hours passed as they searched the cold dark hole with its craggy ledges and fissures, and their enthusiasm evaporated. The chances of locating anything in its depths were slim.

Lafayette called several times for updates and sent encouraging messages to Alex.

"Any news yet?"

"Nothing." Alex responded like death.

"There's still time." The big man sighed.

The Mountain Rescue team leader announced, "We'll be stopping for the day if nothing is found within the next hour." The sun crept toward the craggy peaks, chilling the air as it descended. Everyone present knew that another day and night only lessened a chance of survival. The volunteers packed up supplies and a heavy gloom filled the air.

Back in the interrogation room at the hospital, Beaver waited impatiently. His lawyer berated him for not following his advice, but Beaver would not listen. The pain from his injured shoulder where Alex had shot him throbbed.

Deputy Green entered the room carrying a piece of paper, saying nothing to Beaver.

Beaver watched him, waiting for something to happen.

Finally, Green said, "You've been lying to us."

Beaver slammed his hands on the table. "Bullshit!"

"You shot Jason."

Beaver tried to surge to his feet, but the officer behind him had other ideas, so he settled back into his chair, muttering, "I did not shoot my own brother!"

JP leaned in, lowering his voice. "When you dumped Colt's body, he was still alive."

"I didn't know."

"Dumping a live body down a quarry is attempted murder. It would be first-degree murder if he were dead, but he is alive."

"You're lying!" The lawyer stood up, fisted hands supporting him on the table.

"Salido just called. We found Colt Forester with some broken bones, suffering from hypothermia but very much alive. He swears you shot Jason," JP embellished, hoping to get Beaver to crack and confess.

"He's lying!" Beaver shrieked.

"We have his word." JP spun the tale, wanting to see what kind of reaction came from Beaver.

Beaver began to sob. "I didn't mean to. We fought over the gun. Jason stepped in to help, and the gun went off. Oh, my God, it killed him. I didn't mean to! I turned on Colt and hit him hard with the bat. I didn't mean it: he never moved after that. I thought he was dead."

JP began to take the formal confession.

"We want a deal. We can help you with the well fire investigation," the attorney said, attempting to salvage the negotiations—but the deputy gave no promises.

JP took down the details of the confession, most of which lined up with Jenny's observation. Coming out of the darkness, Colt had approached the two men at the well. He drew his gun and ordered them to get away from the well machinery. Beaver swung the bat and fought with Colt, wrestling the gun from him. At gunpoint, Beaver and Jason robbed Colt of his cash. Jason took Colt's watch and put it on.

Colt lunged at Beaver, trying to get the gun back and, when Jason jumped in to help Beaver, the gun discharged, killing Jason. In a fit of rage, Beaver beat Colt with the baseball bat as he shoved him in the truck. Panicked, Beaver, who knew no one would look for his reclusive brother, dumped Jason's body in the line of the fire, hoping it would burn up from the explosion, forgetting Jason was wearing Colt's watch.

As he drove away from the explosion, Beaver decided to dump Colt's motionless body far away, where it could not be connected to the well fire and likely would never be found.

As volunteers packed up for the day, out of the cold darkness, one of the rescue team yelled, "Over here! I see something." Lights were directed toward the caller and everyone gathered near the cavern.

Several paramedics descended in the direction of the caller. Rumor immediately passed to the people at the entrance to the quarry.

"They've seen something," one of the coordinators informed Salido.

A member of the Mountain Rescue team ordered, "Get a stretcher."

The team scurried like spiders down into the cavern and waited for a stretcher to be lowered. Powerful lights on long lines illuminated the cavern. Near the bottom of the quarry, on a precarious ledge, a motionless body was spotted. The team up above assessed the situation and devised a plan to retrieve the body.

Near the edge of the cavern, Alex paced like a caged tiger. She was certain Colt was dead, but people had survived longer in the rubble of earthquakes.

A paramedic finally reached the still form. Everyone waited. Carefully, the body was examined. The skin was cold and there were obvious fractures.

A voice announced, "I've got a pulse."

Word spread up the lines to the team at the opening. "He's alive."

Cheers erupted.

Alex trembled as she texted Carter, Lafayette, and Schaeffer. As the rescue team prepared to move Colt, seconds dragged by like hours.

"His back may be broken; stabilize his neck," the lead paramedic ordered. Colt was covered in warm blankets and moved to a board and onto a stretcher that would be raised by pulleys. After what seemed like an hour, the basket stretcher was slowly raised out of the depths and onto the ledge at the entry to the quarry.

Alex, numb with shock, waited off to the side, allowing the emergency team to do its work.

"Oh, my God," she said over and over as Colt's motionless body was moved from the stretcher into the back of an ambulance. She tried to get closer, but officials held her back. "Where are they taking him?"

Bull waited and watched. Alex was pale.

"There's a chopper waiting down below to take him to Glenwood Springs," the paramedic explained.

"Will he make it?" Alex asked cautiously.

"I don't know; he must be pretty tough." The young mountain rescue volunteer squeezed Alex's hand hopefully.

"I want to ride with him."

He shook his head. "Sorry, we can't take you in our chopper. Only emergency personnel."

"We'll follow."

The ride to Glenwood was tortuously slow. Alex pondered her next action while Bull drove in silence.

"Schaeffer, it's me." Alex had already told Schaeffer about the mistaken identity of the burned body, but this news was shocking. "They found Colt's body dumped in the Marble quarry. He's unconscious, but alive."

"Thank God..." her friend began, but Alex cut her off.

"I need your help."

"Anything."

Alex had come up with a plan. "Can you put your hands on the power of attorney so I can talk to the doctors?"

"Of course. Do you want me to come?"

"Wait until after we speak with the doctors at the Glenwood hospital."

"I'm here if you need anything," Schaeffer said.

Alex remembered one more thing. "Please call Fran and update the team."

"I'll let Trey know, too." Alex knew Schaeffer would take care of everything, which is why Alex relied on her.

"Ask him to meet me in Glenwood with the chopper."

"It's done."

"I don't know what I would do without you," Alex told her.

At the hospital, Alex received a copy of the legal document showing she had medical power of attorney for Colt. Schaeffer had managed to find the file and emailed it immediately. In the emergency room, a swarm of doctors and nurses attended to an unresponsive Colt. After he was evaluated, an MRI was taken to assess the condition of the brain and swelling.

A doctor in scrubs came into the family area where Alex and Bull waited anxiously.

"Who has medical power of attorney?"

Alex raised her hand. "I'm Alex." She showed him the document.

"Thank you. He has a severe concussion and trauma to the brain stem but, thankfully, not too much bleeding. There is some swelling as well as extreme dehydration and hypothermia. But the cold probably kept him alive."

"What are his chances?" Alex asked apprehensively.

"His situation is very fragile, but he somehow survived the fall."

"I want the truth," Alex insisted.

"More tests are ordered and I will let you know. He's in a coma, which we want."

A pendulum of grief, fear, and anxiety swung wildly. After mourning Colt for days, she was now faced with his life and death again.

"Do you want something to drink?" Bull offered, coming up behind her to press a hand to her shoulder.

She reached back and returned the squeeze. "No, I don't want anything. I'm not sure what to do."

"Would you like to talk to Dr. Thomas, the neurosurgeon who treated Laura? He's a friend."

The offer meant a lot to her, knowing his circumstances. She looked up at him with gratitude. "That might be helpful. I'll wait to see what the brain scan reveals."

CHAPTER 39

Several weeks later, Mike Carter and Blue Davies sat in the Brown Palace Hotel cigar bar, with its dark wood paneling and stuffed leather chairs.

No leads had been found in the murder of Ferrell Brandt, and Blue was in charge of the case until they connected it to Salido's jurisdiction. No prints of any kind were on the dagger-style letter opener, and no witness from the hotel had seen anyone enter or leave the room. The staff had been questioned to no avail and no clues showed up on video. Clients were methodically interrogated, but no one offered evidence that helped lead to a killer. Brandt's phone and calendar contained no incriminating appointments and the letter opener was traced to a common manufacturer.

"Did you find the woman who left her panties?" Carter asked Blue.

"Yes," Blue said, "she said he was alone and alive when she left." Tracking down the prostitute who had been in Brandt's office had been easy.

"You trust her?"

"She admitted being in the room with Brandt, but she had a sound alibi. She went to another job."

Carter leaned forward, blowing out a ring of smoke. "Someone will back up her story?"

"She's a good person. Been around Denver for years. It's not her." According to Blue's investigation, the doormen at the hotel had seen her go and come from Brandt's suite more than once.

"Any other leads?"

Blue shook his head, looking disappointed. "From what I can gather, Brandt was universally despised, which complicates everything."

"Who had motive?"

Blue shrugged, rolling his cigar between his fingers. "Who didn't? I spoke to his clients—they all hated him. The prostitute says the other girls wouldn't go to him anymore, and she had decided that this was her last time."

"What a prick." They chuckled and ordered another round.

Carter leaned back, the leather chair creaking beneath him. "What about his big-money clients?"

"No one liked him. The Sloanes said they were getting ready to fire him."

"Convenient how all these people paid him but now they all claim to detest him."

"Any leads on Aaron Jeffries?" Blue asked.

"Aaron Jeffries has completely dropped off the radar screen." Carter was baffled. "I talked with Salido."

"About?" Blue asked.

"Beaver swears that they were forced by Jeffries to sabotage the well."

"He would say anything to get a plea." Blue knew firsthand the depths to which desperate defendants would go to try to buy their freedom.

"They said Jeffries was being coerced by Nancy Parker and Brandt, but I can't put any evidence together," Carter said.

"Nancy sounds slippery."

"Like everyone else, she had nothing good to say about Brandt."

"For instance?"

"Said she was scared of him. She said he was capable of anything, whatever that means." Carter tried to make sense of the information.

"She's in the business of selling influence—wouldn't place a bet on her truth." Blue reached over and took a long pull on his bourbon. "Brandt's silence is convenient for everyone," the experienced homicide investigator reflected.

"Beaver swears that Colt attacked them when he found them at the well site, and that his gun misfired," said Carter. Sheriff Salido had willingly shared information with Carter. Once Alex was no longer a suspect, he hoped Carter and Blue could help him with the missing links in the case.

"Misfired?" Blue scoffed at the idea. "You can't believe that."

"Well, they weren't out there in the middle of the night by accident with explosives, that's for sure."

"He's told multiple versions of the story. He dumped his brother's body, hoping it would burn up in the fire. Then he dumped Colt's body. Come on." Blue's skepticism was well-founded. "He tried to kill Jenny. Don't believe a word he says."

"There's still a missing piece."

"Where's the gun?" Blue asked.

"Probably in the bottom of the quarry," Carter speculated, "but I doubt it will ever be recovered."

"You have Scott's confession?" Blue prodded.

"Yes, but he's back-pedaling. And where does Brandt fit in?" Carter was puzzled.

"He was up to no good, even if you can't prove the connection." Blue concluded.

"Lafayette gave me his file...the list of his enemies is enough to choke on."

"You'd have to get at the back of the line if you wanted to kill him." Blue smiled, knowing it was the kind of case that would probably go unsolved. Instead of grieving friends and family, everyone around Brandt was cheering.

"Any idea about how to track down Jeffries?"

"He's gone," Blue predicted.

After Colt was stabilized, he was airlifted to the Denver Health Medical Center, and Dr. William Thomas, the neurosurgeon, took over. For more than eight weeks, Colt was kept in a drug-induced coma to allow his brain to heal.

Visiting the hospital became a regular routine that Alex grew to enjoy. She and Lafayette would drink coffee and talk to Colt about the business as he lay in silence. They read the newspaper aloud, and Lafayette told him all about Samantha, who was crawling around the office. Alex had learned from Jenny that Colt had gone to the site to try to help with the well on that terrible night. Even if he had relapsed, he was trying to do his job. Knowing that he had not deserted their project helped quell the fury she felt following their fight and his initial disappearance.

Conversations with the doctor helped Alex understand the severity of the injury and the miraculous potential healing powers of the brain. Hours of waiting gave her time to process the traumatic events. Slowly, she accepted the possibility that he might never be whole again, even though snippets of encouraging news came from the doctors who treated Colt. Numerous fractures were healing nicely. His pupils were responding more normally, and the swelling in his brain was slowly lessening. But he was still in the induced coma. With what she knew of Bull's experience, Alex tried to quash expectations.

CHAPTER 40

A lex and Bull stood on a mountain ridge in the Thompson Divide studying the magnificent terrain. He had managed to salvage her wells, and they were now producing large amounts of natural gas.

"We are planting new trees in this area and working with Salido and the forestry service to do everything possible to restore the burned area of forest," Alex told Bull. She pointed out the new saplings. Their love of the mountains had brought them together with a shared desire to restore and preserve the beautiful habitat. Less successful was Alex's effort to convince the sheriff of the ongoing threat Aaron Jeffries posed. He was a red herring as far as Salido was concerned.

Alex knew better. Jeff Ashton, the cunning and devious murderer, had managed to escape with a new identity—Aaron Jeffries. He might have a new name, but his lethal intentions remained. Alex knew he carried a vendetta that would not be forgotten and, as long as he was alive, he was a threat.

"Riggs must be happy," Bull said.

Alex tried not to stare at his windswept profile, his tousled hair, and chiseled jaw.

"Yes. We are going to drill some wells in West Texas, which he's excited about. And he is bidding on some offshore leases in the Gulf of Mexico."

Bull stared off into the distance. "What a great partner."

"We are having fun," she said, smiling. Riggs didn't have any children and Alex was quickly becoming his family. They talked almost every day, sending deals back and forth. He shared his experience and wisdom from a lifetime in the oil fields, and she brought him up to date on all the latest technology. Together they were a formidable team. More than anything, they just plain liked each other.

With the sun setting at their backs, Alex and Bull held hands, enjoying the vista before their return home. Not far away, Trey and Brutus waited to ferry them back to Denver in the chopper.

It was a time of suspended love. Alex and Bull both knew that time was ticking like a bomb, and in the countdown there would be change. The chances of Colt coming out of the coma were slim, but every day that went by was in his favor. Little movements and responses brought glimmers of hope and every hopeful breath engendered fear.

Alex climbed into the copilot's seat and adjusted her headset as Bull slid in next to Brutus in the back.

"How's Jenny?" she asked Trey.

"Good," he answered over the roar of the propellers. "We are talking about her moving to Denver. Brutus wants her to be part of the family." His grin was wide.

Alex's face lit up with joy.

"She's a kind person. Everyone buckled in?" Alex moved the yoke and they were off.

Weeks later, Bull and Alex awoke together at daybreak. The smell of Colombian coffee filled the room. Alex, naked and sleepy, was wrapped in white cotton sheets, her long dark hair spilling over the pillow. They were in the new penthouse Bull had purchased, just around the corner from Alex's office, their own private love nest. It was an escape from the rest of the world, and there, they were beginning to build their own story.

Alex rolled over and caressed Bull's lean body, which responded to her touch. She held him and stroked him until he could not wait another moment.

"Want to play?" she teased.

He kissed her passionately, smothering her with his mouth. He caressed her breasts, driving her wild with pleasure. She welcomed his passion and tenderness and relished his erotic loving. He gathered her in his arms and moved into her, all warmth and love and arousal. He rocked her gently and rhythmically until they shivered with delight.

Alex rolled over and sighed. "You were going to bring me a coffee?" she playfully reminded him.

"You interrupted the mission." Bull stood up and stretched his sculpted body, then pulled on some pants. He bent over and kissed Alex on the cheek, then went to find the coffee.

The phone rang and the familiar name of Dr. Thomas came up on the caller ID.

"Hi, Doc."

"Good morning, Alex."

"How's the patient?" Alex hated asking the question.

How much damage had occurred or what condition Colt would be in, if he came out of the coma, was unknown. Any progress would be a miracle, and the chances of his being severely handicapped were high. Doc Thomas patiently had discussed the probable scenarios for his recovery so many times she could not remember them all. She was mentally prepared to oversee his care and manage the physical therapy, whatever he needed. She loved Colt, and she would not abandon him. She also knew that she would live her own life. That decision was made before the accident. She would not go back.

"Are you sitting down?" the doctor asked playfully.

She looked at the bed. "Not exactly."

"I have someone who wants to speak with you."

Alex froze like a piece of granite and her heart thundered as she tried not to react. "Okay..." Slowly, Alex rose and walked to the bedroom window, searching the horizon.

"Hey, baby." Colt's raspy voice was weak from having a tube down his windpipe for months, but he sounded like himself. "Where've you been?"

Alex's knees gave way. Holding the phone to her ear, she knelt on the floor. "I'm here. Oh, my God, don't move."

"I don't think that's an option. They've got me hog-tied." There were countless tubes and hoses coming out of his body. Whatever the future brought, Colt's humor had survived.

"I am coming right away."

Dr. Thomas came back on the call. "He'll be in and out for some time," he told her. "This is not a straight line."

"But he sounds coherent," Alex said.

"He doesn't remember the accident, and who knows what else, but he can recover—I'm encouraged."

"Thank you. Oh, my God, thank you." Alex put her hand over her mouth, awed by the news.

"There's still a long road ahead, Alex, but this is good news."

"I'll see you over there in just a few minutes."

Bull stood motionless, a coffee cup in each hand as he watched Alex frantically scurry around the room. She gathered up her clothes, then hurriedly slithered into her pants. The silence was unbearable.

Bull placed her coffee on the bedside table as Alex finished dressing. Then he said, "I'll have them pull the car up."

"Thanks. I have to go help." Disheveled hair and no makeup would have to do. She grabbed the coffee and gulped some down.

"I know." He leaned over and kissed her on the top of the head.

"I'll be back, promise." She kissed him on the cheek and picked up her handbag.

Bull said nothing as Alex disappeared into the morning.

EPILOGUE

Denver, Colorado
MONTHS BEFORE

Aaron Jeffries appeared outside a service exit of the historic Brown Palace hotel, eyes darting right and left. He entered the alley, clutching his newly minted passport and the envelope of cash given to him by the diabolical lawyer, Ferrell Brandt. With his new identity, Jeffries could escape, disappear and never come back to Colorado. He fingered the scar that ran down his face to his neck, something the plastic surgeon had not been able to repair completely. The gouge was crooked and deep; even now, years later, he could feel the homemade knife cutting to his bone.

As Aaron scurried down the dirty edges of the dingy alleyway, the desperate thought of leaving every memory of Denver and the nasty lawyer far behind drummed uncontrollably in his mind. Out of the shadows, a dark man appeared. The hooded figure bent and moved closer, his mummified face concealed by gauze and sunglasses.

"Jeffries?" The man called to him with a muffled growl.

Jeffries stopped abruptly, fear vibrating through his veins, his eyes searching for an escape. He was an expert escape artist but, in an instant, the hooded stranger was over him, consuming him. He carried a black snub-nosed pistol and a large envelope. Jeffries' soul quaked.

"What do you want?" Jeffries trembled, but he knew many people wanted him dead. The plastic surgery and new name were not enough to protect him from the kind of people he had crossed.

"Brandt can't be trusted. Take care of him."

Jeffries sucked in a breath. "I'm finished."

"You're finished when *we* say you're finished." The threat was an order that came from powerful underbelly people that were accustomed to having their way. Jeffries had been manipulated. He was a pawn, but that was about to end.

Jeffries tried to get around the man. "I'm leaving."

"Not if you want to live! That passport will be flagged—you'll be picked up by the feds before the morning."

"The feds got me the new passport." Jeffries shot back. "I am free."

"We own the feds. You'll be back in jail or worse before nightfall." The otherworldly voice hissed through the gauze mask.

"I've done my part." Jeffries squealed like a pig. The sky crackled as dark clouds gathered. Only steps away, normal people walked the streets of Denver in the shadows of the Rocky Mountains. They shopped for groceries and drove carpools, oblivious to murder, crime and punishment.

"You and Ferrell Brandt created a mess. Now you have to clean it up." The man shoved a large wad of cash into Jeffries's gut. "Don't leave any evidence. Then get out of the country and never come back"

Like an apparition, the hooded messenger was gone.

Jeffries stood in shadows in the alley looking at the service entry to the hotel. It was an ancient fortress of a hotel that was a historic monument to the city of Denver. Motionless, he remained frozen in place. An escape route was not clear. He could try and melt into the city of Denver until he could create another escape plan. But that would be dangerous. He would be foolish to think they weren't watching; even now, they were following him. Their power and influence ran through the veins of the business community and into the heart of government power. The hooded stranger was waiting—it was no accident. Jeffries had to create another exit strategy.

He looked west to where the peaks of the jagged Rockies rose above the tops of buildings and he knew in the crevasses of his mind that this day would come. There was no choice. Ferrell Brandt, the lawyer who had helped mastermind his release from prison, knew too much. Brandt knew too much about the rich and powerful people he had helped and crossed. He had mutated from an asset to a liability.

Jeffries wanted to run, but the instinct would not serve him. This threat was real. His newfound freedom would be ripped away. He had to make a choice now.

A plan came into focus. Jeffries, dressed in non-descript clothing and sunglasses, went to his old car and rummaged in a duffle bag. Surrounded by the towering office buildings of Denver, he was trapped. Close by, car horns honked. A garbage truck clanked. After some time pondering the distasteful options, he re-entered the elegant 19th century hotel wearing a Broncos cap and a grey overcoat. He slipped into the back of the foyer of the grand hotel and studied the elevators through dark glasses.

The lobby area filled with American period antiques was conveniently empty. A man with olive skin in a black-and-white uniform pushed a large dust mop around the perimeter of the lobby.

A maid, with large calves and wearing a hair net, polished the brass railings and dusted the antiques with precision. Dark woods and old brass harkened the hotel's elegant past. In its day, the Brown Palace was the grandest of ladies. Jeffries continued to scour the expansive lobby as he looked up the open atrium that revealed the stairs that lead all the way to the top floor. No one was watching. His mind calculated the next moves. He searched for security cameras but saw none. The collar on his coat was turned up, and the cap pulled down low, covering as much of his face as possible. He could not be recognized. Aaron felt feverish heat rise. With surgical instincts, he formulated a plan.

He studied the lobby from the shadows as if it was a minefield. Several well-dressed guests passed by. He waited patiently with a tourist map in his left hand. When the lobby area by the elevator was empty, he moved like a wisp of smoke and entered the elevator. Slowly the doors closed. A hand jutted in to interrupt the doors closing. Jeffries pressed the close button harder and the doors came together. Like drying cement, the antique elevator ascended toward the twelfth floor where Ferrell Brandt resided.

Jeffries despised the henchman lawyer who had masterminded hundreds of creepy and shady deals. The secret list of clients he manipulated and answered to was one of wealthy business leaders and powerful politicians. He made sure people owed him favors. For Aaron Jeffries, paybacks were overdue.

The doors opened and Aaron Jeffries, a most-wanted man, peered out of the elevator and into the elegant hallway. An unattended service cart sat near the end of the hallway. He moved toward the cart.

A door opened and a maid stepped out. Jeffries whirled around and moved back away from the cart toward the elevators. He rounded the corner out of sight. He waited and listened. He heard a door close. After a few moments, he peered down the hallway again. He pinched a pair of rubber gloves from the cleaning cart and pulled them on as he approached the elaborate entry to the lawyer's twelfth-floor office residence. His eyes searched for a witness, but fortune provided no one.

Standing in front of the antique doors, Aaron knocked, a warm sense of pleasure oozing through his vessels. A shuffling sound could be heard coming from inside the apartment. Jeffries searched the hallway, eyes darting, bulging wildly. No guests or staff appeared.

"What do you want?" the lawyer's voice snarled through the door.

"I left my phone..." Jeffries had said his final words to Brandt only a short time before, and picked up his passport and money, which terminated their relationship.

"I'm busy." But the bolt slowly turned.

"Let me in. It will only take a second," Jeffries demanded through the door.

Brandt cracked the door open a sliver. Jeffries slammed the door open and barged in forcefully. With gloved hands, he grabbed the slight lawyer by the throat, forcing him back inside the suite. Jeffries crammed a gun in the lawyer's ribs as he secured the door.

"The office! Not a sound." Aaron marched him through the reception area of the residential office suite where Brandt lived and conducted his illicit affairs.

Two fluted glasses and an open bottle of champagne sat on the coffee table in front of the large windows. Discarded red panties under the glass coffee table were rolled inside out. Jeffries ignored the scene as they entered the refined office. It was filled with leather bound books and fine art acquired with other people's money.

As Jeffries studied the room, his eyes locked on the safe door that gaped open. He clearly remembered it being closed after Brandt gave him his passport and arrogantly let him leave.

The feeling of power welled up inside him like a stoked furnace. "Don't move!" Finally, he controlled the throttle. For too long, he had been at the lawyer's mercy. He had begged and pleaded and promised his life to attain the lawyer's needed assistance in securing his release and pardon from the prison. He had promised and compromised to get his new identity. But the lawyer's aid turned to demands that became a treacherous anchor around his neck. Brandt forced him to take risks that almost destroyed his newfound freedom. Threats had become blackmail from multiple sources. No more, he thought.

"I gave you the passport and money," the lawyer pointed out nervously. "We had a deal."

Aaron looked around the room, getting his bearings. A plaque from the Denver Bar Association honoring Ferrell Brandt for service was prominently displayed. A marble paperweight from Sloane Enterprises, one of the most powerful conglomerates in the world, sat on the edge of the desk. It read *In Appreciation for Service*. A framed degree from Harvard Law School hung on the wall behind his desk. All this, Aaron absorbed in an instant. This was not premeditated and he had to be insidiously clever. No trace evidence. The desk was free of clutter except for a few pieces of mail and an ornate letter opener.

"Sit down." Ferrell Brandt sat in his large desk chair. "Hands on the desk." Slowly, Jeffries moved around behind the lawyer. Ferrell Brandt, the balding lawyer with twitching lids who had wielded so much terror, the man that blackmailed him and used him, now in a blue smoking jacket, trembled with fear.

"I'll give you whatever you want," Brandt said, the words vibrating with anxiety. His confidence was steam disappearing into the air.

"Shut up and don't move."

"Diamonds. There are diamonds and cash in the vault." Sweat formed on the nasty lawyer's brow.

"Shut up."

Just then, a dark-haired woman with a perfect figure and smeared makeup and a bruised cheek appeared in the doorway. A small trickle of dried blood clotted in her left nostril and her lip was swollen. "I want my money."

Ferrell looked at Aaron, who lowered his face and turned away from

335

the woman's bruised face.

"Pay her and get her out." Jeffries ordered in a low, disturbing tone.

Ferrell pulled out a large roll of one hundred-dollar bills. In slow motion, he peeled off a few hundreds.

"More," Aaron hissed. Ferrell Brandt gave her the rest of the wad of money. "Get out of here. Can't you see I am in a meeting?"

The woman backed away, looking at Jeffries, then disappeared from the room. *Click click* went the heels of her shoes on the hard floor. *Creak.* The door opened. They waited in silence until they heard the front door close.

"I won't tell the Sloanes anything. Take the…"

In one swift, elegant motion Jeffries clamped his left arm around Brandt's neck in a lethal chokehold, simultaneously grabbing the ornate dagger-style letter opener set with semi-precious stones. In one fluid movement, he buried the blade deep in the lawyer's neck.

Brandt wriggled for several seconds as blood spurted out and ran down his neck to the floor. In a few more seconds, he was still. Brandt's lifeless, bald head slumped forward onto the desk like a rag doll.

Quickly, Aaron Jeffries removed the synthetic gloves and stuffed them in his pocket before putting on a clean pair. Jeffries moved to the safe. He gasped. An unexpected treasure trove stared back. Neat stacks of gold bars filled the shelves. Hundred-dollar bills were banded in neat stacks. He meticulously searched the safe, pulled the bills out and started counting. How could he transport the loot?

He dug deeper into the vault. Behind the precious bars, there were rows of small envelopes containing diamonds wrapped in tissue paper. He opened one of the rectangular pieces of tissue paper to find flawless, gleaming stones. Tremors rippled through his body and his hands quivered as if with a palsy. This was his freedom. An added bonus, he thought, a well-deserved payday and there was a good chance no one would even know that the precious stones and gold bars were there. Brandt had them in the safe for a reason. The currency and the gold and diamonds were all non-traceable. They were Brandt's secret fund. And gold could be turned into cash in small increments without leaving tracks. Diamonds were even more liquid.

It was like a shooting star that he found Brandt with the safe open.

He loaded the cash, most of the bars and all the diamonds into a carrying case he found in the safe closet, closed the safe door, turned the lock, and stealthily slipped out of the suite, leaving Brandt's body resting at his desk. A wicked grin spread across Aaron's face. He and his stash would vaporize. He was a free man at last.

℘

PRESENT DAY
MEMPHIS, TENNESEE

Judge Thompson walked off the plane at Memphis International Airport and headed toward the cabstand, pulling a small piece of luggage. An old black man with bloodshot eyes driving a dated cab offered her help with the door. He was bent, worn, and kind.

"St. Jude Children's Research Hospital," the judge directed. "Please take the 240 Loop." It was a route no one wants to know well. She looked at the Denver paper and reread the article about Colt Forester, the missing oil man who had miraculously survived. Aaron Jeffries, a person of interest, was still at large, and there were no clues in the mysterious death of the Denver lawyer, Ferrell Brandt. She, like many others, was thankful he was dead.

In silence, they drove until the cabbie put on a B.B. King tune. They passed a large billboard with a photo of Elvis advertising Graceland. Memphis was still a music mecca. The cabbie sped around the freeway until he saw the distinct pink buildings on the edge of downtown. The Mississippi River was low, brown, and snaky as it passed under the new bridge. The river deposited all of the upstream sins and debris along the shores of Memphis.

The cabbie pulled up in front of the main entrance to the massive hospital complex, Danny Thomas's gift to the world and the only children's cancer research hospital of its kind. After paying for the ride, the judge entered the building. Without asking directions, she went to the ward where brain cancer patients were treated. Lots of little hairless, pale-skinned children played while doctors and nurses moved around the halls. There was nothing reconcilable about children and cancer. She walked into the ward, observing the small patients.

Suddenly, an eight-year-old boy holding a red caboose noticed her and ran over. His face burst open with a smile, and they held on tight.

"Granny, you came!" His face was lit with excitement.

She smiled down at him. "I always come on Fridays."

"But I was afraid you might not make it."

"I'm here." She hugged him tight.

A thin young woman with a baby on her hip walked in the door. "Hi, Mom," she said to the judge.

They hugged. Judge Thompson stepped back and looked at her daughter. Her eyes harbored fear, and large tears tumbled down that she quickly wiped away.

"Michael, we get to have ice cream today," the young mother told her son.

"I want chocolate." His voice was enthusiastic. "Granny came for the weekend."

"I know," his mother said, shifting the baby's weight a little. "She always comes."

Michael focused on his train cars.

The judge hugged her daughter again and slipped an envelope of money into her purse. "This will help." They embraced. "When does John deploy?" the judge asked, referring to her son-in-law.

"He leaves for Afghanistan on Tuesday."

They sat on the floor with the baby and Michael, who was playing with the train unhampered by his portable IV.

"I thought you should have an engine!" The judge handed him a new engine for his train set, and the boy jumped up and down with excitement. He hitched the shiny engine to the front of the other train cars.

"Thanks, Granny."

She patted his head. "You're welcome."

"It's going on a long trip."

"Where's it heading, Michael?"

"It takes the children to heaven," Michael said in a matter-of-fact tone, as if she should have known. "Choo-choooo, chugga chugga…" he said, making train sounds and smiling with joy.

THE END

To find out what happens next, look for the new book in the Alex Sheridan series, coming soon.